SOUL OF SMOKE

BOOK I

DRAGONSWORN

CAITLYN MCFARLAND

OLIVERHEBERBOOKS

PUBLISHER'S NOTE: This is a work of fiction. Names, characters, places, and incidents either are the product of the author's imagination or are used fictitiously. Any resemblance to actual persons, living or dead, business establishments, events, or locales is entirely coincidental.

Soul of Smoke 2024 © Caitlyn McFarland

Cover design by Hannah Sternjakob

Edited by Kristy S. Gilbert, Kate Rene Gleason

Published by Oliver-Heber Books

0 9 8 7 6 5 4 3 2 1

For Chaela, Joss, and Kairi.
You are dragons.

CHAPTER I

KAI

K ai stood at the brink of the precipice, the toes of her worn hiking boots hanging over the edge. One wrong move would plunge her down the sheer cliff face to the rock-strewn valley two hundred feet below. A shiver of adrenaline thrilled from the bottom of her feet to the base of her neck. She threw out her arms and inhaled the pine-spiked autumn air. It was late September, and the higher elevations of the Rockies were a motley mix of yellow, orange, and dusty green. Snow capped the high peaks in the distance. Not far off, a stream laughed in its rocky bed.

Freedom.

Kai blinked, and the sun disappeared.

"What... ?"

The wind whipped as something passed overhead, huge and dark. Fear and the sudden feeling that something was *wrong* overwhelmed her. She teetered forward, and her foot slipped. The rocks and trees two hundred feet down suddenly looked too close.

"No!" Kai twisted and managed to fall backward onto solid

ground, scraping her palms on the pebbles that littered the hard dirt. She scrambled away from the drop, collapsed on her back several feet from the edge, and threw an arm over her eyes, breathing hard.

"Kai! What the hell? Are you okay?"

Kai winced and pulled her arm away from her face, squinting against the brightness of the sky at the looming silhouette of Juliet King, her best friend since preschool and roommate since college.

"You just gave me a heart attack!"

"Yeah. Me too. But did you see that?" Kai pushed herself into a sitting position and scanned for the helicopter or rogue Cessna or whatever had buzzed her, but the sky was clear. Nothing except a few scattered clouds.

"I saw you almost fall off a cliff. Like an idiot." Juli prodded Kai not so gently in the thigh with her toe. "Any normal person would've gone over. I told you I wasn't going to put up with this. I know you have to 'find yourself,' but you've got to stop taking stupid risks."

Regret washed over Kai. She climbed to her feet and dusted herself off. "Yeah, I know."

She hadn't been thinking about anything but the moment and the rush. The wind, the view, the feeling, so much like flying. Every once in a while, Kai just wanted to feel *something* other than lost.

Her messy bun had been knocked askew. Kai didn't want to see the look of disappointment in Juli's eyes, so she flipped her head upside down and smoothed her long soot-black hair into order with her hands, then straightened and wound it into a bun again.

Juli sighed, a long=suffering sound only the responsible friend in a twenty-year-long friendship could make. "It's fine. Just don't do it again."

"Deal."

Juli gave Kai a narrow-eyed look. She was the kind of woman people liked to describe as "a cool blonde." Slender. Tall. Sleek. *A face like art, a glare like an ice pick,* Kai's mother used to say. It was good they'd been friends since preschool, because there was no way Juli, who'd graduated summa cum laude in pre-med early, would put up with Kai, who had dropped out of law school after her second year.

Their friendship was a study in contrasts. Juli: the tall, golden, graceful blonde who radiated competence like the sun did light and barely tolerated physical activity. Kai: the short, dark-haired adrenaline junkie athletic enough to run, flip, dance, or climb circles around most people but who avoided responsibility like the plague.

Not all responsibility—not like paying rent or holding down a job. Only responsibility for others. Responsibility like becoming a lawyer and having clients' lives depend on your ability to argue a point and think on your feet.

That was the great secret Kai had realized partway into school: if no one ever relied on her, Kai could never fail them.

She hadn't quite figured out what to do with her life since then.

"You ready?" Juli put a hand over her eyes and scanned the sky. "We need to get moving if you want to make the summit."

"Yeah." Kai shouldered her pack, which she'd set to the side before walking to the edge of the cliff, and they carried on walking side by side up the mountain.

"I was being careful, you know," Kai muttered. "Something startled me."

For a long moment, there was no response. Just the sound of dirt and gravel crunching beneath their boots. Then Juli said, "Your idea of what is risky and what isn't is not normal."

One side of Kai's mouth turned up in a wry smile. "I know."

After about five minutes, the path curved around a tall cluster of boulders and meandered toward a pile of scree at the foot of a cliff. At the cliff's base, a flash of color caught her eye—a scrap of sapphire-blue fabric that shifted in the breeze.

Kai squinted, and her stomach dropped like a stone. It wasn't just a scrap of fabric. It was a torn jacket. A woman sprawled at the bottom of the cliff, her leg twisted at a terrible angle, blood matted in her dark red hair.

"Juli!"

It took less than a second for Juli to follow Kai's gaze and leap into action. "Follow me! If she's alive, she needs help."

If she's alive. If she's alive.

They reached the girl and Juli crouched at her side to check her vitals while Kai dug a first aid kit out of her pack.

Kai pulled the kit out and handed it to Juli, then crouched next to her and absorbed every detail she could. "She looks so young."

Aside from the long blue jacket, the girl wore a high-necked black shirt and charcoal-gray pants tucked into black boots. Not hiking boots—they were taller and more finely made. The whole outfit was just off. Too fine for someone to wear this deep in the wilderness at the end of a difficult hike. Aside from the clothes, she was draped in jewelry. Gold bracelets, rings, multiple earrings, and no less than three necklaces, all hung with crystal or polished slices of colorful stone.

The feeling from the edge of the cliff returned. *Wrong. Something is wrong.* And, *this could have been me if I hadn't caught myself. This could have been me.*

"I don't understand." Juli wasn't speaking to Kai, but was examining the girl's head wound, utterly perplexed.

"What is it?" Kai asked.

Juli wiped gently at the wound again, clearing away blood to reveal pale pink skin. "It's like she's been lying here for days. Her injuries have started to heal. See? There and there, where her skin is pink? It's knitting together. And her bruises, they're dark, like they've had time to develop. But that's not possible. You see her clothes?" Juli traced her finger over the blue jacket and lifted it for Kai to see. There was bright red blood on her fingertip. "That's fresh. Extremely fresh. And it was below freezing at this elevation last night. If she'd been out here, she would have died of exposure."

"And she's not dead?" Kai asked, just to be certain.

"She is most certainly not dead."

Kai helped Juli clean and bandage the girl's wounds as the sun sank toward the horizon. In all that time, the girl didn't stir. Juli started muttering about brain damage.

When they'd done what they could, Kai stood and twined her fingers in the carabiners on her belt, clicking one open and shut, open and shut. Her eyes fixed on the neck and left sleeve of the girl's long coat, which had been covered in dozens of inch-wide pentagons cut from thin leather and layered over each other in rows to look like scales. "What do we do?"

"We make a litter."

"And drag her down the mountain with a broken leg?" Kai shook her head. "No. Some parts of the path are way too dangerous for that."

"Then what do you suggest?" Juli snapped.

Danger. Something wrong. Flee.

Kai checked her phone but knew there would be no reception. She looked over the empty mountains as if an ambulance might manifest. They hadn't seen any other hikers all day, and there was no sign anyone else had been there recently. Not only did that mean there was no one near to turn to for help, it meant this girl had just appeared.

5

Like she'd dropped out of the sky.

Kai remembered the massive shadow that had buzzed her earlier. Maybe it had been a plane or some other kind of gliding or flying thing. Maybe it had wrecked on the cliffs a hundred feet overhead, and this girl had fallen from there.

Juli sighed and rose. "We have to go down. Maybe all the way to the parking lot."

"It's a three-hour hike," Kai protested. "There are cougars up here. Bears. She could wake up disoriented and fall again. We can't leave her."

Juli pulled a space blanket out of her backpack and tucked it around the girl's body, then stood again and looked at Kai.

Without speaking, they both knew what had to happen. Someone had to stay. With a lifetime of Girl Scouts and a handful of wilderness survival courses under her belt, Kai was the only real candidate. Still, she could see the hesitation in Juli's eyes.

"Maybe we both stay until she wakes up," Juli said. "We can help her out of here if she can walk."

Kai gave Juli a wry smile. It was a look that said, *I'm good. I've got this.*

Juli's return glare said, *I don't want to leave you up here alone.*

Kai shrugged. *I'll be fine.*

It wasn't real telepathy. But then, people who'd been friends for twenty of their twenty-four years didn't need magic to read each other's minds.

Juli shook her head, still resisting.

Kai smiled. "Come on, Jules. I promise I'll be here when you get back."

Juli's nostrils flared, but she nodded. "All right. I'll be as quick as I can. Try to get some water in her. If she starts to vomit, roll her on her side."

Kai nodded.

Juli moved as if to leave, then turned back one more time. "Be safe. No risks. Use your bear spray if you need to."

"No risks," Kai repeated. "I'll be safe."

But as Juli headed down the path, Kai couldn't help but think of the flying shadow and shiver.

She didn't believe in cryptids, but she'd seen enough of the world to know how much of it was unexplored and wild. How much still remained hidden from human eyes.

So she waited, and tried to convince herself that there was nothing in the yawning vastness of the mountains that could possibly be bigger or more dangerous than bears.

CHAPTER 2

KAI

The warm day had ebbed into chill twilight when a moan shredded the gathering dusk.

Kai looked up from a small pile of sticks she'd hoped to turn into a fire. The girl was awake and moving feebly. She touched her bandaged head, then fixed a confused gaze on her blood-smeared fingers.

Kai crouched at her side. "Don't move. You're hurt."

The girl's glassy gaze roamed, unfocused, her eyes a surprising saturated turquoise. She spoke, but whatever sounds she was making did not amount to a language Kai understood. The girl groaned and clutched her broken leg, inhaling sharply through her teeth, then spoke nonsense again, louder.

Kai leaned into the stranger's line of sight, and the girl's eyes finally fixed on her. Kai gave her a little wave. "Hey. Do you speak English?"

The girl blinked. "English?... Yes. Who are you?" Her accent was difficult to place. It sounded British, but more musical.

"Kai Monahan." Kai lifted her water bottle, unsure

9

whether she should offer it to the girl or just stick it in her mouth. "Do you remember what happened?"

"Remember..." The girl's eyes widened, depth and clarity returning. She surged upright. Her leg collapsed under her and she gasped, her face contorted in pain. "I have to warn them!"

"Whoa! Listen, help is on the way."

"*Blaenoriaid, ni allaf weld.* I can't fly like this." The girl groaned and pressed a hand against her forehead.

"Fly?" Kai looked up at the looming cliff, brow furrowed. Maybe the mystery woman had crashed up there and stumbled away from the wreckage, disoriented. It could explain the clothes that clearly weren't for hiking, and the fact that she had no visible form of transportation.

The stranger seized Kai, her fingers digging into Kai's shoulders like claws. "Help me!" She leveraged herself up, nearly pulling Kai to the ground. "They're in trouble. Rhys!"

"Stay here. Sit down. Help is coming." Kai disentangled herself. "Were there more of you? Are they up there?" Not that Kai knew what she would do if they were. Juli was coming *here*. It would be better to wait.

The girl tried to stand again, and this time she succeeded, leaning awkwardly to one side. Kai grabbed her elbow. "You're going to hurt your leg even more."

"Damn my leg! I have to get back to my family!" In a weird trick of the dying light, the girl's eyes seemed to luminesce, like tropical water lit from below. "Rhys—how did Kavar know? Ancients, let him be safe. Let all of them be safe."

Kai tried to regain control of the situation. "Listen to me. My friend already went for help. She'll be back in a couple of hours with rangers, maybe a helicopter. If your family is up there and they're hurt, we'll help them too."

The girl made a sound remarkably like a growl. "My people will have no help from yours. Let. Me. Go."

With astonishing strength, the girl wrenched free, hopped a few steps, then turned her ankle on a loose stone and went down hard. She let out a cry and started to crawl, dragging her broken leg behind her.

"Stop!" Kai fumbled to pick up her pack and swing it over her shoulders. "You hit your head. You aren't thinking straight."

The stranger ignored Kai and forged forward on hands and knees. Kai watched for three excruciating heartbeats, expecting her to stop or collapse. But she didn't; she just kept on crawling and sobbing.

"Well. Shit." Kai glanced back down the path, hoping to see Juli. Listening for a helicopter.

She was alone.

No risks.

It was more of a risk to let the injured young woman crawl away than it was to stay here. At least if Kai went with her, she could make sure the stranger didn't fall off any more cliffs.

With a frustrated grunt, Kai kicked some stones into a rough arrow pointing up the path, then jogged to the struggling woman. With luck, they were only moments ahead of the rescue.

Kai wasn't tall, but years of high-level competition in rock climbing and gymnastics had made her strong. She caught up to the young woman, hoisted her to her feet, and shouldered under her arm. Standing, the stranger towered over Kai. She had to be almost six feet tall.

She glared down at Kai in annoyance, her face bone white, her voice hoarse with pain. "I don't want your help."

"You won't get anywhere without it."

For long seconds, the girl hesitated, and Kai was certain she'd try to shrug her off again. Finally, she nodded. "All right. Just... If you see something coming from the sky, let me go and hit the ground. Do you hear me?"

It never hurt to humor people. "Sure. Hit the ground. What's your name?"

"Deryn. Let's move."

They set off, managing a hobbling gait. Deryn fell silent, and Kai didn't restart the conversation. They followed the path upward along the base of the cliff, but it was slow going.

After fifteen minutes of scrambling along the scree and when Deryn nearly fell for the umpteenth time, Kai let out a grunt of frustration. "There has to be a better way up. If we find a low spot, I can climb."

"There's a way up. It's close." Deryn's face was even paler than before, and her breath came in gasps. "A little farther."

They were near the top. Ahead, the cliffside path disappeared into a hazy bit of cloud. The fog rolled around Kai, cutting off her view of the valleys and the darkening sky.

Abruptly, she *knew* she was going the wrong way.

She stopped.

"No! Keep moving!" Deryn said.

"This is wrong." Kai shook her head and tried to back up, but as strong as she was, Deryn was stronger. She clamped her arm down, fastening Kai to her side.

"Keep moving."

"No!" Kai tried to duck out from under Deryn's arm. Panic drove coherent thought from her mind. Her heart threatened to beat out of her chest. "I can't go this way!"

Deryn made a noise of disgust. Still using Kai as a crutch, she forced both of them forward. She was *incredibly* strong.

"No! No!"

Deryn jerked Kai around in front of her, hands squeezing Kai's shoulders so hard Kai let out a cry and was forced to hold still.

"Listen to me," Deryn hissed, eyes flashing turquoise again. "I know you don't understand what's going on. I know you're frightened. But my brother's life is on the line and that *matters*. You can save the world today, Kai Monahan, but you must ignore your fear and keep moving forward."

Brother. Brothers. *My brothers. Liam and Colm. I'd walk through this for them.*

Kai took a gulping breath and nodded. Slowly, Deryn let her go and put her arm around Kai's shoulders again.

They climbed higher. Fear curdled in Kai's throat, choking off her scream. It felt like wading through waist-deep mud. Just when the fear climbed to such a pitch that Kai thought she'd have to turn back or throw herself off the mountain, brothers or not, the feeling...snapped.

The panic was gone.

"What happened?"

Deryn gave her a tight smile. "You pushed through."

It was full dark now, the night lit by a full moon hidden somewhere above the peak. They'd climbed far higher than Kai had realized—nearly to the summit. But it was surrounded by cliffs. She and Deryn stood before a crack in a sheer stone wall barely wide enough for one person.

"Through here. This is how we get to the top." Deryn braced her hands on either side of the crack and levered herself up. It didn't work, and she fell backward.

Kai caught her. "If you crashed, how do you know how to get to the top?"

"I've been here before."

Stifling unease, Kai climbed into the crack and helped Deryn up. The ravine was twisted, narrow, and filled with stones and debris. When they came across a pile of waist-high boulders, Kai thought they'd have to turn back. But Deryn gritted her teeth and hoisted herself over the rocks.

Then they were through, falling over each other into clear night air on the very peak of the mountain. The stars were back, the air crisp and cold. The moon hung full and fat in the sky, edging everything in silver. A hilly meadow stretched in front of them, tall grass and wildflowers rolling in shimmering waves beneath the chill breeze. It was as if the summit wasn't a point—which Kai could have sworn it was—but a shallow bowl, like the top of an ancient volcano. One so vast, Kai couldn't see all the way across it now that night had arrived.

As soon as she was on her feet, Deryn cupped her hands around her mouth. "Rhys! Ashem!"

At first, there was nothing but silence. Kai slipped under Deryn's arm again, helping her forward. Every few steps, Deryn repeated her call. Finally, someone answered. It was incomprehensible at first, a muffled shout from the distant dark. Then someone jogged over the top of a small rise, nothing but a silhouette among the stars. Deryn sagged in such relief she nearly fell and took Kai down with her.

"Rhys," Deryn whispered.

The girl's companions were alive. Not just alive, but mobile. Kai tried to feel relief too, but mostly she felt the same growing unease she'd had since the flying shadow buzzed her.

Wrong. Something is wrong, and if I don't get out of here, something is going to happen to me.

Deryn left Kai, reaching out to the still-distant figure and babbling in that language again. So fast it sounded like music. "Rhys! Rhys! *Rydych chi'n fyw.*"

"Deryn!" The figure answered with a man's voice, sharp with fear and surprise. He began running toward them, legs stretching in ground-eating strides.

"That's your brother, right?" Kai asked.

Deryn's smile was fierce, white teeth catching the moonlight. "Yes. That's my brother."

The figure resolved into a man who moved with an ease and grace Kai had never seen outside of professional athletes.

14

Such ease, in fact, that he couldn't have been in a plane crash. He couldn't have been in an accident of any kind.

Kai cleared her throat. "Great. He looks okay. We can gather whatever others there are and head back to the base of the cliff."

Deryn met Kai's gaze, but didn't speak. Kai tried to say something else, but the words evaporated from her lips. A strange, electric heaviness settled on the air, like the world drawing breath before a storm.

When she looked for the source of the feeling, she only saw Rhys.

He came to a stop before them, mostly shadow. Taller than Kai had even expected. Even in the dark, she thought his thick hair—just long enough to tell he'd run his fingers through it several times—glinted red like his sister's. He grasped Deryn's shoulders, speaking fast and low. She responded, and he cursed. It was in that other language, but cussing was cussing. He took Deryn's face in his hands and tilted it, turning both of their bodies toward the moon to examine her wound.

Kai's breath caught as the light silvered the planes of his face. Rhys was jaw-dropping. Not the too-polished, generic, smooth handsome of a model or influencer, but a striking, classic, rugged kind of handsome that came with a narrow face, high cheekbones, and defined jaw.

But it wasn't just his face that twisted her heart and stopped her lungs. It was his expression. The furrow between his brows when he examined Deryn's wounds. The concern in his eyes. The smile as Deryn said something flippant—just the barest curve that eased one side of his stern mouth. As soon as she saw that smile, Kai wanted to see another. She had the strange, urgent desire to hear what it would sound like when he laughed.

Of course, that was the moment he chose to notice her. For

an instant, Kai swore his eyes sparked with blue fire. With secrets and stars.

Then he turned back to his sister. "Deryn," he said in the same tone Kai would've used to warn someone about a spider on their shoulder, "*Pwy yw hwn?*"

Deryn shot off a rapid succession of words. Rhys tensed, his smile disappearing. Then he scooped his sister into his arms. He stood for a moment, looking down at Kai. Then he shook his head and finally switched to English, his voice low and mellow yet resonant with command. "Follow me. We'll have you back to your friends soon enough."

He turned and strode back the way he had come. Bemused and slightly offended at being left behind to follow like a puppy, Kai trotted after.

They waded through the grass and up a small rise. Only a few steps behind the siblings, Kai noted an orange glow and the scent of woodsmoke on the air just before they strode over the hill. Then she reached the top and stopped short again.

There was no horrific plane crash. There were no people in need of immediate help. This was a camp. A handful of domed tents in a circle with a firepit between. Pots and pans were stacked neatly on a log near the firepit, as if they'd just missed a communal dinner. Kai counted the tents. Seven.

Seven tents. No wreckage.

I am in deep shit.

She should leave, but she was drawn forward. If she left now, she'd never know who these people were, never know how they got here, or what they were doing on top of a mountain in a crater that was supposed to be a peak. Just a few minutes, a few answers, and then she'd slip away.

"Ashem!" Rhys called.

A man threw back one of the tent flaps, caught sight of Rhys and Deryn, and strode toward them. Nearly as tall as

Rhys and a little more broadly built, he looked older, maybe thirty, with light brown skin, thick black hair that was pulled back from his face, and a neatly trimmed black beard that emphasized his square jaw. He was handsome in a more elegant way than Rhys and—from the way his brows drew down over his eyes at the sight of them—far less friendly.

Ashem asked a question in the mystery language, his voice a calm, velvety baritone.

"Nothing good," Rhys responded in English. He carried Deryn to the campfire at the center of the tents, where a stocky blond man sat near the fire. He rose and moved to support Deryn as the other two men helped her sit on a large stone.

Kai hung back, her arms folded protectively across her chest. There were four strangers now, three of them men. Ashem said something commanding to the blond. At first, the other man hunched closer to Deryn, shaking his head. Ashem repeated himself, but this time the words were barked like an order. Scowling, the blond stood and hurried toward the tents, calling out to others Kai had yet to see.

Deryn grimaced. She, at least, still spoke English. "I was hunting to the southeast. I thought I saw someone veiling, so I went to check. Demba came out of nowhere. I lost my bag, my singstone—"

"Demba?" Ashem, perhaps transitioning to English unconsciously, let loose an impressive string of obscenities. "Where? Was he with Kavar?"

Deryn shook her head, clenching trembling hands. "I didn't see Kavar, but he has to be close. I managed to lure Demba into a cloud bank and got away, but not before he injured me. I crashed, blacked out. I don't know how long I was there."

Kai shifted her weight, a nervous, jangling energy pulsing through her at Deryn's words.

Rhys stood and shot Kai a glance, his expression unreadable. "I'll take Deryn and go. We can regroup at the rendezvous on the coast."

A muscle jumped in Ashem's jaw. "I *warned* you this would happen."

"It shouldn't have. No one knew where we were going. No one even knew we left!"

"Then Eryri has a spy," Ashem snapped.

"A spy? That's not—"

But Ashem wasn't listening. "Tell the others. We leave *now*."

Baring his teeth, Rhys turned on his heel and headed for a tent.

Ashem made a sharp gesture at Deryn. "Put out the fire. If they're still in the area, they could see it. A barrier doesn't make us invisible."

Deryn rubbed her face, obviously exhausted. "I haven't done my ritual in a few days. I'm running dry."

A lean man, taller even than Rhys, appeared from beyond the fire and dropped a bundle next to the firepit. It fell with the clang and clatter of metal, cutting Deryn off. Ashem growled something at the man, who laughed and shrugged. The newcomer glanced at Deryn, his face going serious when he saw her leg. But when he bent to get a better look, Ashem barked orders in the mystery language again.

The man laughed and raised both his hands in surrender. Then his eyes fell on Kai. They widened in surprise. He stepped over the bag, catching his toe on the fabric. It spilled open, and Kai caught a glimpse of half a dozen things that looked like sword hilts. She didn't have time to examine further, however, because this new man approached her, and her breath caught in her chest for a second time.

Rhys was striking. Ashem was refined. This, whoever he was, was the most beautiful human being Kai had ever seen.

Flawless face, perfect bone structure, unruly black hair, eyes that shifted in the firelight so she couldn't quite tell what color they were. She thought about backing away, but by the time she found the presence of mind to move, he was already next to her, wearing an easy expression that—despite the bizarre situation she'd found herself in—gave her the comforting feeling she'd found a friend.

"*Noswaith dda.* What's your name?" He asked in a voice rich as chocolate.

Kai fidgeted, hesitated. But she'd already told Deryn. "Kai Monahan."

"Kai." He breathed her name like a sigh or a song. "You've found us at an interesting time. But don't worry, we'll make sure you get home all right."

"Cadoc!" Ashem barked. "Get moving."

The beautiful man winked at her, gave Ashem an exaggerated salute, then jogged toward the tents in the same direction Rhys and the blond man had gone.

As he moved, Ashem's gaze finally landed on Kai. "Blood of the Ancients, what is *she* doing here?"

Kai bristled. "*She* brought Deryn back. You're welcome."

Ashem bit out a word that sounded filthy. He called toward the tents, and two more women and a man appeared. That made eight. Not an unreasonable number of people if they were a group of friends on a weekend campout, but she had the feeling they were not.

Kai glanced at the bag that Cadoc had dropped by the fire. It still looked suspiciously full of swords.

Ashem gestured at Kai and addressed one of the newcomers—a woman with a mane of curly hair. "I need to take care of this. Take charge of these idiots and get us ready to leave here in ten minutes. Griffith can shift and—"

He broke off, his brow furrowing. His eyes lost focus.

"Kavar is close." He blinked, returning to himself. "Deryn! Why isn't that fire out?"

Deryn had both hands stretched toward the fire. A fine mist seemed to gather in the space between her palms, gleaming and changing shape like a golf-ball-size glob of water. Kai's mouth fell open. It had to be a trick of the fire, or the moonlight.

"I'm trying." Deryn snapped. "I haven't done my damn ritual in three days!"

"Damn it, Deryn!" Ashem made a sharp gesture at Rhys as he and Cadoc rejoined the group. "Take care of it!"

Rhys lifted one hand toward the fire, fingers extended as if inviting it to dance. The flame, which had been crackling merrily, snuffed out.

"What?"

Kai's surprised question hung in the silence.

"I'm sorry. *What?*"

No one answered.

"Get going," Ashem said. "We may still be able to sneak away."

There was a distant rushing, like wind passing over a sail. Slowly, the people around the fire raised their heads. One by one, they turned.

A raw, primal fear whispered at the back of Kai's mind, and she couldn't bring herself to look. She did not want to see what they saw.

She drew a shaky breath—the only sound except for that distant, rushing wind.

Rhys stood opposite Kai, his gaze fixed on the sky behind her. In the darkness, his eyes luminesced. No imagining it. No convincing herself it was pretend. Rhys's gaze met hers, a magnificent starfire blue. Then he looked back to the sky. "It's too late. They're here."

Unable to bear it a second longer, Kai twisted on the log.

A wave of distortion, like a heat mirage, passed over the wavering moon. Between one blink and the next, the effect melted away, revealing a dozen impossible shapes.

The earth seemed to tilt. She pressed her fingers into her eyes. But when she looked again, they'd only grown larger. Vast and serpentine, some bat-winged, some feathered, and some wingless, undulating through the sky.

Dragons. Actual, real *dragons*.

"Impossible," she whispered.

And then the people around the fire were running. Not away from the shadows, but toward them, Ashem in the lead. He pulled ahead, and darkness deeper than the night coalesced around him, swirling like a storm. Just as Kai thought he'd been consumed, the darkness burst forth like a negative image of the sun.

Where there had been a man, a sixty-foot dragon, black as pitch, roared a challenge to the sky.

CHAPTER 3
RHYS

R hys spared one glance for the pretty human girl staring, mouth agape, at approaching death. If she had sense, she would get down and pretend to be a stone. Sense, however, was generally lacking among humans. He didn't expect her to survive. Which was too bad. There was something about her face. Her body. Her eyes. Something that tugged at his attention when it was needed elsewhere.

He glanced at Deryn and fought down a surge of anger at himself. He'd been the one to insist Ashem let her come on this training excursion, so far from their island home in Eryri. It was his fault she was in danger. He crouched in the beaten-down grass, bringing his face level with hers. "Deryn, Kavar may not know you made it back to camp. They won't be looking for you. Hide."

Her lip curled. "Get sundered!" She stood, wounded leg shaking. "I can still fight. I'll finish any of them that hit the ground."

Rhys bared his teeth. She could never just *listen.* "You have to stay safe. If something happens to me—"

Her irises ignited, glowing turquoise. "*You* have to stay safe."

She was going to hate him, but she'd left him no choice. Rhys rose and pulled power inward, focusing it until his blood buzzed and hissed, boiling in his veins. If he could only do one thing for certain in this battle, he would save his sister. "Deryn, REMAIN HUMAN. You aren't needed in this fight."

"No!" Her injured leg buckled, though by now the bone should have healed nearly enough for her to walk alone. "No! Take it back!"

Ignoring his sister, Rhys sprinted after Ashem and the others, his feet pounding over uneven ground as the knee-high grasses of the meadow whipped and clung to his legs. Deryn screamed obscenities at his back, but he didn't care. Not as long as she was safe.

A tingle of magic and an explosion of light signaled Cadoc's transformation; a dragon the red-orange of flame clawed his way into the sky. Morwenna transformed next, then Griffith, Ffion, Evan. Six dragons ranging in color from mirrorlike silver to midnight blue leaped from the hillside, churning the air with vast wings.

Rhys fought through the buffeting winds of their takeoff. Reaching the top of the rise, he flung himself open, pushing himself higher and wider and *more* until he touched the fires that burned along the borders of his being. Flame erupted, consuming, reforming, and expanding. The transition jarred, as always.

Dragon.

He opened his jaws wide, roaring, digging his talons into the ground. Bunching his haunches, he spread his wings, then leaped after the others. No time for self-recrimination, no time to wonder how this attack fit into the wider scope of the war, or if Owain was lurking somewhere in the night. If Rhys wanted answers, he'd have to survive.

Less than five hundred yards away, a dozen enemies swooped toward the meadow. Rage ignited in Rhys's belly at the sight of them. Led by Ashem's brother, Kavar, they called themselves the Sovereign's Talon, and they had stolen much Rhys held dear.

Rhys strained his wings, pulling for as much altitude as he could get. As the enemy approached, Rhys identified Kavar flying ahead of the others. It was easy enough—in his dragon form, the other Azhdahā was nearly identical to Ashem. Demba, the dragon who had attacked Deryn earlier that day, flew just behind Kavar in the vee formation. It had been nearly a decade since Rhys had seen Kavar or any member of the Sovereign's Talon. A decade since they'd met in battle. A decade since Iain died.

The two lines of dragons collided. Ashem and Kavar crashed together in the center, clawing, biting, and writhing until it was impossible to tell which was which. Cadoc twisted, spiraling below an oncoming enemy and searing the blue dragon's unprotected belly with flame. Ffion and Griffith raked past huge, bronze Demba, who snapped, nearly taking off the end of Ffion's silver tail.

Thought flew from Rhys's mind until there was nothing but the night wind and the enemy and the fire scorching his gut. He roared, and the bronze dragon turned toward him. Demba roared a challenge in return.

Rhys would have his revenge.

CHAPTER 4

KAI

K ai shoved the heels of her hands into her eyes and
rubbed hard.

Again, the dragons didn't go away.

She let out a breath, her body so packed with adrenaline
she might ignite. It couldn't be real. None of this could be real.

Wind from dragon wings struck her hard, and she staggered to one side. She couldn't blink, couldn't take her eyes
from this scene of dreams and nightmares. The full moon
appeared from behind a cloud, and Kai spun, trying to see them
all at once, straining toward the beasts that wheeled and
swooped overhead.

It was terrifying, yes, but exhilarating. The most terrifying,
beautiful thing she'd ever seen: dragons blazing through a star-
encrusted sky.

They roared over the meadow like the heart of a storm, all
crackling energy and shrieking wind. Someone had to hear this.
Juli, or rangers, or random campers.

Metal crashed behind her, and Kai whirled to see Deryn
clutching one of the swords from the bag. Her long red hair

flew every which way, and she shrieked words Kai couldn't understand, shaking the sword at the sky.

One of the dragons skimmed too close, and Kai threw herself onto her belly. Terror took over from wonder. She had to escape. She raised her head, then pushed herself onto hands and knees to see above the madly waving grass. Dragons were everywhere. There was no way to reach the tunnel she'd come through without being seen.

Kai scanned the field, looking for another way out, but her gaze caught on Deryn instead. She'd left the fire. The idiot was limping right into the middle of the fight.

"Deryn! You'll be killed!" Kai stumbled toward her and tried to yank the sword from Deryn's hand, but Deryn snarled and shoved her back. She was inhumanly strong, and Kai landed hard on her behind next to the smoking, dark firepit.

"Run!" Deryn's shout was barely audible above the noise. Her turquoise eyes pulsed with light. "There's nothing you can do but die. Go, before they notice you!"

"Not if you're staying!"

The swords Cadoc had dropped were still there, gleaming in the dark. Kai hefted one as she stood, surprised by how heavy it was. It was sheathed in ancient leather, but the hilt winked with rubies and milky white stones.

Roars deafened her, and the snap of jaws and whoosh of wings thrummed through her skull. The air was bitter with lightning and sour with the scent of sulfur. There were dragons in the sky. There was a sword in her hand.

Kai knew she'd lost her mind, and she laughed.

The damp scent of earth swirled into her nostrils as two dragons crashed to the ground so close she had to jump to one side. Their talons gashed deep, soil-bleeding gouges into the meadow, and their bodies leveled the tents. They snarled and writhed. The blue dragon raked its claws across a green dragon's hide. The green roared, blood spurting from half a dozen long gashes in its flank. A tiny silver dragon zoomed past, unleashing a spear of lightning from delicate jaws and scoring a direct hit on the blue, which jerked to the ground. The hair on Kai's arms stand on end.

This is real. The thought sank in for a long moment, only to be interrupted by an angry shriek. Deryn had reached the top of the hill and she was still moving, making for the thickest part of the fight.

Kai sprinted after Deryn, the unfamiliar weight of the sword pulling her to one side. But thanks to years of intense athletic training, she reached Deryn in less than a minute and grabbed for her arm, but the tall girl shrugged away.

Frustrated, Kai slammed her sheathed blade between Deryn's shuffling feet, putting the girl's life above her injured leg. Deryn went down with a shout of pain.

Kai wrenched the sword free. Its sheath went flying. She pointed the naked, gleaming blade at the sky, where black dragons spewed clouds of yellow vapor. "Those are dragons, you crazy bitch!"

Deryn snarled and fought to rise. "*I'm* a dragon!"

"Not right now you aren't!"

A thunderous roar of pain sounded from above. Kai looked up, only to be blinded by a column of fire. She shielded her eyes and shouted at Deryn, "Come on!"

"Get away from—" Deryn's eyes flicked up, then widened. Kai followed her gaze.

One of the dragons had spotted them. At first, Kai thought it was Ashem, because it was one of the black ones. Then she heard Deryn's strangled whisper.

"Kavar!"

The black dragon dove straight for them, silver eyes flashing. Deryn stiffened, her mouth wide in wordless terror. Kai's entire body went numb, freezing her to the spot.

Wind whistled. With a booming thud, a dragon whose scales glittered like blood slammed into the black dragon, knocking it off course. The black dragon Kavar recovered, twisting in the air like a cat. The crimson dragon swiped at the other with wickedly long claws, but missed and overbalanced.

Seeing an opening, Kavar darted forward and buried his teeth in the red dragon's shoulder.

"No," Deryn whispered. The fear and pain in that single syllable filled Kai with dread. "Rhys! *No!*"

The crimson dragon—the one that was Rhys—let out a howl of agony. He convulsed and plunged earthward like a stone.

Deryn screamed.

Instinct took over. Kai seized Deryn's arm. With strength born of adrenaline, she hauled the taller woman out of the way. They made it several yards before an earth-shaking crash sent both of them flying. Kai lost her grip on Deryn and landed on the sword, driving the hilt into her stomach and knocking the wind out of her.

"Rhys! Rhys!" From the volume of Deryn's cries, *she* was having no trouble breathing.

Kai coughed and gasped, seconds ticking away while she tried to catch her breath. The earth shook as the black dragon landed between them and Rhys with its back to them. The vast nothingness of his inky hide wasn't a dozen feet from where Kai gulped for oxygen like a landed trout. He was so close, she could hear the sibilant hiss of scales when he moved.

Air trickled into Kai's lungs, dry and musky, a scent that could only be dragon. She pulled herself to her feet, dragging the sword with her.

Deryn had lost her sword when Kavar landed. That didn't

stop her from running at him, screaming a war cry. Exasperation warring with terror, Kai ran after, expecting at any second to see Rhys's red scales on the other side of the black dragon's bulk.

But when they reached the other side, there was no red dragon, only Rhys the man. Rhys, unconscious. His shoulder was a bloody mass, and Kavar was curling one clawed foot around his torso.

"Rhys, wake up!" Deryn screamed.

With a brain-rattling roar, another red dragon swooped from the sky, aiming for Kavar. Kai felt a moment of relief. This dragon would save Rhys; she wouldn't have to do anything.

Then an emerald beast with rainbow-feathered wings slammed into their would-be savior in midair. Both spun out of control and crashed into the ground a hundred yards away. The red dragon struggled, but his enemy had him pinned.

Kai's heartbeat boomed in her ears.

Thump-thump. The red wouldn't get to Rhys in time to stop whatever was happening.

Thump-thump. Unarmed, Deryn wouldn't be any help.

Thump-thump. None of the other dragons, outnumbered and too caught up in survival, had noticed Rhys.

Thump-thump.

Time slowed; sounds fell to silence. The sword's jewel-studded hilt was slick in Kai's hand. Helpless tears streaked Deryn's face as Rhys lay motionless on the churned earth, trapped in a constricting cage of two-foot talons.

Help was not coming.

It had to be her.

Kai charged, leaping through the clinging grass before her brain registered she was moving. She tightened her slippery hands and raised the sword high, praying one of the good dragons would notice what was happening and do *something*.

It occurred to her at the last instant that she didn't even know if Deryn and the others were "good" at all. Then her blade flashed down, met resistance, and plunged through midnight flesh. It hit bone, and the impact reverberated through Kai's shoulders. Then the blade slid around bone and sank to the hilt. The tip came out on the underside of the dragon's clawed hand, wetly gleaming in the moonlight. Everything blurred but the bloodstained blade.

She let go.

Time slammed back into motion as Kavar jerked his injured limb up, wrenched the sword out with his other claw, and hurled it away. Sound came rushing back as he let out a grinding, shrieking roar. Kai threw herself to the ground near Rhys's unconscious body, barely dodging a rake by the dragon's good foreclaw.

Flat on her back, she could only stare at the car-sized head that hovered above her, luminous silver eyes filling her vision. Black lips curled back in a snarl, revealing a gaping maw full of pointed white teeth as long as her forearm and covered in slimy yellow spittle.

Something *pushed* against her mind, the pressure growing until her brain felt it would burst like a smashed grape. She screamed and clawed her fingers into the dirt, as if the earth could anchor her sanity.

That's right, ape. Scream, a voice oozed through her brain. It forced its way into her mind, prying her open. Almost idly, it flipped through memories. Her vision doubled as her true eyes watched silver ones loom closer while random images flashed through her mind. Her parents. School. Her brothers. Juli. She squirmed and gagged, bile climbing into her throat.

Kai Monahan. His mental voice was oddly flat against her brain. Black nostrils flared. *You smell crunchable.*

The pressure in her head doubled. Kai thought she

screamed again but wasn't sure. The black head darted toward her, jaws gaping wide.

A few feet away, there was a groan and a soft curse. Kai rolled her eyes to the side in time to see Rhys push himself up onto one elbow, a gaping wound down his torso sheeting blood. He raised an open palm toward the black dragon.

"You won't... take any more lives... under my protection."

There was a wave of heat. A blast of flame. Fire that burned white hot, searing into Kai's retinas.

Another chest-rattling roar. Voices that bounced around inside her head.

Everything went blessedly dark.

KAI WAS COLD. Her head throbbed. Beneath her was hard, uneven ground covered in something soft. She rolled, and the movement triggered a sensation like a knife twisting in her brain.

Disoriented, she lifted her head. She was on a shallow slope surrounded by dark, narrow pines and carpeted with their prickly castoffs. The gray light of dawn filtered through the forest. Twenty feet away, several people huddled around a figure on the ground and spoke in the mystery language.

Memories swamped her. Finding Deryn. Trekking through the weird fog. Rhys and his starfire eyes.

The battle came flooding back, and her stomach lurched. *Dragons.* The last thing she remembered was Kavar popping open her mind like an oyster. She rolled to the side and vomited.

Taking short, shallow breaths, Kai rolled onto her back again. After half a dozen tries, she managed to push herself up on her elbows and squinted at the huddle of people.

"I couldn't put out the fire. I'd used all my magic."

Kai nearly fainted in relief when she recognized Deryn's voice. The tall girl separated from the group, led by the tiny woman with a mane of loose curls. As they moved, Kai caught a glimpse of the prone figure at the center of the circle.

Short red hair. Pale skin. A horrifying wound that ran from one shoulder down to his opposite hip. Rhys?

Deryn's hands were curled into tight, white-knuckled fists. "He's dying and it's my fault. Why do I always forget to do my stupid ritual?"

Kai's stomach lurched again and she swallowed bitter bile. She'd tried to save him. Had they failed?

"We've been traveling. It's easy to forget," said the woman, Ffion. She had dark brown skin and didn't look much older than Kai, except her eyes. In Kai's addled state, she thought she could see the wisdom of ages in those eyes, the same way she had imagined she saw the invisible weight of too much knowledge on Rhys's shoulders.

"It's not your fault." Ffion squeezed Deryn's shoulder. "You won't forget again."

"Won't I?" Deryn's voice was small and sad.

The small woman pushed Deryn gently forward, a look of calm surety on her face. "No. You won't. Come on, *bach*." Her voice was fluting and birdlike. "We'll get to the waystation and Ashem will make the antivenom. Rhys is strong. He'll make it." Though Ffion's face was serene, her voice wavered.

Kai felt something in her chest unknot. For the moment, Rhys was alive, though his skin was ashen and he lay utterly still. If Ffion hadn't said otherwise, Kai would've thought he was dead.

She looked back to the huddle, recognizing more of the people—or more of the dragons, she supposed—as they did their best to care for Rhys.

Beautiful Cadoc was there. He knelt at Rhys's side, leaning on the fallen man's injuries with a blood-soaked rag. The rag was probably Cadoc's shirt, because he wasn't wearing one. Cadoc's own hands were stained red to the wrists. A red-orange tattoo swirled over his shoulder and down his right arm like flame. Foreign words fell from his lips, fast and angry and apparently directed at his fallen friend.

A woman with foxlike features and short, dark brown hair knelt by Rhys's head, stroking his cheek.

"Leave off, Cadoc." A huge man pushed Cadoc gently aside and took his place. The giant's right sleeve had been torn, revealing that he also had a tattoo, though his was reminiscent of vines, the twining green tendrils edged with bronze.

Cadoc rose and started pacing. He caught sight of the blood on his hands and stopped short, staring. Abruptly, he stalked off through the trees in the direction Deryn and Ffion had gone, returning a moment later with his hands clean. Ffion followed close behind.

"Where's Deryn?" The blond man—Kai had forgotten about him, there were so many of these people—leaned to one side as if he might be able to see past Ffion and Cadoc.

Ffion held up a hand. "Leave her for a moment, Evan. We need to bandage Rhys's wounds while we can. Here, Griffith." Ffion grasped her shirt and tore, handing strips of fabric to the giant with vine tattoos. The form-fitting gray top now ended jaggedly just below Ffion's ribcage, emphasizing the curves of her small waist and full hips. Two blood-encrusted red lines extended down her abdomen. At the base of her sleeve, Kai saw a glimmer of silver.

The blond—Evan?—gently shifted Rhys while the giant man and tiny, curly-haired Ffion wrapped strips of shirt around Rhys's wounded shoulder. When it was done, Evan handed

Cadoc the bloody rags they'd used to stanch the wound. Cadoc took the rags in his hands, and they burst into flame.

The world darkened for a moment before Kai got a hold of herself. "Do not pass out," she muttered. "Do *not* pass out."

Dragons. Magic. Blood and maiming. She squeezed her eyes shut until the world stopped spinning.

When she opened them, Cadoc was watching her. He dusted ashes from his hands and approached, and Kai's throat went dry. *I should have run. I should have gotten away when I had the chance.*

Cadoc crouched a few feet away and offered his hand. This close, his eyes were the clear, startling color of amethyst. She could also see that the pattern on his shoulder and arm she'd thought was a tattoo was actually comprised of thousands of tiny scales that glittered like iridescent lines of fire.

"It's all right, *brânwen*. We met, remember? My name is Cadoc."

The man of the chocolate voice. "I remember." Kai eyes darted from his hand to his purple eyes, her fist pressed to her chest.

His mouth curved into a weary smile. He had full lips. Even now, he was striking. "And you are Kai. Or shall I call you Lady of the Lake for turning up with a sword when it was so badly needed?"

Against her will, the sharp edge of her fear dulled as Cadoc once again put her at ease. "Kai."

He nodded gravely. "Kai, a few hours ago, you saved my best friend's life." He nodded in Rhys's direction without breaking their gaze. "I swear by fire and by the blood of the Ancients, you are safe with us."

Kai reached up before she fully realized what she was doing. His fingers closed around hers, and she let him pull her to her feet. Dizzy, she put a hand out to catch herself, and it landed on his chest.

"Sorry," she mumbled. Her head throbbed sharply, and she bit the inside of her mouth against the pain.

His serious expression flashed into a wicked grin. "I expect it took a massive effort to resist me as long as you did."

"Leave her alone, Cadoc."

Kai jumped as tiny Ffion appeared on her other side. The short woman—well, only two or three inches shorter than Kai, but Kai was unused to being taller than anyone—took Kai's arm, and Kai noticed a beautifully worked band of silver and jewels around the small woman's biceps. Ffion patted Kai's shoulder and gave Cadoc a narrow-eyed glare, as if she suspected him of mischief. "She's been through enough."

"We've all been through enough," the woman with the fox face hissed from her place at Rhys's head. "Why should we treat her like glass?"

"She saved his life, Morwenna," Cadoc snapped.

There was an earth-rattling thump from somewhere in the woods. Kai tensed, but next to her, Ffion relaxed. Ashem appeared from under the trees with Deryn close behind, walking with barely a limp. She moved to blond Evan and leaned against his side. He pressed a kiss to her temple and wrapped an arm around her waist.

Kai started a list of dragon traits in her mind. Scale tattoos. Healing. Strange eyes. She also started a list of dragons.

Deryn, obviously. Crazy bitch. The reason Kai was here. Younger than the others. Maybe nineteen?

Ashem, the leader. Handsome. Scary. Black dragon. Older than the others. Near thirty, if Kai was right.

Rhys, the almost-dead one. Eyes like stars. Presence like a storm. Red dragon.

Cadoc. Handsome flirt. Red scale tattoo. Another red dragon?

Ffion. Tiny with wise eyes. Kind. Silver scales?

Evan, the burly blond one who clearly had a thing for Deryn.

Morwenna, the one with vulpine features who looked like she hated everything.

And the last one, who was practically the size of a mountain. What name had Ffion used? Griffith. Griffith with a scale tattoo like twining vines.

Ashem's gaze flicked around the group. "It appears that we've lost them. At least, I don't sense Kavar. Change forms. I know a place in these mountains. It's ancient. If we're lucky, Owain and Kavar have forgotten it exists."

"You can't be serious," Morwenna snapped. "We have to get him home!"

Ashem's lip curled. "It's too far. He won't survive." He jerked his head at Evan. "You and Morwenna fly south back to Eryri. Get Commander Tane's Ironscale Vee and bring them back here as a security escort. If we can remain hidden until your return, there's a chance Kavar will think we snuck past him and his Talon and are flying for Eryri."

"When he knows Rhys is as injured as he is?" Morwenna's perfectly arched brows pinched together. "We should just contact—"

Ashem cut her off with gesture and a glare. "Our singstones and all of our things were left in the meadow. The meadow the Talon now occupies. Unless you have yours?"

She looked away, jaw clenching. "No."

"So we have no way of contacting anyone. By now, Owain knows Rhys is wounded and stranded, and that I was stupid enough to allow Deryn to come. We will need help."

Morwenna opened her mouth to protest again, but Ashem cut her off. "Go!"

"We'll be back soon." Evan slid his arm from Deryn's waist.

Morwenna tossed her hair, speaking through gritted teeth. "Get the singstones back and contact us if you can." She stared at Rhys as if memorizing the sight of him. "Don't let anything happen to him."

Ashem nodded. "Wind carry you well."

"And you." Evan put a hand on Morwenna's arm and pulled her away. They walked beyond the nearest trees and out of Kai's line of sight. A moment later, the pines rustled in a sudden, brief gust of wind. Two dragons, one midnight blue, one red-black, flashed across a patch of sky and were gone.

"Cadoc, Griffith, bring Rhys," Ashem commanded.

The two men hefted Rhys carefully between them and headed into the trees.

Ffion tugged Kai gently in the same direction. Kai dug her heels into the carpet of pine. "Wait. I need to get back. My friend will be worried."

Ffion glanced worriedly from Rhys back to Kai. "I'm sorry. You can't go back right now. There's no time."

Kai leaned away from Ffion. "No time? I stabbed a *dragon* with a *sword* for you people. Take me back!"

Ffion tugged again. Kai tried to wrench her arm free, but she might as well have tried to pull a building down with her bare hands.

Ashem noticed the commotion. He strode over, scowling, and lifted a hand toward Kai. "We don't have time for this."

Kai cringed, but it didn't stop the sickeningly familiar sensation, like someone cracking open her mind. She tried to scream, but everything went black again.

CHAPTER 5

KAI

D arkness. Warmth. The smell of stone. Soothing, mellow notes plucked on a guitar.

Something was wrong in her head. It didn't hurt, exactly, but it felt like it might if she moved.

Kai opened her eyes and saw a ceiling covered in the most gorgeous mosaic she'd ever seen: a lush forest beneath a full moon. In the forest, dragons.

They're everywhere these days.

She turned, careful not to move too fast. Little shocks of pain zinged through the base of her skull. Her vision blurred and sharpened like a camera that wouldn't stay in focus.

A lean, beautiful man with disheveled black hair and amethyst eyes sat an arm's length away, rocking a heavy wooden chair on its back legs like a bored kid at school. Long, artistic fingers flowed over the neck of an acoustic guitar, picking out an intricate, mournful melody.

A name drifted out of her brain and attached itself to the man.

Cadoc.

In a gut-wrenching flash, she remembered. *Dragons.* The violence and violation of Kavar in her mind.

Waking up in the pines.

Rhys bloody and unconscious.

Cadoc holding fire in his hands.

She bolted upright. Heavy blankets that smelled musty with age slithered down to bunch around her hips. Agony bloomed between her temples. She tried to scream, but emitted a choked garble instead. Nausea burned in her stomach, and bile rose in her throat.

"Easy, *brânwen.*"

A ceramic bowl slid into her lap, and a cool hand gathered loose hair away from the base of her neck. She clutched the bowl as her stomach constricted and heaved. She didn't have much to lose, which made it worse.

"Ow." She whimpered, tears of pain streaming from her eyes. She was still wearing her hoodie. She touched the pocket, but there was nothing there. She'd stuck her cell phone in her pack the night before. As far as she knew, that pack was still sitting next to the firepit in the meadow where the dragons had fought. Kai bit back a whimper.

The bowl shifted, and a cool goblet of water seemed to materialize in her hands.

"Rinse and spit."

Fighting her rising panic, Kai swirled water in her mouth and spit into the bowl, which was whisked away. Black strands of hair fell around her face.

"Cadoc," she croaked. Moving tentatively, she raised her head. If it had to be a dragon, at least it was the one who had promised she'd be safe.

He rose with the bowl in hand, smiling that smile that made her feel like things might be all right. "At your service."

His voice was light: half teasing, half serious. His accent made it sound like music. Musical chocolate.

Kai looked around. She lay in a massive bed covered in blankets and furs. The air was cold, but she was warm. The smell of age and dust was everywhere. There were no windows, but every inch of the walls in the room had been carved into fantastical, three-dimensional designs of trees covered in flowering vines, a continuation of the forest scene above. A few carved animals peered out from between them here and there. Hundreds of tiny fires burning in nooks and crannies lit the room like fairy lights. The floor was a dozen shades of green and gray marble pieced to look like patches of moss and a scattering of stones, polished until it shone.

"Are we in a castle?"

Cadoc's smile was crooked. "More like a palace. At least, what remains of one."

"Remains?"

"It's older than old. A complex of rooms, halls, treasure chambers, and tunnels under your 'Rocky Mountains' that dates back to the dawn of dragon time. It was falling out of use right as we started coming into contact with your people. Human-sized rooms are almost all that's left of it, in fact, because they were newer and closer to the top. The rest is collapsed. Retaken by the mountains and lost to time. Lost to us as well, until some scouts rediscovered it and Ashem decided it might be useful."

"Oh." That felt like too much to mentally sort through at the moment, so Kai set it aside.

When she'd woken earlier, it had been dawn. What time was it now?

Juli was going to kill her.

Kai tried to swallow the nasty taste in her mouth. "My head hurts."

Cadoc gave her a concerned once-over. "Are you going to be sick again?"

Kai grunted a negative and rubbed her eyes. If she held still, the aching subsided, but her thoughts skittered out of reach. All but one.

Kavar. He'd been in her head and left his name behind like a scar. For a moment she thought she'd lied to Cadoc about not being sick again. She opened her eyes to ask for the bowl, but he was already moving toward a heavy wooden door in the far wall.

"I won't be a moment. You're going to be all right. Just remember to breathe." He pulled open the door, giving Kai a glimpse of a hallway outside. More mosaic. More carved stone. More tiny lights. Then he was gone.

Kai put her head on her knees and breathed deeply. She was in an underground palace with a bunch of strangers, who were also dragons. She'd stabbed a dragon named Kavar with a sword. Juli—and by now, Kai's family—were probably out of their minds with worry. There would be search parties out. They'd be terrified, uncertain of her fate. Shit, shit, shit.

Cadoc reappeared, his hands empty. He must have gotten rid of the bowl. He grinned at Kai and stepped to the side of the doorway, as if performing a magic trick. Ashem appeared behind him: dark, built, and scowling. Pushing past Cadoc, he sat rigidly in the chair next to Kai's bed. "You're awake."

"Stay out of my head." Kai pressed her hands against either side of her head, as if that might keep him out.

Ashem leaned forward, resting his elbows on his knees. His eyes were the color of molten gold but held none of Cadoc's warmth. Everything about him, from his posture to the way he moved, screamed "military." His brow creased in a clinical-looking frown, eyes dispassionately roving over her face and body.

44

Something *other* brushed her mind. Kai yelped and pressed her hands tighter against her head. Her pulse boomed in her ears and bile rose again in her throat. She fought it down, concentrating her entire will on keeping him out of her head.

"No! Get out!" The gorgeous room wavered around the edges.

Ashem's frown deepened from vague to annoyed. Cadoc knelt next to the bed, his voice soothing. "He's trying to help."

Kai pushed harder against the disturbance in her mind, teeth clenched. "I don't want his help! Give me an ibuprofen and I'll be fine!"

Ashem didn't withdraw. His touch was soft and deft, not like Kavar's, but close enough. The mental pressure grew, and her breath turned to sharp, ragged gasps.

"No!"

"Leave it, Commander." Cadoc didn't snap, but it was the closest Kai had heard him come so far. "She's whiter than snow."

Ashem pinned Kai with his lion eyes. "Do you want this headache?"

"I'll deal with it if it keeps you out of my head!"

Ashem glared. She glared back. Finally, his mental touch withdrew. "Deal with it, then." He stood, addressing Cadoc as he stalked toward the door. "Rhys should regain consciousness soon, if it worked. Pray to all of the Ancients it did." He exited, slamming the door behind him.

Kai exhaled, sagging against the wall.

"Rhys is lucky he wasn't killed," Cadoc muttered. He had the guitar back in his hands and examined the wooden body closely. "We might all be dead, if not for you."

"Well... I'm glad you're not. And I'm not. I think." Kai looked down, taking stock of her body, her clothes. She only had what she'd been wearing—a sea-green hoodie that Juli had picked out because it matched Kai's eyes, jeans with a couple of carabiners threaded through the belt loops, and a white tank top. She wiggled her toes, determining her socks were still intact, and assumed her hiking boots were somewhere near the bed on the floor.

"So, Rhys... he's alive?"

Cadoc picked up his guitar. His fingers rippled over the strings like water, but his voice had a hard edge. "Kavar didn't have much venom left by the time he bit Rhys. He'll survive." He sounded sure, but threw a worried glance over his shoulder at the closed door.

Kai leaned her head back against the soft pillows behind her and followed Cadoc's gaze. The door was wooden and ornately carved. It looked heavy. If it was locked, there'd be no way out of this room short of dynamite. "Am I kidnapped?"

Letting out a surprised laugh, Cadoc shrugged. "A little."

Kai frowned, her unease growing. "A little?"

"Yes."

"I don't understand."

"Yes means yes, *brânwen*." He plucked another complex tune on the guitar, his fingers a blur. "We brought you with us because you saved Deryn and Rhys last night. We owe you."

Kai rubbed her head. "You owe me, so I'm kidnapped."

"Would you rather we'd left you in the meadow to be squashed or eaten?"

Kai blanched. "No. But I'm alive, and so are Deryn and Rhys and all of you, so thanks and you're welcome. When can I leave?"

Cadoc smiled. "Not quite yet. Demba and the rest of Kavar's vee are flying all over this half of Turtle Island looking for us. We have to lay low for a bit."

"Turtle Island?"

Cadoc's brow furrowed, then cleared. "Oh, that's right. It's North America now. It changes so frequently."

"The name of the continent?" Kai was only half listening. Her heart sped again, thinking of her parents. Her brothers. And Juli, who would tear the dragon-infested mountains apart looking for her. Instead of waiting for his answer, she asked a couple of her more pressing questions. "How long is 'a bit'? And what's a vee?"

"A bit is probably a day or so. We—that is, we dragons—will be here until Evan and Morwenna get back, but there's no reason I can't fly you home, as long as we don't get caught. It's only a couple of hours south, if it's anywhere near where you found us."

Kai relaxed a fraction. "Not too far if you're flying, I imagine. We can't go now?"

Cadoc laughed again. "No such luck, I'm afraid. But soon." He stood, pulling the strap of his guitar over one shoulder. "You're all right?"

Not in the least. "I'll survive. Can you tell me what 'vee' means?"

"A vee is a group of ten to fifteen dragons raised and trained together from childhood. It's our basic military unit." He rose. "Now that you're awake, I'm going to step out. When I said you're a little kidnapped, I really did mean a little. As I said, we're in a palace complex. It's ancient and quite interesting. Feel free to explore, except for the dangerous parts. We dragons will all be hovering around Rhys's room for the most part, until he gets better or he... Anyway, he's just down the hall, so that's where I'll be if you need anything." He opened the door and pointed to the right. Then he pointed to the left. "That way is the exit, if you want to take a look outside. There's rather a steep step out front, though. Mind you don't fall."

47

With a wink, he disappeared and closed the door behind him.

"Wait," she said to the closed door. "How do I know which are the dangerous parts?"

But Cadoc, obviously, was gone. Kai threw off the blankets and scooted to the edge of the bed. She half-heartedly straightened her bedding, but the thing was huge. At least the size of a California king. She might have considered doing a better job—Juli certainly would have—but her head still hurt and she hadn't eaten in who knew how long, so she did what she could and walked out into the hall. Cadoc had said there was an exit. If the dragons—holy shit, *dragons*—wouldn't take her home, she would just take herself.

She held her breath for a moment when she tried the heavy door, but it wasn't locked. It didn't even have a doorknob, just a bar that slid into a slot in the stone wall. She pulled it open and stepped into the hall, her eyes going wide.

The hall wasn't just a hallway, it was a *hall*. Vast, with polished marble floors and carved white walls and a ceiling that arched some fifty feet overhead. It was so wide, she imagined it must have been made for dragons.

A scattering of heavy doors lined the sides of the white walls, each surrounded by an arch of stone etched with runes. Fist-sized gemstones were sunk into the archways at intervals, glittering in hazy shafts of light that slanted down from above. Kai looked up, but the source of the light was hidden. It might be mirrors, or magic, or even windows somehow carved into the mountain above.

Voices echoed down the hall from a door that had been left partially open. Kai recognized Ashem's impatient bark and decided that must be where they had Rhys. Cadoc had said the exit was in the opposite direction, so that was the way she turned, praying she didn't get lost.

Thankfully, there weren't any twists and turns to get lost in. The massive hall led to wide, shallow stairs that descended into a chamber so vast, Kai could hardly see the other side from where she was standing. What she could see, however, was the huge archway—wide enough for three dragons, at least—that yawned open, showing the blue sky.

Kai scrambled down the stairs and into the huge chamber. The floor was an unbroken polished black that reflected small points of light from the ceiling a few hundred feet above, and Kai felt like she was stepping onto an ocean of stars. The walls of the chamber were also black. But instead of the intricate carvings in the hall and her room, they'd been left rough-hewn, with only the outlines of false columns carved into the stone at intervals. Larger fires burned in hollows within the columns, casting a little more light around the room.

However, Kai didn't have time to feel the appropriate awe at the size and grandeur of the place. Instead, she made a beeline for the arch that showed the sky. As she passed beneath it and outside onto a ledge, the temperature dropped from comfortable to cold.

Outside, the sun was so brilliant it momentarily washed out her vision. Her eyes adjusted, and color slowly seeped into the haze of white. Her mouth fell open. Cadoc had said the palace complex was underground, but she hadn't expected this.

A large, flat ledge as wide as the archway extended out about thirty feet before dropping off in a sheer cliff. Over a hundred feet below, the cliff became a more gradual slope populated with pine and aspen. She backed away from the edge and walked to one side of the platform, looking for a path traversable by humans. There was none. She walked to the other side. Still nothing.

She was trapped. The ledge was a perfect landing platform for flying creatures, but offered no way for a land-bound human to escape. Damn it. No wonder Cadoc had been so nonchalant about letting her wander around.

Her eyes watered. She told herself it was the wind, not tears, and tried to at least gauge where she was. Mountains stretched into the misty blue distance, snowy peaks rising and falling like frozen ocean waves in the endless wilderness.

Yeah, no. Aside from being in the North American Rockies —which she only knew because Cadoc had told her—she didn't have a clue where she might be. "Only a couple hours" from where she'd found the dragons, but how fast could dragons fly? A couple hours could mean anything from a few miles to a few hundred miles. Maybe more. Cadoc had also said that where she'd found them was south of here, which narrowed it down a little, but not much. She could be anywhere from Colorado to Canada.

Kai shivered beneath the cloudless dome of sky, then leaned over the edge again, assessing. She'd been rock climbing since she was a kid. A climb from here would be possible, but dangerous. If she had the right gear, she would've considered it. But without gear, without direction, there was just no way.

She had been kidnapped by dragons. Until they decided to set her free, she was at their mercy.

CHAPTER 6

RHYS

Rhys burned. Fire licked his insides with tongues of icy flame; his bones cracked and sizzled. Time didn't exist, only dark and pain and cold.

Something pricked his arm. Warmth. Blessed heat. It seeped through his veins and into his shoulder. The soul-searing cold began to melt. The blackness drew back from his mind, and coherent thought unfurled like wings.

He woke with a gasp, bursting through the last frozen crust of unconsciousness. Rhys shot up, his last memory was of battle, of Kavar sinking long, yellow teeth into his shoulder, of thinking he was dead.

The movement sent pain crackling through him, making his eyes water. Through the blur of unshed tears, he saw an ornate room. A fire. A bed. His friends.

Ashem scowled above him, a syringe in his hand. "Lie down."

Rhys complied, dizzy. "Where are we?"

"One of the palaces of the Ancients. The one I told you I wanted to turn into an outpost. The upper level is livable enough. Especially since I've been personally stocking it with necessities for the last two years."

Ashem tugged on the bandages and Rhys bit his tongue, stifling a groan. Across the room, Cadoc leaned against a wall, glaring. Ffion and Griffith were there as well, watching him.

"Where's—"

The bed moved, and suddenly Deryn loomed over him. She was kneeling next to him on the mattress, her face contorted with rage. "You *used* it on me! If Kavar hasn't killed you, be sure I'm about to finish the job!"

Despite his exhaustion, Rhys gave her a patronizing grin. "I have to protect my beloved baby sister."

Deryn slapped him. Rhys grunted in shock. She pushed away from him, rolling off the bed and onto her feet next to Ashem. At least her leg had healed.

She folded her arms across her chest. Her long hair hung loose around her shoulders. When she spoke, there were suppressed tears in her voice. "I'm glad you're alive, but I am so, so angry at you."

Embarrassed, Rhys touched his cheek. "It was that bad?"

From where he and Ffion stood at the end of the bed, Griffith regarded Rhys with eyes like still, green pools. "You were in the fords of the river, boyo, and we almost didn't get you back."

Rhys tried to move, and pain ricocheted through his right shoulder and diagonally down his chest and stomach. His right arm wasn't much better, heavy and numb as stone. "We owed them blood."

Deryn bared her teeth, looking feral. "You won't let me risk myself, but you fly straight into danger. Ashem's spent all day trying to keep you alive."

"It took longer than I thought to create the antivenom. This place has limited resources." Ashem prodded the healing skin of Rhys's abdomen with two fingers. "Did that hurt?"

Rhys shook his head. The motion set the room spinning. "Good."

"How about this?" Cadoc punched him hard on his unbandaged left side.

"*Uffern dân*, Cadoc!" Rhys gasped. He rubbed his ribs, remembering to use his left hand.

Cadoc was unrepentant. "You should've left it to us. I've spent my life watching your back. Iain *died* saving you. Don't demean our sacrifices with your stupidity."

Rhys clenched his jaw against angry words and the pang of grief at Iain's loss, still fresh. Ten years might be a long time for humans, but for a dragon, it was nothing.

"Idiot." Ashem's voice came out as a growl. "I told you it was too dangerous for both you and Deryn to travel this far from Eryri." He looked like he wanted to throttle someone. Rhys thought that someone was most likely him. "I *told* you."

Rhys closed his eyes. "Seren didn't foresee any problems."

As Seeress, Rhys's other sister, Seren, wasn't supposed to have allegiances, especially not to family—meaning Rhys shouldn't have been asking her personal questions about her visions at all. But he had, and even though she shouldn't have answered, she'd done her best to tell him all she'd seen. Nothing stood out as a warning.

"Her visions are so twisted up in symbols we'd hardly know if she had." Cadoc's guitar *bonged* as he collapsed against the wall, and he cradled it to his chest, looking for damage. "You're lucky Kai was there."

"The human girl? Did she live?" Rhys had only woken long enough to see her inexplicably there, Kavar bending toward her, jaws wide.

"She stabbed Kavar." Ffion glanced up at Griffith, a small smile on her face. "She saved your life and almost got eaten for her trouble."

Rhys put a hand to his face. "I saw her with the sword. I saw Kavar try to kill her."

"It's my fault." Ashem's voice was gruff. "They might not have seen us if it weren't for the fire. I never should have allowed it."

The others exchanged looks. The fire had been allowed because the "mission" was nothing but a glorified holiday: secret and safe. This part of the world was well outside Owain's territory. None of them had been cautious. But no matter what they said, Ashem would blame himself.

Rhys shifted on his stack of pillows. "It's my fault Deryn was there. I should have made her stay in Eryri."

"You could certainly try," Deryn snapped.

"It happened." Ffion's gray gaze zipped from Rhys to Deryn to Ashem, and her voice was firm. "It's over. Now we need to worry about getting home without getting killed."

Rhys looked around again, and his fingers tightened in the blankets. "Where are Evan and Morwenna?"

Ashem said, "I sent them back to Eryri to bring Tane and the Ironscale Vee. Our singstones are still in the meadow, and likely so is Kavar. You stunned him and we managed to get enough of an edge over the others to escape. But it's likely his vee is still in that meadow with all our gear. We have no way of contacting anyone."

"So we're going to stay here until they can make the entire trip there and back? It's five thousand miles each way." Rhys gave his head a small shake, then clenched his jaw against the protest the movement elicited from his torn shoulder. "We can't stay here that long. We're too exposed. We should go back."

Ashem got a familiar forbidding look on his face. "No."

Rhys pushed himself higher, sweat popping out across his brow. "If Kavar was injured that badly, he may have commanded his vee back to Cadarnle. We could be hiding from nothing."

Ashem's brows contracted further and he opened his mouth to speak.

Ffion's light voice cut off whatever Ashem was about to say. "Will Kavar steal what we had at the camp?" She ran her fingers over the wide, delicately-worked platinum cuff around her right bicep. Griffith had given it to her at their pledging ceremony, and she always toyed with the diamond-studded coils when she was troubled. "I had records in my things I'd rather not lose."

Ashem shrugged. "Kavar has always done whatever takes his fancy. He'll rummage through our things. He may destroy them. But steal? I don't know. Kavar has never been one for material possessions. I'm inclined to think he'll leave them, but shield the meadow out of spite so you can't find it. But I am Azhdahā. He cannot hide it from me."

"I wonder if your own twin brother realizes you're Azhdahā like him," Cadoc commented drily.

Ashem shrugged. To Rhys, the gesture implied both Ashem's apathy and the innate superiority of his clan.

But Ashem was right. Each of the ten remaining dragon clans had their own magic, and he and Kavar were the only Azhdahā left. Anyone who tried to locate a place shielded by Azhdahā mind magic would suddenly find they needed to be somewhere else. They'd fly right over. If they were human, they'd run away screaming, repelled by forces they wouldn't be able to explain. The only people who could enter that meadow without a guide, a miracle, or a will as strong as the heart of a star were Ashem and those he permitted.

They all stood around a few moments longer, looking at Rhys and each other.

"I'm not dying today," Rhys said. "You can all sit down. Or leave so I can sleep."

Cadoc made a show of searching his pockets. "Aw, we aren't leaving, boyo. Not when we came so close to losing you forever. I'm sure we can find a way to pass the time." He finally produced a reed pipe, raised it to his lips, and began a jolly tune. It was so at odds with the tense atmosphere that Rhys smiled.

A face intruded in his mind. A girl. Pretty. Maybe even beautiful. Pale skin, ink-black hair, and eyes like a green sea. After so long in Eryri—the isolated archipelago of mountainous islands in the South Pacific that he and nearly two thousand other dragons called home—it had been almost shocking to see someone he didn't recognize on sight.

Shocking, and fascinating.

He touched the bandage on his shoulder. Never in ten thousand years would he have thought he'd owe his life to a human. "What happened to the woman? You didn't say."

Cadoc's gaze cut to Ashem. The tune turned even more absurdly merry.

"She's here." Ashem's voice was a flat counterpoint to the song.

"What?" Rhys shot up. He gritted his teeth against the rending pain in his shoulder. Warmth oozed beneath the bandage, and red blossomed on its white surface. He must look pathetic. "Damn it. Why did you bring her *here*?"

"Damn Kavar. This will take a full week to heal. Stop moving." Ashem examined the bandage, his tone long-suffering. "I'll have to change it again."

"Ashem. The human. Why is she *here*?"

"Should I have left her to Kavar?"

"Of course not."

"She saved your life and Deryn's. Perhaps she saved the

world." Ashem glared at Cadoc, whose song had morphed to an aggressively cheerful dancing reel.

Rhys had barely seen the human woman, but for some reason, knowing she was there made him glance around again, as if he might have missed her presence in the room. "Where is she? How is she?"

Ashem made an indifferent gesture toward a heavy wooden door and bared his teeth at Cadoc. "Cadoc ap Brychan, I swear on the blood of the Ancients that I will grind that pipe into powder and make you eat it!"

Cadoc winked at Ashem and stuffed the pipe back into his pocket. "All things considered, I think she's done beautifully. I, for one, plan to delight in her company for as long as she's here."

Deryn had wandered to a chair. Cadoc flopped down in one next to her and strummed a chord on his guitar. He chuckled at the expression on Ashem's face and plucked a somber ballad. "There's no life without music, Commander."

Ashem didn't stop glaring at Cadoc. "Do not tempt me to kill you."

Cadoc winked at him. "I can't help it. I am so very tempting."

"Ashem," Rhys said, pulling the attention of his near-apoplectic commander away from his idiot friend. "The human?"

None of your concern, Ashem said directly into his head. This, along with the ability to create shields, was the magic of the Azhdahā. Though all dragons could communicate mind-to-mind in dragon form, only Ashem and Kavar could do so as humans.

Rhys held Ashem's gaze. *We can't draw the attention of the humans.* Though Rhys couldn't actually send the thought, Ashem would be able to "hear" it.

It's too late to worry about that. They'll think she went missing in the mountains. Speaking of which...

Ashem cleared his throat and spoke aloud. "About the human girl."

Cadoc perked up. "Woman."

Ashem sent his gaze skyward with a sigh. "She's here because she saved Rhys and Deryn. Don't tell her anything." He hesitated, then spoke again. "The unheartsworn males—Cadoc and I—should see if she can be sworn." He looked like he'd rather cut off his own wings.

"Rhys isn't heartsworn," Cadoc said.

Anger immediately washed over Rhys. "I will *not* heartswear to a human. We know exactly where that got my father. Where it got all of us."

Deryn's face looked pained. "Rhys, Mother was—"

"Not someone I will waste another moment of my life thinking about," Rhys snapped. At her hurt expression, guilt welled up inside him. "I'm sorry, Deryn. I know you were close."

Deryn shook her head. "Close just means she betrayed me more."

Ashem glowered at Cadoc, who lifted his hands in surrender. "Sorry I suggested it."

"Not Rhys," Ashem said. "He's right. It's too complicated. Once we've made sure she can't be heartsworn, we'll take her home."

Rhys shot Ashem an incredulous look. "Do you think it's wise for any of you to bring a Wingless mate back to Eryri, given the state of things?"

Ashem shrugged. "We're at war, and heartswearing means extra magic and extra strength. The whining of a few malcontents hardly matters if I'm better able to do my job."

Cadoc gave a dramatic sigh. "Alas, the fair raven is not for me. I've touched her twice and nothing happened."

"Skin to skin?" Ashem asked. "Nothing interfering?"

"I know how heartswearing works, Commander. I'm not a child," Cadoc said.

Deryn leaned over and flicked Cadoc's ear. "The *fair raven*? Sounds childish to me. Tell me, Cadoc, do you write your horrid poetry beforehand or does garbage spew from your lips as you speak?"

Cadoc dodged away from her and winked. "I write it down, love. I'd hate to deprive the world of my words when I'm gone. Anyway, looks like you're her only shot, Commander."

Ashem's face soured further, and Rhys had to hide a smile.

Griffith cleared his throat. "There's also the matter of food," he rumbled.

"There's some food here. If we stick within a few miles, we can hunt deer."

Rhys's own empty stomach roiled, and he realized that he was starving. *Another reason to leave here,* he thought at Ashem.

Ashem threw up his hands, snarling at Rhys. "Fine. We will check and see if we're hemmed in. And when we find out we are, you will all be put through the workout of your life.

"Ffion, Griffith, you two *carefully* range out about a hundred miles and see if any other dragons are in the area. If things are clear, we'll fly for Eryri. However, in the very likely case that we must stay here until help comes, we need food. We have some staples, but no perishables. Deryn, your leg should be healed tomorrow, so tomorrow morning you and Cadoc may hunt in the valley below here, where I can watch you. Cadoc or I can take the human girl home after that."

"*If* she isn't heartsworn to you, Commander," Cadoc said,

"I've already volunteered to take her back. But you never know. It could be love."

Ashem spoke through gritted teeth. "Take your musical twiddlings and go sit the first watch."

"Anything to please you." Cadoc swept a bow to the room and left.

Rhys touched the bandages across his chest. "Ashem. There's the matter of the mantle ritual."

"No."

"We're exposed. I—"

"*No*," Ashem repeated. He leaned over the bed, one hand sinking into the mattress as he leaned in close, speaking through clenched teeth. "You have internal injuries from the venom. You have no idea how close to death you linger, even now. It. Will. Kill. You. Do you understand?"

Rhys's nostrils flared, but he nodded. "What about lesser magic?"

Ashem pulled back and skimmed his gaze over Rhys as he considered. "You can perform the ritual for fire as soon as you can move well enough to do it. A day or two, I expect."

Rhys tested his arm. It would probably be two days, but he'd try tomorrow all the same. "Thank you."

Ffion and Griffith approached Ashem, and the three of them spoke softly. Deryn climbed into the massive bed and curled up on the other side, her back to Rhys. He reached over the few feet of mattress between them and touched his sister's hair in silent apology. *Forgive me for all of this, because I cannot. Not when I brought you so close to harm. I'm so sorry, Deryn.*

Though she couldn't hear his thoughts when they were both human, Deryn lifted her hand from where it rested on her shoulder and grasped his fingers, squeezing for a moment before she let go. But she didn't turn, didn't speak. He would be forgiven, but he wasn't yet.

Rhys settled back, his thoughts lingering on the human girl. Human mates weren't uncommon, but Rhys would rather declare himself Unsworn than be bound to one. The Council would fly into a rage if Rhys turned up with a Wingless mate. Politics aside, humans were too changeable, too unpredictable, too apt to betray.

His mother had been human.

His lip curled. Thrusting thoughts of *her* into the deep recesses of his mind, Rhys settled deeper into his pillow, looking one more time at his sister before he let his eyes drift closed. As long as she was in danger, he wouldn't rest easy. He had to get her back to Eryri. She was his main concern, not some random human girl.

At most, Kai Monahan would only be around a day or two, no more than a blink. Staying away would be no challenge at all.

CHAPTER 7
KAI

K ai returned to her room hoping to find Cadoc, but it was empty. She grasped one of the carabiners attached to her belt loop and rubbed one thumb across the smooth metal bar. He was probably still with Rhys and the others. At least they had each other to talk to.

Shrugging off the sudden, overwhelming feeling of isolation, Kai walked back down the echoing hall to the massive black chamber, with its impossibly high ceiling and its reflective floor and all those little lights that made her feel like she was floating in space.

She wanted to get a better look at those natural stone walls.

She stepped off the stairs and examined the raw stone. It was full of interesting cracks and crevices that a climber might make use of, if they had the time. Reaching up, she slid her hands along the wall until she found natural handholds. Her shoulders unknotted. Her headache dulled. She exhaled. As easy as breathing, she lifted her foot to a little outcrop and pulled herself up.

Someone laughed, warm and rich. Kai sprang down from

the wall, landing in a crouch. Cadoc stood behind her, guitar over one shoulder. "What are you doing?"

Kai's cheeks heated. "Nothing."

"Climbing the walls already? You haven't even been here a day."

"It's good rock," Kai said defensively. On the ground, her headache returned. Her stomach cramped, reminding her that it had been too long since she'd eaten something and kept it down. "Is there anything to eat?"

He cocked an eyebrow, then walked toward a shadowed alcove on the opposite side of the cavern, motioning for her to follow. As he approached, fires sprang up, illuminating a short hall that led, incredibly, to a huge kitchen. Granted, it looked like a kitchen straight out of medieval times, with rough wooden countertops, open hearths featuring meat-roasting spits, several sinks the size of baby bathtubs, and a wooden table large enough to host a Viking feast. But it was still recognizably a kitchen, and that made Kai feel a bit less desperately lost.

Something that could only be described as a cauldron sat in one of the hearths. It even had wood stacked beneath it.

"We haven't had time to cook anything yet, but I think you and I can get something started."

Cadoc pulled a wooden bowl off a set of shelves, which were filled with an assortment of plain bowls, plates, and fat round cups. Another shelf sat next to it covered in sculpted glass goblets and flatware of fine porcelain, silver, and gold.

"Were we expected here?" Kai asked.

Cadoc smiled. "Who knows when it comes to these ancient places." He walked to an open wooden bin built into one of the walls, and bent to lift out a couple of sacks.

"I'll make you a deal, Kai Monahan. You stand at the

entrance and watch for murderous dragons to come flying through the sky toward us, and I'll make you food."

"That sounds good to me."

Kai wandered back out into the star-flecked cavern, standing just inside whatever spell or dragon magic kept the warm air in. It took about an hour, but soon enough, Cadoc emerged from the short hall with a steaming bowl. He handed it to her, and Kai peered inside. It was full of beans and rice. She sniffed it and caught the faint smell of spices.

"This is what dragons eat?" she asked dubiously.

Cadoc shrugged. "When there's nothing else to be had."

"Do dragons use utensils?"

Cadoc handed her a wooden spoon.

"Thank you." She shoved a lump of rice and beans into her mouth, pleasantly surprised at the taste. It was smoky, like cumin, and had just the right amount of salt.

Cadoc watched her, a smile hovering around the edges of his mouth. "There will be meat tomorrow. Venison, most likely. Griffith is incredible at cooking venison."

"I'll look forward to it."

Cadoc smiled, then looked out to the red light of sunset spilling across the floor of the main cavern. "No enemy dragons?"

"None that I saw."

"Good. Then I relieve you of your watch. I'll have to sit mine outside, or Ashem will get in a snit."

Kai hesitated. She had nothing else to do here. No one else to talk to. And whatever the technicalities of her kidnapping were, it could only help to know about the people who'd brought her here. It would be better than passing the days sitting in her room. Knowledge was power, especially knowledge about people and how they worked. This was as good time as any to start collecting it.

Besides, who wouldn't have a thousand questions upon discovering dragons?

She smiled at Cadoc. "Can I sit with you? I'd rather not be alone."

His sensuous mouth curved. "Until the end of time, love."

Kai almost choked on her rice. Men who looked like Cadoc shouldn't say things like that.

Cadoc noted her flustered face, winked, and jerked his chin in a follow-me motion. They walked onto the ledge, which was far colder than the interior of the cave. Kai clung to her warm bowl, eating the food slowly while Cadoc swung one leg over the edge and pulled his guitar into his lap. His fingers ran like liquid over the strings and he started to sing, the notes of the guitar intertwining with the rich tenor of his voice.

And what a voice he had. Kai didn't understand the language—but she could *feel* the words, all longing and sadness. It went on for a long time—long enough for her to finish her food and set the bowl aside.

When the song was over, she let out a breath. It misted in the air before her. "That was beautiful."

He let out a short, self-deprecating laugh. "Thank you."

"What language was that?"

"Welsh." He caressed the guitar.

"Is that where you're all from? Wales? The mystery language is Welsh?"

"Yes. Though it's been a long time." His voice was soft, and he stared into the distance at something beyond the moonlit valley.

"Question."

Cadoc smiled. "Yes?"

"Why do you speak Welsh and English and not...dragon?"

He laughed. "Dragon?"

Kai nodded.

"We—dragons—have a language. It's fairly dead, but we write in it a bit. When we're actually dragons, we talk in here." He touched his forehead with a finger, then Kai's. His fingers were warm, and she did her best to suppress a shiver. Of what, she wasn't sure.

Cadoc continued. "We speak whatever language our clans raised us speaking, mostly local human languages, and we try to keep up as times change. But it's been a long time since I've been back to dear Cymru."

"You sound like you miss it."

"I do."

Sadness tinged his voice, and Kai searched for a way to cheer him up again. "Do you know any songs I might know?"

Cadoc's sadness dropped away. He gave her a stern look, taking up the guitar again. "Darlin'," he drawled in an awful American accent, "I know *all* the songs." He strummed a chord and sang the first line from the Beatles' "Blackbird" in a ridiculously high falsetto. Kai laughed, then sang along with him. After another line, Cadoc stopped singing, though he still played, alternately strumming and plucking to accompany her.

She caught his eye, surprised to see genuine pleasure on his face. After a few more lines, he sang again, harmonizing. Silence crashed over them when the song ended, and Cadoc stared an instant too long before he started to laugh. Kai laughed with him.

"You've got a voice like fine gossamer, *brânwen*."

Kai snorted. "Thanks. You too."

They laughed again, and Kai shivered. The sun had set, the light changing from orange and red to the washed-out grayscale of a nearly full moon. Frigid night sank into her bones.

"Are you cold?"

"I'm all right."

"That is an untruth." He set the guitar aside and took her

hands. Grinning wickedly, he exhaled warm breath on her fingers. A wave of tingling heat pulsed through her body. She gasped.

"Better?"

She could see the moon in his amethyst eyes. For a moment, they stared at one another. Then he let go. "If you need a little warming, that trick works like a charm. No good for anything serious, though. If you're too cold, it does more harm than good."

"It's magic." She couldn't keep the wonder out of her voice.

"You like that, do you?" He put a palm up between them, and a white flame appeared. It darted along his fingers, rolling over and between them like a magician's coin.

"I do. I'm so curious about it, but I don't want to drown you in questions."

Cadoc shrugged. "Drown away. We have plenty of time."

Kai considered, staring out into the vast distance. This was what she wanted, but she had to be certain of the consequences. "If I ask and you tell, won't I be a risk? I could tell other humans all about you."

Cadoc chuckled. "Not to put too fine a point on it, but no one would believe you."

Kai thought about this, then laughed. He was right. "Fine then. I'll drown you. How does magic work? Does it make you tired?"

"Tired? Not so much. Every dragon has... let's call it a well or a battery. The well must be filled. The battery must be charged. We do this with a ritual, which differs from clan to clan, dragon to dragon. Once the ritual is performed, we have enough power to do magic until said well runs dry. Sometimes you can go weeks between rituals. Sometimes, like when you're a soldier in the field, you must be vigilant about performing it daily so the well is always at its fullest. This"—he rolled the flame between his fingers again—"is but a drop of power. I could do this all day, for a few days, even, and still have enough magic to call on."

"What about transforming?" Kai asked.

"Transforming is something else. It can get tiring, but we can usually go back and forth a handful of times a day. More, if we push ourselves."

Kai followed the flame with her eyes as he tossed it up, made two, and started to juggle. "So if you were a dragon, you could shoot flames from your mouth and your claws and just immolate everything in sight?"

He caught the little flames and sent them flying around her in a rush of warm breeze. "No. Clan Draig can't manipulate magic as delicately as this when we're in dragon form. We're more about brute force. Breath weapons only. Those are usually enough. But some other dragons have the wherewithal to do other magic while maintaining the dragon. Most notably the Azhdahā. They are, in all forms, exceedingly deadly." Cadoc closed his hand and the little flames died.

Kai blinked away their afterimage, still wishing to see more. "That was incredible."

"I'm a talented man, *brânwen*."

Kai tilted her head. "Another question. Brahn-wen. What does it mean?"

He reached over and twisted a strand of her hair around his finger. "Raven. For your hair. Fair raven. White raven. A symbol of victory and good luck. Perhaps not according to the mythology, but according to me." He let his hand drop, then picked up the guitar and played again, for once refusing to make eye contact.

The song ended, and he began another. Not liking that they had fallen into an awkward silence, Kai touched Cadoc's wrist when he finished the next song.

He raised an eyebrow.

"Another question again. What's this?" Kai pushed up his sleeve. Red-orange scales glimmered in the moonlight. Beneath her hand, the design was pebbled and warm. She wasn't sure why that surprised her, but it did. She resisted the urge to trace it with her fingers and released his wrist.

His eyes followed her hand, and cleared his throat. "An indicium. We take human bodies, but we are always dragon. They're same color as our scales. Some have them on the right arm, some the left. Doesn't seem to matter which."

Kai laughed, once again caught up in the magic. "This is fascinating. Dragons. I bet you have your own entire history. I'd love to hear stories."

"About dragons?"

"If you don't mind."

He laughed. "You're asking the wrong person. Ffion is our resident historian and scholar. Or I suppose you could ask Griffith. I imagine he knows whatever she does."

"Why?"

"They're heartsworn."

Kai waited for the word to make sense. It didn't. "Heartsworn?"

"He's like her...ah...husband. Except that's not really the word."

"They're married?"

Cadoc shook his head. "They're heartsworn. Married, or mates. But not really either. It's...more."

"More than mates? What does that mean?"

Cadoc laughed. "You haven't drowned me yet, but that is a question with a long answer." He stopped playing and tinkered with the tuning pegs, then gave her a wink. "Care to trade the rest of it for a kiss?"

Kai snorted. She liked Cadoc. He had no shame. "I'll just ask Ffion."

He sighed. "The sting of rejection. Alas. Though it will be a few days before you can speak to her. Tomorrow, she and Griffith will be out scouting to see if the coast is clear."

"Out?" Kai's brow furrowed. "Why can't they take me back?"

"Because if the Talon—Kavar's vee—*is* flying around out there, the last thing either of those two needs is worrying about the human girl on their back. If things are clear, we'll take you home once Ffion and Griffith return."

Slowly, Kai nodded. Things were going to be a shit show by the time she got home. She just hoped Juli would forgive her one day. And her parents. And everyone who had to spend the next few days believing she was dead.

A tune even more poignant than the first coiled through the air. He didn't sing; the haunting, heartbreaking notes spoke for themselves. When it finally ended, Kai felt like she was waking up from a trance.

Cadoc nudged her. "I've kept you late enough, I think."

Kai protested, but he put his hands over hers, engulfing them, warming them. She hadn't even realized she was cold again. "I appreciate your company, *brânwen*, but you should go to bed. My watch will be over soon, in any case."

"Fine." She hesitated. "Will you play that song again before I go? The first one?"

He smiled, and it was beautiful enough to break hearts. "I'd love to."

Music drifted into the air.

CHAPTER 8
ASHEM

B ecause Ashem was monitoring his surroundings—listening alone required only a tiny trickle of magic, and he was rigorous about the morning ritual that filled his well of power—he sensed Kai Monahan's mind several seconds before he heard the sound of her feet. Frankly, it was about time she was up and moving about. She'd slept through the morning rituals each dragon performed in solitude. She'd slept through the others leaving on their various missions. She'd slept through breakfast. He was beginning to think she'd stay asleep if he picked her up and tossed her into the half-frozen river that snaked around the base of the mountain.

Not that he would...without reason.

Because of her *sensitivities*, Ashem did not delve into her mind. He didn't listen hard enough to pick up her thoughts, and he couldn't have discerned her exact location even if he wanted to. His magic didn't work like that. He was merely aware that she was conscious and had entered within some fifty feet of him. His scowl deepened. He mentally prepared himself for what he was about to attempt.

Ancients, please do not let this girl be my heartsworn.

She came through the hall and into the room, starting when she saw him at the long table.

"Good morning, Ashem." She watched him warily.

He folded his arms across his chest and jerked his head toward the cauldron hanging in one of the fireplaces. "There's food."

"Thank you." Kai reached for the waistband of her pants. Apparently not finding what she was looking for, she closed her hand into a fist. Ffion had found some old clothes in one of the rooms. A loose pair of pants and a flowing shirt a few thousand years out of date, but preserved by magic. The loose fit only emphasized Kai's boyish figure. He said another prayer that she was not the one. A man wanted something to hold on to.

Kai half turned away from him. "So...everyone is gone?"

"Yes."

Silence.

"Your...accent is a little different. Are you not Welsh like the others?"

Stars, he hated small talk. He went to the sink to clean his bowl.

Kai sighed. "All right. We'll just be quiet, then. Can you hand me a bowl?"

Ashem grunted and pulled a wooden bowl down from the high shelf. He held onto it for a moment, looking from it to her.

Just get it over with.

He held up the bowl. Kai watched him expectantly, as if she thought he would move forward to hand it to her. He didn't. Instead, he shook it slightly.

"What are you doing?"

He shook the bowl again.

"Okay." Kai gave him a strange look and walked over to

74

SOUL OF SMOKE

retrieve the bowl. At the last second, he reached up and skimmed his fingers across the pale, freckled skin of her cheek.

Nothing happened. He let out a long, low exhale of relief.

"Ashem, what are you doing?"

He dropped his hand. "None of your concern."

"Well, it is my face."

Ashem scowled. His experiment concluded, he left the kitchen without another word to the human.

"Excuse me?" she called.

He ignored her, strode down the main hall, all the way to the end, then took a second hall just as large as the first down an incline and deeper into the mountain.

He'd go to the half-ruined library and spend the day watching records of old battles and working out new drills for the vee. That would occupy him, since Rhys wouldn't need him for a few hours and he'd already strengthened the barriers around the old palace. If anyone other than the members of his own vee happened upon it, they would suddenly remember they needed to be somewhere else. It took an incredibly strong personality to break through a barrier unaided. No one had ever managed it before, except Kavar. But that was more because he was Azhdahā—and Ashem's twin brother—than because of any particular personal strength.

Ashem was so wrapped up in his thoughts, he didn't realize the human girl had followed him until he stood in the dark, half-tumbled archway that led to the ancient library. A library where he'd stored a few things of his own.

"Wow. What's in there?" Kai peered past him into the darkness.

Ashem nearly jumped out of his skin. He hated being startled. It meant he hadn't been paying attention, which meant he hadn't been doing his job. He spun on Kai, using his mind to

75

put pressure on hers at the same time as he spoke. "Don't follow me."

"I don't have anything else—ahh!" Her face went bone white, and she clutched either side of her head. "Get out of my brain!"

Surprised at the depth of her reaction, Ashem withdrew. Kavar must have hurt her far more than he realized. "Your boredom is not my problem. I've fed you. You have clean clothes. Go find something to do. Away from me."

He turned his back on her before she could respond, striding into the dark. Though it was low, her voice echoed after him as she turned away and walked back up the passage.

"Okay, bye. Asshole."

CHAPTER 9

KAI

"Asshole," Kai muttered again, wandering back up the hall after leaving Ashem in a tantalizingly secret-looking ruined room. A room that begged to be explored, but it was dark, and Kai didn't want Ashem swooping out at her like a giant, angry bat. Not if it meant he might invade her mind again, leaving her trembling and caught in memories about Kavar.

So much for making him part of her mission to learn everything she could about dragons.

She touched the place his fingers had grazed her cheek. What had that been about? She shook her head, deciding she'd rather not know.

The echoes of her own footsteps were all that greeted her when she entered the vast, light-filled main hall.

Deserted with dragons. Alone with Ashem. Confined in a cave.

A slightly open door caught her eye, and Kai remembered Ashem wasn't her only option for company. Rhys was still here.

Rhys, with his heavy presence and stern mouth. He was stuck in his room. He might be as bored as she was.

Kai approached his room, uncertain. As she moved closer, the air grew pleasantly warm and heavy with the rich scent of smoke. Not like a campfire, but like some exotic perfumed wood burning.

Quietly, she peered inside.

Her eyes traced the room first. Where the walls in Kai's room depicted a nighttime forest, his were more like an alpine grotto, with natural cave-like lines and the suggestion of pine trees in the distance. The floor was gray marble, the ceiling a mosaic of white mountain peaks.

Rhys sat in profile with his left side toward her, cross-legged in the middle of the floor. He wore nothing but loose pants, his torso heavily bandaged. She'd been right last night—his hair was the same deep red as Deryn's. Thick and mussed again, like he'd slept on it.

A golden bowl sat in front of him, its exterior etched with a thousand wavering lines in a flame pattern. Inside the bowl, a single tongue of fire flickered on a small mound of embers, which sent up faint white spirals of smoke.

Kai sucked her bottom lip between her teeth at the sight of him. She shouldn't look. He was injured and...meditating? No, this had to be the magical "well-filling" ritual Cadoc had mentioned.

But she couldn't tear her eyes away. There was something uncannily *right* about drinking him in. As if the sight of his body was familiar, or should be. Like it was absolutely natural and good for her to memorize every detail of him.

Rhys wasn't bodybuilder huge, but he wasn't small either— every ounce of him perfectly right for his frame. Every ridge and dip of muscle so defined he could've been carved from granite. Faint scars traced much of his skin, with a few nastier ones visible here and there. He had a soldier's body. A warrior's body. Or maybe a knight's. Maybe that was why he looked so good sitting on the floor doing whatever ritual he was doing.

Her eyes moved over the ridges of his back, over the lines of his upper arm. Rhys was a fire dragon, wasn't he? Like Cadoc. How warm would his skin be beneath her palms? How would it feel to have his entire, hard body pressed against hers?

Heat flared in several inconvenient places. Rhys was a stranger. An injured stranger. It wasn't okay to linger on these kinds of thoughts about him, no matter how much he made her want to dive into the dirty fantasies and roll around in them like a raccoon in a dumpster.

He looked like he was trying to sit straight, but hunched a little, favoring his wounds. Rhys clutched a thin-bladed golden knife in his right hand. As Kai watched, he attempted to lift his arm and pass the blade through the flame. He closed his eyes, muttering guttural words that sounded more suited for a dragon's mouth than a human's.

Halfway through the motion, he winced, clutched his right shoulder, and dropped the knife into the bowl. Sparks burst into the air and the fire flickered and went out. Rhys cursed, then plucked the knife out. It clattered to the stone floor in a spray of ashes.

Kai must have gasped or shifted, because he turned suddenly, his eyes finding her.

"Kai?" There was mild surprise in his voice, as if she'd had an appointment and showed up a few minutes early.

Guilt seethed in her stomach, more for the dirty thoughts than for interrupting. Worse, heat flared beneath her skin, and she knew she'd just gone beet red. God damn her pasty skin. "Sorry! I can go. You're busy."

"No, it's all right. This is the third time I've failed anyway." He braced his good arm against the floor, then cursed again. "Can you give me a second? Getting around at the moment is a little undignified."

"I could help." Kai pulled the door open wider.

"No!" Rhys cleared his throat, then spoke more softly. "No, thank you. I'd like to maintain what dignity I have left."

"Of course." Kai stepped outside, halfway closing the door. When Rhys called out a minute later, she re-entered the room.

Rhys had moved to a massive bed piled high with blankets, with posts and a head and footboard carved from heavy, dark wood.

He was watching her. The bright blue of his eyes was equal parts terrifying and compelling. Despite how awkward it would've been, she nearly backed out of the room.

Then Rhys shifted and winced, breaking eye contact, and Kai felt like an iron band had been released from around her lungs.

It was a good thing he'd looked away, because she was staring again. From this angle, she could see the taut lines of his chest and stomach where he wasn't covered in bandages. Even more fascinating was the scale tattoo—indicium—that swirled like flame up his arm and down the entire right side of his body, ending at the base of his neck and disappearing beneath the blankets pooled at his waist. She might have thought it was ink, but she'd seen Cadoc's up close. Where his indicium was a warm, orangey red, Rhys's scales glittered crimson as blood. A small, ancient-looking book was open beside him, half buried in rumpled covers.

Kai's stomach clenched. It really didn't help that he'd moved to a bed, or that the covers looked like that, or that Rhys apparently liked to read. She wasn't sure what was wrong with her. Yeah, she liked to look at attractive men, but Rhys was lust-inducing in a way Kai had never felt before and wasn't prepared to deal with. She would rather face Ashem.

"So..." Rhys let the word hang in the air, and Kai realized the silence had dragged on an awkwardly long time. "How can I help you?"

She cleared her throat. "So... Everyone else is gone. I've just been left to my own devices in this place with no idea of where I am or when I get to go home."

Rhys frowned. "Ashem isn't here?"

"Oh, Ashem is here. But he doesn't like me and I don't like him delving into my brain without permission." An involuntary shudder rolled through her at the memory. "He doesn't like that I don't like it. We're avoiding each other."

Rhys frowned. "He's entering your mind when you've asked him not to?"

Kai swallowed and shook her head. "Yeah. I asked him not to. It reminds me of Kavar." Another shudder.

"I'll speak to him," Rhys said.

Kai scoffed. "I don't think he takes orders."

A smile played around the corner of Rhys's mouth. "No. But sometimes he'll take suggestions from me."

"Then sure. Thanks." It wouldn't work, but it was nice of him to offer. Kai gestured at the golden bowl and dagger on the floor. "In the spirit of helping each other out, do you want me to pick that up for you?"

"No. It will burn you."

"I see." Kai noticed then that the room had lost some of the heat from before, but the air around the bowl still rippled with it. Fascinating. She turned her attention back to Rhys and was surprised to find him studying her intently. Warmth rose to her cheeks. "If I'm intruding, I'll leave. I didn't mean to bother you."

Rhys hesitated, then said, "You're no bother. I just don't

81

find myself in the company of humans very often." He hesitated again, then, "Come here."

It wasn't a command, but neither was it a request. Again, there was that pressure to his presence, the heaviness of air before a storm.

Kai moved cautiously toward the bed. There was more than just the scent of woodsmoke here. Something deeper, wilder. Like earth and blood, and something nameless and masculine that made her want to breathe in deep.

She stopped at the foot of the bed, and for a moment they simply studied each other. Rhys's fingers played absently across the pages of the book at his side. "I wanted to thank you for what you did in the meadow."

Kai reached for her carabiners, but they weren't there, so she smoothed her palms down her thighs. "It's not a problem. I couldn't just stand there."

His smile faded. "You could have. Or you could have run. You risked yourself for Deryn. And for me. It was brave."

Kai gave him a tight-lipped smile. "It was instinct."

"Instinct to pick up a sword and slay a dragon?"

"I didn't slay him."

Rhys's face hardened. "Maybe next time."

Kai huffed an incredulous little laugh. "Maybe."

Silence fell again, then Rhys shook his head, as if remembering himself. His wry smile returned. "Slayer or not, you saved my life. I guess that makes you my knight in shining armor."

Another laugh escaped her, this one surprised and genuine. "Yeah. Just call me Saint George."

To Kai's delight, he laughed too. She found herself asking the question she hadn't asked Cadoc. "You aren't planning on another battle anytime soon, are you? I'm all out of swords."

He regarded her with those unnerving starfire eyes, and the

almost-smile of his laugh pressed into something grimmer. "I'm not planning on it."

Kai nodded. Since she was on this path, she figured she might as well press forward. "Why did they attack you?"

Rhys shifted his right arm, blanched, then ran his left hand through his hair, mussing it before smoothing it down. So that was why it always looked a little mussed. It worked for him, and the motion made the scaled design over the right side of his chest glimmer faintly, which only highlighted the muscles of his chest. Kai forced herself not to bite her bottom lip and slide down the slippery slope of dirty thoughts again.

"We're at war," Rhys said in a weary voice.

"Oh." It was the obvious answer, she supposed. But dragons at war, flying around and trying to kill each other a few hours outside of Denver? It didn't compute. Someone should have seen them. "War over what?"

He raised an eyebrow. "Power."

"Just normal war things, then. Humans and dragons have something in common."

Rhys smiled. Not wickedly, like Cadoc might have. A heavier, more tired smile. How could a man who looked so young—only a year or two older than her—have such a heavy smile? Of course, he could be any age. Maybe dragons lived forever.

"I guess we do."

He didn't drop her gaze. Her pulse quickened, part hormones, part panic. Talking to Rhys was not like talking to Cadoc. With Cadoc, everything was a game. He smoldered because he meant to smolder. But there was nothing put-on about Rhys. He was real, and that made him more mesmerizing than Cadoc could ever hope to be.

Unwilling to leave yet, Kai reached for a carabiner, only to remember—again—that she wasn't wearing her own clothes.

She backed toward the door, out of things to say. "I should go. I suppose I'll see you again before I leave?"

Something flickered across his blue eyes. Was it disappointment? "I suppose you will, George. Thank you again. Truly."

She nodded. "You're welcome. Truly." With a pang that was both relief and regret, Kai escaped.

CHAPTER 10

RHYS

The following morning, Rhys woke to a scent that made him groan. Someone was cooking meat. *Thank the Ancients, real food.*

Rhys threw off the covers. He'd spent enough time in bed. Using the wall for support, he managed to get on his feet.

Cadoc yanked open the door when Rhys was still five feet from it, making his way along the wall like a decrepit old man.

"What do you think you're doing, wind-for-brains?"

Rhys bared his teeth at his friend. "Walking, until you nearly knocked me over, *twp*." Rhys braced against the wall, breathing hard.

Cadoc offered a hand. "Ashem is going to pop a vein when he sees you. Out of bed before he explicitly allowed it." Cadoc tutted and shook his head. Then he caught sight of the golden bowl and dagger Rhys had used for his flamecaller ritual, still on the floor. He'd finally managed it this morning, and magic swirled inside him, its comforting warmth as familiar as his own heartbeat.

Cadoc let out a low whistle. "Damn, boyo. You really do have a death wish."

Rhys took Cadoc's offered hand and pulled himself upright. "Ashem can eat his wings."

Cadoc gripped Rhys's arm, braced him, and peered into the hall. "It's clear."

They started down the hall and got halfway through before they heard footsteps. Rhys let go of Cadoc. It took more effort to stand alone than he expected, but he gritted his teeth and refused to look weak.

Griffith came around the corner with a bowl in his hands. His eyes widened. "Ashem is going to throw you off the ledge."

"He's more than welcome to," Rhys said. "If I stay in bed another second I'm going to shrivel into a husk."

Griffith shrugged congenially and turned, leading the way toward the kitchen. Rhys and Cadoc followed more slowly. So slowly that Rhys almost forgot about his pride and let Cadoc prop him up. But he was almost to the kitchen. He *would* make it the rest of the way.

"*Twp*," Cadoc muttered under his breath.

"Ass."

They reached the short hall that led from the star-filled cavern to the kitchens before they heard Ashem explode. "He's *where?*"

Ashem burst out of the kitchen and caught sight of Rhys, then let out a long string of curses. "Get back in bed, you idiot!"

Rhys stood to his full height. "I don't think I will, Commander."

Ashem's lip curled, and he switched from swearing at Rhys in Welsh to swearing at him in Old Persian. Rhys exchanged a look with Cadoc as the tirade went on. Cadoc, of course, was mouthing along with some of Ashem's longer and more familiar curses. Ashem noticed, stopped, and jabbed his finger at the kitchen, glaring between the two of them. "Get in there and eat."

When Ashem had turned around, Cadoc muttered, "He does not lose with grace."

"I can hear you, you warbling fuck boy."

Cadoc burst into guffaws and one corner of Rhys's mouth turned up. Rhys paused next to Ashem and gave the commander a meaningful glance, then pushed a thought toward Ashem, whom he knew would pick it up. *Kai said you were in her head.*

She startled me. It was instinct.

She's been traumatized, Ashem, and we owe her. Do me a favor and keep out of her mind.

Ashem narrowed his eyes. *That is a stupid thing to ask.*

I'm asking it all the same.

Ashem grunted. *Fine.*

Promise me, Rhys pressed.

Ashem rolled his eyes. *Fine! I promise. I won't dig around in the girl's head.*

They entered the kitchen, where everyone else was clearing up after breakfast.

Kai sat at the long table, prodding her food unenthusiastically. Her dark hair was piled in that messy bun on top of her head. Her eyes were downcast, sooty lashes hiding her pretty sea-green eyes. She looked small sitting there among the dragons, even though she was more or less the same size as Ffion.

For an instant, Rhys had the ridiculous, overwhelming urge to put himself between her and the others. To make sure she was comfortable, that she'd slept well, that she liked the food. He found—strangely—that he'd been looking forward to seeing Kai.

She looked up as they approached the table and Rhys straightened, ignoring the weakness in his muscles and the dull agony in his shoulder. She gave him a small smile before looking away too quickly and turning a brilliant grin on Cadoc.

Rhys suppressed a grimace. Of course she smiled at Cadoc. When it came to charming women, Rhys didn't even try to compete. No sane man would.

Once, Cadoc had nearly drowned himself pearl-diving in the Philippines "for a friend." He'd found a pearl—golden and perfectly round. It was an impressive gift. But Rhys hadn't seen him with a woman for months after that. Obviously that particular "friend" hadn't appreciated his efforts as much as Cadoc had hoped she would. It was the one time Rhys couldn't remember the object of Cadoc's affection throwing themselves at his feet.

"Now that we're all here"—Ashem glared at Rhys—"Griffith, why don't you tell Rhys the news?"

Rhys sank into a chair and gripped the table to hide his shaking hands. "What news?"

Griffith cleared his throat. "Ffion and I spotted Demba and several other members of Kavar's vee patrolling the area. It's unclear if they're staying in the meadow or not, but they're searching for us."

"I was right, as I knew I would be," Ashem declared. "We aren't leaving until Evan and Morwenna get back with reinforcements, so settle in."

Rhys cursed under his breath. There were groans all around. Kai frowned from Ashem to Cadoc. "Cadoc said he was going to take me home."

Ashem shook his head. "No one is leaving."

Kai's face went pale. "I have to go home. Do you know how worried people will be? What kind of resources people could be wasting looking for me? I can't stay here."

"Drills," Ashem announced, ignoring her. "We're stuck here, but we won't waste our time. Everyone but Rhys."

Cadoc cast Rhys a baleful look, which Rhys didn't notice until he managed to tear his gaze from Kai, who was clearly distressed.

"Lucky, boyo," Cadoc said. "What I wouldn't do to get out of drills."

Rhys jerked his head at his injured shoulder. "I'll trade you."

Cadoc snorted. "I'm not that witless."

"Wait." Kai came around the table to stand directly in front of Ashem, her voice deadly calm. "You have to take me home." She turned to Cadoc. "You said you would take me home."

An awkward silence fell over the room, and Rhys winced inwardly on Kai's behalf. Of course she wanted to leave, but she was caught up in things far more dangerous than she knew.

"He does what I tell him," Ashem snapped. "If you're going to make noise about it, go somewhere I can't hear you. Rhys, if you insist on being out of bed, you can watch us drill. Cadoc, bring him a chair."

Obviously uncomfortable, Cadoc turned away from Kai and reached for a chair. "Sorry, *brânwen*, I'm just a soldier."

Griffith offered Rhys a hand. Rhys took his wrist and hauled himself up, making his unsteady way out of the kitchen and back into the starry black cavern near the entrance.

Cadoc dropped a chair next to Rhys, and it thudded hard against the ground. "I feel like a worm. I did tell Kai I'd fly her home."

Rhys shrugged with his good shoulder. "If Ashem says we're grounded, there's nothing we can do."

Cadoc gave him a look.

"No." Rhys shook his head, ignoring the uncomfortable prickling of his pride. "Ashem is right. If Griff and Ffion say it isn't safe, it isn't. Not for you or her."

Cadoc glanced at Kai. She had followed them, which made sense. There wasn't anything else for her to do.

"All right." Cadoc gave Rhys a twisted smile. "Enjoy the show, my feeble friend."

Rhys growled. Cadoc laughed as he went to join the others in the center of the vast room.

Kai walked back into the kitchen, face expressionless. Shaking his head, Rhys lowered himself into the chair. His body shook, and he clenched his jaw at the weakness. Pathetic.

Ashem arranged the others in a row, then separated Cadoc and Deryn when their elbowing nearly devolved into a wrestling match. At his shout, all five of them, Ashem included, sprinted toward the far side of the room. When they reached the rough-hewn wall, they spun and sprinted back toward the open archway. They ran the length of the cavern a few dozen times, laughter fading into panting. After they had gone back and forth fifty times, Ashem arranged them in a line in the center of the cavern and truly put them to work.

"I think this was supposed to be yours?"

Rhys looked up in surprise. Kai stood uncertainly a few feet away, a bowl in her hands. She held it out toward him. "We all got distracted in the kitchen. I think it's cold, but it's better than nothing. It's venison I think. And rice."

"Thank you." Rhys tried not to stare at her smattering of freckles, her soft pink lips, the openness of her expression. Guilt ate at him. She'd helped them, and in repayment, they'd kidnapped her. They were holding her against her will. But she wasn't afraid, or hiding, or closed off. She was offering him food.

Rhys looked at his hands, rubbing his thumb against the tips of his fingers. "I'm sorry that you can't go home. Tact is not Ashem's strength."

"I already know he's an ass."

Rhys laughed and reached for the bowl. Distracted, he realized a second too late that their fingers were about to touch. He jerked back, and the bowl fell to the floor with a crash, food and ceramic shards scattering everywhere.

Kai recoiled, her cheeks turning bright pink. Her flush deepened as Ffion called over to see if she was all right.

"Well, that was a waste," Kai muttered, waving at Ffion without looking at her. Wetness sparkled along the rims of her eyes.

Perhaps she wasn't as immune to her situation as he'd thought. Shit, he was an idiot. He should have been watching her hands.

He faked a grimace and clutched his right shoulder in response to Ashem's questioning look. "I—ah—reached forward too far. Hurt my shoulder. My fault." In a quieter voice directed at Kai he said, "I'm sorry."

Kai's brows drew together. "Don't worry about it." She knelt and began to gather broken fragments.

With a groan, Rhys leaned forward in the chair to help with what he could reach, ignoring the way his body ached. Neither of them spoke, and Kai kept her hands far from his, making it obvious she knew Rhys's movement had been no accident.

His stomach growled, and he swore internally. He truly was hungry, but he'd rather pull out his scales one by one than ask Kai to bring him more food.

His stomach growled again.

Kai stood, hands full of broken bowl, and walked to the kitchen.

He didn't realize he was watching her, admiring her slight curves and the focused, graceful way she moved until she disappeared around the corner. Drawing back from thoughts of Kai like they might burn him, and experimentally rolling his sore shoulder, he turned back to watch the others.

They'd arranged themselves into pairs for sparring. Griffith and Cadoc faced off against each other on one side of the cavern, Ffion and Deryn on the other. Apparently Ashem was saving the real show—Ffion versus Griffith—for last.

"Here." A bowl banged down on the arm of his chair. Kai raised her hands and backed up, settling against the wall a solid five feet away.

Rhys stared at the bowl. It was full of food. He grabbed it before it could fall. "Why—"

"I'm having a shit day, but it's not like I need to spread it around. Besides, you can't even walk to the kitchen by yourself, and I can hear your stomach from here." She shrugged. "It's cold."

"That's...fine." He looked into the bowl. Venison stew. He sniffed it. Bland venison stew. Cadoc must have been in charge of cooking. But it could have been worse. It could have been Deryn.

Balancing the bowl on his palm, Rhys reached inside himself to the swirling maelstrom of power and pulled out the tiniest thread of magic, channeling the energy into the bowl. In seconds, the food was steaming. He picked up the spoon. After a moment of awkward silence, he said, "Ashem promised to stay out of your mind."

Kai's eyes widened. "You talked to him?"

Rhys nodded. "We owe you. He knows that. I want you to be as comfortable as possible. Given the circumstances."

Kai snorted. "Given the circumstances. Yeah. Well... Thanks, I guess."

Rhys nodded, and silence fell again.

"Won't they cut each other?" Kai asked suddenly.

Rhys looked back to the sparring. At some point, Ashem must have retrieved weapons from some storage room, because Deryn and Ffion each held a pair of long, thin daggers.

"They're doing a form." Rhys took a bite of stew. He'd been right: bland.

Kai gave him a sidelong look. "A form?"

Rhys swallowed. "The motions are choreographed. We know them by rote."

Deryn blocked Ffion's high, spinning kick, then used their combined momentum to throw an elbow into Ffion's back. Ffion dropped, avoiding the blow, and swept her foot toward the backs of Deryn's knees.

"They're going so fast," Kai said.

"It's a game. See who can go faster without making a mistake. A point every time you nick the other person."

As if on cue, Deryn let out a hiss. A thin line of blood welled up on her left bicep. Ffion bared her teeth in a fierce smile, twirling her blades. "Too slow, Princess."

Deryn cursed and whirled into motion. Ffion matched her speed without any apparent effort, and they became a blur moving back and forth across the cavern. Then Ffion let out a surprised "Ouch!" They stopped. Blood seeped from a shallow slice across her collarbone. She touched it and smiled at Deryn. "Very good."

Deryn made a simpering face and curtsied. Ffion laughed, and they lunged at each other again.

"They cut each other on purpose?" Kai's voice was incredulous.

Rhys glanced at her, but she wasn't looking at him. Too quickly, he was immersed in studying her again. The exact formation of those freckles, the graceful curve of her neck, the dip in her collarbone. The smoothness of her skin.

He cleared his throat and forced himself to look away. Nothing about the way she interacted with him had invited him to ogle her like a horny teen. "We heal quickly."

"I noticed that Deryn's leg isn't broken anymore." Kai turned thoughtful eyes on him. "Why aren't you better?"

Rhys's mouth twisted and his voice came out dry. "Azh-dahā venom is potent."

Across from Ffion and Deryn, Cadoc and Griffith fought hand-to-hand. Cadoc was fast, but Griffith was twice his bulk and heartsworn. Cadoc didn't stand a chance.

"Ashem is venomous *and* he can read minds *and* he can do magic as a dragon. Damn."

Rhys resisted the urge to reach beneath the collar of his shirt and fiddle with his bandage. "The Azhdahā are formidable."

"So Cadoc said," Kai replied.

"You've spoken to Cadoc?" Rhys asked. He didn't know why he did, but the words were already out.

"A few times." Kai scooted a little closer. "He mentioned clans several times, but there was so much else to ask about, we didn't delve any deeper."

He raised an eyebrow. "You won't be among us long."

"So?" Kai scooted closer again. She was almost within normal speaking distance. "Call me insatiably curious."

Something about her was completely disarming. Maybe because Rhys knew what it was to be hungry for knowledge about everything, everywhere, all the time. "An insatiably curious human among dragons could get into quite a bit of trouble."

A smile curved half of her mouth. "My best friend always says I'm too fond of taking risks."

Enchanted, Rhys returned her smile. "Well, George. What would you like to know?"

Kai scooted even closer, now only about two feet away. She was sitting on the floor, and she tilted her head up at him, smiling a little. A breeze blew in through the cave mouth, and

Rhys caught the distant smell of snow mingled with a sweet, spicy scent that could only belong to her. It went straight to his head like a drug.

"Clans," Kai said, completely unaware of the war she'd set off inside him to control his thoughts. How long had it been since he was with someone? Was that his problem? He was usually too busy to think about sex. It had to be all the forced rest in addition to the presence of an attractive stranger.

"In the meadow," she continued. "Some of those enemy dragons didn't have wings. Are they a clan?"

"I—" He swallowed. *Don't get distracted. She's human. You can never have her. You can never even touch her.* "There are three serpent-dragon clans, two clans with feathered wings, and the rest of us are—"

"Bat-winged?" Kai supplied.

"Reptiles are older than bats. Perhaps bats are dragon-winged."

"Perhaps." Kai tilted her head, smiling. "Which clan are you?"

He chose the least complicated answer. "Clan Draig."

"Clan Draig," she repeated. "Does everyone in Clan Draig breathe fire?"

He pointed at himself. "Fire." He indicated Ffion and Deryn. Their arms were bare, their scaled indicia gleaming from the backs of their wrists to their shoulders. Azure for Deryn, mirrorlike silver for Ffion. "Ffion's element is air. Though she's got some blood of Clan Bida. Deryn's element is water." He indicated Griffith, whose indicium was green. "Earth."

Kai squinted at Ffion, who had Deryn trapped beneath one arm. "Bida? That's different from Draig? But you all have different powers."

"All Draig magic is all elemental, though. It works on the

same principles. The Bida are a clan from the Sahara. Their magic is completely different."

Kai considered this. "Ffion is Draig and Bida. How does that work? Is her magic a combination of both?"

Rhys watched Cadoc twist out of Griffith's grasp. "Combinations are possible, but Ffion takes more after her mother, magic-wise. She has a sister back home who's better at Bida magic."

Kai tapped her lips. "There's so much to know. No wonder Cadoc didn't want to go into every single detail."

"Didn't want to what?" Distracted by the sound of his name, Cadoc had turned. Griffith seized the opportunity and kicked his knee out from under him. Cadoc landed hard on his back, gasping.

Griffith laughed and pulled him to his feet. "You've got to stop being such a fool when girls are around, boyo."

Cadoc winked. "There's nothing wrong with a little harmless flirtation." He pulled off his sweaty shirt and tossed it aside, winking at Kai. Kai shook her head, but Rhys saw the way her eyes followed him as he and Griffith squared off again.

Rhys smothered a spark of irritation. Of course she was watching Cadoc. She'd smiled at him like he hung the sun earlier. Another reason to squelch the unreasonable, unwelcome, unfulfillable interest in her that he couldn't seem to stop from growing.

"Why do their scales only cover their arms?" Kai asked.

Rhys hadn't been listening. "Sorry?"

Kai turned her frown on him and gestured at his shirt. "Yours take up the entire right side of your body. Theirs don't."

He cleared his throat. "I—uh—it happens like that. Sometimes."

"Hm." Kai raised a brow and skimmed her eyes down

Rhys's torso, then down further still. "Does it take up the *entire* right half of your body?"

Damn it. He refused to let his body react to that look as if it were a touch. "No." He indicated the area from his shoulder to his lower abdomen.

"Hm," Kai repeated, her eyes narrowed as if she could see through his shirt.

Cadoc struck inside Griffith's guard. One, two thuds of his fists against skin before Griffith could block. Cadoc tried to bring his knee up into Griffith's stomach, but the large man recovered and blocked him with a hand, shoving Cadoc's leg hard to one side and using his other hand to push Cadoc off-balance. Cadoc staggered, and Griffith wrapped him in a bear hug, grappling him to the ground.

Rhys shifted restlessly, glad Kai had looked away. The longer he sat here next to her, the more he wished he was healthy enough for drills. Sitting around left his mind too empty for anyone's good.

"Switch!" Ashem barked.

Cadoc groaned and lay flat on the floor. Ashem made an exasperated sound. "You broke him, Griffith."

"Sorry, *awenydd*." Griffith held out a hand and hauled Cadoc to his feet. "It wouldn't be so easy if you weren't so skinny."

"Sure, mate. It has nothing to do with the fact that you're sworn and I'm not." Cadoc bled from a cut above his eye, had a bruise on his right cheek, and was grinning like an idiot. He slapped Griffith on the back.

Griffith laughed. "As if the Ancients would ever curse any poor soul to become your heartsworn."

"Stars save our entire species from *that* fate," Deryn said loudly as she settled next to Rhys. She and Ffion had also finished their match.

Cadoc staggered over and sat on the other side of Kai. She picked up a towel from a stack Ashem had brought out of the lavatory and pressed it to the cut on his face. Rhys smothered another spark of irritation.

"You're an angel, *brânwen*." Cadoc tugged a strand of Kai's dark hair. Rhys gave him a flat look. Cadoc saw and chuckled.

"She's a sucker," Deryn muttered as Kai sat down again.

Cadoc leaned back against the stone wall, holding the towel in place. "Don't be jealous, love. I'll always treasure our time behind that squatty old barn in Gwynedd."

Rhys burst into surprised laughter. Across the room, so did Ffion and Griffith. Even Ashem cracked a smile. Deryn shrieked in outrage.

Cadoc leaned over to Kai and said in a whisper loud enough to be a shout, "She quite literally leaped off the roof onto my head. Wouldn't let me up until I kissed her."

Kai pressed both hands to her mouth, but that didn't stop the sound of her laugh.

"I was barely old enough to fly!" Deryn's cheeks had gone pink—Rhys wasn't sure if it was outrage or embarrassment. "I should've stabbed you instead and saved myself from a lifetime of annoyance!"

Cadoc leaned back against the stone, his expression blissful. "Sweet Aderyn. I reckon you still taste like strawberries and dirt."

"She was a determined little thing," Ashem observed drily.

Rhys barked a laugh.

Deryn leveled one of her daggers at Cadoc. "I will murder you."

"Don't," Rhys said, his voice dry. "I'm not up to protecting him at the moment."

"Rhys defends my virtue, which was forced from my virgin lips as a lad," Cadoc whispered loudly to Kai.

Rhys had to put his good arm out to keep Deryn in place. She shoved at him, but stayed where she was. "Nothing about you is virgin or virtuous, you fire-belching git!"

"Enough!" Ashem shouted. When they quieted, he turned to Ffion and Griffith, still in the middle of the floor. "Begin."

"Poor man doesn't stand a chance," Cadoc muttered, studying Griffith.

"I don't know how heartsworn pairs do it, fight when they're in each other's heads like that," Deryn muttered. "It's like they have to have a whole fight inside their minds before they start."

"Why?" Kai glanced from Cadoc to Rhys in confusion.

Rhys opened his mouth to explain, but Ffion darted inside Griffith's guard and drove the heel of her palm at his jaw. Griffith jerked his head up at the last second, stepping back. Ffion drove forward again, coming at him from the side. This time Griffith turned his dodge into a low spin kick in an attempt to knock Ffion's legs out from under her. Instead of falling, she jumped over his sweeping leg. The whole thing took less than a second.

"Holy shit," Kai squeaked. She leaned forward, eyes wide. Tendrils of soft hair fell across her face. Rhys had the sudden, ridiculous urge to reach out and brush them behind her ear. He tightened his hands into fists, grateful when she moved the wavy black strands herself.

Cadoc chuckled. "I told you it would be a show."

Skin smacked against skin, and Rhys turned back to the fight. Ffion had gotten behind Griffith and was landing a series of sharp blows to his back.

"Holy shit," Kai repeated.

"Though she be but little, she is fierce," Rhys murmured.

Cadoc nodded. "And Griff would never hit her."

"Then how is this fair?" Kai asked. "She's hitting him."

99

Deryn shrugged. "She's not hurting him. It's a game. See if she can touch him a certain number of times before he pins her."

Ffion and Griffith sped until every movement was a blur. Each of Ffion's punches seemed to find an answering block from Griffith even as all his attempts to catch her met with her slipping out of his reach.

After thirty minutes, Ffion suddenly sprang forward and hooked her legs around Griffith's waist, then planted a fat kiss on his lips. "I win."

Griffith wrapped his arms around her and kissed her deep and hard, and Rhys looked away. What would it be like to love a person the way those two loved each other?

His eyes trailed to Kai before he wrenched his gaze away. His time to heartswear would come when it came. If it came. Even if he heartswore, it didn't guarantee love. The only thing he knew for certain was that would never be with a human woman.

Never.

"All right, enough." Ashem shook his head in disgust. "Cadoc and Deryn, get up here. Griffith, with me. Ffion..."

Ffion, cheeks flushed, slid from Griffith's arms with a giddy giggle. Griffith shot Ashem a warning look and opened his mouth, but Ffion stopped him with a hand on his arm.

"I've marked some records for study in the library." Ffion smoothed her hair. "If that's all right with you, Commander."

Ashem nodded, giving the pair of them a narrow-eyed glare. Rhys studied them as well. They were always happy, but something else was going on.

"There's a library?" Kai watched Ffion don the small pile of jewelry she'd removed to spar.

Rhys caught himself tracing the outline of Kai's profile and looked away.

"Half a library," Ffion said. "It's at the end of the hall, turn right, then down a second hall. The archway is partially collapsed."

"Oh. I saw that, actually..." Kai fell silent and stayed that way for a long while, staring into space.

Rhys cleared his throat. The others had returned to sparring or, in Ffion's case, left. He was alone with Kai again. He should let the silence be.

He couldn't. "What were you doing in the mountains?"

Kai shrugged, looking at nothing. "Just hiking with my roommate."

More silence.

"What do you do when you aren't hiking?"

Kai arched her eyebrows. "I work at a climbing gym. I climb."

"Climb...?"

Her soft lips twisted with wry amusement. "Rocks."

Climbing rocks did not sound like something people should do for fun. "And that's your work?"

Her smile faded, and Kai shook her head. "For now."

"What will you do later?"

She laughed without humor. "Nothing. Because I'm stuck here." She looked longingly toward the archway that led to the outside world. "There isn't any way you could force Ashem to let me go, is there?" Before he could respond, she shook her head. "Let me guess. You're *just a soldier*." She made air quotes around the last part of the sentence.

Rhys glanced over at Ashem. "I—"

"It doesn't even matter," Kai cut him off. "Even if I get home, Juli will murder me. My life is over either way."

"Juli?"

"My friend." Kai laughed quietly. "More than that. My family. We did a project in fifth grade about ancestry. Turns out that we're something like first cousins eight times removed."

"I see." Rhys hesitated, counting myriad small scars on the backs of his hands. He'd gathered them over a long, long life of training and war. Kai's hands were similarly scarred. Had that come from climbing rocks? "Kai..."

She looked up at him, and he was caught off guard, somehow, by those dark-fringed sea-green eyes. By the guarded expectation in her face. By that scent that still swirled in the air. He couldn't remember what he'd been about to say, so he just pushed up from the chair, still shaky. Still infuriatingly weak. He had to get away.

"I'm going to rest."

"Oh. Of course." She smiled, but it didn't reach her eyes. "It was good to talk to you again, Rhys. Thank you for listening to me."

The earnestness of her gratitude did something inside his chest. Something he refused to examine too closely. "Whenever you need."

CHAPTER II
KAI

K ai jumped when Cadoc slid her plate away from her after dinner. He took it and the last few dishes from the table to put them on the counter next to Griffith, who was washing them. Once the plates were delivered, Cadoc plopped down next to her again.

"Thanks." The food had been more meat and rice. Salad had never been her favorite, but she was starting to crave green things. "Liam and Colm could learn from you."

"Liam and Colm?"

Kai's mood dipped further. "My brothers."

He smiled ruefully. "I am sorry, *brânwen*. I wish I could take you home."

"You could."

Cadoc shook his head.

Kai tamped down her frustration.

"I understand why you want to go."

Kai looked at Cadoc in surprise. He was still smiling that rueful smile. "It's not easy to be far from the ones you love. To never know what's happening to them, what they're doing, what they're thinking..."

His eyes went distant and sad.

"Is someone you love far away?" Kai asked.

Cadoc shook himself, his smile slipping back into place like a mask. "We're all far from home. I'm sure we're all missing someone."

"Even Ashem?"

Cadoc chuckled. "Him? Never. The commander has a heart of stone and is complete within himself wherever he goes."

Cadoc still sounded melancholy, and Kai cast about, looking for a way to cheer them both up. "I was thinking, I've been here two days now, and I still haven't seen most of this place. Care to give me a tour?"

Cadoc grinned and winked. "I'll give you a tour of anything you want."

"I can imagine worse ways to pass the time." Kai waggled her eyebrows, not at all serious because she knew he wasn't either. When he'd spoken of missing someone far away, there had been true longing in his voice. Whoever Cadoc was missing, they had a deep hold on his heart.

Cadoc laughed and pushed back his chair, offering her his hand. "Stars, we're going to get each other in trouble. Come on. I haven't been in this place any longer than you, but I've heard stories. Let's see what we can find."

Kai took his hand and let him pull her to her feet. She followed him out of the kitchen and down the vast hall, which was dim now with night. At the end of that hall was the one that angled downward. The one she'd followed Ashem into before he'd told her to get lost.

"I've been here," Kai said. "This is the ruined library?"

Cadoc nodded. He'd shortened his strides to keep pace

next to her. "Sure, but libraries are for boring people like Ashem and Rhys."

"Ffion goes there," Kai said.

"Ffion is a perfect being. In her, liking boring things is a quirk, not a flaw."

"But in Rhys?"

"Horribly boring. Don't ever let him get started on politics and history."

Kai laughed. "I happen to like politics and history."

"Oooh. Well then. Perhaps he's the one who should be giving the tours."

Kai hid a grimace. Being close to Rhys pressed some kind of "inhibitions and decency be damned" button inside her that should not be pressed. She slid her arm through Cadoc's. "No, thanks. I'd rather go with you."

They'd descended the tilted hall past the library's half-fallen opening, and it was getting truly dark.

"Why's that?" Cadoc asked. "Rhys is wonderful. Even if he is dead boring compared to me."

Kai thought of Rhys's eyes. Of the way his attention made her feel like she was the only person in the room. Hell, the only person in the world. She searched for the right words, knowing —despite what he said—that Cadoc loved Rhys deeply. These people, from what she'd seen, all loved each other that much.

"Rhys is...burdened?" Kai sighed. "That probably sounds ridiculous. He just has—" *Don't say a body or a face or a voice.* "—a gravity that I find intimidating."

She might have had the same kind of gravity, once, had she pursued certain paths. But as it turned out, being a responsible and ambitious adult was a double-edged sword. One she wasn't prepared to wield. Despite Juli's pained sighs every time Kai refused to go back to law school, Kai was perfectly happy making other people happy by teaching them how to climb rocks instead of doing things like, say, getting dangerous criminals released from prison on a technicality because they'd fooled her into thinking she knew them.

"How insulting!" Cadoc pressed a hand to his chest, his incredulous tone pulling Kai from dark thoughts and memories. "I'm the very *soul* of gravity."

Kai laughed, leaning her head against him for a moment. "Sorry, Cadoc. You have burdens, I think. But, like you said earlier, they're far away."

Cadoc paused then. A small hitch in his step that nearly made Kai trip. His laugh this time was surprised, and without much humor. "You are far more observant than I realized, Kai Monahan."

Kai flinched, hoping she hadn't put her foot in her mouth. Cadoc's company was the only thing keeping her sane. "Sorry."

"Not at all. I think I admire you greatly. I'll just have to be more careful what I say in your presence."

With a wink, Cadoc snapped his fingers. A ball of golden fire blossomed above his hand, throwing red-and-gold light all around the dark hall. Cadoc's fire didn't flicker like a torch, but neither was it as steady as a flashlight beam.

He flourished the fire and said, "Behold the work of the Ancients."

Kai's lips parted. The stone walls were carved in undulating lines that depicted serpentlike dragons flying through the clouds, painted in vibrant blues and greens that faded to deep gray and black in the shadows.

She approached, running her fingers reverently over the carvings. Each of the dragons' scales had been picked out in meticulous detail, each painted a slightly different shade of iridescent color. She'd never seen anything like it. Aside from the exquisite artistry, the place was so clean. When she looked back the way they'd come, the opening to the hallway above was a distant gray blob of fast-dimming light. They'd walked farther than she thought.

"Why isn't there any dust?" she asked.

Cadoc swirled his long fingers, setting the ball of fire spinning, and grinned. "Magic."

"I cannot even tell you how much I would love magic that made it so I never had to dust again. My roommate is obsessed with spotlessness."

"It is terribly convenient. A favorite of mine. Shall we carry on? If what I heard Ashem telling Ffion is correct, things are just about to get interesting."

Kai fell into step next to Cadoc again. After another moment, the hall ended, letting them out in an empty, echoing space so vast, Kai wondered if they'd stepped outside into pitch-black night. Here, Cadoc's golden light only illuminated the ground around them. The air was abnormally still; it smelled like leather and aged paper.

"Hello!" Cadoc called.

Long seconds later, his voice echoed back to him. *Hello... Hello... Hello.*

"I think it needs to be told someone is here." Cadoc exhaled and twisted his wrist so his palm faced the floor. The ball of light disappeared into his hand like he had sucked it back into his body. Blackness closed over them like water. For a breathless, silent second, Kai drowned in darkness.

"Cadoc?"

"Watch, *brânwen.*"

In the distance, a white light flared. A circle of flame blazed into being on the ceiling of the cavern, moving like a gunpowder trail in a cartoon. Another circle rippled to fiery life. It passed through the first and out again, like links in a chain. There was another flare of light, this one almost above her head—another circle forming. They took shape all over the ceiling, all joined like chain mail, slowly lighting the enormous space.

And what a space. It was vast almost beyond comprehending. As if the entire center of the mountain had been hollowed out. Ledges ran along the sides of the walls in neat rows, with dark, arching caves dotting each one at intervals. Most, it appeared, had been blocked by falling rock, but not all. Every bit of the walls looked like art—carved and painted, or shining with intricate mosaics, or in some places glittering with depictions of dragons or nature picked out in precious stone.

Wonder sparked inside Kai—something she hadn't felt so profoundly since she was a child who believed in Santa Claus, waking up to find presents under the tree on Christmas Day. No matter what else happened after this, she had seen magic. Whether the dragons would call it that or whether it was more like science to them, she had never been so perfectly happy to be in awe.

"Impressed?"

She tore her gaze from the... room? Chamber? City? It was large enough to fit a town, at least. Cadoc was grinning again, his hands in his pockets.

She grinned back. "I am."

"I told you I am a talented man." He stepped closer, and Kai had to tilt her head to look at him. Her heart gave a little jump at the look in his eyes. Lonely, wistful, longing. Maybe his heart did belong to someone else, but maybe that wasn't someone he could be with. Maybe Kai and Cadoc were both just isolated and confused and happy to be in each other's company. Maybe there would be worse ways to pass the time than to let herself fall into those amethyst eyes, or let him kiss her with those lovely, smiling lips.

Cadoc, however, was not the dragon she would choose to kiss.

"I'm sure you are." Kai put a hand on his chest, pushing him gently back.

His smile turned rueful. "Maybe later." His chocolate voice was meltingly soft.

"Maybe." Kai patted his arm, half sure she was crazy for not taking what he offered. "Is this as far as we go? It's getting late."

"Not quite. I know at least one of these has been used for storage in more recent years. Let's take a peek before we head back."

"Sounds good to me."

They walked into the chamber, which was so large their footsteps didn't echo back to them—only louder noises like shouts or laughter. Cadoc led her to the first of the archways on ground level, lighting the short, darkened hall with his floating ball of fire as he led her inside.

The room at the end of the hall was lit like the larger chamber, though it was much smaller—only the size of a college lecture hall. Stone rows fell away from them in tiers. There were carvings here as well, mostly of clouds and birds. It looked like a sort of intimate dragon amphitheater. One that had been taken over by packrats.

The room was filled with... everything. Tall shelves leaned against walls, old crates were stacked high, huge statues draped in sheets stood here and there. Some of the things she saw were dragon sized, but there were human artifacts everywhere. A tall, ancient stone covered in cuneiform stood next to a desk-sized record player with what looked suspiciously like a Fabergé egg sitting on top. A pile of yellow-black rocks dominated what would have been the amphitheater stage. Paintings leaned against stacks of leather-bound books. Gorgeous antique furniture in dozens of different styles was piled haphazardly with bolts of fabric or old toys. A delicately painted silk screen, possibly Japanese, was draped in gorgeous red-and-gold fabric that looked as if it might be an Indian sari. There were military artifacts too. Suits of armor from across the world, stacks of weapons, flags Kai didn't recognize.

"Is this some kind of museum?"

"Don't you know anything about dragons?" Cadoc flung his arm wide, encompassing the room and all it held. "This is a hoard. One that must've belonged to a specific dragon, years ago, and was left because they either lost interest or died. Ashem has added a few of the more modern bits." He gestured to a stack of camping gear in one corner. "But for the most part, it's been here at least a hundred years."

"I thought a dragon's hoard was treasure." She gestured at the bracelets, armbands, and pendants he wore. "I thought you were wearing the hoard."

"The jewelry is for various sorts of magic. Amplification, mostly. Storage. Records. But this is history, *brânwen*, and history *is* treasure." He jerked his head toward the pile of rocks. "Though if you're looking for something with a bit more glitter, that is gold ore and uncut gems."

Kai gazed at the centuries-long history of several countries on display, feeling suddenly young, ignorant, and small. A suspicion had been creeping up on her for a while. One she was almost afraid to have confirmed. "Cadoc, how old are you?"

"Old."

She folded her arms, waiting.

He gave her a small, almost sympathetic smile. "Let's just say your people write my birth date with a BC at the end."

The air seemed to go out of the room. BC? She'd expected something outrageous, like *Two hundred, brânwen,* or *I was born in 1555, love.* Not *Your people write my birth date with a BC at the end.* That was beyond comprehension.

"How long do dragons live?"

His voice was gentle. "Too long, I think. But relatively

speaking, I'm not much older than you. All of us in the vee are roughly the same age. Except Deryn, who's a bit younger, and Ashem, who's a bit older."

Kai couldn't help herself. "I feel like you should be wiser."

Cadoc laughed, a rich, full-throated sound. "You're not the only one."

"Really, though. When humans depict ancient creatures in fiction, you're always borderline alien. As if we can't comprehend you because you've lived so long."

Cadoc shrugged one shoulder. "Time ebbs and flows. The days blend. We see many friends come and go, especially when those friends are human. But I don't think that makes us alien. Perhaps more patient. Perhaps more likely to see patterns in the history of humans, whose lives are so much shorter than ours. We are still flawed creatures who have friends and families, who love and fight and f—"

"I get it."

Kai scanned the pile of camping gear and more recent things that Ashem had deposited. She'd almost lost hope when she spotted two of the things she'd been hoping to find: a lantern and a large coil of rope. She waded into the chaos and picked up the lantern, almost whooping with joy when she flipped its switch and the light blinked on. Apparently, even Ashem used batteries.

Cadoc folded his arms, his expression mock severe. He tilted his head at the ball of fire still floating at his side. "Not good enough for you?"

"We aren't always together."

"We could be." He wiggled his eyebrows.

Kai snorted. "You are a silver-tongued devil."

Cadoc leaned toward her, eyes wicked. "Silver? Never. My tongue is made of gold."

Kai burst out laughing. She took his arm, and they left the

remains of the ancient dragon palace and climbed back into the upper halls. Kai clutched her lantern the whole way.

Ashem might have grounded the dragons, but he wasn't *her* commander. She'd grown up in the Rockies; camping was almost as natural to her as climbing. With the things in the hoard, she just might be able to make it home.

When they were all asleep, she would come back.

Two HOURS LATER, Kai snuck back into the heart of the mountain. Her memory was good, so it didn't take long to find what she needed. She was grateful for that. Without Cadoc, the trip was creepy. Shadows jumped and jittered, making it look like the ghosts of dragons slithered along the walls. The items in the hoard, too, seemed full of ghosts and watchful eyes.

Free to dig through the equipment, Kai found a large backpack and stuffed it full. Knives, blankets, a couple of small, tightly-rolled tarps, and even a couple of sets of extra clothes. Ashem had probably stored them here for Ffion, but they'd fit Kai well enough.

But her best find was the rope: three lengths, lighter and stronger than any she'd ever used. She shoved as much as she could into the pack, then hid the lot of it in one of the crates beneath a pile of water-smooth silk. She wasn't desperate enough to run. Not yet. But Ashem had refused to send her home once. There was no guarantee he wouldn't make that same decision again.

If he did, she would be ready.

CHAPTER 12

KAI

While the dragons did their magic well-filling rituals, then trained again the next morning, Kai returned to the half-ruined library archway.

She lifted her lantern and stepped inside the silent, dusty room. Like the door that led inside, half of it seemed to have collapsed. The rest wasn't filled with books like she'd expected —though there were a few small bookshelves near the door. Instead, most of the shelves were designed like wine racks, honeycombed with spaces meant to hold something small. Spaces that were completely empty.

With a sigh, Kai walked farther into the room, exploring more of the shelves. Most of the aisles between shelves were dragon sized, wide enough to be two lane roads. But there were some smaller, human-sized alcoves. About halfway around the room, in an alcove hidden from the entrance by shelves, Kai found a long wooden table littered with papers and surrounded by chairs. In the middle of the table, a glass sphere with an open top sat on a black cushion, reminding Kai of the candle holders her mother liked to fill with silk flowers and colored stones.

In the shadows at the far end of the alcove were more of the honeycomb shelves. But unlike the others, these weren't completely empty.

She tilted her lantern and peered into one of the shallow holes. Light glinted off something small and angular within —a round-cut diamond the size of her thumbnail. She pulled it out and blinked in surprise, then looked in the next cubby. A fat rectangular ruby sat inside. The next one contained a huge emerald, and the one after that another diamond. Several of the cavities housed a single gemstone and had markings scratched below each—dragon letters, Kai assumed.

She replaced the diamond and lifted out a darkly glittering sapphire, rolling it between her fingers. *There must be hundreds of thousands of dollars stuffed in this wall.*

She returned the sapphire and pulled out a pink diamond, then an emerald the size of a robin's egg. After she put them both back, her fingers lingered. If the dragons weren't using these, her parents certainly could. Or Juli, who was in a mountain of debt after medical school. Maybe she'd ask Cadoc, and she could take one or two of them home.

Sighing, Kai turned to go. Then her eye caught on the clear glass sphere.

A diamond hovered in its exact center, unsupported by anything except, possibly, magic. Intrigued, she walked around the table, setting her lantern beside the black cushion. Magic was all around in this place, of course, but not usually the kind she could see.

What would happen if...

She raised one finger and touched the cool, smooth glass of the sphere. It released one clear, shivering note. The diamond pulsed, and a wave of light and tingling energy rippled outward.

As it passed, a three-dimensional image unrolled in the air above the table. A gray sky capped a strip of desolate beach. On the right, a dark ocean foamed with whitecaps, and a hazy mountain range disappeared into the distance on the left. Dragons as varied in color and shape as tropical birds were scattered through the sky, tangled in vicious battle.

It was a picture of some kind. A still shot, like the holograph of a photo. At the center of the scene, a red dragon battled a white one. The white dragon was slightly larger, its snowy scales streaked reddish black with blood.

Kai stepped forward, and the image leaped to life. The white dragon lunged and slashed its claws down across the red dragon's collarbone. The red dragon's mouth opened in a soundless roar. It darted forward, claws flashing, but the white dragon feinted out of the way.

A sound reached Kai's ears—slow, uneven footfalls echoing from the empty library walls. Startled, Kai sprang forward, hoping another touch would turn the image off. Her fingers brushed the smooth glass.

The dark cave disappeared, and Kai found herself blinking in cloud-filtered sunlight. Waves crashed in an inexorable rhythm against the stone beach. The ground vibrated, and there was a deafening roar. Disoriented, Kai spun.

Life-sized dragons, one crimson, one white, were trying to kill each other on the beach less than a dozen feet away.

Her insides shriveled. Dozens—maybe hundreds—of dragons shrieked and roared overhead in a scene that made the battle in the meadow look like a playdate.

She yelped and ducked as the white dragon's tail whistled inches above her head. Scrambling away on hands and knees, she found her escape blocked by a silver dragon charging up the beach. Its roar thrummed through Kai's body, buzzing in her teeth. *Shit, shit, shit! How did I get here?*

Kai threw herself to the side, and the silver dragon's charge missed her by inches. But her head slammed into something hard. She fell back, groaning, and tried to see what she'd hit. There was nothing in front of her but a few more feet of beach and the ocean beyond.

Her breath hitched; her heart pounded in her ears. She put her shoulder against the invisible barrier and shoved. The surface didn't move. It was full of holes, like the honeycombed shelves. But she didn't see any shelves, just open air.

She spun, pressing her back against whatever it was.

The silver dragon had joined the fight on the crimson dragon's side. Unnoticed above them, a black dragon swooped out of the sky, jaws open. Bile rose in Kai's throat. It had silver eyes. Without meaning to, she shouted, "Watch out for Kavar!"

At the last second, the silver dragon noticed Kavar and tackled his crimson ally out of the way. Kavar slammed down onto the silver dragon instead, sinking his teeth into its neck.

In the air, a slender red-black dragon faltered in its flight. A wailing keen rose from her throat, a pitiful sound that rent Kai's soul.

The silver dragon collapsed. A shimmering haze rose around him, and then only a slender young man with a long nose and disheveled brown hair lay on the beach between Kavar's claws, his eyes empty and staring.

The red-black dragon fell drunkenly from the sky.

"Stop." A male voice cut through the chaos, hard and commanding. Silence rang in Kai's ears as the scene froze once again. "Minimize."

The ocean shrank away. The light dimmed. Kai was still in the library, but now there were fires burning at intervals along the alcove walls. Her breathing ragged, body shaking, she pushed herself up. The image of the dragon-filled beach hovered over the table, rotating slowly.

Shaking, she spread her fingers along what had been an invisible barrier, glancing at it out of the corner of her eye.

The honeycombed shelves. She'd been trying to crawl through shelves.

Across the alcove, Rhys leaned against the edge of the paper-strewn table, holding his injured shoulder with his good hand. He was breathing hard and his jaw was set. His broad shoulders seemed to take up the alcove's entire width. The sleeves of his simple dark blue shirt were pushed up, revealing the veined muscles of his forearms. On the right one, his indicium licked over his skin like motionless flame.

For the first time, Kai noticed that the only jewelry Rhys wore was a gold chain around his neck with flat, rhombus-shaped pendant. The pendant held a round, yellow stone in its center. Lines radiated from the stone like a small sun.

"Are you all right?" Rhys asked, voice rough and low.

"I..." Kai lifted shaking hands. She could feel every throb of her heart, but she took an unsteady breath. Safe. She was safe. Not being attacked by dragons.

"Kai?"

His voice was soft around her name, which did nothing to slow her speeding heartbeat. She balled her out-of-control hands into fists. *Safe. Not being attacked. Safe.*

"Kai." Rhys stepped forward, leaning heavily on the table. He didn't look like he should be out of bed, let alone all the way down here by himself.

She forced herself to nod and stand, almost afraid he'd try to touch her if she didn't. Then she remembered the way he'd jerked back from her when she tried to hand him that bowl of food.

"Sorry. I'm fine." She forced her breathing into something

more even and tilted her head at the hologram-like image rotating above the sphere of glass. Her hands were still unsteady, and she didn't want him to notice. "What is that?"

"That is a record."

She opened her mouth to ask what it was a record of, or how a video had found its way into a diamond, but instead her eyes snagged on the way his big hand was splayed over his injured shoulder and she asked, "Are you all right?"

Rhys dropped his hand and nodded, meeting her gaze. The impending storm pulsed in the air between them. Standing, he took up more space than she remembered. Tall and broad, his jaw more defined for the dark stubble that had started to grow there. "I'm fine."

She rubbed her fingers absently across the skin of her throat, willing herself not to get caught in his eyes, so intensely blue. "What does the record show?"

Rhys was silent for a long moment, some suppressed emotion flitting across his face. When he spoke, his voice was rough. "It was supposed to be the battle that ended the war."

"The same war you're still fighting?"

He looked at his hands and a terrible, haunted expression crossed his face. "The same war." He visibly gathered himself and when he spoke, his voice was colder than she'd heard it. "But it's not a human concern."

"Okay..." She walked around the table and turned off her lantern, which was useless in the now brightly lit room. She made sure to keep a few feet between them, but she could still feel that intensity. That pressure.

Rhys touched the sphere. The scene expanded again. The stone walls disappeared, and the bloodstained dragons were suddenly life-sized. Kai took an involuntary step toward Rhys and braced herself for the noise and terror of the battle, but the scene didn't move. They stood on the beach, lush green mountains to one side, gray ocean on the other.

"What's—" She turned, and then cut off. She'd misjudged that last step, and he'd half turned toward her.

He was so close, she could feel the heat that radiated from his body. She lifted her eyes a solid foot to meet his electric blue gaze. He looked just as surprised as she was, but he didn't back away. His throat bobbed.

His scent was clean and wild, like wind through the mountains and something masculine and melting that sank into her bones. That sizzled in her blood. That fogged her mind.

"Kai..." He lifted his hand as Ashem had, as if he would brush his fingers across her cheek.

"Yes?" Kai's entire world contracted into that moment. The movement of his hand. The anticipation of his touch. He wasn't even making contact, and it felt like she was burning.

Then Rhys's expression changed, his jaw tightening. He closed his fist, dropped his hand, and moved away. "Never mind. It's nothing."

"Okay." Annoyed and embarrassed, Kai shifted her attention back to the scene.

Not looking at her, in what seemed to Kai a rather determined way, Rhys moved his fingers, and suddenly the overcast sky surrounded them. They were above where the slender dragon with red-black scales had crashed. A green dragon with a snakelike head and feathered wings in every color of the rainbow dove toward her, one foreclaw raised. A projectile that looked as if it were made of bone hovered in the air between them.

Kai's breath caught. She'd always thought it would be thrilling to stand unsupported in the sky, but even though she knew it was an illusion, fifty feet of nothing between her and the beach made her head spin.

Rhys, who had turned away from the two dragons to gaze at the scene as a whole, glanced at her. "Minimize."

The illusion shrank so it hung over the table once more. Kai leaned on the table. She didn't know how much more adrenaline her body could take. "Did you know that silver dragon?"

"Iain." Rhys lifted his hand, as if he would touch the image of the body on the beach. "He died saving my life."

"You were the red dragon?"

Rhys nodded.

"I'm so sorry."

Rhys's voice took on a hard edge. "War has a high cost. I've paid less than many."

"If you keep bringing up this war, I'm going to assume you want to tell me about it."

"It's—"

"Not really a human concern," Kai finished.

Rhys looked slightly off-balance at her quick response. "I... Yes."

Kai pointed to the hologram. "Who's the white dragon? Can you tell me that?"

Rhys reached into the glass sphere and pulled out the diamond. The image disappeared, leaving the alcove drab and unadorned.

"Owain."

Kai hesitated, then remembered what he'd said about the war the day before. She asked, "Is he the one who wants power?"

Rhys's fist closed around the diamond, his knuckles white. He met her eyes briefly, then dropped the gem onto a cushion of black velvet. "Yes." He walked to the bookshelf next to the door and ran his fingers absently along spines.

Rhys pulled out a book. "Do you read?"

"Depends on the book."

He nodded. "Some of these are in English. You can borrow them if you like. Just be sure to put them away. Ffion is meticulous and Ashem is insufferable."

The subject change was obvious, but Kai didn't think Rhys was someone she wanted to push. "Thank you."

"It might be best if you stay away from the records."

The idea of experiencing another dragon battle, even a virtual one, made her feel faintly ill. "Don't worry, as of right now I have no desire to go near that thing."

He glanced over his shoulder, a wry half-smile on his face. "That's not the same as promising you won't, George."

To her annoyance, Kai's heart thumped at the sight of his smile. Yes, he was handsome. Yes, he turned her brain into dumpster diving raccoons. But his smile... That did something else to her. Something too frightening to even begin to think about. "I know."

Pulling out another book, one of the less age-darkened volumes, he came back toward her.

Again, she noticed his pallor, and the dark circles under his eyes. "You should go get some rest. You look like you could use it."

Rhys's smile twisted into an expression of disgust. "I probably could."

Kai laughed. "Getting twitchy?"

He ran a hand over his jaw, the skin of his palm rasping quietly against the stubble. "Is it obvious?"

Kai shrugged. "I know the look. I saw it in the mirror every day after I had a bad fall off a boulder and got laid up for six weeks with a broken leg. I was losing my mind by the time I got my cast off." Scanning the shelves herself, she was surprised to see some familiar titles. She picked up *The Hobbit* and stuck it under her arm, then retrieved her lantern. "I guess we're leaving?"

He nodded, and Kai saw him surreptitiously checking the title of the book she'd grabbed. She thought his mouth curved up on one side, but the fires on the walls went out. A golden ball of flame appeared at Rhys's shoulder, much like the one Cadoc had used, and it threw his face into shadow. They left the library and walked up the tunnel in silence. Rhys moved with slow deliberation, but otherwise seemed all right. Hyperaware of him at her side, Kai didn't feel like the silence was awkward. In fact, it was kind of nice.

They reached the black cavern where everyone had been practicing just as Ashem roared Rhys's name.

"I'm here." Rhys nodded for Kai to lead, and she went down the wide, shallow stairs first. The dragons stood in a cluster at the archway to the ledge, staring out. Cadoc came over and offered Rhys a hand, but Rhys waved him off.

Kai looked into the sky. "What is it?"

Rhys went rigid. "Sunder me."

Confused, Kai squinted into the cloud-smudged blue. At first, she saw nothing. Then her eyes landed on a white bird circling in the distance. Except it wasn't a bird. It moved wrong, as if its wings were attached differently. And it had a long, whiplike tail.

With dawning horror, Kai realized it was a dragon. A white dragon. Familiar to her. As if, by viewing the record, Kai had somehow brought him here. "Is that...?"

"Owain." Rhys's voice was grim.

"What do we do?" Deryn squeaked. For once, her voice was completely free of snark.

Rhys held up his good arm, and Deryn moved close and leaned against her brother's side, half holding him up, half hugging him. Kai faintly heard him whisper into her hair, "We'll be safe here."

Kai folded her arms tightly across her chest, wishing she

had her brothers here, having to settle for hugging herself. Her mind was thrown back to that beach and the battle. To Rhys's friend dying. Though she'd only known the dragons a handful of days and her relationship with some of them wasn't exactly stellar, the thought of them fighting, getting injured, maybe dying, turned her heart to ice.

"We do nothing." Ashem fixed each of them with a golden glare. "The only person who can locate the barrier around this cave, let alone break through it, is Kavar. Owain won't be able to find us without him."

"Why?" Kai whispered, not caring how ridiculous it was. Owain was too far away to hear her, even if she shouted.

"Why is he in the middle of the sky?" Ffion asked, moving a dark corkscrew curl out of her eyes. "He has to know we can see him. He isn't even veiling. He's going to be seen by humans."

"He wants to be seen," Rhys growled. It was hard to tell in daylight, but Kai thought his eyes were glowing.

Cadoc bared his teeth. "He thinks we're stupid enough to show ourselves if we have a chance to catch him."

Silence fell. Kai's shoulders and neck tensed as Owain circled closer. The tension grew into a slow, headache-inducing sort of fear. At length, the dragon was joined by another, huge and bronze. Then another, glittering and green. But she only caught brief glimpses of each as they seemed to shimmer out of existence. "How—?"

Rhys glanced down. "They're veiled. It's how dragons hide from human eyes, though we can still see each other. There are"—his gaze flicked across the sky—"half a dozen of them."

Kai jerked, her legs spasming with the instinct to run. That was stupid. There was nowhere to go. "Is Kavar one of them?"

Rhys looked to Ashem, who shook his head. "No. But even if he was, I wouldn't know. The Azhdahā use barriers instead of veils. You encountered a barrier when Deryn brought you to our camp. It's a mental trick that repels unwelcome eyes and minds. They're the only ones who can hide from other dragons."

"And there's a barrier around us?" Kai rubbed her neck, trying to dispel some of the tension. Barriers, veils, mental shields, records, hoards. It was getting difficult to keep track of dragon magic.

Ashem spoke. "Unless Owain has gotten ahold of the mind-hiding magic our people are working on, Kavar is nowhere close. Though, since we were attacked when no one should have known where we were, it's very possible Owain has gotten ahold of other information he shouldn't have."

Kai licked her lips. The dragons outside drew closer. Being kidnapped by dragons hadn't bothered her as much as it should have. They were *dragons*. She had gotten to spend time with creatures of legend, to see magic. That was amazing, but not worth becoming collateral damage. "Owain is the leader on the other side of your war, isn't he? Why would he care enough to personally search the mountains for one little group of soldiers?"

They all looked at her, expressions blank, as if she had just said something exceptionally stupid.

Rhys broke the silence, saying with a wry smile, "There aren't many dragons left. Every single one makes a difference."

Abruptly, Ashem seemed to notice Rhys was pale and sweating despite leaning on Deryn. He cursed in a language Kai didn't know. "Griffith, get him something to sit on before he collapses."

"I'm—" Rhys started.

"Just sit," Cadoc interrupted.

Griffith came back with a chair. Deryn helped Rhys sit, not

teasing him for once even though he growled beneath his breath the whole time.

Every pass brought the white dragon closer to the cave. After half an hour, they came close enough that Kai could make out the way the dragons' veiling distorted the air like heat mirages. She reached out and found herself gripping Cadoc's arm.

He smiled wanly and squeezed her fingers. "It's all right, *brânwen*. We'll all get home safe. You'll see."

Finally, after an eternity, Owain and his dragons flew out of sight and didn't return.

But for the first time, no matter how hard she tried, Kai couldn't make herself believe Cadoc.

She wasn't sure she'd get home from this at all.

CHAPTER 13

KAI

The next morning, Kai woke with a restless energy she couldn't shake. Between Owain's flyover, Ashem's scowls, and Rhys's...whatever it was Rhys made her feel, she had so much leftover adrenaline from the day before she thought she might explode. Rhys wasn't the only one getting twitchy from being stuck in this cave.

She walked out into the black cavern, trailing her hands along the rock walls. She went outside first, as if some kind of bridge to lower ground might have manifested overnight. It hadn't. Rain fell in cold drops, rolling down the back of Kai's neck. White mist trailed cold fingers down the mountains, pooling in the valley below. Kai hugged herself to keep from shivering. There were no roads she could see, no cabins, no smell of smoke from campfires, only endless peaks, mist, and icy, wet wind.

At least today there weren't any dragons.

Voices reached her from around a curve, where the mountainside hid a small part of the ledge. She leaned forward, peering around. Rhys and Deryn sat there, half hidden by some tumbled boulders. Apparently, Kai hadn't risen as early as she'd thought.

She backed into the cave and looked out at the mountains again. It struck her how absolutely delusional she'd be to consider leaving here on her own. Her throat closed and her eyes burned with unshed tears of frustration. Last night, home-sickness had filled her so full she thought she might drown. The feeling ebbed as morning arrived, but it hadn't vanished entirely.

Chilled, Kai backed further into the starry cavern and paced its perimeter. The walk turned into a jog, then a full-on sprint. After a few laps she stopped, putting her hands behind her back, arching and breathing deep. Running wasn't enough.

She pressed one hand to the rough-hewn part of the wall, and her fingers rested on a narrow strip of stone. She needed a rush. She needed height. Mats or no mats, she was going to climb.

She sank her fingers into a crack above her head, then lifted her foot and settled her toes on a small irregularity at about knee height. In seconds, she lost herself.

Peace. Focus. A place for fingers, a place for toes. Balance and lift, body tight. Get through this tricky spot. Arms and legs burn. So, so good.

She was twenty feet off the ground in a particularly tricky position when voices broke her trance. Rhys and Deryn appeared from the ledge, heading toward the hall. Deryn made a few quick swipes at the air, as if she held an imaginary knife. She said something in Welsh, and Rhys laughed. He gave her a playful shove, then rolled his injured shoulder.

He looked good. Much better than he had yesterday. Though he still had a long way to go, Kai might not have noticed if he hadn't been walking next to Deryn. The girl moved like a cobra.

Kai pressed her body against the wall, willing them not to see her. Suddenly, her need to climb felt silly. She stayed as still as she could, hoping they would hurry up and get out.

No such luck. They paused and Rhys held up his good hand, curling his fingers into a fist and moving it slowly in the same twisting strike Deryn had, demonstrating something. Kai's arms shook. The leg that held her weight trembled. *If I can get into a better position...*

She slid her fingers up the wall, seeking a crack, a hole, any inconsistency that would let her shift herself. If she could get weight on both her legs...

Her fingertips grazed a promising handhold just barely out of reach. She risked a glance up. If she could get a grip on the small shelf of stone above her, she could get high enough to wedge her other foot into a crack. To reach the handhold, she'd have to jump off her already shaking leg.

She jumped.

"Kai?" Rhys exclaimed.

She started, missed the handhold. For a frozen moment she hung by the fingertips of one hand, her other arm windmilling uselessly. Climbing accidents she'd seen flashed through her mind: bloody, swollen faces, shattered bones, dented skulls, days and days in the hospital.

I shouldn't have climbed so high. I shouldn't have...

She fell.

With an *oomph*, she came to a stop feet above the ground. The heat of a body pressed against hers; strong arms cradled her to a firm chest. She looked up into eyes the color of a starfire. The feeling of latent, electric power washed over her. Even weakened, Rhys's strength was frightening.

She tried to say thanks, but her voice wasn't working. All she could do was shake and gasp.

A bemused smile curved Rhys's mouth. "Breathe, George. I've got you."

Kai found her voice, weak and wheezy. "I guess you're the knight now."

His smile deepened. "Better a knight than a king."

Deryn made a derisive sound.

Rhys shifted Kai, wincing. He held most of her weight with his good arm, his injured side supporting her legs. Still, a wet, red stain was spreading on the fabric of his sky-blue shirt.

Deryn frowned at Rhys's shoulder, then at Kai. "What were you thinking? A fall from that height could have killed you."

"She would have reached that bit of stone if I hadn't startled her. My shoulder is my own fault."

Kai's cheeks heated, and she became abruptly aware of the hard planes of his chest and abdomen where they burned against her side. Of how good he smelled. How warm he was.

She wasn't alone. Rhys's gaze slid hesitantly, almost unwillingly, over her body, and she swore she could feel his heart beating hard and fast against where her shoulder was pressed into his chest.

He smoothed his thumb over her sleeve. "Can you stand?" He'd been so careful to avoid touching her that Kai couldn't help but notice he wasn't in any hurry to put her down.

Kai swallowed and fought the urge to raise a hand to his face. To end this madness and stroke her hand over his cheek. Maybe finally making contact would break the spell.

No. No way. There was no breaking the spell of a man like this. Maybe if her interest was only physical, but it wasn't. Everything about Rhys pulled her to him. But she was leaving, and he was a dragon, and Kai hated complicated things, so she kept her hands to herself. "I'll be fine."

Deryn muttered something about idiot brothers. Ignoring

her, Rhys set Kai on her feet, his fingers lingering. Kai's shirt had hiked up to around her belly button, but with his hands on her waist, just above the hem, she couldn't pull it down.

"All right. Good," he said, his voice rougher than usual.

He dropped his hands.

His fingers grazed her right hip, no more than the whisper of skin against skin.

A pulse throbbed through her body, like standing too close to speakers at a concert. Without warning, a wave of force threw her back against the wall. She managed not to hit her head, but the rock gouged into her back. "Ah!"

Rhys staggered as if he'd felt the blast as well. His went as dark, as blank as a TV without a signal.

Kai recovered, twisting to check for broken ribs. Not feeling any, she glanced up at Rhys.

He was unmoving, eyes wide, staring at nothing.

An uncomfortable prickling started in Kai's stomach. "Rhys?"

"Rhys? Oi!" Deryn snapped her fingers in front of his face, then looked from him to Kai's pushed-up shirt. Her face went white. "Oh no. No!"

Rhys's eyes snapped into focus. He was looking at her, his pupils dilated so far only the barest hint of blue iris could be seen around the edges, glowing bright.

Cold fear rose in Kai's stomach. "What's wrong with him?"

The thunderstorm feeling swelled, turning the air chokingly thick. Though he wore a man's body, there was nothing human in Rhys. Only the dragon looked out of those eyes.

"Kai, listen to me," Deryn's voice was too calm. Too careful. "Whatever you do, whatever he does, do *not*—"

Rhys lunged.

Kai ducked to the side, bracing for impact, confusion and

fear overwhelming higher thought. The expected attack never came. She opened her eyes.

Deryn had thrown herself between them. She braced against her brother, teeth bared, muscles standing out in taut cords on her slender arms. Her eyes were ablaze with turquoise light; her face drawn with some inner conflict Kai didn't understand.

"You don't want this, *fy mrawd!*" Deryn heaved Rhys backward. He staggered, but only fell back a step before feinting left, then lunging right.

Kai tensed to run, but Deryn moved like a striking snake. Somehow she was between them again, her shoulder in her brother's chest, stopping him despite the difference in their size.

Deryn shoved, throwing Rhys back again. Before he could recover, she flung out her hand the way a police officer might command traffic to stop. With an ear-splitting groan, the floor cracked and rent at Deryn's feet, polished stone parting and crumbling into an abyss.

A geyser burst into the air, drenching them all in cold spray. It fountained higher, stretching and spinning until it formed a translucent bubble-like shield of swirling water that surrounded Kai and Deryn, blocking them from Rhys.

Rhys raised his hands in front of him, blank face contorted by the water shield. Light sparked between his fingers, growing into a ball of spinning flame. Deryn swore. She set her feet and raised her arms above her head like a priestess summoning a long-dead god.

Kai cowered behind her, fighting for breath and utterly confused. *He's trying to kill me. I'm going to die.*

She couldn't stop her scream as Rhys flung the fireball. It exploded against the watery shield, denting the bubble inward. Clouds of steam billowed. Deryn made a strained sound somewhere between a screech and a growl and thrust her hands down and forward. The bubble sprang outward, the last of the flames curling away to nothing on its surface.

Distorted shouts came from somewhere beyond Rhys. Cadoc, Ffion, and Griffith sprinted toward them, their words unintelligible through the water. Relief washed through Kai. Rhys would stop now. He had to stop now.

Instead, he raised his hands again. This time, instead of forming a fireball, a jet of flames spewed from between his splayed fingers. Water hissed and steamed, turning the air unendurably sweltering.

Deryn's stance grew unsteady. Flames raged outside the shield, which shrank by the instant. Kai hunched, damp hair clinging to her forehead and the back of her neck, another scream building inside her. She shoved it down, catching Deryn and supporting her as the taller girl sank to one knee, sweat drenching on her forehead. The bubble of water continued to shrink. Soon it would be gone.

Rhys was going to burn them alive.

One coherent thought flitted through her brain: *I want to go home.*

The jet of flames faltered. For a split second, Kai could see. The others had reached Rhys. Griffith was trying to drag him away. Deryn's shoulders relaxed. The bubble became less stable. Then Griffith's clothes caught on fire and he let Rhys go to beat at the flames. Rhys renewed his attack. Deryn shuddered and let out a sob.

The flames faltered again. Through the wall of water, Kai could see Cadoc beside Rhys now. Instead of trying to pull him away, Cadoc clasped his hands over Rhys's wrists. A glowing trail of flame twisted between Rhys's fingers, over his wrists and into Cadoc's hands, shrinking the jet of fire.

Ffion hovered, gesturing sharply at Cadoc to stop. Cheeks

flushed and eyes glazed, Cadoc shook his head. His lips moved, but Kai couldn't hear over the rush and sizzle of water and flame. She thought he looked at her, the ghost of a grin on his lips, and remembered his promise.

I swear by fire and by the blood of the Ancients, you are safe with us.

Face a mask of frustration, Ffion darted from the room, sprinting toward the hall. Kai heard her cry rising above the noise. "Ashem!"

At last, the flames fell away. Rhys struggled, but Griffith grappled him in a bear hug. Cadoc had fallen to his knees, his hands curled against his chest. Deryn collapsed. The water bubble fell, soaking her and Kai.

Kai looked up. Rhys struggled in Griffith's arms, and she found herself locked in Rhys's flame-blue eyes. Eyes filled with rage and desperation. With a roar, Rhys threw Griffith off. He raised one hand, aiming at Deryn and Kai. Fire sparked between his fingers.

Suddenly his arm fell. His eyes rolled back in his head. Griffith caught him and lowered him to the floor, unconscious.

"What. Happened." Ashem's deep voice echoed in the silence. He strode toward them, Ffion at his side. Some still-functioning part of Kai's brain registered that Ashem must have knocked Rhys out with his magic.

"He's heartsworn." Deryn's voice was blank. She pushed herself up, teetered around the two-foot-wide crevice she'd ripped in the floor, collapsed onto her knees, and touched her brother's face. "Damn you, Rhys. You should have let her fall."

"He's *what?*" Cadoc stared at Kai, all humor gone. "He can't be."

Ffion's brow creased. "A Wingless mate." She glanced at Ashem. "How many will go to Owain over this?"

Ashem frowned and shook his head.

"Mate? Heartsworn?" Kai echoed. "That's what Ffion and Griffith are. That's a dragon thing."

"Not always," Ffion said softly, something like pity in her wise gray eyes.

Kai's stomach clenched in a hard knot. She flashed back to falling. Rhys catching her. The tips of his fingers brushing her skin. That's why he wouldn't touch her. "Rhys is heartsworn to *me*?"

"He can't be," Cadoc repeated softly.

"Oh, can't he?" Deryn shouted, "I saw him. Just like when it happened to Ffion and Griffith. Blank eyes and a second later it looks like he's trying to eat her!"

"I am *not* heartsworn." Kai tried to sound commanding, but her voice shook. Her hand went to her carabiners. Open, closed, open, closed.

"No," said Cadoc. "You aren't. Not yet."

Rhys moaned and stirred. Kai tensed.

"Why is he waking up?" Deryn demanded.

Ashem scowled. "Because I want him to."

Cadoc looked at Rhys, then back at Kai. She'd expected concern. Instead, he seemed detached. She gave him a questioning look, but he turned away. Kai felt like she'd been slapped.

Rhys took an unsteady breath and opened his eyes. The radiant light was gone. No longer blank, those starfire eyes fixed on Kai like she was the last breath of life in a dying world.

"Kai," he said, dazed. "I..."

"No!" Kai barked. She wasn't heartsworn. She was human. She was going home.

None of them seemed to care.

CHAPTER 14

RHYS

Fire had always belonged to Rhys: a weapon, a tool, a toy. He had never felt what it was to burn. Now an inferno raged where his heart used to be.

Kai stared at him, wide-eyed and frightened. He'd thought he wanted her before, but now... He suppressed a groan. He was gripped by a churning need to know her. Possess her. Touch her. It was as if he'd been living in a dark room, and when someone finally turned on the light, he discovered half of him was missing. *The stories lie. This isn't love. This...*

It was *need*. Pure, incandescent need.

That was why he desired her. Why he felt drawn to her even though they barely knew each other. It was the mate bond. Whispers of heartswearing magic stirring between them before they'd ever touched.

Griffith hauled Rhys to his feet, but Rhys shook off his friend's steadying grip and put a hand to his forehead.

This wasn't happening. She was leaving soon. Going back to her human family in her human home. She didn't belong in this world. In his world.

This would break everything.

He hadn't meant to touch her. He'd barely registered the smooth softness of her skin before a wave of magic rolled over him. The world had gone black, then white, then red. A vast emptiness of soul yawned open inside him, an emptiness only she could fill. Instinct had screamed that if he didn't possess her in that very instant, he would be consumed. Gone into ash, into dust, into nothing.

He remembered attacking Deryn, but barely. He gritted his teeth so hard his jaw ached. He would have killed his own sister for keeping him from his mate.

Mate. He thought he'd be ready when it happened. He'd thought he was prepared. He'd been a fool.

Human. She's human. Like my mother. She had no idea, like my mother.

The others stood around them in a loose semicircle, tense and waiting. Cadoc swayed next to Rhys, sweat dripping from his temples. He'd taken Rhys's power and drawn it into himself to save Deryn, but Rhys could channel far more magic than Cadoc.

Rhys grabbed his arm when it looked like Cadoc would fall. "*Twp.* You could have died. What were you thinking?"

Cadoc's grin was a shadow. He wiggled his fingers. The skin of his hands was red and blistered, but it seemed no permanent damage had been done. "As long as these work, boyo, I'm golden."

Guilt and embarrassment burrowed into Rhys's chest. He'd never lost control before. He turned to Deryn. "Are you hurt?"

She put a hand on his shoulder, her expression pained and knowing. "It's not your fault. No one can control heartswearing."

"I am *not* heartsworn. *We* are not heartsworn." Kai's voice was furious, and she clenched the carabiners hooked through her belt loop with a shaking, white-knuckled fist.

He met her gaze for an instant before she looked away, but it had been long enough to see her fear.

I could have her. I could complete the bond. All it would take was a kiss. Even weakened, he was so much stronger than her. If he wanted, there would be nothing she could do.

The thought turned his stomach. *Curse instinct and biology. I will* not *be my father.* He rubbed his chest over his heart. The need was turning into an almost physical ache.

He switched to Welsh and forced his face to relax. "If she's to swear to me, I want her to do it on her own. I will not repeat my parents' relationship." He met each of their gazes in turn. "Don't tell her anything that will put pressure on her. Absolutely nothing." Suddenly, the need *was* pain, a white-hot spear through his heart. He fought not to double over. *Blood of the Ancients.*

"What's wrong?" Ashem asked sharply, still in Welsh.

Rhys shook his head. "It...it hurts."

Ashem swore.

Ffion's brows pinched. "I understand not wanting to pressure the girl, but if she's going to make an informed decision, there are things she should know."

The ache in his chest sharpened, and Rhys swore. It would be bad enough to ask Kai to leave her life behind and be his mate when she thought he was a soldier.

How could he condemn her to heartswear to a king?

Not only a king: a target. One of two people standing between Owain—his own cousin—and the murder of the human race.

Kai wanted freedom. She liked to climb rocks. She wanted to smile at Cadoc, who made her laugh.

Rhys couldn't make her laugh. The only things he could offer were responsibility, the mistrust of his people, and war.

If Kai knew who he was, maybe she'd accept their bond willingly. But Rhys didn't want her to agree because he was king. Even if she believed he was the only thing standing between humans and total destruction, telling her that—and that his sanity depended on her—felt like coercion.

He'd seen what resentment did to his parents. If Kai didn't choose Rhys for himself, they would face the same fate.

But perhaps if she could be convinced to heartswear to him —just him, not his crown—she might find it easier to adjust. And Stars, was it so wrong to hope to be wanted for himself?

Ashem didn't bother with Welsh. "You don't have a choice, Rhys. Do it and be done."

"Do what?" Kai snapped, backing up a step, looking like she'd fight them all to the death if she had to.

She threw a pleading look at Cadoc. Rhys closed his eyes, clenching and releasing his fists at a burst of sudden, unreasonable rage that she would look at Cadoc for help instead of him.

Another pain speared through him, worse than the last. With massive effort, Rhys focused on Ashem. *Do it and be done.* If he kissed her now, without explaining, she'd have no idea what was happening until it was over.

Because until he kissed her, Rhys was heartsworn to Kai, but she wasn't heartsworn to him.

"Do what?" Kai repeated, louder.

Rhys stepped forward, wanting to comfort her, but she scuttled back.

"Oh hell no! Don't you come near me."

"I shouldn't have stopped you," Deryn murmured in Welsh. "I just... Our mother and father."

He shook his head. "I'm glad you did." With a hope he didn't feel, he added, "Maybe it won't be like it was with them."

Ashem grasped Rhys's shoulder, and this time he spoke Welsh as well. "It's stupid to act like she has a choice. It's selfish. The Council won't like it, but they'll live. You might not. Even if you insist on this idiocy, you can't give her more than a few days."

"Then I'll give her a few days," Rhys growled.

"Translation?" Kai demanded.

No one answered.

Rhys wanted to sit. He hadn't recovered from the Azhdahā venom yet, and now this.

"Listen," Kai said, so obviously trying to sound confident, "I know things aren't perfectly safe, but you all were right. I'm in over my head. None of this is my business. It's time for me to go home."

"Home?" Rhys had to fight the urge to stride forward and grab her, tie her down, do anything to make sure she didn't leave him. Ever. If she didn't complete the bond, his fate would be insanity and death. He couldn't afford to die. *Fuck, this is monstrous.*

Ashem must have been listening to his mind, because his grasp on Rhys's uninjured shoulder tightened. "Your departure has been delayed," he said to Kai. "Things have become complicated."

"Complicated?" Kai's voice rose to a near shriek. "I don't give a damn about your complications. Rhys just attacked me. Take me home!"

Ashem gestured at Ffion. "Take her outside and explain what you can."

Ffion pursed her lips. "Rhys needs to explain. They're in this together."

Ashem indicated Rhys's injured shoulder. "He's bleeding, Ffion."

Rhys tore his eyes from Kai. Blood soaked his sleeve, dripping down his arm. As if it had been waiting for him to notice, the wound throbbed, joining another pain in his chest. This one lasted longer than the others. Suddenly light-headed as well as exhausted, he felt his knees give out.

Cadoc caught him. "Steady, boyo."

Rhys pushed Cadoc away and forced himself to stand straight. He could not be weak.

Hang on, Ashem spoke into his mind. "Griffith, take Deryn to the kitchen and get some food in her. Cadoc, help me get Rhys to his room."

Cadoc nodded, but shot a long look at Kai, an emotion swirling behind his eyes that made Rhys want to growl and flame him to char. He tamped it down and straightened. "I can manage." He forced himself to turn from Kai, heard Ffion murmur to her in her soft, chirping voice.

He left the main cavern, the fire inside him burning hotter with every step. The pain no longer stabbed—only stayed. Burning. Raging. The farther he got from her, the stronger the agony grew. He made it halfway down the hall before he collapsed.

CHAPTER 15

KAI

C adoc, Ashem, and Rhys were barely out of sight when the others began to whisper frantically to each other in Welsh. Ffion turned to Kai, concern furrowing her brows. "I'm going to explain. One moment."

"Sure." Too full of furious, terrified energy to wait, Kai strode out onto the ledge and sat. The rain had turned to snow. Fat, slow-falling flakes that were too soft for her mood. She pulled up her hood and yanked her hoodie tight around her, then moved to the edge and sat on the wet stone, her feet dangling a hundred feet above the ground. She glared out over a landscape quickly disappearing behind a curtain of white, replaying the moment in her mind. The touch of Rhys's fingers, the burst of energy, the attack, the sweltering heat inside Deryn's water shield as it shrank and Deryn fell to her knees—

Ffion settled on her left like an alighting bird. "What a morning." Her voice was sweet and calm.

"Yeah. What a morning," Kai repeated, her voice dry. She kicked her feet, bouncing them hard enough against the cliff to send little shocks of pain through her heels. "What did Ashem mean, 'do it and be done'? Was Rhys trying to kill me?"

"Kill you?" Ffion sounded appalled. "No. You've never been safer in your life."

"Safe?" The word came out high and harsh. "Really? Because having fireballs and flame jets aimed at me didn't *feel* safe."

"Hmm. Perhaps not." Ffion tapped her fingers against her lips. "In all your conversations with Rhys and Cadoc, did they tell you anything about heartswearing?"

Kai shrugged, irritable. "Cadoc said it's dragon marriage, but 'more.' You and Griffith are heartsworn."

Ffion sighed, the light, breathy sound sending a puff of fog into the air. "When humans say they're married, it's symbolic. Words and paper. Heartswearing is magically and physically binding. It's real and permanent. They are not the same."

Kai gave Ffion a disgusted look. "Like hell. Family and love don't need magic to make them real. Or permanent. Or binding."

Ffion frowned thoughtfully. "I apologize. Of course they don't. But heartswearing, as I've said, is significantly less...intangible. To be heartsworn comes with physical and mental consequences. When Rhys came into contact with your skin, he became bonded to you. Magically and permanently."

Kai slammed her heels down. Chips of rock spun into space. "I am *not* married to Rhys. That is not how this works."

"Kai... This is so sudden. So strange to have to explain." She took a steadying breath. "I know you don't understand, but this is it for Rhys. He'll never be able to be with anyone but you. Well, he could *be* with someone else, I suppose, but he couldn't have what you two could have together. Heartswearing doesn't allow for choice."

It took Kai a full ten seconds to find words. "You don't get any say in who you spend all of your thousands of years with? None at all? How do you know you'll love them?"

Ffion's gaze went far away. "You don't."

Confusion, fear, and anger heaped up inside Kai, tangling into knots that made her head ache. This whole situation was impossible. Yes, she liked Rhys, when she wasn't intimidated by him. Yes, there was something that drew her to him. Sparks. The feeling of an impending storm. But that didn't mean she was going to be his wife or his mate or his "more." Not when they'd just met. Not when he was dragon/man who shouldn't exist. A soldier likely to die in some invisible, ancient war that wasn't supposed to be her concern.

Kai pressed her hands to her temples. No wonder Rhys hadn't wanted to touch her. "Can it be broken?"

"Technically, yes. But the consequences are extreme."

"What are they?"

"Pain. Madness. Sometimes death."

Kai closed her eyes. If they had told her this could happen with a touch, she would've worn ten layers of clothing the entire time. "What if you get heartsworn twice? Are you required to be with both of them?"

"That doesn't happen as far as I know." Then her face turned thoughtful. "Though there is lore..." She shook her head. "Rhys only has sisters, in any case." She looked thoughtful again, then said decisively, "Definitely not. I mean, you can *choose* to be in a polyamorous relationship if you'd like. Some do. But you'd only be heartsworn to one."

"Good to hear you all have some choice about something." Then something Ffion said gave her pause. "Rhys has sisters? Plural?"

"Rhys is the oldest and Deryn is the youngest."

"Is the other one heartsworn? Is that why she isn't here?"

Ffion shook her head. "Seren is a gold dragon—our Seeress.

Rare, powerful, and sacred. Her powers allow her to catch glimpses of the future. She never leaves the island." Ffion's mouth curved in a small, wry smile. "Or at least, she isn't supposed to."

Kai rubbed her face. "But is she heartsworn? See, this is why this is insane. I didn't even know Rhys had another sister, or anything about her. I don't know anything about his family at all."

Ffion's lips pressed into a thin line. "You're right, Kai. You should know about his family. No, Seren is not heartsworn. She isn't allowed to heartswear. If she does, she loses the Sight. She's the only gold dragon we have. The first in thousands of years."

Kai rubbed her temples. Honestly, it sounded like this Seren, if she couldn't heartswear, had it better than everyone else. "What about you and Griffith? Did you know each other?"

Ffion smiled wistfully. "We've known each other since we were children. I love Griffith now, of course. But I didn't love him when it happened. Heartswearing doesn't guarantee love."

"Did you love someone else?" Kai didn't realize how personal the question was until it hung in the air between them.

Ffion hesitated, watching the snow fall. "I thought I was in love with Ashem. I had hoped... But it was just infatuation. Ashem never reciprocated."

"Ashem? Yikes."

Ffion laughed. "I agree now." She looked at Kai, her eyes full of sympathy. "As I said, Rhys has no choice. But he's trying to give you time to adjust. It's more than Griffith and I had. When two dragons who are compatible touch, the bond is instantaneous."

Distracted from her internal maelstrom, Kai gave Ffion a searching glance. "That must have been difficult."

"It was...surprising."

Kai closed her eyes and took a breath, trying to imagine feeling whatever it was Rhys was feeling. "I respect that this has happened to you. I still don't understand why it happened to me."

"Dragons do, sometimes, become heartsworn to humans."

"But I don't feel what Rhys feels."

"With a human-dragon pairing, only the dragon is heartsworn instantly. For the magic to affect the human, the bond must be completed."

Kai crossed her arms and shivered. The cold was getting to her. "What completes the bond?" Not that it mattered. Not that it was something she would ever consider.

Ffion gave Kai the aggrieved look of a disciple about to share something sacred with an unbeliever. "A kiss. If Rhys kisses you, or you kiss him, you will also become heartsworn."

Kai couldn't help it. She snorted. "A kiss? Ffion. This is not a fairy tale. Please, tell me you're joking."

"I'm not."

"How did this even begin to happen? What, was there some old dragon story about kissing humans the way humans tell stories about kissing frogs? And then someone tried it and it worked? This is ridiculous!"

Ffion shrugged, obviously uncomfortable.

Kai shifted on the cold stone ledge. "Explain something to me. Why is this a thing? Why does heartswearing exist at all?"

"The Ancients."

Kai's brow furrowed. "The dragons who built this place?"

"Yes. It's some old magic. Call it a curse if you'd like."

"Why would they do that to their own species? Take away choice? Make people miserable?"

Ffion shrugged again. "We don't know. There are theories about genetic diversity, or optimal pairing in a population that

147

was increasingly small. But for whatever reason, dragons can only produce offspring with their heartsworn."

Kai rubbed her temples. "What does any of this have to do with humans? And how could it possibly benefit your species to pair-bond with another species that lives a fraction as long as you?"

Ffion sighed. "As far as the age problem, you won't like the answer. A human who completes heartswearing to a dragon gains a dragon's lifespan."

"Yikes," Kai said again.

"As for why we involved humans to begin with, I only have more theories for you, more scraps of records older than time. My guess is that the Ancients combined dragons' genetic material with humans' so we'd survive. Our population has been through several bottlenecks, and there was some cataclysmic event a few hundred thousand years ago that nearly wiped us out. Maybe a disease, maybe something else. Perhaps the first human-dragon DNA was combined for immunity reasons. Or maybe our numbers had dwindled so much that, once we realized humans were intelligent, this was a step dragon ancestors took to ensure our survival. You see, most dragon pairs only produce one or two children. Wingless-dragon pairings can produce four or five."

"Wingless?"

"Human mates."

For a second time, Kai pressed her fingers to her temples. "Wouldn't the children from humans be human? Especially if all this...mating...is going on while human? I'm assuming I'm not going to turn into a dragon. Not that I'll be doing *any* mating with Rhys." Kai's cheeks flamed. She was surprised not to see steam rising into the frigid air.

Ffion's face took on the pained expression of someone forced to talk about a sibling's sex life. "No, you won't become a dragon. Our genetics are dominant. All offspring are dragons."

"Of course they are. Wow. You don't want much from me, do you? Marry this random man and have lizard babies with him."

Ffion's mouth twisted in obvious offense. "Please don't call us lizards."

"Fine. You're not lizards. You're insane, virgin-kidnapping monsters. Which I'm not, by the way. Does that matter?" Kai hugged herself, refusing to look at Ffion as she rubbed feeling back into her arms and hands. Her butt had gone numb a long time ago.

"No." Ffion inhaled like a mother praying for patience with a badly behaved child. "Human legends aside, you can see why becoming heartsworn is important. For Rhys, it's rather essential. It won't be easy at first, being away from your family, but there are benefits..."

Kai had heard enough. She stood. "You know I'm not doing this."

Ffion rose as well, standing like a barrier between Kai and the snowy world beyond the mountain. "We need him, Kai. If you don't complete the bond, he'll be... Damn it, Rhys." She shook her head, as if searching for words. "Distracted. So distracted he'll be unable to function at full capacity. We can't afford for him to be wounded again, or worse. He's important."

"And my life isn't?" Kai heard her voice rising and took a calming breath. "What exactly will happen to him if I don't agree to this?"

"He won't let me tell you."

"Why?"

Ffion shrugged. "Come. Let's see if Ashem has stopped the bleeding, and you can ask him yourself."

Ffion walked away. Kai hesitated, looking out over the

snow-obscured wilderness. Somewhere out there, her family and Juli were looking for her. She had a life. A small one, but one she lived.

With a pang, Kai realized she was truly kidnapped.

Rhys... She liked him, she thought. She was definitely drawn to him. But this was too much. He had to listen to reason. He *had* to let her go.

Kai sat on the cliff as long as she could bear the cold. Finally, ignoring the impulse to slip over the edge and take her chances free climbing down an icy cliff in the dark, she went inside to face the dragons.

CHAPTER 16

KAI

Kai didn't have to see him. Even before she reached Rhys's room, she could feel his presence. Power rolled off him in waves stronger than ever, tingling in her fingertips. Ffion stood in the doorway and motioned Kai inside.

Kai took a breath and held it, torn between thoughts of home and thoughts of Rhys. Heartswearing might be "real" and "magical," but if it took away Rhys's choice in who to spend his life with, it was also messed the hell up.

But the memory of the way he'd stared, need naked on his face, made it hard to breathe. No man had ever looked at her like that. It was wrong, but now that the danger was more distant, Kai realized to be so desired was a heady, intoxicating thing. To be desired like that by Rhys...

Kai shivered, anticipation and dread warring inside her. Ffion motioned again, tipping her head toward the interior of the room with more urgency.

Her fingers twined in her carabiners, Kai stepped across the threshold.

The small fires in the nooks of the carved walls had been extinguished. The only light came from the hearth at the far side of the room. Low music drifted from the corner. Cadoc sat in the shadows, plucking softly at his guitar. He didn't look up.

Rhys sat in a chair before the fire, shirtless, the golden flames drawing him in stark lines of light and shadow that emphasized his tautly muscled form. His head drooped, and he had his elbows on his knees, hands clasped between. Remnants of dried blood streaked his arm and smeared his chest. Clean white bandages obscured the pattern of crimson scales on his torso. The rhombus pendant he always wore dangled from its chain, glinting gold and yellow.

He looked like an ancient warrior king, his shirt a blood-stained banner draped over one thigh, his head bowed with the weight of a battle fought and lost.

Kai would be lying to herself if she didn't admit the sight of him arrested her. That she wanted to be the one to go to him and take his face in her hands and smooth the weariness from his brow. To wrap her arms around him and comfort him and find comfort in him when he wrapped his arms around her.

His eyes found hers, cerulean irises glowing like eclipsed stars. His lips formed her name.

Kai's heart gave a hard lurch, and she fell back a step. He wasn't completely the dragon, not like he'd been a half an hour before, but he wasn't completely human, either. Dangerous. The sight of him brought on a wave of sudden, unavoidable certainty. She didn't love him now. Not even close. But she knew as sure as the stone beneath her feet that if she let him, this man could mean more to her than anything in the world.

If.

Ashem stood behind Rhys, tying off the bandages. "—says no and you're going to be an idiot, you'll need something to help you sleep. I can knock you out, but I can't hold you under all night every night. And besides, unconsciousness is not true sleep. I'll have to go back to the meadow."

Rhys nodded, his gaze still fixed on Kai.

Ffion waved Kai farther into the room. "Talk to him. I'm going to save Griffith from Deryn." A bittersweet smile twisted her lips, and she went through the archway.

Rhys sat up and rubbed his chest, shrugging off Ashem's hands.

Kai folded her arms, keeping a wary distance. "How are you feeling? Are you... Does it hurt?"

Rhys hadn't taken his eyes off her. It was unnerving. She hugged herself tighter.

"I'm fine." His voice was rough but even.

"*Gwaladr*..." Ashem murmured.

Rhys made a quick slashing motion with his good hand, and Ashem fell silent. "Did Ffion explain?"

Kai nodded.

"Do you understand?"

"As well as I can."

Rhys ran a hand through his hair and then smoothed it down. He took a breath and let it out in a rush. "Will you become my heartsworn?"

Cadoc plucked a sour note.

Kai tried to keep her voice gentle. "I'm supposed to go home."

Rhys closed his luminescent eyes. "I fully intended for you to go home before this. I can't... Will you heartswear to me?"

Fear slipped down her spine, because he had asked twice instead of accepting what he knew to be the answer. She didn't know him well, but she knew it was unlike him. Just like lunging at her had been so unlike him. "We don't even know each other. You can't ask this of me. How can you ask this of me?"

Rhys's voice took on a quiet edge. "Believe me, the last thing I wanted was to be mated to a human."

Kai swallowed a hysterical laugh. He was Mr. Darcy, proposing to her despite her inferior family and birth. She dug her nails into her palms and couldn't help a sarcastic, "But what about all the babies I can make you?"

Rhys made a strangled sound. Cadoc stopped playing. Ashem scowled at Kai and folded his arms across his chest. Like when he'd looked at her yesterday as he'd run his fingers over her cheek.

Realization dawned, and she touched her face where Ashem had. "You! That's why you touched my face. You were seeing if I was *your* heartsworn and you never even bothered to ask. You—you—" She couldn't think of words vile enough.

Ashem shrugged. "We become stronger when we're sworn. It would have been irresponsible for me not to try."

"*Irresponsible?* Do you know what consent is, you bat-winged jackass? You can't force your dragon mating magic on a woman because you *get stronger!*"

She rounded on Cadoc, prepared to yell at him too. He knew and hadn't warned her. She'd touched him dozens of times. But seeing his stricken expression, her rage wobbled, threatening to collapse into tears. "Why didn't you tell me?"

Cadoc stood and took a step toward her. Rhys tensed, and Cadoc came to an abrupt, ungraceful halt. "I'm sorry, *brânwen*. I'm so, so sorry. The chances—I didn't think it would happen."

Kai took a shuddering breath. She would *not* cry.

Rhys closed his eyes, breathing deeply. When he opened them again, the glow was muted. "Please."

Kai raised her hands in a helpless shrug. "Please? I—no. Rhys, I'm sorry. I can't."

Rhys stood suddenly, knocking over the chair. "You won't.

That's the choice you're making, even after everything Ffion told you?"

A ball of fear formed in Kai's stomach, but she stood her ground. "Yes."

He growled. For a moment, she thought he'd lunge at her again. But he didn't. He strode out into the hall, and Ashem followed more slowly.

Kai put face in her hands. "Please tell me this is some kind of horrible dragon prank."

Cadoc approached, his voice soft. "I wish it was. Are you all right?"

Kai took her hands from her face and looked up at the genuine concern in his beautiful amethyst eyes. She reached toward him. "I'm—"

"Cadoc!" Ashem stood by the door. His voice ricocheted off the walls like a gunshot.

Kai jumped. Cadoc froze like he'd been caught playing with someone else's toy. He stood jerkily and went to retrieve his guitar from the corner.

"Cadoc?" She was dangerously close to weeping.

Without looking at her, Cadoc gave a small shake of his head and strode past Ashem out of the room.

Kai glared at Ashem. "You don't dictate who I can or cannot talk to."

Ashem raised an eyebrow. "I dictate whatever keeps this group functioning, as I have done for a thousand years. If you have any brains or any heart, leave Cadoc to write songs about his misery and heartswear to Rhys."

"If *you* had any heart, you'd take me home!"

Ashem shrugged. "I don't have a heart. I have a duty."

Kai bared her teeth and marched past him.

Back in her room, she flopped down onto her mattress and its pile of blankets and pillows. If the dragons wouldn't take her home, it was time to take herself. She'd prepared. She could do it. Maybe tonight, with everything that had happened, she wouldn't need a distraction.

KAI ADJUSTED the heavy pack on her back and swore. She'd waited until they were all asleep. She'd slipped down into the hoard with no problem. Unfortunately, Ashem hadn't forgotten to set a watch like Kai hoped. Cadoc sat just inside the entrance, playing his guitar. It always seemed to be Cadoc.

Outside, the snow had gone, and the moon sparkled off the white landscape—though not as much snow had stuck as Kai expected. That was lucky. She'd rather not try and make her way through the mountains in snow. She shifted, and something inside the pack clinked.

Cadoc didn't turn, but he spoke. "*Nos da, brânwen.*"

Kai swore.

Though the moon was waning, she could see when he lifted his gaze from the guitar to look at her, one brow raised. "That's one I haven't heard."

She thought about slipping off the pack and leaving it at the bottom of the incline that led to the cave mouth, but that wouldn't fool him. Hoping he'd understand, she came out onto the ledge. "I'm feeling creative."

"It's been an inspiring evening for that kind of creativity." He looked at the pack, then at the coils of rope in her hands. "Going somewhere?"

She shifted, trying to get the pack into a more comfortable position. "I can't stay here, Cadoc. I'm not going to give up my life. Leave my family and friends with no word of what happened to me."

"What if you're giving up a better life by going?" He strummed a few more notes on the guitar.

Kai laughed, her voice harsh. "I'd rather die in a few days out there than suffocate over the course of millennia in here. I can't do it. My family and friends think I'm dead already. They're suffering."

"Who becomes heartsworn to whom—or doesn't, or can't, in some cases—often causes suffering." Cadoc's voice was flat.

Kai frowned, trying to untangle what he'd said. "I'm not sure what you mean."

He shook his head. "Nothing. Just know that this particular facet of dragon magic often causes heartache."

"It must." Maybe that was the problem with his faraway love. Maybe they had touched and not heartsworn. Maybe they were sworn to someone else.

Kai wanted to ask Cadoc for help. It would be so easy for him to change into a dragon and glide down through the silent night with her on his back. He could probably drop her off at the nearest city and be back before his watch was up.

"Cadoc—"

"Don't ask me, Kai. Please."

She dropped the pack and sat hard on the ground next to him, covering her face. "Please. You can't take me away from my life. You can't make me be with Rhys. I saved him. I saved Deryn. All I want is to go home. Please. You swore by fire and the blood of your Ancients that I would be safe, Cadoc."

Warm hands closed over hers, pulling them gently down. Cadoc's amethyst eyes were agonized. He brushed dark strands of hair to the side and stroked her cheek with his thumb. When he spoke, his voice was filled with pain. "Rhys is a good person, *brânwen*. The best. Believe me."

Kai tried to speak. She took one breath, then another, but words wouldn't come. Finally, she slid sideways, burying her face in Cadoc's shoulder. He wrapped his arms around her and held her as she wept. When she finally pulled away, his shirt was soaked with tears. He didn't let her go, and Kai thought his eyes might be shining with unshed tears of his own.

"I'm sorry. I didn't want this for you."

Kai became acutely aware of how close he was, how he smelled like fresh-cut wood and lemon oil. There was none of the pull she felt from Rhys, none of the pressure, but Cadoc was comfort, pure and simple. There was nothing she wanted more in the world than comfort.

Even though the sensible part of her whispered that it was wrong, that this wasn't something either of them truly wanted, she found herself leaning in, closing the distance between them, tilting her face toward his.

His gaze dropped to her lips. In a voice filled with misery, he murmured words Kai didn't understand. He brought a hand to her cheek, not moving toward her, but not moving away. His eyes closed, as if he were torn with indecision.

So Kai made the decision for him. She kissed him. After a second, he kissed back. It was a gentle kiss, as soft and sweet as music.

It was the kiss of a friend, and nothing more.

Cadoc broke away. "I can't—" His eyes widened.

With a jolt of fear, Kai realized the air had the heavy feeling of an impending storm.

Rhys.

In the blackness of the cavern, two neon-blue points hung in the dark like lonely stars.

Cadoc scrambled up, pulling her with him. He gently pushed her toward the interior of the cavern, but she didn't move. She didn't want to face Rhys.

"Get away from the ledge," Cadoc said.

"What—"

An enormous ball of flame erupted where Rhys stood. In the instant before she shielded her eyes from blinding brightness, she saw the silhouette of a man. When she could see again, Rhys was gone. She looked up, higher and higher, until she met the starfire eyes of a dragon.

Cadoc's voice went very soft. "Kai, if I don't transform now, Rhys is going to kill me."

CHAPTER 17
RHYS

"*Hoffwm i ddim wyt ti ei berthyn e*," Cadoc whispered. *I wish you didn't belong to him.*

They had kissed.

Rhys's control slipped. Like a match to dry leaves, the flames of the transformation consumed him, rage burning away conscious thought until nothing but instinct was left.

"Stop! Rhys, stop! Just listen!" Kai came toward him, her hands outstretched.

His head swayed as he drank in the sight of her. Loose hair fell past her shoulders in soft black waves, framing a frightened face as pale as milk. Tiny. So tiny. But strength coiled in the lines and curves of her petite form. To his dragon eyes a white halo surrounded her, radiating from her body.

Heartsworn. Mine.

Beyond her, heat and light exploded. The enemy had become dragon with scales like fire beneath the moon. With a roar, Rhys leaped over Kai's head as the enemy dove off the ledge. Rhys roared again, plunging after him into the night.

Cadoc. The traitor had broken something deeper than law, and the debt could only be paid in blood.

CHAPTER 18

KAI

Kai whirled to run for help, her eyes wide with horror, and smacked into a warm, solid wall. "Griffith!"

"What happened?" His voice was sharp and hard, a startling contrast to its usual measured rumble.

"Rhys... He saw Cadoc...and me..."

Griffith growled something in Welsh and went out to the ledge. Kai didn't know what he'd said, exactly, but she heard "Owain."

Her heart constricted. The white dragon. He was out there somewhere. Looking for them. Waiting, perhaps, for this. Roars that shook the night. Fire in the sky.

Kai stumbled back from Griffith until she hit the cold stone arch of the entrance. She pressed her knuckles to her mouth, where Cadoc's kiss had faded in less than a breath. "Oh my—"

Outside, a stream of flame lit the sky. Dragon fighting dragon.

Griffith didn't waste breath on her. He bellowed for the others. Then his eyes glowed, radiating the green of sunlight on lake water. He pointed. "Stay there. I need room to change."

Terrified, Kai nodded.

Griffith backed away. His image distorted and faded, as if a cloud of dust passed between them. When it settled, the massive green dragon remained. Deryn, Ffion, and Ashem appeared from their rooms in various states of wakefulness. Griffith explained what happened with his dragon mind speech, which Kai could still hear, as it seemed to always be sort of generally broadcast. They all turned to look at her just as he leaped into the sky. Ffion's gaze was filled with sympathy, Deryn's with contempt, and Ashem's with mixed rage and exasperation. Another fire lit the sky outside.

"Go!" Ashem growled.

They transformed and flew into the night.

Whatever happened was quick. Another plume of flame blossomed in the distance, then nothing. A few minutes later, the bulk of returning dragons blotted out the stars. The others flanked a red dragon who struggled to stay in the air, though it was too dark to tell if it was Rhys or Cadoc.

The red dragon came in first, collapsing to the floor and dragging himself toward the back to make room for the others. His scales glittered like blood in the starlike fires of the ceiling.

She might not have seen the dragons transform many times, but she'd spent days staring at their scaled markings. This was Rhys, his scales crimson as blood. Cadoc's would've been the red-orange of fire.

The others landed. With rushing wind, roaring flame, and a surge of magic so strong Kai felt it tingle like effervescence in her blood, they resumed their human shapes.

Griffith reached to Rhys's shoulder. But Rhys shrugged him off and took two long steps toward Kai, rage and pain etched in the rigid lines of his face. "Why?"

She shrank against the wall, terror lacing her throat tight. Somehow, she found the courage to answer. "Because I am confused and terrified, and since you touched me, he is the only person here who is treating me like I matter."

The rage fell from Rhys's face so only the pain remained. He stared at her for two hard breaths, then strode into the darkness.

Kai ran to Griffith. "Where's Cadoc? Is he all right?"

Griffith's voice was hard as iron. "He's gone." He reached for Ffion, and the two of them followed Rhys into the shadows. Deryn spat a single Welsh word at Kai and left with them.

The adrenaline was wearing off, leaving Kai weak and shaking. She turned to Ashem. "Gone?"

His golden eyes flared with tightly contained rage. "I told you to leave Cadoc alone. Rhys would have killed him if the fool hadn't flown off as fast as he did. Do you understand now, you stupid human girl? Heartswearing isn't a frivolous human relationship based on nothing but emotion."

"I am a *person*," Kai shouted, pouring every ounce of confusion and frustration and rage into the words. She pushed herself away from the stone. "What I need is every damn inch as important as what he needs!"

To her shock, Ashem seemed to be trying to control his temper. When he spoke, he didn't yell. It was worse. His voice was calm and deadly quiet. "While I attempt to respect the free will of idiots as often as I can, nothing is as important as this. I am nothing. Cadoc is nothing. You are nothing. And if you don't heartswear to Rhys, everyone you love will be *nothing*."

Before Kai could answer, he went after the others.

Numb, Kai retrieved her pack and sat against the wall, praying to see the shape of one final dragon outlined against the stars. Praying one second of stupid indiscretion hadn't ruined a friendship older than anything she could comprehend.

"Come back, Cadoc," she whispered into the night.

He did not.

CHAPTER 19

RHYS

R hys threw a ball of fire into the hearth. Flames exploded from the point of impact, clinging in patches to the ornately carved wall. He denied himself the indulgence of sinking to his knees, curling in on himself to contain the guilt. Maybe if he let it rage, it would burn him away.

They were all there, in his room, watching him. Deryn paced, her long curtain of dark red hair shielding her face. Griffith stood like stone, arms folded over his blacksmith's chest. Ashem and Ffion murmured to each other.

"He doesn't have a singstone." Rhys stared into the flames.

"No. None of us do." Ashem's voice was tight, angry with all involved. "And he's not answering when I try to contact him directly."

Rhys clenched his fists. "Where is he?"

"I'm burning as much of my power as I can to track him, and even with that, he's almost out of my range," Ashem said. When he extended himself, Ashem could sense the mind of someone he knew for several miles.

"Blood of the Ancients, he hasn't turned around?"

167

Ashem shook his head.

"He won't," Ffion said. "Not tonight. He needs time. He's obviously attached to Kai."

Griffith made a small noise of dissent. Rhys looked at him, but his massive friend only shrugged. "I have watch tonight. I'll keep a lookout for him."

Rhys rubbed his temples. "No. I'm going after him."

Deryn stopped pacing, her eyes aglow. "You are not."

"You think you can stop me? Owain is searching these mountains, and Kavar will rejoin him any time now. If Cadoc is caught, he'll be killed." Rhys strode toward the door only to find Griffith in his way.

"Move, Griffith! It's my fault he's out there!"

"It's his own fault." Deryn got in Rhys's face. "Give me those hellfire looks all you like, *fy mrawd*. You aren't going anywhere after that lovesick idiot."

Rhys stood to his full height and glared at each of them in turn. "If I want to go, I will go."

Ashem shrugged. "You will. And then you will collapse. Unless you want to ask Kai to go with you. How far away from her did you make it before you fell out of the sky? Five miles? Eight?"

Flames sparked into life around Rhys's hands. "We can't just let him leave! We're the only family he has!"

Only a heavy silence answered. Finally, Griffith said, "Our first duty is to you, Rhys. To our king."

Rhys slammed a fist into the stone, knocking a divot into the ancient carvings. "Damn my being king! If anything happens to Cadoc..."

If anything happened to Cadoc, the only person Rhys could blame was himself.

CHAPTER 20

CADOC

C adoc landed on a summit, gulping crystalline air and trying to clear his head. His wing gave a twinge of pain, and he craned his neck to assess the damage. Singed and blistered, but not bad enough to stop him from flying, as long as he didn't have to maneuver much. He was lucky Rhys had missed.

You screwed up good this time, boyo. You've made a true mess.

He scrutinized the stars, trying to get his bearings. Rhys had fallen behind twenty minutes ago, but Cadoc hadn't been able to bring himself to stop. Bone-deep guilt and anger, not to mention embarrassment, had kept his back toward home. Lovers had never come between him and Rhys before. He'd been a fool to let it happen now.

A distortion rippled across the stars that made up the Flame constellation. Cadoc stilled, watching it pass across the sky. Two other distortions followed, forming a V. Dragon soldiers in battle formation. Either it was Owain and his people, or there were rogues in the area.

Cadoc lifted his wings, preparing to return to the cave, but hesitated. If there were other dragons this close, it would be better for him to find out where they were camped and who they were.

Taking off on aching wings, he followed the dragons north, away from the cave and the rest of the vee. The strangers flew for five or so minutes before they dove out of sight below the peak of a mountain. Cautiously, Cadoc soared to the summit and landed.

Below, two Quetzals and a Naga skimmed over the pines, their outlines blurred by their veils. The lead Quetzal was female; her vivid, feathered wings prismed the moonlight into pastel rainbows that scattered off frozen rocks and patches of snow. Silent and alert, their heads swept back and forth as they scanned the mountain wilderness.

Midway up the mountain, his quarries disappeared. Trying to look at the spot made Cadoc dizzy, and his eyes kept trying to slide away from it. He recognized the effect. They'd gone through a barrier, which meant Kavar was close, or had been when he set his magic up in that spot.

Glancing around for others, Cadoc leaped from the summit and soared to an overhang just above the place they'd vanished, making sure to stay upwind so the Quetzals wouldn't smell him. He thought of transforming, but the inevitable flash of fire would give him away. Instead, he crouched low and inched along the top of the overhang. Finding a place where he could ease down, Cadoc descended the slope. He crept to an upthrust rock and felt the familiar mental tingle of an Azhdahā barrier passing over him.

That was far easier than Ashem let on it would be.

He peered around the rock. A cave mouth had blinked into existence, set back on a small rocky shelf in the midst of what had previously appeared as an unbroken stand of dark green pine.

The lead Quetzal female was still standing. The other Quetzal, a male, sat back on his haunches. Their bright green scales and rainbow-feathered wings were a vivid contrast against the muted snow and stone. The Naga, its lemon-yellow scales also bright, wound the bottom of its snakelike body around the thick trunk of a nearby pine. It toyed with a few bits of long brown grass and a pinecone it had pinched delicately between two claws.

What are you doing, Ranvir? the female Quetzal broadcast her thoughts. *We don't have time for your tinkering.*

The Naga clicked its jaws lightly together, its version of an annoyed shrug. *There is more to life than blood for some of us, Izel.*

Cadoc's blood froze. Izel. Owain's master of torture. He'd never met her. Her reputation was terrifying enough that he'd never wanted to.

Izel snorted. *Not until the wrongs of the past are righted and the true ruler sits on the throne in Ancient Eryri.*

The male Quetzal growled. *If Rhys is isolated and injured and Aderyn is with him, we'll find them soon enough. Ashem can only have so many supplies. We could kill both of them tomorrow.*

Ranvir wound the grass into the minuscule grooves on the pinecone. It would have been nearly impossible for any dragon except a Naga, whose power lay in fine craftsmanship and their ability to charge inanimate objects with magic. *I'm not sure what I'd do without war anymore.*

Izel tucked her snakelike head and nosed her feathered wings. *You'll have plenty of war, Ranvir. Owain should have killed Rhys and Aderyn when they were children two thousand years ago. Not only are they formidable warriors now, the humans outnumber us hundreds of thousands to one. Even the rogues are banding together, saying they don't want any king at all. Our troubles only multiply the longer Owain tries to find his relic instead of taking action.*

The Naga tilted his head, examining his work. *Don't be so quick to write off relics. The Sunrise Dragon that Owain seeks has more magic twined into its molecules than you could ever comprehend. As for the rogues, they have wind for brains. The Warbringer is hardly a leader any sane dragon would follow.*

Cadoc recoiled. Warbringer? That wasn't possible. She'd been dead for nearly a thousand years.

Cadoc backed uphill. He had to get back to his vee. He had to tell Rhys. If he could reach the top of the overhang, he might be able to take off without them hearing. But his dragon body was large, and he hadn't spent enough time in it lately. His tail hit a sapling. It broke with a sharp *crack* that echoed through the valley.

Who's there? Izel's mental voice was sharp as needles.

Cadoc went very still.

Who's there? Izel repeated, low and menacing. Cadoc heard the slide of scales across stone coming his way. In seconds, she would be able to see around the boulder. As long as he didn't fly straight, he should be able to avoid the dart-like poisoned spines Quetzals could shoot from joints on their foreclaws.

Steeling himself, Cadoc launched. Wind screamed past as he thrust his wings down, and at the protest of the blackened skin of his injury, smoke streamed from his nostrils.

Izel, there! Fire Draig!

Cadoc thrust down again, then again, cursing gravity. He rose above the mountain, too slow. The small-bodied Quetzals had already sprung after him. He cut through the air, his longer wings giving him an advantage despite his injury. Hoping they would lose sight of him in the dark, he veiled himself and pushed hard for speed.

Eerily silent on their feathered wings, the Quetzals followed, and the Naga swam through the air behind them.

Cadoc changed course to shake them, but time dragged on, and no matter how much he twisted and turned, they paced him. Slowly, it sank in that he wouldn't be able to escape. All he could do was get within range of Ashem and pray the Azhdahā was still awake.

Cadoc maneuvered again and again over the next quarter hour. He wove between mountain peaks and flew so high his wings trailed cloud, but still the Quetzals followed. Clouds were gathering thicker now, and he wondered if he'd lost his way. The Quetzals were close, barely two lengths behind. Cadoc didn't think his injured wing would last more than another five minutes.

Finally, Ashem's blessedly livid voice bounced off the inside of his skull. *There you are! You wind-for-brains idiot! Get back here! That's an order.*

Cadoc's breathing came hard and ragged. *I can't.*

Don't be a fool. Rhys is fine. The girl—

Kavar's vee is chasing me. If I come back, I'll lead them directly to you.

In an instant, Ashem's voice went from angry friend to commander. *Where? How many?*

Three. I followed them to a cave hidden behind a barrier fifty miles northwest of yours. Owain is—

Cadoc cut off with a grunt of pain as one of the Quetzal's bone darts lanced through his injured wing. The poison seeped into the delicate membrane and spread agony like fire.

Cadoc? You're twenty miles east. We'll be there as soon—

No! Cadoc swallowed against pain and sudden fear. Knowing what he had to say didn't make it any easier. *We're too few already. Stay in the cave. Wait for Evan and Morwenna.*

Ashem swore long and loud. *Can you lose them?*

Cadoc didn't answer.

Cadoc?

Cadoc flared his wings as a Quetzal darted in front of him, hissing as the motion stretched his burn and the gash left by the dart. Curling his lips, Cadoc spat fire at the male Quetzal, igniting his feathers. The smaller dragon caromed toward the ground, a flaming beacon that cracked several trees and hit the mountain slope with a dull *thud.*

A gut-twisting, muscle-wrenching spear of agony shot through Cadoc's midsection, and he roared. Izel, the leader, had gotten beneath him with one of her poisoned spines. He belched fire after the Quetzal, but she dodged. Her shorter wings and smaller size made him look like a lumbering monster.

Ashem spoke again. *Don't be a martyr, Cadoc! Draw them closer. We'll meet you midway.*

Cadoc banked away from the cave. *No. Listen to me. Owain is searching for a relic called the Sunrise Dragon. And I heard... Damn it, it seems impossible, but I heard one of them mention the Warbringer.*

The Warbringer is dead. Come back. We'll meet you. We can handle three.

No. I won't risk any of you because I was a fool. Keep them safe, Ashem.

He folded his wings into a steep dive, knowing the female Quetzal would follow. The tenuous connection with Ashem severed; he'd passed just close enough to Ashem to be in range for a moment, and now he was away again.

Just as well. He didn't want Ashem to overhear what happened next.

There was another stabbing pain, this one in his back. Another dart. He roared, a red haze fogging his brain. It hurt. Fuck, it hurt. He writhed in the air, out of control.

The Naga was on him then, his claws raking Cadoc's

unburned wing, his jaws chomping at Cadoc's side, his teeth glancing off hard scales but bruising the muscle beneath. The Naga wound around Cadoc, searching for the softer flesh of his neck and belly.

Be still! The Naga's mental voice was hoarse and sibilant.

Eat shit and choke! Cadoc wrapped his limbs round the Naga's sinuous body, digging his claws deep. He stopped fighting and let his weight drag them down. At the last second, he opened his wings, roaring in pain as the rushing air and the weight of the Naga strained the burn and his new wounds. But the tactic worked. He'd flipped them, and now Cadoc was on top.

With an abrupt, bone-snapping thud, they crashed. Snow exploded around them as they slid downslope, scraggly pine trees splintering around them. The Naga screamed, but the sound turned to a gurgle. Cadoc roared again as branches pierced his wings and stabbed his body.

The Naga thrashed, dark blood bubbling at the corners of its mouth. Cadoc tried to shove it away, but the Naga's teeth sank deep in his forearm.

Sweet dreams, fire eater, it hissed.

All the sweeter, snake, because they begin with your death. Cadoc managed to rise to his three uninjured feet and staggered off the dying dragon. The Quetzal's darts were still in his gut and back, and his forearm burned. Soon, the sleep venom from the Naga's bite would take hold.

He was dead.

Cadoc wrenched out the Quetzal's poisoned bone dart with a claw, but couldn't reach the one in his back. He tried to run, to take off, but he only stumbled hard into the ground.

Snow crunched. The female Quetzal landed. She curled her lip at Cadoc, then bent her head to examine the Naga.

Well served, Ranvir. Be free in death, she intoned. One long,

175

wickedly curved claw sliced across the soft part of the Naga's throat. Blood spewed, spattering its yellow scales, steaming in the snow.

The Quetzal wiped her bloodied claw on the ground. To Cadoc's poison-addled mind, she seemed to move in odd bursts.

She turned her back on the Naga, whose body flickered and became human as he died. Examining Cadoc, she raised a claw as if to slit his throat as well. He closed his eyes and tensed. Fear pooled in his belly, making his heart jump no matter how he told it to stop. It was a good death. A warrior's death. His parents had died serving Rhys's father. He'd make them proud.

Pain pricked the corner of his eye. Cadoc jerked his head back as best he could, blinking away a trickle of blood that clouded his vision.

Amethyst eyes and fire-red scales. I know you, Cadoc ap Brychan. She bared her teeth in a fierce smile. *How perfect. We're combing the mountains for members of the false king's vee, and you fly right to us. The rest must be around somewhere.*

Cadoc couldn't answer. He couldn't breathe. He tried to push himself up, but the smaller Quetzal knocked him back with a sharp shove of her shoulder. His vision blackened at the edges, and he felt himself shrinking. Too many injuries. His body was making him human, trying to heal faster.

Excellent. You're far more portable this way. Let's get you into the pit.

CHAPTER 21

RHYS

R hys burned. Relentless pain radiated from his chest, seeping into the rest of his body. He threw off the sweat-soaked blankets and sat up.

Kai.

The farther he was from her, the more exquisite the ache. A different kind of pain accompanied that thought, a twinge he didn't expect: rejection.

Anger flared. At himself, for being so stupid. At Kai, for her selfishness. At Cadoc, for his betrayal. He pressed the heels of his palms to his eyes. Trying to distract himself, he reached for his father's journal. He ran his fingers over the embossed design on the front cover. There was comfort in the familiar gesture as he opened to a random page. The leather was wearing thin. Soon it would fall apart completely.

The tithe arrived today. Fifteen human girls and none worth a second glance. They'd better come up with something better, or the people of Gwynedd are going to find themselves without protection...

Rhys flipped forward a few pages. His father had, in

general, been a decent king and a good leader. But he hadn't been very generous when it came to humans.

One week since becoming heartsworn. Mair isn't bad to look at. Not as juicy as her cousin, the little peach Dumos ended up with, but not bad.

Rhys grunted, glad Kai hadn't come with a sister. Though heartswearing to humans tended to happen if a dragon spent too much time among them, it was almost guaranteed within certain human bloodlines. The last thing any of them needed was another Wingless mate.

When the heartswearing took hold of me, she tried to run. She didn't care who I was or who she'd become once we were sworn. When I pinned her and got the kiss, the wench actually bit me hard enough to draw blood. She managed it right in the middle of the swearing. I got a good laugh out of it. She hasn't shown much backbone since.

Rhys snapped the book shut, wincing when the delicate pages clapped together. The journal was on record, but there was something about having the actual book in his father's handwriting, even when it revealed his father to be less than admirable.

She hasn't shown much backbone. If only his father had known. Mair had beaten him in the end. She'd gone to Owain to sunder the heartswearing, and both Rhys's parents had ended up dead.

Rhys rubbed his chest, feeling his father's pendant beneath his shirt. If his aim was to relax, thinking about his parents did more harm than good. He tried to lie down again, only to find himself out of bed less than a minute later. It *hurt.*

Next thing he knew, he had hauled open the heavy door to Ashem's room—the Azhdahā had chosen one with a desert scene—and was shaking the commander awake. He'd passed

Cadoc's room on the way here, and his friend hadn't returned. Guilt closed a tight fist around Rhys's heart.

"Rhys?" Ashem got to wakefulness so fast, Rhys wondered if he'd truly been sleeping in the first place. The Azhdahā peered at him, dark brows furrowed over golden eyes.

"Cadoc hasn't returned."

For some reason, Ashem winced. "No. He has not."

"Have you heard from him?"

Ashem hesitated, then shook his head. "No."

Rhys sighed, rubbing his forehead. He hadn't wanted to ask for help, but he couldn't stand or sit or lie down or breathe for the pain. "I, um... I can't sleep."

Ashem pushed disheveled black hair off his forehead. "Sunder it, Rhys. Why are you doing this to yourself?" Instead of waiting for an answer, he pushed out of bed and padded barefoot out of the room. Rhys followed him down the hall. In the black cavern, he noticed a blanket-swathed lump next to the wall.

It was Kai. She had fallen asleep in the same spot he'd seen her last. Someone—likely Ffion—had covered her with a blanket.

"What is she doing out here?" Rhys rubbed fingers across his chest. The pain had plateaued, but it hadn't gone. Need twisted inside him. He wanted to go to her, touch her, wake her, lay her in bed and—

He shut down those thoughts before they went any further.

Ashem made a sharp, dismissive gesture and led Rhys into the kitchen. He rummaged through one shelf, then another. Finally, Ashem swore. "I told you there wouldn't be a sleeping draught here strong enough for this. I'll have to retrieve my pack from where we were attacked and pray Kavar had no interest in the more obscure vials in my medical kit. Which he likely did not. He was never one for medicine. Or any other topic that required study. I'll take Ffion. Ancients know she's smarter than the rest of you combined."

Rhys shook his head. "No. There's too much risk."

Ashem scowled at him. "You need sleep. You still aren't well."

Rhys forced his face into a neutral mask. "I'll live."

Ashem grunted, then asked, "The pain lessens when you're near her?"

Rhys nodded.

With a sardonic smile, the Azhdahā said, "You could ask her to sleep in your bed."

Rhys closed his eyes, willing himself not to let his mind go there. "And while I'm at it, I'll ask if Owain will off himself and end the war."

"Then I'm going to the meadow. If I can't make her swear to you, I can at least help you sleep."

Rhys's mouth pressed into a grim line. Force a woman to heartswear or allow Ashem to risk his life and Ffion's. What a choice.

At least Ashem and Ffion were able to make a choice. Rhys couldn't take that ability away from Kai.

Not yet.

They headed back through the cavern, and Rhys's eyes fell on Kai again. "Will she be warm enough?"

"She'll be fine." Ashem was terse, then silent as they climbed the shallow stairs and entered the wide hall. Terseness and silence were normal for Ashem, but there was something pronounced about it tonight.

"Is something wrong, Commander?"

Ashem winced. "No."

Rhys stopped. Ashem never winced. "You're lying. You have heard from Cadoc. Something happened."

Ashem scowled and kept walking. "No."

"Where is he?"

"I haven't heard anything," Ashem snapped.

Rhys hesitated. He might have pressed Ashem further, but as he put more distance between himself and Kai, fresh pain speared his chest. Through gritted teeth, Rhys said, "Promise you'll tell me if you hear from him."

Ashem didn't make eye contact. "I'll tell you anything you need to know."

———

HOURS LATER, Rhys sat in his tangled blankets, jaw sore from clenching his teeth against the pain. When he couldn't take the ache any longer, he stood and headed for the cavern. Night still slanted through the slits high in the hall ceiling. As he walked by Kai's room, the pain let up for a moment. Someone, probably Ffion or Griffith, had moved her from the entrance into her bed.

He made himself walk by without stopping.

Griffith kept watch near the cave mouth, just inside the spell that kept warm air in. Instead of sitting, he worked through a form with a massive oak staff that whistled as he whirled it through the air.

"You're up late." Griffith stopped to lean against the staff, sweating, green eyes bright beneath the brown hair plastered to his brow.

"As are you," Rhys replied.

Griffith's face was grim. "I don't have it in me to sit still tonight."

Rhys rubbed his chest. "Neither do I."

"If I could, I'd go after him."

"We could go together," Rhys said, only half joking.

Griffith smiled. "All right. Shall we strap Kai to your back or mine? The condition being, of course, that you explain to Ffion."

Rhys laughed. "I'm more terrified of her than Owain's entire army."

"As am I." Griffith grinned and whirled the staff. He jerked his head toward the wall, where another staff leaned against the stone. "Are you going to stand there, or are you going to work?"

They'd been friends their entire lives; there was no need to ask how Griffith had known he would come.

Rhys rolled his injured shoulder. The lingering weakness of Kavar's venom still made his limbs feel like lead, but he was tired of sitting on the side while his friends kept up their training. "I can go a few rounds."

With the first *clack* of the staves, the world drifted away like smoke. Action, reaction. Block, parry, block, thrust, the back-and-forth of feet across stone. No incomplete heartswearing. No Kai. No missing Cadoc—

Griffith called a halt half an hour later when Rhys buckled to his knees. He leaned his forehead against his staff, panting and frustrated. Even against Griffith, he should be able to manage two or three times longer.

"We're just resting," Griffith said. He offered a cup of water, and Rhys gulped half of it down in one long pull. "Truly, though, how are you?"

"Out of control." Outside, the snow had stopped. Mountain peaks glowed white, reflecting the light of moon and stars. Rhys turned away and took a deep breath. It didn't dull the pain. "I don't know if I'm making the right decision. Cadoc—"

"Did a stupid thing. I've lived through heartswearing, Rhys. Instinct takes over. It wasn't your fault."

"He's half in love with her. I think she may feel the same about him." Rhys hadn't meant to sound so bitter.

Griffith chuckled. "I can't speak for her, but Cadoc isn't in love with Kai. He just wanted to be. He lost his heart to someone else a long time ago."

Rhys raised an eyebrow, skeptical.

Griffith shook his head. "It isn't my place to tell."

Rhys didn't respond. It was hard to believe Cadoc could be in love and never mention it. The only thing he talked about more than romance was music, though food took a very close third. Of course, Rhys knew he was less than observant at times, not able to read the subtleties in others as much as he should, as a king. It was possible the signs were there and he'd simply missed them.

Silence was easy with Griffith, and this one stretched. Finally, Rhys licked his lips, where salty sweat mingled with cool water. "Griff. What was it like? For you and Ffion?"

Griffith leaned on his staff, his face thoughtful. "Quick. And unexpected. Like being struck by lightning, I imagine. She wasn't thrilled at first." He smiled. "I like to think I changed her mind." It was rare for a dragon to heartswear to someone in their own vee. Instead of forming the bond during a ceremony in Eryri, they'd sworn during a reconnaissance mission over the Chukchi Sea.

Rhys smiled as well. "Thoroughly. I assume Ashem informed her about tomorrow, and she told you. Are you worried about her going?"

"Ashem will keep her safe."

Griffith's tone was confident, but there was worry beneath. Rhys licked his lips again and changed the subject. Ffion and Ashem would be at risk tomorrow because of him. Like Griffith, he had to believe they would keep each other safe. "I've felt the lightning. I wondered more about...after."

Griffith straightened and arched, the bones in his back cracking. "It's...entirety. Completeness. Finality. You are half, only you don't realize it. Then you're whole."

"Isn't it strange? To have someone else in your mind?"

Griffith shrugged with one shoulder. "When you're sworn, it feels wrong not to have them there. But there are levels of intimacy. If you want, you can close each other out." He shook his head. "I know some who live that way. I don't think I could."

"But you love Ffion."

He smiled, glancing toward the hall, where he must be able to feel Ffion sleeping in their room. "Ffion is my soul. Without her, I am not."

Rhys pushed himself back to his feet. "I don't know if I can love like that."

Griffith gave a rumbling chuckle. "You've only known her a few days. There's plenty of time for love."

"Or hate, if we're like my parents." All Rhys could see when he closed his own eyes were her fey green ones, the scattering of freckles over her nose. Her lips, sweet and full. Ancients. That was lust, not love. Lust had caused him enough problems. "What am I supposed to do? Take her to Eryri and hide her? I didn't choose this. I don't want this, and neither does she."

"The wind blows where it will. We can only control our wings." Griffith's expression turned thoughtful. "Once you're sworn you'll be able to handle a bit of distance. Maybe Kai could go home while you settle things in Eryri. She could see her family, put her life in order, say goodbye." He laughed quietly. "You could meet her father and brothers."

Rhys thought of the distance between the island in the Pacific and Kai's home. A wave of nausea rolled over him at the thought of her so far away. At not being there to protect her. She was only human, after all. Vulnerable, defenseless, small, and so extremely short-lived.

Unless she completed the heartswearing.

Rhys rubbed his chest. The motion pressed the gold pendant against his heart. "Even sworn, I don't want her that far away. Humans are so...breakable."

"She won't be human. She'll be Wingless."

Rhys shook his head. Without Cadoc's constant music, his thoughts were too loud. He looked through the archway into the night. Any second he expected to see the tell-tale heat shimmer that surrounded a veiled dragon or a flash of fire, or to hear Cadoc's voice in his head.

He whirled the staff. It was as heavy as stone. "Let's go again. I can manage a little longer."

CHAPTER 22

JULI

J uliet King stared into the rising sun. The light burned her eyes, but it kept her from crying. How many days since Kai had disappeared, now? She didn't care to count. They were talking about calling off the search, but she wouldn't. Not if she had to turn over every damn stone on this mountain by herself.

Blinking, Juli looked around at the area where they'd found the unconscious girl. Everyone else was far below. They'd already looked this way. Scoured this whole section, actually, since it seemed like Kai had created an arrow of stones that pointed this way. But she couldn't shake the feeling that if Kai had gone anywhere, it would be up. Juli was determined to try the peak one last time.

She put one hand on the rough stone of the cliff base, not seeing or thinking, the cool rock slipping away beneath her fingers. The days trekking up and down the mountain had taken their toll. And now... Now most of the search and rescue people were saying Kai was dead.

Dead.

The path turned, angling upward. A bank of fog rolled in.

I have to turn around. Something is wrong!

Startled, Juli tried to shake off the feeling. There was nothing wrong here. There was still path left to explore this way. She pushed forward.

I have to turn back. If I keep going this way, I'll die! She can't be here. No one would come this way!

Juli gritted her teeth. Her mind went fuzzy, and she tried to remember if she'd come this way before. There were memories of this, memories of trying to come up the mountain and being turned around. The fog sparkled around her in the sunlight, threatening to swallow her whole if she removed her hand from the base of the cliff along which she walked.

I will not turn back. I will keep going. Kai is this way.

No, her mind gibbered back at her. *Wrong!*

Her steps slowed as if she waded through mud. Bile rose in her throat. Juli took another step, then fell forward, gagging and retching.

Go back!

"I will not!"

She didn't know how much time passed in the mist. Maybe a minute. Maybe days. She rocked back and forth on her hands and knees. With a cry of agony, she scooted her hand an inch forward. Then she scooted her other hand. Then her knees.

I will go this way! Every section on the map had to be searched. If she kept moving this way, she could put an X on the personal map she kept in her bag. The one that kept track of the places she had re-searched after everyone else gave up.

Juli would not give up, and she would not rely on strangers. She could trust only herself and Kai's family—who had arrived mere hours after Juli made the gut-wrenching phone call—to be truly thorough. The sheriff was here because it was her job.

The volunteers were here to make themselves feel good. They didn't care about Kai.

And then, without warning, the resistance dropped. It was such a shock that Juli staggered forward. Juli came fully back to herself, panting, her hands and knees bloody with scrapes.

The mist had cleared a little, and she looked around. She was in front of a deep ravine in the cliffs above, whose rocky floor sloped upward. There was no ravine on her map. Suddenly, after days of despair, she *knew* she was going to find Kai.

Through the ravine, she thought she heard the echo of a roar.

She gritted her teeth. She had bear spray. It would take more than wild animals to deter her now.

She clambered up. Ten minutes later, she stepped out into a brilliantly sunlit meadow that didn't make any sense. This mountain had a peak, not a flat top. And if it didn't, why hadn't the helicopters seen this place? Why had no one searched it?

The wind whispered through knee-high grass, carrying the scent of autumn and earth. Close by, a small hill rose above the rest of the meadow. Here and there, swaths of dirt were visible. One huge, brown scar ran through the center, as if something enormous had crashed and skidded. It wasn't Kai, but it was more than anyone had come across so far.

Hope quickening her heartbeat, Juli headed for the hill. It would offer a better vantage point.

She came over the top of the rise, shocked to discover a wreck of a camp surrounding a stone firepit. She counted eight tents, half of which were scattered and broken, looking as if they'd been bulldozed. Some of the marks looked a week old, the dirt inside pale and dry. Another, closer by, looked very, very fresh.

Wary but curious, Juli jogged down the hill. Stepping over

the rocks ringing the firepit, she held her hand over the ashes. Cold. Cautiously, she touched the top layer, sending up a gray, smoke-scented puff. Still cold. She curled her fingers into the gray dust beneath. Cold. No one had lit a fire here for days. Nothing stirred in the meadow but the wind.

Then the sound of a woman's voice, high and tuneful as birdsong, made Juli start.

A man replied, his voice deep and resonant. The skin on the back of Juli's neck prickled. The sliding, musical vowels and precise consonants reminded her of water flowing over rocks in a stream.

So, there were people here. They could know Kai's whereabouts...or they could be the ones who had taken her. Juli pulled her hand from the ashes, dusting off her fingers. Suddenly, her decision to come here alone seemed extremely ill-advised, but there was nothing for it now.

She crept toward the tents until she saw them fishing a loaded backpack out of the wreckage of one of the tents. The man looked a few years older than Juli—perhaps in his early thirties, bronze-skinned and dark-haired. His face was handsome in a way that made her mouth dry. The woman, who looked to be Juli's age, was short, with a long mane of complexly braided dark brown hair, dark brown skin, and a practical, kind expression.

Juli exhaled, long and low, as she studied the man, who had the body of a UFC fighter. Nice to look at, certainly. Not so nice if he tried to fight or run after her.

She touched her pocket, feeling the hard ridges of the Kubaton Kai had bought her for her birthday.

He could certainly try.

Abruptly, the man put one hand out to stop the woman and froze, his gaze fixed on the spot where Juli hid.

Her heart pounded. He didn't see her. He *couldn't* see her. A cold sweat broke out on her forehead.

"Come out," he growled.

The man and woman were both staring now. Juli didn't move. The man started toward her.

Shit. He *did* know where she was.

Juli let her pack slide off one shoulder and stood, ready to hit him with it and run. "Stay back!"

The man stared at her as if she had two heads. "How did you find this place?"

"With my feet," Juli snapped. "Who are you?"

He turned to the woman next to him, anger in his voice. "The other one was with Deryn. This one should *not* have been able to get through."

The small woman gave him a flat look and slung one of the packs piled at her feet onto her back. "Just be glad she didn't make it through twenty minutes before she did, or she would've had much the same introduction to us that Kai did. Aled fought like beast."

The hair on Juli's arms stood up. "Did you just say Kai?"

The man gave his companion an exasperated glare, then turned to Juli again. "Leave this place."

"No. You said my friend's name! Where is she?" Her eyes fell on a bag slung over his arm. Disturbingly, it looked like it was full of swords.

Then Juli's eye caught on a smaller bag at his feet. A faded, dirty blue backpack.

"That's Kai's bag!" She took a step forward, her hands half raised, ready to snatch it. "Tell me where she is this instant! The police are coming up the ravine. They're right behind me."

"No one is coming up the ravine." The man folded his arms, staring her down with his lion eyes.

Juli folded her arms as well and tilted up her chin. "I guess we'll see who's right when you go to prison for kidnapping."

"Ashem, there is *no time*," the woman said. She said something else in a fluid, musical language, never taking her gaze from Juli.

He shook his head. The woman put her hands on her hips, pointed north, then back at Juli. From the sound of it, the man was getting a thorough dressing-down. He might have the kind of voice that could command armies, but under the tiny woman's tirade, his resistance visibly crumbled. They went back and forth a few more times before he made a clear "do what you want" gesture. Juli was about to interrupt when they finished.

"We know where Kai is," the man growled.

Juli remained standing through sheer force of will while relief and terror rocketed through her. "She's alive? Please, her family and I will do anything to get her back."

The woman shook her head. "It's not that easy. But I believe"—she glared at the man—"the people who love her should know she's safe. She should have a chance to speak with you. We can take you to her, if you'd like. It's your choice. Though I must make it clear that Kai can't come home."

"Why not?" Relief warred with desperation. She could see Kai. And if she could see Kai, she could save her. Juli stepped closer to Ffion. "What do you want? Money? We'll come up with it, however much." Even if Juli had to beg her drunken, negligent mother.

"What happened to the police?" The man's full lips twisted into an impatient frown. He glared at Juli, his eyes roving down her body for a moment before he brought them back to her face. "You want to see her?"

"Yes!" Juli could have stomped her foot. How many times did she have to say it?

The man's expression was unchanged. "You are not making a wise decision."

Juli met him glare for glare. "It's mine to make."

She stepped forward, about to insist. Then her eyes fell on something that had been hidden a moment ago.

A body.

The broken, wrecked body of a man, half buried in the wreckage of the camp. Fear flared in her gut, and Juli started to scramble away. "Who is that?"

"An enemy," Ashem growled.

"You killed him! Oh my God. Have you killed Kai? Who are you people?"

The man didn't stop advancing toward her. "You've chosen. We must leave before other members of the Talon return. Let's go."

"Wait!"

Juli felt an odd, gentle pressure inside her head. Before she could finish her sentence, everything went dark.

CHAPTER 23

CADOC

Blackness rolled back from the world. Cadoc blinked damp grit from his eyes and groaned as he registered the pain of his injuries one by one. The Quetzal had not been careful with him.

Below him, the ground was stony and bitterly cold. His hands were bound in front of him with a rope of twisted metal wires. Finely wrought iron chains wound through his fingers and wrapped over his palms. He'd never worn chains like this before, but he knew their purpose well enough. Iron was used in everything from keeper-boxes, which hid magical trinkets, to lining the cells in the lower levels of Eryri, where king and Council sent their most dangerous enemies.

It blocked magic.

He wouldn't be able to use his fire.

"Cadoc ap Brychan."

Until the man spoke, Cadoc hadn't realized he wasn't alone. A testament to how badly he'd been hurt, he supposed. Now he looked up and saw an older, blonder, more polished version of Rhys who towered between Cadoc and a rope ladder that led through a narrow hole in the ceiling. About the same age as Ashem, he exuded an aura of power that made the air thick as syrup.

"Owain." Cadoc pulled his legs under him and struggled to his feet, then shoved his tangled, dark hair out of his eyes. Owain wasn't short, but he still had to tilt his head up to meet Cadoc's gaze. Owain's irises were white, ringed with dark gray. Even before losing his fire and becoming the white dragon, he'd had those bizarre eyes. "Get it over with."

Owain's only reaction was to give him a half-smile, unnervingly like Rhys's, but cold. Someone snorted, and Cadoc realized two people stood off to the side. One was Demba, a tall, ebony-skinned Bida with a vicious reputation. The other was a woman with golden-brown skin and a fierce scowl.

"You are stupid, Cadoc ap Brychan o'r Draig," she said. Cadoc recognized the voice of the Quetzal who had captured him. Her lip curled. "I find it hard to believe you're one of the false king's vee."

Cadoc sneered, his voice ringing as he spoke. "Rhys is the true king."

Owain gave Cadoc a sickly smile. "What a declaration. Untrue, of course, but I wouldn't expect any less from my cousin's most loyal friend. He's strong, Izel," Owain said, his gaze never leaving Cadoc. "In fact, he's perfect. You couldn't have done better."

Izel snorted, glaring with proud, black eyes. "Is he?" She took a knife with an obsidian blade from the belt slung low on her hips. She stopped in front of Cadoc, then slashed the blade over his collarbone.

Cadoc flinched, but didn't make a sound. The slice burned, but it was no more than a cut. Worse would come.

He refused to break eye contact as Izel raised the knife and placed the point of the blade on the left side of his chest.

Leisurely, inch after excruciating inch, she dragged it diagonally across his chest. He didn't move, didn't step back. His shirt parted, and so did his skin. Blood dripped hot down his cold flesh. Cadoc bit his tongue, his breathing ragged.

"That was for Ranvir. He was a glorious warrior."

Cadoc smirked. "Gloriously dead."

Smiling, Izel ran a finger through his blood and brought her finger to her mouth.

She licked it. Cold nausea rolled through Cadoc's stomach.

Izel stepped close, as close as a lover, and raised the knife to slice a long cut down his left cheek. Ignoring the burning line of pain, Cadoc turned his palm up. The chains stopped him from summoning fire, but they still grew hot.

He wrapped his fingers around Izel's arm. She yelped and tried to pull away. When he didn't let go, the yelp turned into a scream. Cadoc bared his teeth. "Apparently I'm not the only stupid one here."

Everyone in the room disappeared. No sound, no warning. They were there, and then they were not. Cadoc gasped and let go of Izel's arm before he realized her arm still felt very real in his hand.

Owain, Demba, and Izel winked back into existence. Cadoc blinked. Izel backhanded him across the face, and he fell to his knees, her many rings leaving scores down his right cheek.

An old man with a round face and huge, dark eyes emerged from the shadows behind the others, his arms pinioned by two other dragons of Kavar's vee. Cadoc didn't know him, but if what just happened was any indication, Owain's other unwilling guest had Clan Wonambi blood.

Owain and Demba wrestled Cadoc to his feet and slipped a hook into the metal cable around his wrists. Then they hauled on a chain strung through another hook in the ceiling, yanking

197

his hands above his head. Cadoc's heels left the ground; he could barely settle weight on his toes. The metal cable bit into his wrists, and it became hard to breathe.

Izel stood behind them, grinning, blood dripping from the blade in her hand. She yanked on the slash in Cadoc's shirt and tore it off.

Owain frowned at Cadoc. "You know how this works, ap Brychan. You're fast. You're a skilled fighter. I'd rather have you on my side than waste you."

"Go burn your wings. Ah, that's right. You can't."

Genuine displeasure crossed Owain's face. "You could save hundreds, Cadoc. Tell me where to find my cousins. If I kill them now, the war will end."

Despite the way Izel's slashes burned and the cut across his chest throbbed to the skies, the rest of him was without pain. Cadoc tried to capture the feeling in his memory, so he could return to it. Shelter in it when they really got started and everything became pain. "I'd be killing hundreds of thousands."

Owain shrugged. "Millions. Billions, I hope, though we'll probably keep a few. You don't count the life of every ant you smash when you land."

"Humans are not ants."

Owain raised an eyebrow. "They're useful gene donors and child makers, but they've barely been around long enough to see their first monuments go to dust. Their legacy is nothing. If we die, the earth loses a million times more history."

"Then why don't you let your Quetzal draw her claw across your throat? Your death would save hundreds of dragons." Cadoc bared his teeth in a humorless grin. "You have to turn it on, don't you? That feeling of power you ooze like a boil."

As if speaking had called it forth, the air around Cadoc seemed to thicken and grow heavy like syrup once more, and he struggled for breath. "It comes when it's summoned," Owain said, his voice dry.

Shoulders burning, Cadoc tried to stand taller, put more weight on his feet. "He doesn't have to summon it. Anyone who stands near him can recognize the true king. Power rolls off him like rain. You're nothing but a puddle."

Owain smiled, then turned to Izel. "Tell me when he's broken."

He ascended the ladder and hoisted himself gracefully through the opening and out of sight.

Izel prodded the old man, and Cadoc blinked in sudden recognition. The old man wasn't as old as he had first appeared, and he wasn't a stranger. "Uwan? You... You were dead."

Uwan refused to look at Cadoc, staring instead at the floor as Izel pressed the tip of her obsidian blade into his throat. Blood trickled red against his dark skin.

"Begin," Izel said.

Uwan shook his head. The movement dragged the blade over his neck, and the trickle turned into a stream. Izel sliced a shallow groove just under his right eye. "Begin, or lose your eye."

Cadoc jerked against his chains. "Oi! I thought I was here so you could stick knives in me. Leave him alone."

Izel's eyes held all the compassion of a dead fish. "Patience, fire eater. Your turn is coming."

Her knife flashed toward Uwan's face, and he cried out as part of his ear went flying. He put a hand to the side of his head, and blood dripped between his fingers.

The cold nausea returned, bringing fear with it. Cadoc inhaled, willing his breathing to steady, calling to mind Rhys's face, then Ashem's and the rest of them. He saw Uwan's years of suffering in his shaking, sparsely fingered hands, in his skin crisscrossed with white scars, in the strained, aged face. He spoke through gritted teeth. "Do it, Uwan."

Izel went very still, her knife half raised. For the first time, Uwan met Cadoc's eyes.

"Do it," Cadoc repeated. "I'm clever enough to know what's real."

Uwan shook his head, but this time it was more pity than denial. In a gravelly voice as familiar to Cadoc as childhood, Uwan said, "Stay strong, boy."

Cadoc blinked. Instead of Izel, he was looking at a tall, slender man. For a moment, his heart stopped. "Dad?"

Izel, now wearing the face of Brychan ap Hywll, smiled. Cadoc had been young when his parents died on a mission for the king. Too young to truly remember his father's face, or know his voice. But he'd spent long enough staring at records that it was a shock nonetheless.

The man who could not be his father smiled. "Well, *bach*," he said in a voice that resonated in Cadoc's brain like a long-forgotten song. "Let's get started, shall we?"

Cadoc recoiled. "Ancients, Uwan."

Cadoc's not-father flipped his hand, spinning a long obsidian blade end over end before he caught it. "It ends when you tell me what I need to know, son." The man leaned close. "Where's your vee?"

Cadoc didn't speak.

"Come now. You'll be helping us. Helping the real king, helping me."

Voice rough, Cadoc said, "My father never supported Owain or his genocide."

"You're wrong, boyo. You were too young to know. This is right. Owain is the true king. Now, tell me where to find the false king."

Resisting the urge to roll his shoulders, which were now on

fire with pain, Cadoc closed his eyes. Suddenly the knife bit between his collarbone and arm, piercing flesh and muscle. His eyes flew open, and he let out a bitten-off cry.

The man who could not be his father had a sympathetic look on his face. "No going away, son. You stay here with me and tell me where to find those liars who pretend to be your friends."

Cadoc didn't speak, didn't move, only looked into the man's amethyst eyes. The knife went into his other shoulder, and Cadoc bit his lip hard as he felt the blade sink into his flesh.

"Tell me where they are!" the man shrieked, yanking out the knife. Blood flowed in its wake. Cadoc sagged, would've gone to his knees if the chains hadn't held him up. His breathing went shallow, and he felt light-headed and sick.

"Sorry, son." The man smiled, the expression made more chilling by the blood spattered across his cheek. He raised a hand and smoothed damp hair from Cadoc's forehead. "It's important. You know it's important. Let's end this war together."

Cadoc jerked his head back. "You are not my father. You're just a bitch who likes to see people bleed."

The man buried his fist in Cadoc's gut so deep it took Cadoc long seconds to remember how to breathe. He hung from the chains, twisting and gasping for air.

His father crouched, peering up into Cadoc's face. "You follow a false king. Give Owain what he needs to take back the throne, or I'll take it. One way or another, you will break."

Still gasping, Cadoc shook his head. His father punched him again. Cadoc tried desperately to curl in on himself, but couldn't.

"Say it! Owain is king!"

Cadoc closed his eyes, trying to breathe. The blade slashed across his right cheek this time. "Open your eyes and *say it!*"

"I...won't." Cadoc spat a gob that clung to his father's shirt.

Smile still in place, Brychan drew back his arm and slammed his fist into Cadoc's face. Cadoc's head snapped to the side and he saw stars.

His father shook out his hand and laughed. "Looks like you need more time to think about it. See you in an hour, boyo." He turned to leave. "And the hour after. And the one after that."

CHAPTER 24

RHYS

R hys knew Kai was on the ledge. The closer he got to the opening, the less he hurt. She'd been there all morning, staring at the sky. At the sight of her, desire curled low in his belly. He was exhausted. Griffith had finally given up sparring around dawn, but Rhys hadn't slept.

There she was: the source, the solution. Standing in the freezing wind looking for another man.

Rhys ran a hand through his hair, then smoothed it down. It wasn't possible for him to send thoughts to Cadoc while human, let alone over a great distance, but he formed one and shot it into the void anyway. *Stay safe, idiot.*

Maybe Ashem was right. Do it and be done. Maybe Griffith was right too, and he could kiss her, then send her packing. He wasn't sure how long he'd be able to hide the new strength heartswearing would give him from the Council and the dragons living at Eryri, but surely he could manage a few months. But she'd have to come to him eventually. He'd need her close, no matter what it did to his standing with the others.

He hesitated, then growled softly and trudged up the rough

incline toward Kai. If she went inside, she went inside, but he'd have a few seconds of relative comfort first.

Even with the sunshine, the wind bit deep. He made no secret of his approach, but she jumped and scrambled as far away as the ledge would allow. Her black hair whipped around her face. Her sea-green eyes, red-rimmed from crying, looked more fey than usual. Her borrowed shirt and ever-present hoodie skimmed the subtle curves of her body, and he couldn't help but imagine doing the same with his hands. How smooth would she be? How soft? How warm? His body reacted to the thought of his hands on her, of getting to touch more of her than that one graze of skin, and he had to set his jaw and force the thoughts into the back of his mind.

Kai stared at him, not afraid or angry, but some uncertain place in between. "What would you do if I jumped off this cliff?"

Rhys gauged the distance between the top of the cliff and the ground. "I would catch you."

Kai turned her back to him, standing so close to the ledge that her toes hung over empty space. He couldn't decide if she was brave or stupid. Or about to test his claim.

She twisted one of her carabiners, and in silence he watched her fidget, knowing he should speak, not knowing what he could say. "About Cadoc... I lost control."

She snorted. "Lost control? You don't have any control to lose. Me, then him. I've never been attacked with magic before. Thanks for that."

Rhys moved to stand at the ledge too. Despite how desperately he craved to be close to her, he gave her several feet of space. Pine and aspen made a swaying carpet of green and gold below the toes of his boots. "I didn't attack you."

Kai hugged herself, not looking at him. "Really? As I recall, you'd have mauled me if not for Deryn." She tried to laugh, but it sounded flat.

"I attacked Deryn."

That surprised her, apparently, because she didn't respond. He kept his eyes down, green and gold blurring as his vision unfocused. *Deryn.* She hadn't even been angry with him after, only worried.

"You attacked your own sister to get to me, then your best friend. Ffion was right. Heartswearing is a curse."

His anger flared. "I'm at fault, Kai. But Cadoc knew. He has some share in the blame for what happened to him. So do you. If you'd listened to Ffion, he'd still be here."

She whirled. "If I had *listened?*"

The movement was too fast. One foot slipped, and she teetered on the edge, arms flailing, balance lost.

Faster than thought, he was by her side. He grabbed her wrist and yanked her from the precipice and against his chest, curling his body protectively around hers.

The contact sent a searing, rolling, electric wave of need through him. The heat and scent of her slammed into his senses as he wrapped his arms around her and took two giant steps back from the edge, then settled her on her feet.

"Oh!" Kai let out a belated gasp. Her arms went around him and her hands fisted in the back of his shirt. "Holy shit."

He knew he should let her go, but then...she melted into him, clinging, her face buried in his chest. "Thank you."

"Of course." Rhys heard his own voice, rough as gravel. When she didn't pull away, he held her tighter, closed his eyes, leaned his cheek on the top of her head, and breathed her in.

It was the first time he'd held her like this, full against him. Her head didn't even reach his shoulder. She was compact and strong, and he could feel the energy coiled in her lithe body. Her small breasts pressed against his ribs, and he bit back a groan and fought back more thoughts of what it would be like to see all of Kai. Touch all of her. She made him as drunk as the strongest liquor in Eryri.

Finally, she pulled away just enough to tilt her head back and look up at him. Stormy, sea-green eyes met his from beneath long black lashes. The contrast with her porcelain skin, her rose-pink cheeks that matched those soft, parted lips. One kiss, and he could be whole.

Or, if she didn't want him forever yet, if she only wanted him for a night, there were so many things they could do besides kiss.

Kai's breath caught. For an instant, the hands fisted in his shirt pulled him closer, and she arched her body against his, and Rhys knew—she might not feel the desperate need of the heartswearing, but she felt something.

She wanted him.

Her mouth was so close. So close to his.

Apparently realizing this at the same time he did, Kai went stiff in his arms. Eyes darkening, pupils that were dilating with desire suddenly contracted in fear.

"Rhys. Let me go."

The monstrous side of him growled deep in the depths of his mind.

He didn't want to.

He didn't have to.

All he had to do was dip his head and claim her.

"Please," Kai whispered.

The terror in her voice splashed over him like a bucket of ice water. Rhys relaxed his grip on her and stepped back, breathing hard.

Kai swallowed, licking her lips, her pulse fluttering at the base of her throat. "Maybe you do have some control. Or maybe you just don't need a sacrificial virgin today."

He should leave, he knew. He should get away from her before his tenuous hold on instinct snapped, but despite the close call, the temptation, he wasn't ready to leave her—and he wasn't ready to deal with the pain that leaving would ignite in his chest.

He seized on her words, looking for anything to distract himself as he pressed his back against the cold stone wall and sank down until he sat with his forearms draped over his knees. Anything to look smaller and less terrifying to her, even if it was a lie and he was just as dangerous as ever. Anything to keep her close. "We never killed virgins. We sent the ones who didn't heartswear back to their villages."

"Excuse me?" Kai blinked at him.

He leaned his head back against the stone and willed his heart to slow down. His body to relax. "They were a protection tithe. Some human kingdoms had protection contracts with us. Often one of the terms was that a number of unmarried persons of a certain age be sent to us to see if they could become heartsworn."

"Yeah, well, I gave it up to Mark Belinsky after senior prom. Can I leave now?"

Possessive rage flared in Rhys so fast his knuckles turned white where he gripped his knees. He closed his eyes and forced himself to breathe. She had no idea of the emotions an offhand statement like that could spark. The smell of burning wafted into the air, and he looked down to see scorched fabric where he'd rested his hands. Chagrined, he laced his fingers together.

The image of Morwenna's lazy smile, of her dark hair feathered across his pillow, flashed through his mind. Ancients, he was the biggest hypocrite under the sun.

Kai smiled and raised a brow at the curls of smoke rising from the burned fabric on the knees of his pants. It was small, but she was definitely smiling. "Relax, Spyro. He wasn't that good anyway."

"Spyro?"

"Never mind."

Rhys cleared his throat. "The virgin part was a human idea, not ours."

"Hm. You like them experienced then?" Kai teased.

Rhys swallowed a strangled sound, and the image of Morwenna in his bed changed to Kai, eyes half-lidded, back arched, whimpering his name. Parting her legs and begging for him to taste her, fill her.

Fuck.

"I...don't have a preference," Rhys managed at last. He didn't say that in all of his years he'd only had one partner himself. That's what happened when you spent half your life too busy to think straight and the other half on the run.

They sat in silence another long moment. Finally, Kai said, "I don't suppose you'll go more into detail about your war now that I'm stuck here. What are you fighting over besides power? Land? Some kind of magical dragon crown?"

He rubbed at the scorch marks. The conversation kept wandering close to topics he wanted to avoid. But Ffion was right, Kai should know some things, and war was a safer topic than sex, even if she was just teasing.

"You're closer than you think. There are currently two kings, and they're fighting over a magic we call the mantle, which is the power to command every dragon on earth. It's broken right now. Weak because it's torn between them. One king wants to maintain the status quo with dragons hidden from humans. The other wants to force dragons to commit human genocide."

She stared at him. "Don't beat around the bush, I guess."

"Cadoc does pretty words, not me."

They both winced. Kai recovered first. "Please tell me you all follow the king who wants to stay hidden."

Rhys nodded.

"Thank God. So the white dragon is the genocide one?"

Rhys nodded again. They were on dangerous ground. If Kai found out *he* was the king who wanted dragons to stay hidden, she might feel obligated to heartswear to him, which was the last thing he wanted. Perhaps some would think his reasoning weak, but his father forcing his mother to heartswear had ended in his death, and the deaths of dozens of others. Rhys would do anything in his power to stop history from repeating with him and Kai.

Luckily, Kai's mind had gone in a different direction. "How many dragons are we talking?"

"More than ten thousand, less than fifteen. A third are for staying hidden, a third follow Owain, and a third are neutral. Rogues. Or free dragons, depending on who names them."

The pink drained from her cheeks. "A few thousand dragons for hiding, a few thousand neutral, and a few thousand for genocide. That's a lot of dragons who either don't care what happens to humans or actively want them dead."

Rhys traced the scales of his indicium with his gaze, putting his thoughts in order. For Owain to win, both Rhys and Deryn would have to die. At least their sister, Seren, would be safe. For reasons no dragon knew, the fact that she was the Seeress meant that she couldn't inherit the power of the mantle. "Most of the free dragons just want to live in peace. They want their families to be safe. I can't fault them for that. But if Owain wins, he'll heal the mantle and use its full power to force *all* dragons to go to war with humans. He believes the outcome of that will be a return to old glory. I believe your species would suffer a massive loss of life, but dragons would become extinct. Magic is wonderful, but there are something like eight billion of you, and you have nuclear weapons."

Kai's face was blank. He didn't blame her. If he had the choice to know about the burden balanced on his shoulders or not, he would choose ignorance every time.

"Yeah, no. That makes sense. I'm all for dragons hiding as well. And this mantle, can the kings use it on any dragon?"

Rhys took a slow breath before answering. Figuring out the limitations of a broken mantle and plugging the holes it left in his defenses had taken up most of the first hundred years of his reign. "Any dragon, yes. Once upon a time, an order could be issued during a sunrise ritual that would automatically affect all dragons. But it doesn't work like that anymore. Now, the power is limited to those within range of the king's voice. Once a command is given by one king, it can't be countermanded by the other. Early on, that meant both kings spent a considerable amount of power issuing an order to every single one of their followers *not* to follow any command given by the opposing king."

"Wait. So these kings can just walk around telling people to jump off cliffs if they want?" Kai asked.

Rhys felt his mouth twist in a wry smile. "Only once. Then they have to wait until the next sunrise. But theoretically, yes."

"Why once?"

"The magic is depleted. The king must perform a ritual."

"Oh. Like the magic refill ritual. Cadoc told me about that." Kai nodded wisely.

Amused, Rhys studied the play of light over the lines of her face. She was very beautiful, once he took the time to look. "This one is... more powerful. The amount of magic being channeled is vast." Which was why he hadn't been able to do it since he'd used the mantle on Deryn the night he'd met Kai. In his weakened state, it would have killed him. But he would need to do it again before they left for Eryri. He might not be able to command Owain's soldiers to jump off any cliffs, but the mantle had its uses.

"So you're under this thing's power?" Kai shivered. "It sounds terrible. I'm getting a little concerned about dragons and their lack of free will."

Rhys opened his mouth to reply, but caught a flash of silver in the distance. Ashem's irritated voice sounded in his mind. *Get her out of the way.*

Rhys saw Ffion surrounded by a veil-signifying ripple in the air. Ashem was helping her hide, and Rhys's focus kept sliding away from the distortion.

"We need to move. Ashem and Ffion are back, and they're coming in. It looks like Ffion is carrying something in her claws."

CHAPTER 25

KAI

One king wants to maintain the status quo with dragons hidden from humans. The other wants to force dragons to commit human genocide. Kai couldn't get the words out of her head.

I guess I know who the good guys are.

She stared at Rhys's back as he preceded her deeper into the underground palace, lithe muscles visible through his shirt as he moved. A dark shiver went through her as she remembered what it was like to be in his arms, surrounded by him. Protected by him. To see in his eyes and feel in every tense, hard muscle how he wanted to devour her.

Had he seen how much she wanted to devour him, too?

Kai shook herself. She couldn't let herself want that. Want him. What if he saw her uncontrollable lust and took it as permission to kiss her and take her away from her life?

Keep it in your pants, Monahan, she told herself. *Forget that you're more attracted to this man than you've ever been to anyone in your life. He's not even human. Soon you'll go home,*

*and he'll fly away to his war and you'll never see him or any of
them ever again.*

To Kai's surprise, that thought didn't sit well with her.
What would she do after this? Just go back to her life and never
know what happened to Cadoc? To any of them? Never know
the outcome of their war unless the bad guys won and
suddenly, dragons started killing everyone?

The still air kicked into a roaring gust, and a graceful silver
dragon with mirror-bright scales glided through the entrance,
pulling Kai from her thoughts. Like the other Draigs, her fine,
triangular head was crowned with two tapering horns. A
slender fin ran down the back of her sinuous neck like the
dorsal fin of a fish. She spread her wings for balance. They
were translucent, with fine silver veins visible within, and they
shaded to a more opaque silvery white around her bones.

Of all the dragons, she was the most beautiful, Kai thought.

Ffion landed on her back feet about halfway into the
cavern, a bundle cradled in her foreclaws. She set it carefully
on the ground, and then air swirled around her, kicking up dust
into a shrinking vortex. A moment later, the human Ffion stood
in front of them. She crouched by the bundle.

Before Kai could make out what it was, the wind kicked up
again and Ashem entered the cave. His black dragon form was
spectacular as well, Kai could grudgingly admit. More thickly
built than the Draigs, he had a heavier, almost lionlike face and
a bony frill like a triceratops, with half a dozen small black
horns sweeping back from its edges. Unlike Ffion's tail, which
was whiplike and unadorned except for two spikes at the end,
Ashem's had sharp spines studding its bottom half.

He set several smaller bundles on the ground, including
Kai's old blue backpack, and changed forms in a burst of darkness. Now fully human, he barked something Welsh at Rhys.

Kai moved to retrieve her pack while Rhys joined Ffion,

leaning over the body-sized parcel the silver dragon had carried in. He said something that sounded very much like an expletive. Ffion folded her arms, her expression cool, and said something back. Oddly, Rhys glanced at Kai.

For the first time, he looked uncertain. Then he shook his head. "It was your idea, Ffion. You explain it to her."

Ffion glared at him. "I seem to be the only one capable of explanations."

Rhys had the grace to look ashamed, but only for a moment. "Go on, then."

Ffion glanced at Kai. To Kai's shock, she looked uncertain as well. She unfolded her arms and twiddled the end of a braid between her fingertips before motioning at Kai to approach. Warily, Kai walked toward her.

"So, Kai..." Ffion smiled brightly, but something about it seemed pasted on. "I know it's been difficult for you, being here without any viable way to contact your family and tell them you're safe."

A sense of foreboding came over Kai. But the dragons wouldn't. They wouldn't bring someone else here. Ffion wouldn't. "Yes..."

Ffion clapped her hands together like an excited teacher. "Yes, well. I thought it might be nice for you to visit with someone you love."

"Tell me you didn't." Kai felt sick. She strode to the disturbingly human-sized bundle, which was wrapped in what appeared to be a piece of a tent.

It only took a glimpse of mussed blond hair to know who it was. Kai knelt, a maelstrom of emotions spiraling through her mind. She barely noticed Rhys had come to stand beside her.

"No. Ffion, why would you do this to her?"

Ffion clasped her hands behind her back, her dark cheeks turning a deep rose. But when she spoke, her voice remained confident. "She found the meadow. She cared enough about you to push through a barrier, Kai. I've never seen a human with the ability to do that before."

Kai sat back, rubbing her face. Part of her wanted to rage and scream. That same part wondered if Ffion thought of her as a sort of pet who might like another pet for company. But that was uncharitable. Next to Cadoc, Ffion had been the kindest to her since she'd been here. "Juli is exceptionally stubborn. I'm not surprised she found a way through."

And it was incredible to see her face. Incredible and strange. Worlds colliding.

"You can write some letters for her to take to your family, spend some time with her. When we return to Eryri, we we'll drop her off somewhere she can be found or find other humans easily."

When we return. Because they expected Kai to go with them. But that wasn't what Kai wanted. Not what she was planning.

Kai's pounding heart slowed as she peered down at Juli, her stern features relaxed in Ashem's magically-induced unconsciousness.

Juli. Here. Maybe this wasn't a disaster, but a blessing.

There would be no one in the world better to have at her side when Kai executed her escape.

"Rhys." Ashem flashed something small at Rhys that looked like it was made of silver and quartz. "I contacted Evan. He and Morwenna have been in contact with Eryri. Seren is sending the Ironscale Vee. They'll meet over the Pacific soon and be on their way here."

"She must have seen something," Rhys said.

Ashem nodded. "They'll be here in a few days. It could be as few as two or three, depending on weather."

"That's...good. That's excellent. Thank you, Ashem," Rhys said.

Kai caught Rhys glancing at her out of the corner of his eye, but she couldn't get a read on what he was thinking. Hearing how soon the other dragons would be here, her heart sank.

She only had a few days, and the dragons had no intention of letting her go. Escape was more important now than ever.

Slowly, she nodded. "Well, then. We should wake her up."

Kai rose and stepped back, bumping into something warm and solid. She looked up to see who it was, and found herself captured by a stern mouth and a pair of starfire eyes.

Rhys. He put a hand on her shoulder to steady her and his fingers brushed the skin of her neck. A shock jolted through skin, sinking like fire into her bones. Her breathing quickened, and he didn't break her gaze. God, he was like a magnet. Was that normal? The dragons said she wasn't bonded, so why did she feel so drawn to him?

"Wake her up," Kai repeated, lifting her chin to look unwaveringly at Ashem.

The humorless man folded his arms. "Politeness is the sinew that holds the wing together."

"Do it, Ashem," Rhys said, his voice soft.

Ashem flicked his leonine gaze to Rhys, then Kai. "Let me make one thing clear. The girl can't know that we are dragons."

Kai folded her arms. "Or what?"

Ashem's face was stony. "Consequences."

Kai tilted her head. "What are we going to tell her, Ashem? That you're a cult who lives in a palace-cave inside a mountain? She'll see through that before she's even half awake. She'll want an explanation. She deserves an explanation."

"Explain it another way," he growled, "or she'll be stuck here the same as you. I've promised not to dig around in your mind. She has no such promise from me. If you tell her, I'll know."

Kai opened her mouth to say something else, or to get Rhys to say something, but canvas rustled. Juli was pushing herself up, blue eyes already sharp, chin-length hair mussed.

"Where am I?" Juli demanded, apparently only seeing Ashem at first. "I swear to God you are going to regret this!"

"I already do," Ashem said dryly.

Kai crouched by her best friend's side. Despite everything, a slow grin spread across her face. "You're with me."

Juli eyes widened and she snapped her head toward Kai. "You're alive! I knew you were! I *knew* it."

She threw herself forward, wrapping her arms around Kai and pitching them to the floor. Juli squeezed Kai until she could barely breathe. "I knew it," she repeated over and over. "I knew it!"

Kai sat up, pulling Juli with her. Their arms were tight around each other as they laughed, and the laughing turned to tears, and then Juli put her hands on Kai's shoulders and pushed her back, as if she needed to get a good look at her. "Are you hurt? Where have you been? Kai, your parents are out of their minds with worry! Your mom hasn't eaten in days. You can't just..."

She shifted her gaze and trailed off, taking in the black, starry-ceilinged cavern. Then Rhys. Then Ffion. She scowled when she got to Ashem, then pushed her hands through her hair as if unconsciously trying to smooth it down. In a move that encompassed the deepest reasons Kai loved Juli, she shifted, pushing Kai behind her and addressing Ashem.

"Who are you and what do you want from us?"

"No one and nothing," Ashem said.

"What will it take to get us home?"

Ashem raised expressive dark brows at her. "You'll leave soon enough. Your friend, unfortunately, is staying."

Juli raised her eyebrows right back. When she spoke, her voice was as sharp and frosty as an ice pick. "No. She is not."

Ashem pinched the bridge of his nose. "I've done this enough over the last few days. I have work to do."

"I'll make sure she has somewhere to stay," Ffion said.

They both turned and walked from the room. Kai stood and pulled Juli to her feet. Her friend thrust her finger toward the retreating dragons, rigid as a cat with all its fur on end.

"This conversation isn't finished!" Juli shouted. "Come back here *now*."

Ffion quickened her steps, but Ashem stopped short. His shoulders tense, he turned tightly and marched straight back, not stopping until he loomed over Juli. So close, Kai nearly threw herself between them. From the look on Rhys's face, he was close to doing the same.

"Understand one thing, woman," Ashem snarled. "I give the orders here."

Juli lifted her chin, her voice cool and utterly calm. "Understand one thing, you bastard. Your orders mean nothing to me."

Ashem bared his teeth. For a terrified moment, Kai thought he might turn into a dragon. It would take that much to frighten Juli, and now that he'd faced her, Ashem had to sense that. Instead, he glared at her a moment longer, then turned on his heel and followed Ffion out.

Juli twisted to glance at Kai, her brows drawn together in confusion. "What is going on here?"

Kai swallowed. If Juli found out the others were dragons, Ashem wouldn't let her leave. So Kai gestured at the only dragon remaining. "Juli, this is Rhys."

"Rhys? We're on a first-name basis with our kidnappers?" Juli snapped.

"Rhys ap Ayen," Rhys cut in smoothly. "And I promise, Ms....?"

"King," Kai supplied, which Juli rewarded with a glare.

"Ms. King," Rhys said, "The kidnapping is temporary. We...ah..."

He foundered. Kai wondered if he always had this much trouble finding words. He hadn't seemed to before. Juli could be intimidating, Kai supposed as she watched her friend impale Rhys with a frozen glare. Even if one was a dragon.

"We have a lot to talk about." Kai put a hand on Juli's arm. "But first, know that I'm safe. I've been fed, I've been cared for. None of them have..." She'd been going to say *laid a finger on me*, but that wasn't true. A finger was all it had taken.

Apparently, trailing off was enough for Juli to understand. "We can talk about that when we're alone. If we're allowed to be alone." She shot the last at Rhys with another icy look.

"Of course," Rhys said.

"We'll go to my room." Kai shifted her backpack on her shoulder. Her cell phone should be inside, but it had to be dead by now. Dragon magic was advanced, but apparently didn't extend to standard electrical hookups. Juli might have a phone. If she did, Kai would have to figure out the best way to call for help. She didn't want to bring police or the National Guard or whoever here, where the dragons were. With Ashem's barrier up over the entrance, they wouldn't even be able to find the place. But if she and Juli could get out of the cave and away from the dragons, maybe they could find somewhere with enough of a signal to get out a text or even pinpoint and share their location.

"You have a room?" Juli asked. She glanced up at the cave

again. "I don't understand. Aren't we in a cave? What is this place?"

"I'll explain what I can. Come on." She tugged Juli toward the hall where Ashem and Ffion had disappeared.

"Kai."

Kai stopped and looked back to Rhys. He was alone in the blackness, the reflections of the fires all around him like stars. "If you need me—need anything—let me know. I would be more than happy to do...what I can."

Slowly, she nodded, feeling like this—their first civil conversation since he'd heartsworn to her—was a tightrope. She couldn't afford to fall. So she kept her tone polite but reserved. "Thank you, Rhys. Unfortunately, I don't think 'what you can' covers what I need."

Then she took Juli's arm and led her up the stairs and out of the cavern, leaving Rhys and his storm-heavy presence behind.

SAFE IN HER ROOM, Kai curled up in a chair near the hearth and watched Juli take in her surroundings with a not-insignificant amount of cognitive dissonance. Her friend's mental process was visible as she categorized and labeled everything in the room. From her frown, Juli did not approve. Whether that was about the accommodations themselves—though the bed and furniture were ridiculously luxurious, if old—or simply the fact that this place had the audacity to exist, Kai was unsure. Probably the latter.

"Are we in a cave? Where is this place located? And why have you been kidnapped by an unstable man with interpersonal issues? How do they even get up here? Do they land a helicopter outside, or are there secret tunnels down below?"

Kai considered her answers slowly. Juli could not know about the dragons. "Not really a cave. Still in the Rockies I think, but north. As for the rest, not a clue."

She winced inwardly at the lies, but the truth was out of the question. Besides, Kai wasn't sure about secret tunnels down below. Maybe there were. She and Cadoc had only explored a fraction of the halls and rooms below, and that had seemed like a hub—a space that led to hundreds of others. Between the collapsed areas, the darkness, and the feeling that the ghosts of ancient dragons might lurk in the deep, forgotten places, Kai hadn't explored anything down there. That could take months. Years. It wasn't a viable option.

Juli, who was pacing the room, slashed her hand down in a gesture of dismissal. "Impossible. There is no place like this in North America. The architecture is too unique."

"What continent do you think places like this exist on?" Kai asked, amused.

"There are underground palaces in North Africa," Juli said.

"A look out the archway that leads outside will show you we're not in North Africa," Kai said.

"Hm." It was the noise Juli made when she was annoyed that things would not conform to simple logic. "You've never been to North Africa, Kai. Maybe you don't know what it looks like."

"Maybe not. But what's outside does look an awful lot like the Rockies."

"Hm," Juli said again. "We'll set where aside. Let's go back to why, and why that horrible man said I could go but you can't."

Kai traced the fabric of the chair's upholstery as she considered what to say. Dragons seemed to prefer intricate decoration, because the fabric was thick with flowers and spirals and hidden animals in the negative spaces. "It goes back to the girl we found at the base of the cliff."

"Is she here too? Is she a captive, or one of them?"

"One of them."

"Of course. Was it a trap?"

"I don't think so. She woke up a while after you left. She was worried—*very* worried—about her brother and her friends. I thought they might have been in an accident at the top of the cliff, which would've explained how Deryn—the girl—fell to the bottom."

"No it doesn't. If she'd fallen that far, she would be dead."

Kai leaned her elbow on the arm of the chair and her chin in her hand. "Can I tell the story? Or would you like to?"

Juli gave her an irritated wave.

"Anyway, Deryn was so worried that she started dragging herself across the rocks. She wouldn't stop. I was afraid she'd injure herself further, so I agreed to go look with her."

Juli made a frustrated sound.

"Yes, I *know* it wasn't safe," Kai said. "You weren't there. You didn't see her, and she was too tall and strong for me to get her to hold still. Anyway. We followed a ravine to the peak of the mountain—"

"That's the way I went," Juli said. "And it isn't a peak, is it? It's a meadow. I don't understand that either."

Kai ignored the interruption. "And the rest of the d—of them were there. They had some kind of camp up there. They were... This is so hard to explain, but they're some kind of military group, I guess. They were out training, and they were attacked by their enemies. They took shelter here."

"What, like they're some special ops group out of the UK and they were attacked on United States soil? No. The government would know about that. They'd be here, handling it."

Kai shrugged.

"They lied to you."

Kai shrugged again. "Honestly, the most believable thing I could tell you is that they're laboring under a group delusion."

It *was* the most believable thing she could tell Juli, even if it was nowhere near the truth.

"And they want you to stay with them?"

Kai hesitated, then shrugged a third time. "Yes."

"Hm." Her eyes went to the bright white fires lighting the ceiling. "Are those...fires? Where's the smoke? What does it use for fuel?"

Kai rubbed her eyes. "I don't know, Jules. Don't ask." Kai tried to keep her voice light. She was glad, at least, that Juli was having a very Juli-like reaction. No panicking, just disdain for their kidnappers and common-sense questions.

Juli snorted. "So, what's the plan?"

"Do you have your phone?"

Juli did. But when she took it out, there was, of course, no reception.

"It could be because we're underground," Kai said.

"Or still in the wilderness of whatever continent this is," Juli replied. "I don't have international service."

"We should go out on the ledge and try it."

"Perfect. That's step one," Juli said. "What's after that?"

Kai chuckled a little as she looked at her friend. Juli feared no one. Tough as nails.

And she *hated* rock climbing.

Kai explained about the hundred foot cliff outside the black cavern and how she'd gathered supplies. About the rope, and how a few years ago she'd learned to create a rappelling harness out of rope and a couple of carabiners.

"Absolutely not," Juli said, her face pale.

"It's either that or let them take me somewhere," Kai said.

Juli's jaw set. "Fine. But you'd better make sure you know

what you're doing, because if I die falling off one of your stupid cliffs, I will murder you."

"Here." Juli pulled a map out of her bag, which Ffion had tucked in with Juli for the flight. The map was covered in violent little red X's—the map Juli had marked as she searched for Kai. Seeing it, Kai had another moment of love for her friend.

After examining it, they decided they were beyond anything it showed.

They sat at the table, and Kai drew Juli a map of the palace complex and everything she'd seen.

"Where are the supplies? And the food?"

Kai pointed.

"How many other people are here, and who sleeps where?"

Kai began labeling the map. When she was finished, Juli tapped her finger on the unlabeled room. "What about this one?"

"Oh." Kai's heart twisted. "That was Cadoc's room. He's gone. But maybe he'll come back."

"Cadoc?" Juli narrowed her eyes.

"He was my friend."

"These people kidnapped us," Juli's voice was razor sharp. "They are not your friends."

He was. Kai shook her head. "It doesn't matter. We're leaving. Tonight, if we can."

"Yes we are. Show me where these ropes are again. Can we get enough for both of us?"

Kai tapped the map, and they talked until they had something resembling a working plan.

CHAPTER 26

RHYS

R hys walked into the cavern to hear voices echoing from the hall that led to the kitchen. Surprised, he saw Deryn lurking just inside, out of sight of the people within. The voices got louder as he approached. To his shock, it sounded like Ffion and Griffith. They never argued.

He ducked close to Deryn's ear. "What are you doing?"

"Quiet!" she hissed, making shushing motions. "These two haven't had a row like this in a century!"

Rhys frowned walked into the kitchen despite Deryn's protests. Griffith stood with his back to them, his arms crossed over his chest. Beyond him, Ffion paced, shouted, and waved her arms. "We swore! I swore. We're staying."

"Things have changed," Griffith rumbled.

"No, they have not!" Ffion shot back.

"I've worried enough, Ffion. I could barely focus on my duty before. Now—"

Ffion whipped around, her mouth open to say something. She saw Rhys, and her lips snapped together. Griffith cut off at the same time, turning to face Rhys. Deryn made an exasperated noise from the door.

"What's going on?" Rhys kept his voice casual.

"Nothing." Ffion glared. "A disagreement."

"About leaving." Deryn said. "Why would you leave?"

Griffith looked at Ffion. She shook her head.

Rhys considered them. "Deryn, will you give us a minute?"

"No." She leaned against the table, long legs stretched in front of her. Rhys locked eyes with his sister and waited.

"Fine!" Deryn glared as she headed out of the kitchen, pointing at him with a threatening finger. "But I'll find out sooner or later. I'm part of this vee too."

Rhys waited, listening to her footsteps. They paused just out of sight. "Keep going!"

He heard a sigh, and this time her footsteps retreated until they were no longer audible.

Griffith and Ffion stood side by side, their unified front not at all diminished by their difference in size.

"Both of you know," Rhys said uncomfortably, "that whatever is between you is personal, but if you're thinking of leaving, especially after Cadoc, Ashem should know."

"Ffion is—" Griffith began.

"Fine," she cut him off. "I'm fine." She grabbed a bowl of food from the counter and marched out of the kitchen.

Griffith's gaze followed her, his head turning to track her through the solid rock wall.

For three hundred years Rhys had wondered what it would be like to live half inside someone else's mind like that. This was the level of intimacy he was expected to reach with Kai? He couldn't imagine it.

"Ffion says if I tell you what's going on, she'll strangle me in my sleep," Griffith said, his voice flat. "Give me time. You'll know eventually."

"If she's sick..."

Griffith's dark green eyes were inscrutable. "She isn't." He took his own food and left.

"That was odd."

Rhys rolled his eyes skyward and sighed before turning to Deryn. She leaned in the doorway, pulling her hair into a ponytail.

Rhys ran a hand through his own hair. "Did you hear anything else while you were eavesdropping?"

Deryn shrugged. "No. Ffion's got a beetle in her head over something. You're the one who interrupted them before it got good."

Rhys shook his head. It was hard to keep problems personal in a vee. Griffith and Ffion deserved whatever privacy they could find. He put his hands on either side of Deryn's head and rubbed hard, mussing her attempts at pulling it back. "Stop sticking your nose in things that aren't your business, Aderyn, or someday you'll regret it."

Deryn made a face. "Don't call me that. That's what *she* called me."

Rhys sighed and sank down on in a chair next to the table. "*She* called Seren and me by our full names, and we still use them. Besides, weren't you trying to stand up for her a few days ago?"

Deryn gave him a look so much like the lost little girl she'd once been, it broke his heart. "My feelings toward the woman are complicated."

Rhys pulled his sister in for a hug. "Mother is gone, little bird. Don't waste your energy on the dead."

Deryn sniffed and leaned against him for a moment before she pushed back, brow furrowed. "Speaking of the dead, I am about to strangle your heartsworn."

A protective instinct welled up inside Rhys, catching him

off guard, and he had to clamp down on it. His voice came out rough. "Why?"

"Because you're in pain, you giant idiot. Every moment she's not sworn to you, you suffer!"

"It's not her fault."

"It is! I should've let you bond her. In fact, I think you should do what Ashem said and get it over with. How about right now?"

Rhys glared up at his sister, who had more reason than anyone to know why that would be a terrible idea. "You did the right thing. Maybe Mother wouldn't have broken the heartswearing if Father had tried—" Agitated, Rhys ran a hand through his hair again, then smoothed it down. "If he'd been kinder."

Deryn snorted. "Mother never cared about Father. Trust me." She took a slender dagger out of her boot, leaned against the table again, and began to clean her fingernails. "What do you think Seren will say about your Wingless mate?"

Rhys gave his sister a flat look. "She's a romantic. She'll support anything if she thinks it makes me happy. I'm far more worried about the Council."

Deryn waved an airy hand. "Sunder the Council, or at least the councilmembers I don't like. Seren would be on my side, by the way. She'd tell you to kiss the girl now."

"Seren doesn't know the first thing about heartswearing," Rhys growled.

Deryn sighed and stabbed her dagger into the table. "You know, I used to be so smug that I have the ability to inherit the mantle and she doesn't, that I would heartswear someday and she wouldn't. Now I'd trade with her. Especially if I could figure out how she keeps pulling off her little excursions."

"Excursions." Rhys rubbed his temples, reminded of another thing on a never-ending list he needed to give his attention to. "We're at *war*. Owain is as rabid to get his hands on her as he is to kill us. If he caught her—"

"She's the Seeress, Rhys. Sacred. He'd use her for her visions, not kill her."

"She's our *sister*, not a holy relic."

"And sneaking off is the only freedom she gets." Deryn jerked the knife out of the table and stabbed it down again, chipping away at the ancient wood. "You can't have it both ways. Either she's the sacred Seeress or she's a woman who needs to stretch her damned wings every once in a while. She can look out for herself."

Rhys opened his mouth, but Deryn put up her hands, forestalling his argument. "I didn't come back here to talk about your brotherly overprotection issues." Her face softened. "Please, consider completing the bond with Kai. Today. Now."

"I won't force her." Ancients willing, Kai would come around on her own.

Though now that Ashem and Ffion had kidnapped her friend, there seemed to be less chance of that than ever. Rhys rubbed his chest and wondered how long it would be before he wore holes in all his shirts.

"And what if you have to?" Deryn asked, stabbing the table again.

Rhys snatched the dagger when she yanked it out again, flipped it between his fingers, and flung it at a cabinet across the room. It stuck, quivering. "I'll deal with that moment if it comes."

Deryn sighed and walked over to retrieve the knife. "You're a noble idiot."

"I don't want to be sworn to a woman who hates me. That isn't noble, it's normal. I might be the damned dragon king, but I'm still a person, Deryn."

"A man with needs? Is that where this is going?"

Rhys glowered. "Not when I'm talking to my baby sister."

She quirked an eyebrow at him. "Speaking of your manly needs, what are you going to do about Morwenna? She is going to be livid." Deryn's intonation rose and she dragged out the last word.

Rhys rubbed his face, because he knew Deryn was right and he didn't want her to be. "That ended years ago. It was... She only wanted comfort."

Deryn let out a low whistle. "Shit, *fy mrawd*. You are dense."

Rhys dropped his hands and glared at her. "Iain was dead. We were both falling apart. It was a mistake."

"You should've let Ashem dismiss her from the vee. She's not stable. When she finds out you're heartsworn..." Deryn made an exploding gesture with her hands. "She *hates* humans. She's going to destroy Kai on sight."

Rhys clamped down his protective instincts again, but not before the fires in the wall reacted to his magic and flared.

"Do you have any suggestions?" he asked through gritted teeth.

Deryn thumped Rhys on the shoulder. "Nope. Good luck."

Ashem came into the kitchen, nodding a greeting at them both. Glass clinked as he extracted a bottle of black liquid and a dropper from a pocket. "It's finished."

Rhys stood. "The sleeping draught?"

"Yes. I didn't think I'd have to make this damned poison ever again, but here we are. Because of a human." He drew an infinitesimal amount of liquid into the glass tube, then closed the bottle and put it back in his pocket.

Rhys and Deryn exchanged looks. "You've made it before?"

Ashem grimaced. "For your father. When his heartswearing was broken. It has Naga venom, and a microscopic amount of mine as well. I'll give you the dropper to take to your room. Lay down before you take it. This will knock you out so fast you won't make it to your bed."

Rhys frowned. "You aren't giving me the bottle?"

"Too much is deadly." Ashem avoided his gaze.

It took Rhys a moment to discern his meaning. "I'm not going to kill myself, Ashem. I don't have that luxury."

"Then listen to your own logic if you won't listen to me," Ashem said, as close to pleading as Rhys had ever heard. "If a normal person wanted to ignore their heartswearing to a human, it would be senseless, but they could. You, Rhys, son of Ayen, son of Thân, ruler of Clan Draig and all clans who swore to the ancient treaties, man upon whom the fate of the world depends, *do not have that luxury.*"

"Exactly!" Deryn threw her hands in the air.

Rhys rose, meeting Ashem's gaze. He waited until silence fell in the kitchen. Until the ragged half of the mantle of power he carried in his blood—depleted though it was—made the air thick and roiling with latent magic. Finally he spoke through a clenched jaw. "Then I will wait."

Ashem didn't cower. He pressed, his own power luminescing in his golden eyes. "How long?"

It was the question Rhys had asked himself a thousand times. How long would he suffer? How long before madness? How far, exactly, could he stretch his control? All for a human woman who had no place in his world at all.

"Until we fly for Eryri."

"She still won't be willing," Ashem replied. "If it were me—"

Rhys took the glass dropper from Ashem's hand. "Lucky for Kai, I'm not you. *Diolch* for the draught. I'll take it now."

Ashem gave him a mirthless smile. "*Croeso,* my king. Both of you should get some sleep."

Rhys said goodnight to Deryn and Ashem and made his way to his room, where he sat heavily on his bed.

She still won't be willing.

He grimaced. Unless there was some kind of miracle, Ashem was right.

Rhys pictured Kai's face. The terror that filled her eyes when she thought he might kiss her on the ledge. The thought of holding her in place, pressing his lips to hers while she fought him, or while tears ran down her cheeks, or while she just stood there, hopeless, and accepted it, made him ill.

Rhys snarled and pounded his mattress with his fist. No matter what he did, he lost. He needed to get out of this cave. He needed to fly. Frustration, pain, and yearning, unfulfilled desire churned inside him, building into an inferno that made his hands prickle with unreleased heat.

Desperate for oblivion, he held up Ashem's dropper of sleeping draught and squeezed it onto his tongue. A bitter taste filled his mouth, and his limbs grew heavy immediately. His body slumped. The room narrowed to a point of light, then went dark.

Even in sleep, the drug didn't take away his pain, but it did put him too far out of his skull to care.

CHAPTER 27

ASHEM

A shem paced the ledge that night, taking the watch that should have been Cadoc's, and tried to rein in barely-suppressed fury. He smashed one booted foot into a stone protruding from the uneven ground and stumbled. With a shout of rage, he pulled up the head-sized rock and hurled it over the edge. It shattered against the ground below, and pieces skittered and scattered out of sight.

It didn't stop Rhys being an idiot. It didn't bring Cadoc back.

Cadoc's last words echoed in his brain. *Keep them safe.* Ashem broadened his mind, pushing his mental powers as far as they could go. *Cadoc, you twiddling fool! Blood of the Ancients, where are you?*

There was no answer. Myriad curses in dozens of ancient tongues strung together in a never-ending litany in his mind. Useless. Everything he did, useless. He couldn't bring Cadoc home. He couldn't deliver Rhys and Deryn to Eryri.

Keep them safe. Rhys's father, Ayen, had said the same.

Ashem was supposed to keep them *all* safe. Iain. Cadoc. Rhys. Who would be next?

He pressed his hands to his head. He needed Evan and Morwenna to get back. He needed Rhys and Deryn to be safe. And thanks to Ffion's soft-heartedness, he needed to come up with a plan to get the infernal Juliet King home. He couldn't forget that. He couldn't forget any of it.

Ashem let out a frustrated snarl and turned to go inside. They hadn't seen scale nor wing of Owain or Kavar or any of them in days, and it was too Stars-damned cold to stand out here on watch. He might have grown up in damp, misty Gwynedd as a ward of Ayen's court, but the need for sunbaked dry heat ran deep in his blood.

The fires in the cavern had dimmed. He would have asked Cadoc to check on the spell, which had been wound through the carvings with fire magic. Now he'd have to ask Rhys to do it, and it would take a large amount of magic. Tinkering with Ancient spell workings always did. It galled Ashem to no end that heartswearing, which should have strengthened Rhys, had weakened him instead.

Rage scorched his insides. For a millennium he'd held this vee together. Guarded Ayen's children. He could not fail now.

He settled into his watch, pacing the length of the wide archway. But the *shush-shush* of bare feet against stone caught his ears. Everyone else was asleep, or so he'd thought. But that sound had come from the kitchen. He reached out with his mind and found the icy shell of a natural and unconsciously made mental shield. One he'd encountered and cracked once already.

The infernal Juliet King.

Ashem strode into the kitchen to find her bent double with her head in the bins that held rice and dried lentils and other

236

such things. At the sight of her sweetly curved ass, Ashem felt something he hadn't in several hundred years.

Attraction.

Fuck. No.

She straightened and pushed pale gold hair behind her ears. Stubborn and icy as the caverns of Cadarnle, she didn't have Ffion's hourglass shape, but neither was her body as boyish as Kai's. Instead, she fell magnificently into the perfectly-proportioned middle. Ashem silently cursed again. "Juliet King. What are you doing in my kitchen?"

She spun, holding a blunt eating knife in front of her. "You! Stay away from me!"

He raised an eyebrow. "Ah. You've gotten hold of a deadly weapon. We should guard you more closely."

"Maybe you should, Mr. 'We don't have time for this.' At least the woman was sorry. You didn't even care."

He put his hands in his pockets and rocked back on his heels, shrugging. For good measure, he smiled.

Her expression darkened and she turned her entire body toward him. "Well?"

"Well what?"

"Well, aren't you going to apologize?" she snapped.

He laughed. "For what? Telling you your friend is alive? Reuniting you? On the contrary, Ms. King—you are welcome."

Her face reddened. To one side, Ashem noticed a small sack of beans on the counter.

He frowned at it. They hadn't had beans in days, and the counter had been clean earlier. He wasn't sure how it had gotten there.

For a split second, he wondered if the infernal Juliet King had put it here. Maybe she and Kai were packing supplies, planning some kind of escape. For another split second, he thought about rummaging in Juliet's mind to find out. But he dismissed the thought out of hand. Though Kai had proven willing to fling herself headlong into danger multiple times, even she wouldn't be foolhardy enough to try to climb down a sheer cliff and wander through the mountains this close to winter. Humans didn't like heights.

Juliet King followed his eyes to the bag of beans. She darted for it, but he was faster. He picked it up, balanced it in his hand, then dropped it in the bin. The movement brought his body inches from hers. She smelled like chamomile, soothing and surprisingly alluring for such a gentle herb. He couldn't stop himself from inhaling again.

"Are you *smelling* me?" She bared her teeth, but didn't move to increase the space between them. Her eyes were the most incredible blue. Despite the fact that her hair was a pale blonde, her brows were dark, and she had dark lashes.

Ashem was no stranger to chemicals that changed the color of one's hair—dragons used them too, from time to time—but both her dark lashes and her blonde hair looked natural. Fascinating.

Those big, blue eyes bored into him. "I asked you a question. Are you smelling me?"

"Perhaps." His voice was a deep, rough rumble, but he barely noticed, too caught up in studying the exact shape of her face. Wondering, did she taste as sweet as she smelled? How deep beneath her icy exterior would he have to delve before he encountered heat? The desire to find out grabbed him by the throat. He distanced himself from the emotion and examined it, then concluded it was logical. Juliet King was beautiful, bold, angry, and a novelty. Who wouldn't be captivated?

"Pervert," she snapped. "Get out of my way."

Ashem stepped back, and she stalked away. He couldn't help but watch; she slinked like a cat when she was angry, perfect ass swaying back and forth. That perfect ass would fit perfectly in his hands.

Voice soft but still reaching her, he said, "If I hadn't let Ffion bring you here, you'd still think your friend was dead."

She paused for an instant, then put her chin in the air and marched out of sight, hips swaying hypnotically.

Ancients, it had been a long time since he fucked anything but his own hand. Years. Decades? Too long.

If he had more time, he would enjoy pursuing someone like her. Someone strong, demanding, challenging. Someone who wouldn't make it easy. Women like that were never dull in bed. Either they wanted to relinquish control completely, or they wanted to dominate him as entirely as they dominated every other aspect of their life. Both of those options were amenable to him.

Ashem waited until he was certain she'd returned to Kai's room, then walked into the cavern and stood at the center of the archway, looking out into the night. Thoughts of Cadoc and Rhys closed over him again, but thoughts of responsibility, duty, and strategy kept getting interrupted by the image of the blonde woman tangled in his sheets. On her knees before him. Or pushing him down on his knees before her.

Ashem groaned. To combat the arousal which was entirely unwelcome to him and which he was certain would be abhorrent to Juliet King, he started making mental lists of the things he had to do, determined to fill his mind with anything but her.

He had more important things to worry about than scratching an itch.

CHAPTER 28

KAI

Juli stomped into the bedroom, her hair practically standing on end. She slammed the door and kicked it, then grabbed her foot and swore.

Kai furrowed her brows, bemused. "What's wrong? Where's the food?"

"That *man!*" Juli growled.

Kai bit back laughter at the look on Juli's face. There was only one dragon who could make her snarl like that. "You ran into Ashem?"

"I don't care what his name is!" Juli started pacing the room, hands balled into fists.

"Okay..." Kai drawled. "Is he why there's no food?"

Juli stopped pacing to glare, and Kai raised her hands in a placating gesture.

"I politely suggested he apologize for kidnapping me, and he *laughed!*"

"You told Ashem to apologize?"

"Yes!"

Kai swallowed a garbled laugh and forced herself to keep her face serious. "The nerve."

Juli resumed pacing. "He thinks he can be an ass just because he's the most perfect specimen of the male species ever to grace the planet. God damn those golden eyes. And those lips. And that voice. I want to punch him. I want to punch him right in his stupid perfect mouth and his beautiful nose." She jabbed her fists at the air like she was shadow boxing.

Her description of Ashem brought Kai up short. "I'm sorry, what?"

"Oh, come on Kai. You've got eyes!"

"Juli, my friend, you've gone somewhere I simply cannot follow."

Juli stopped jabbing the air and looked at Kai like she was insane. After a second, her face settled into a more neutral expression and she sniffed. "We'll wait another hour to make sure they're all asleep, and then we'll get what we need from the 'hoard.' Why on earth would you call it that, anyway?"

Kai sighed. "There's a lot of stuff. A hoard of it. You'll see."

Juli tapped her fingers against her lips. "So we'll get the gear and go. Goodbye horrible, gorgeous, stupid man."

Kai nodded, ignoring a twinge of guilt and something deeper. *Rhys.* What was it Ffion said would happen if he didn't complete the heartswearing? *He'll be...distracted.* Which heavily implied there was more to it than that. Whenever she saw Rhys, he was clearly uncomfortable.

Kai shifted. Surely it couldn't be that bad. He would have said something.

Even as she thought it, she had to push away the feeling that she was lying to herself.

Juli yawned. "I'm going to sleep for a little while. Are you?"

"No." Kai ran her fingers along the base of her throat. For the hundredth time that day, she replayed the moment Rhys had pulled her back from the edge of the cliff. The way his whole, hard body had pressed against hers. The way she was gripped with the violent urge to slide her hands up under his shirt and touch his skin, and the fine, glittering scales of his indicium, and then maybe slide her hands into other places to see exactly how far down the scaled design went.

There went her raccoon mind, freediving into the dumpster again. The problem was, it didn't stay there. Because when she undressed an imaginary Rhys in her head, she couldn't help but picture his face. He'd been afraid for her in that moment.

Kai had seen Rhys be tender with Deryn. When that tenderness was focused on her, mixed with all that aching desire, Kai hadn't been sure she wanted to resist Rhys.

Touching Cadoc had been comfort. Touching Rhys felt like salvation.

Juli jerked Kai from her morose, horny thoughts by flopping onto the bed. "Wake me up in an hour. That distraction for whoever is on watch will take a while to set up, and I want to be out of here before sunrise." In seconds, Juli was asleep.

"Okay." *Salvation.* The thought was so melodramatic, but Kai couldn't think of how else to put it. She didn't even know Rhys. And it wasn't like he wanted her because of who she was. It wasn't like he had feelings for her or would miss her when she left. It was just the heartswearing. The dragon mating magic.

Of course he would be fine. Of course she had to leave.

She watched Juli sleep for a while, waiting for the time to pass. When it was about fifteen minutes before she was supposed to wake her friend up, Kai decided to go to the lavatory one more time.

The dragon lavatory was a bit like a public restroom with a shared space for sinks, but with several closed-off rooms containing toilets and a huge sunken pool for bathing. She was washing her hands when she heard someone come in behind her.

Kai froze, her hands still beneath the water that flowed from the open beak of a heron carved into the wall. She didn't want to see Rhys. Especially not in here. Slowly, she raised her gaze to the mirror.

Ffion's drawn face reflected back at her.

"Oh! Hello, Kai." Ffion had one hand on her stomach, the other on her mouth.

"Hey." Kai dropped her eyes to her dripping hands. She wasn't sure how to react to Ffion. She'd brought Juli here, and the emotions involved in that were complicated. "Sorry. I was just leaving." She found a towel, dried her hands, and turned to leave.

"Okay. Goodnight!" Ffion gasped. She sprinted for one of the toilets, not bothering to close the door. A retching sound filled the bathroom.

Kai's complex emotions resolved into concern for the other woman, and she took a few steps toward her. "Ffion? Are you okay?"

Only vomit noises answered. Kai swallowed, trying not to throw up herself. This was why she could never go into health-care. Still, she should make sure Ffion was all right.

Ffion reappeared. She moved gingerly to the sink and rinsed out her mouth; her richly brown skin had an unhealthy gray cast. She looked like she was about to pass out.

Kai moved forward. "Can I get you anything? Do you need Griffith or Ashem?"

Ffion waved her off. "It's just something I ate. I'm fine. I can manage. I need to get back on my watch."

Kai put a finger through a carabiner. She was sure Ffion was lying, but not certain about what. She hesitated, realizing this might be the last time she ever saw the other woman. And then it dawned on her what Ffion had said.

"Ffion, thank you for bringing Juli. Really. I was angry, but I think this will be for the best."

Ffion nodded, obviously too preoccupied to hear the goodbye in Kai's tone. "I'm glad it made you happy. I really do want happiness for you."

"I believe that. I think that you do."

Ffion nodded. Then she pressed a hand against her mouth and looked like she might be sick again.

"Ffion, you can't watch like this. You should be in bed."

The other woman inhaled slowly through her nose. "I can't. Cadoc is gone and Rhys is"—she seemed to catch herself—"still recovering from his injuries. It's only me, Ashem, and Griffith."

"There's me," Kai said.

Ffion's fine brows drew together. "You can't see dragons who are veiling."

"I know what the waver in the air looks like when they're doing it. Besides, it's not like they bothered veiling last time they flew over."

"That's true."

"And we haven't seen them in days," Kai pressed. "Come on, Ffion. Let me do this for you. You obviously need sleep."

Ffion considered. Then, heaving again, she ran for the toilet. When she was finished, she cleaned up and gave Kai a searching glance. "You really don't mind?"

"Not at all."

A relieved smile broke out on Ffion's face. Guilt twisted in Kai's guts, but this was a chance she couldn't pass up. Ffion would understand, and so would Rhys.

"Well, all right. I really could use some rest. Goodnight, Kai."

"Goodbye," Kai murmured. She waited until Ffion had

time to get back to her room before returning to her own. When she got there, she checked the watch on Juli's wrist. Still ten minutes to go. Restless, she paced the room. But there was nothing to do. She could watch for the ten minutes like she'd told Ffion she would, but there didn't seem to be much point.

Finally, Kai sat at the table where she and Juli had made their plans. There was paper and something like a pen. The dragon version of it, anyway. Jeweled and sparkling, like everything they created. Kai picked it up and slid a piece of paper over.

Dear Rhys, you really can't have expected—

No.

Dear Rhys, since we're strangers, it may come as a relief that—

No.

Dear Rhys, I'm sorry.

She propped her forehead on her fist, staring at the blank piece of paper, thinking again of that moment on the ledge. There had been no fear in him, only confidence. He was absolutely certain he could catch her, and he had.

If only Rhys was a normal guy who had walked into the Quarry—the climbing gym where she worked—and asked for her number. Her mouth curved. That would be a change from the scruffy full-time climbers who usually flirted with her. Not that they were bad guys, but it would be nice to go out with someone who didn't live out of his Subaru. Still smiling, Kai closed her eyes.

She didn't know him, but she wanted to. She wanted to see if there was more to the electricity that crackled over her skin when he touched her.

For a few seconds, she let herself imagine what it would be like to let him pull her close again. Slowly, sensually. To let him run his hands up her waist, trail his knuckles over the sensitive skin of her neck, cup her face. An ache formed between her legs as she imagined the way he'd kiss her. Slow and heated and so thorough. Rhys was the kind of man who'd get off on getting his partner off, Kai had no doubt.

The scenario in her mind played out further. He took off her shirt and whispered that she was beautiful. She took off his and slid her hands up the ridges of his abdomen and chest, then pressed a kiss to each whorl and line of his indicium. And then her head would fall back, and his warm lips would press kisses down the vulnerable line of her neck and between her breasts, and one big hand would flick open the button of her jeans and slide all the way down...

Juli snored once and rolled over, and Kai jumped. She groaned and pinched the bridge of her nose.

Great. Now her panties were damp.

Yes, she liked Rhys. She wanted to screw the hell out of him.

That didn't mean she could leave her family and her life behind. Ffion had suggested giving Juli letters to deliver, but that wouldn't work. She could never tell them the truth, which meant she would have to lie and say she'd run off for some reason, just...abandoning them.

It would hurt them less to think she was dead.

Kai sighed. Ten minutes had to be up by now. She lobbed a crumpled piece of paper at Juli from across the room. People who shook Juli awake got slapped.

"What?" Juli flailed in the bed, sitting up and looking around wildly.

Kai grinned at her friend. "Time to go."

Time to put all her doubts in a dark corner of her mind. Time to go back and face a life she'd stopped living years ago, when she realized how big mistakes could be when other people gave you power. Funny that it had taken being kidnapped by dragons to realize she should probably get to living again. Unless she and Juli died of exposure, starvation and/or mauling by wild animals first, of course. Then she wouldn't have to learn life lessons or grow or face anything.

Tempting. Maybe there would be bears. She could run faster than Juli, but that didn't mean she had to.

"All right." Juli yawned, stretched, and threw off her blankets. "Let's do this."

"Yeah. Let's." Kai slung her blue backpack onto her shoulder and led the way down to the hoard to collect their supplies.

CHAPTER 29

KAI

"How can they have all those things?" Juli asked for the umpteenth time as she and Kai stood in the black cavern just inside the archway. "Those things belong in museums."

"Yeah, I know, Jules. Now remember, this is going to be uncomfortable." Kai sawed through a piece of rope with her pocketknife, cutting it into two equal lengths. She let one drop and tied the ends of the other together, yanking hard.

Juli frowned. "Not as uncomfortable as being kept prisoner in a cave for the rest of your life. Seriously, Kai, are they some kind of bizarre cult?"

"Something like that." Deftly, Kai pulled the sides of the loop together around Juli's hips, then yanked up the part that hung behind her legs so the whole thing looked like a woefully inadequate diaper. Kai took one of her carabiners and threaded it through each of the three points she'd made with the rope.

"This is going to hold, right?" Kai heard the nerves in Juli's voice. They'd gone rappelling before, but they'd had real harnesses and belay devices and anchoring equipment, and the cliff had been a quarter as high, and Juli had *still* hated it. So Kai didn't respond, her mouth twisting into something that probably wasn't a reassuring smile.

Real equipment would have made her less nervous too. She pictured the bottom of the cliff a hundred feet below. At least most of the snow had melted. And they wouldn't have to worry about being caught. Not if they were fast.

Kai secured her own makeshift harness with a second carabiner, twirling the metal between her fingers until it locked. She stepped out into the freezing air, pulling close the thick, old fur coat she'd found in the hoard. Her debt to Cadoc kept adding up. Without the things they'd found down there, they never would have been able to make the descent.

She picked up her backpack and threaded one end of the longest rope through the straps. She wouldn't tie it, but would hold one end in one hand and allow rope to slide through the other, feeding the pack slowly down. The dragon rope was longer, lighter and stronger than anything she'd used. She knew climbers who would kill for rope like this. "You're sure we've got everything?"

Juli nodded, and Kai shoved the pack over the edge, letting the rope slide through her gloved hand as planned. The bag disappeared into the darkness, bouncing a little as it hit protruding parts of the cliff. A few minutes later, the rope stopped sliding. Kai let the loose end fall down the cliff, then hauled the whole length up. She repeated the process with Juli's pack. It stuck for a minute, but with some maneuvering Kai managed to shake it loose. Finally, both packs were on the ground. The first parts of the plan were going off without a hitch.

"Come check this," Juli called in a carrying whisper.

Kai hauled the rope up again and walked over to the anchoring ropes. Juli had tied them about ten feet apart, each around the base of its own boulder on the ledge. Kai knelt, examining Juli's knots. They were perfect, of course. When Juli did something, she did it flawlessly.

They walked back over to the ledge. The moon was nearly gone now, leaving the night so dark it was impossible to see. Juli stood a foot back from the edge, leaning over to gaze down into the icy darkness. At least it wasn't windy.

"Are we really doing this?" Juli asked.

"We don't have to. *You* don't have to," Kai said. "I won't make you. But I'm going, Jules. There's no other way I'm going to get to leave."

Juli nodded, barely visible in the dim light from inside the cavern. "If you go, so do I. Let's do this."

Kai picked up Juli's rope and tied a knot around the carabiner hooked to her harness, going over and over it in her mind to make sure she'd gotten it right. If she messed up and Juli fell, Kai would never forgive herself.

She tied another knot and pointed at Juli's carabiner. "Lock it."

Juli dutifully turned the metal until it was screwed in tight.

"Remember, this angle will brake." Kai demonstrated, pulling the rope close to her hip. Then lifted the rope. "This will let you slide. It's going to kill your arm by the time we get to the bottom. *Do not let go.*"

Kai had expected a flippant show of bravery, but Juli only nodded, her lips pressed together. Kai didn't blame her. They'd both been climbing and rappelling, but it was Kai's thing. Juli only did it because they were friends. The same reason Kai helped keep their apartment so ridiculously clean and went swimming so much in the summer.

The thought brought a worried smile to her lips. What kind of state would the apartment be in when they got back? Probably dusty as hell. Juli would make her clean for days.

At the same time, she saw Rhys's face—jaw set, perfect body rigid, eyes intense in the dim light of the fire—asking her to become his heartsworn. She'd never see him again. Probably never see dragons, or magic.

The thought filled her with a dull, bitter ache.

Though she thought she'd made her decision, Kai wavered, torn for an eternal instant between home and the cave. Real life, or dragons.

No. Rhys would get over it. Even if he didn't, a hundred years wasn't that long for a dragon. Even if heartswearing was unbreakable, when she died, he'd be free.

She pulled off her gloves and retrieved the lantern from the floor, tying it securely to one of her belt loops. She gave one last tug, testing the anchor. It was solid.

Kai met Juli's gaze. For all her fear, Juli was unwavering. They nodded at each other. At the same time, they stepped backward over the edge.

The hardest thing about rappelling was getting around the ninety degree angle made by the edge of the cliff. Kai managed it smoothly, then ignored the way the rope dug into her thighs and butt while she waited for Juli to get situated.

"You were right," Juli said through clenched teeth. "This is uncomfortable."

"Are you okay?"

Juli gave a tight nod, and Kai shifted the rope, allowing it to slide a little through her glove as she pushed off the cliff face. Juli's descent was jerky, going from too-fast drops to abrupt halts, but she didn't fall.

The dark air swirled with the cold scent of unfallen snow. The stone beneath her feet was uneven and unyielding. Kai fell into a trancelike state: release, jump, brake, release, jump, brake. She didn't think about badly tied knots, unsteady anchors, or what would happen if her numb hands slipped. Foot after foot, they descended through the sky.

Sooner than she'd expected, Kai hit the ground. Only then did she feel the ache of the places the rope had bitten into her flesh and hear the harshness of her own breath. For a long moment, Kai stood, looking up at how far they'd come. A slow grin broke over her face as Juli landed, safe and sound, beside her.

Juli collapsed against the cliff face, her heavy breathing uneven, then sat hard on the ground.

"Jules, we did it." Kai started to laugh. She danced around at the bottom of the cliff.

She could fly. She was invincible. She could do anything.

If they could get down the cliff, getting home wouldn't be a problem at all.

"Ugh. Stop." Juli looked like she was about to throw up. "Save your insanity for when we find people. We need to put as much distance between us and them as we can before they wake up." Juli picked up one of the packs and slung it over her back.

Still grinning, Kai let her harness fall from her hips. She picked it up, along with Juli's, and stuffed them into her pack with the long rope. They both pulled on their gloves and blew into their hands.

Juli frowned at the swath of visible sky. They'd landed in a clear spot at the base of the cliff, but now they'd be heading into a forest of dark pine and spindly aspen. "From what we could see from the ledge, the river is west, straight ahead. We follow it south. Do your best not to leave a trail."

Kai opened her mouth to say a trail wouldn't matter and then closed it again, a little sad. Outside the cave, the real world settled around her. To speak of dragons seemed suddenly ridiculous. She untied the lantern and handed it to Juli, then looked up at the top of the cliff, twisting the carabiners once again clipped to her belt.

This is it for Rhys. He'll never be able to be with anyone but you.

Kai pushed Ffion's voice all the way down into the depths of her mind. They were dragons. They had magic. They had to be able to figure it out.

THEY WALKED FOR HOURS, the only sound the crunch of their shoes over dead pine needles and thin soil. Kai's legs burned from the steep downhill angle, and her right arm was stiff and achy from controlling the rope during the rappel. At least she didn't need to worry about falling asleep on her feet; the freezing air wouldn't let her.

Kai was about to ask Juli if they'd gotten off course when the sound of running water reached her ears. They stepped out of the trees and onto the bank of a river, its dark water gleaming in the light of the lantern.

Juli let her pack drop and stretched her arms, grimacing. "If we keep following the river it will take us to a city eventually."

"Eventually, as in, 'it could just go to the ocean or fade away into a bunch of streams or go underground into an aquifer,'" Kai said, staying beneath the overhanging branches of the trees. The forest around them was turning from black to gray as the first signs of dawn filtered between the mountains.

Juli snorted. "Then we'll walk down the coast until we find someone."

"If we don't get caught."

Juli's confidence was unshakable. "We won't. We have several hours' head start and both know how to move around the forest without leaving a trail. Do they have dogs I don't know about?"

Kai shook her head. "No, but—"

"Get your head in the game, Kai. You were practically raised in the mountains when you weren't flipping around on a balance beam. Clearly, we have the advantage." Juli's face, always intense, went stormy. "I won't *let* them take you again."

Kai sighed. "Then we'd better keep going."

They followed the rushing water, staying as close to the edge as they could in the uneven mountain terrain. Thankfully, there was a bank on their side instead of some kind of sheer ravine.

By the time the sun was fully up, Kai was stumbling.

Juli came to a halt next to a jumble of boulders. One had come to rest on top in a way that formed a hollow just large enough for two people. "Let's stop. We need to rest."

Kai was so tired her vision blurred, but she shook her head. They couldn't have gone more than five miles. A dragon could fly that in a minute. "It's not far enough."

"I say rest." Juli took off her pack and threw it into the little cave between the stones.

"Seriously, Juli."

"Seriously shut up and get in."

Too tired to argue further, Kai did as she was told. They squeezed inside and Juli pulled blankets out of her pack and the space blanket from Kai's blue backpack, which she'd forced Kai to pack "in case of emergency" on the fateful day of their last hike. That day seemed like a lifetime ago now.

"Just an hour," Kai said. "We won't be safe until we're out of the mountains."

At least, she hoped they'd be safe then. She had a vision of Rhys striding up to their apartment and pounding on the door. A smile flitted across her face.

255

Exhausted and cold, she drifted to sleep.

CHAPTER 30
RHYS

Fire.

It started as an annoyance and grew until it was unbearable. Rhys's heart was a white-hot pit. Flesh burned. Bones melted. He was nothing but flames and darkness and pain.

With a yell, he wrenched himself out of bed. He hit the floor on hands and knees, then hauled himself up with fistfuls of sweat-soaked blankets. His breath harsh and uneven, he doubled over.

The door flew open.

"Rhys! What happened?" Deryn knelt in front of him and tried to make him look at her.

He couldn't bear to be touched. He jerked away, moaning through clenched teeth.

"Ashem!" Deryn screamed, her voice throbbing through his skull. "Ashem! Something is wrong with Rhys!"

"What's happened?" Ffion came in with Griffith behind her, his broad frame filling the door. She put a soothing hand on Rhys's back.

He shrugged her off. "Don't," he managed to grunt.

"It's Kai," Ffion said. "It's got to be. I'll find her."

Griffith shifted closer, but didn't try to touch him. "Hold on, boyo."

"What happened?" Ashem snapped. Rhys felt his mental touch, but Ashem withdrew as fast as if he'd stuck a finger stuck into flame. He swore long and loud. "Where is the girl? This ends now."

"She's gone!" Ffion was back, panting and pale. "They're both gone. Ropes are tied to the boulders outside on the ledge."

"How?" Ashem demanded. "Even Kai Monahan could not be so reckless! Did she think she could just tie a rope to a rock and slide down?"

A sudden chill gripped Rhys. If Kai had tried to climb over the cliff—if she had died—

He shoved Griffith out of the way and staggered out of his room, down the hall, through the black cavern, and out onto the ledge. His heart in his throat, Rhys leaned over the edge.

Nothing. No small, broken body, no blood, no sign of Kai at all except the trailing ropes. Rhys dropped to his knees, the relief almost as keen as the pain. She was alive. Or at least, she hadn't died going over the cliff.

"How?" Ashem repeated, examining the ropes.

"She climbs rocks for fun," Rhys gasped. "Maybe you'd know that if you had ever bothered to speak with her instead of barking about how inconvenient she is."

"It's my fault." Ffion stood nearby, a stricken look on her face. "I... I was sick last night. Kai offered to watch for me. I let her. I didn't know—I trusted her."

"I don't blame you, Ffion." Rhys's body was incandescent with pain. He sank to his knees, his breath misting in the air as he let out a humorless laugh. "And I don't blame her."

Gone. Escaped. She had gone over a cliff to get away from him.

It might kill him, but Rhys couldn't help admiring the guts it took to run from dragons by rappelling hundreds of feet in the dead of night with nothing but ropes and a few carabiners. He would bet she'd taken supplies, too. Planned the whole thing, seen Ffion sick, and seized her chance. Bold, meticulous, and clever.

She would've made a good queen.

"I do blame her," Ashem snarled. "Sundering humans! Ffion, you and I will talk about this later."

Even bent double with pain, Rhys let out a weak laugh. "In two thousand years I've never seen anyone get the better of you, Commander. Now two human girls have done it twice in less than a day. I think it's safe to say we underestimated them."

The pain doubled, and Rhys gasped.

"Change," Ashem commanded. "You chased Cadoc almost ten miles before you collapsed. The dragon can deal better with the pain, and they can't have gotten that far on foot."

Rhys dragged himself to his feet and lurched back into the cave. He opened his mind. Power washed over him. Fire sprang up around him, his self widened, and the agony shrank—still beyond anything he'd endured before, but it was no longer all-consuming.

"Better?" Ashem, small in his human body, stood in front of Rhys.

Not much.

Ashem nodded. "At least you're coherent." He looked at the other three. "We're going after her. Rhys will be able to find Kai. You two stay with Deryn."

Should he go after her? She wanted so badly to leave. If it were him, and he was the one facing giving up his life, his family, his home, he would have done the same thing.

Ashem knew him too well. He shifted, and when he saw Rhys hadn't taken off, he growled into his mind, *If you don't find her, Kavar will.*

What do you mean? Rhys demanded.

Take off, figure out which direction she ran in, and I'll tell you.

Shit. *Shit.* Ashem didn't make idle threats or tell lies. He wouldn't invoke Kavar unless Kavar was a threat.

Rhys leaped from the cliff without another thought, his right wing barely twinging as he spread it wide to catch the air. He pushed himself upward, circled once. When the pain lessened, he broke the circle, angling southwest.

Do you sense her? Ashem glided a few lengths below him.

Rhys growled in acknowledgment and angled his wings in the right direction. *Southwest. I don't know how far. Now tell me what you meant about Kavar.*

For a long moment, Ashem was silent. *Then he said, I lied the night Cadoc disappeared. He contacted me.* Something about Ashem's mental voice was off. Nervous. Unsettled.

Shock rippled through Rhys, warring with the pain. *Where is he? Why didn't you tell me?*

Ashem took a moment to answer. *Owain is still in the mountains. We have to be careful.*

I know he might still be here.

There's no might or maybe. He's here. Cadoc told me.

The thought of Owain and Kai wandering around the same mountains sent a jolt of terror through his heart, but there was still that strange tone to Ashem's mental voice. *If you spoke to him, why hasn't he returned? Did you send him back to Eryri too?*

A long moment of hesitation, then, *He's been captured.*

Rhys felt as if his insides plummeted to the rocks a thousand feet below. Cadoc captured. Kai with no idea, no weapon and no one to protect her. Ashem might as well have torn him in two. Rhys snapped his jaws. *I should char your hide! I told you we needed to go after Cadoc! He might already be dead!*

Cadoc is a soldier. I did what I had to. Despite his words, Ashem's voice was ragged.

Blood of the bloody Ancients, Ashem. If Cadoc was still alive, Owain was torturing him. They had to rescue him. But if they didn't go after Kai *now*, she might be captured too. Or killed in a thousand other ways. It ached that she didn't want to be with him. He wished he could let her go. But he couldn't stand by when she was in this much danger.

Rhys shifted his flight southward, following the river below. The pain was less in that direction, though nothing could ease his deep sense of foreboding for his friend.

CHAPTER 31
CADOC

C adoc wasn't sure how long it went on. As promised, Izel returned every hour. At least, he thought it was Izel. She never wore her own face. One time it had been someone else, an air Draig, which meant electricity instead of knives.

His body became nothing but layer upon layer of agony, his vision blurring, his mind numb. Blood dripped steadily from the tip of his nose, plopping too loudly into a red pool at his feet. Once, hazily, he thought someone was with him, holding a bowl beneath him, collecting the blood as it fell. Quetzals had blood magic. It made them great healers. It also allowed them to bestow powerful curses.

He doubted healing was what Izel wanted it for.

The ladder rattled as someone descended. His torturer wore his father's face again.

"Morning, boyo." Brychan grinned.

Cadoc said nothing. His father's grin widened. "Or maybe it's afternoon. Or the middle of the night. Would you like to know how long you've been here?"

Cadoc didn't respond. The knife came out, and his father

carved a burning slash across his chest. "You've got to speak when you're spoken to, son. Don't be rude."

There was a shuffle from the small hole above. A pinched, gray man scrambled down the unsteady ladder and whispered excitedly in Brychan's ear. Brychan laughed, then straightened and gave Cadoc a sickening smile. His eyes went up, following Cadoc's cable-bound wrists to the hook that held them aloft. The hook dangled from a chain that could be raised or lowered by a winch in one corner, controlled by a lever. Almost gleeful, he pulled the lever all the way back, releasing the chain.

Cadoc collapsed, doing his best to cover his head as the heavy links rattled and fell, battering his shoulders and back. When he looked up through swollen eyes, Brychan was gone; Izel stood in his place. Uwan was in the corner, hunched and silent.

Izel bared her teeth at Cadoc. "It's been a pleasure, but we have a new guest, and I'm eager to visit him."

With that, she unhooked the chain, leaving Cadoc's bindings and the delicate, magic-blocking iron chains wound between his fingers. She barked at Uwan, who scrambled ahead of her out of the pit, leaving Cadoc alone.

He waited for the next torture session, but no one came. Each second stretched into agonizing eternity.

He rolled and let out a short cry of pain. Moving at all was difficult; movement without severe pain was impossible. His shoulders were the worst. The first time he tried to move them, he screamed. Inch by agonizing inch, he brought his hands down to his sides. He should have been healing faster, but lack of food and water prevented it. Gingerly, he curled into a ball to keep warm. The fire inside him guttered, his magic wavering in and out of reach. He'd never known cold until now. It felt like emptiness.

The thought crossed his mind that Izel could have been

lying. She might have left because Ashem had tracked him here. Maybe his friends were outside, trying to get to him. Hope kindled deep within him that the torment might be over. He tried to smother it. Hope was infinitely more painful than despair.

The rope ladder slapped the floor of the pit. Cadoc bit his swollen tongue to prevent a groan. They were back for him after all. He clenched his fingers, and the fine anti-magic chains on his hands clinked softly.

Someone descended. There was a harsh laugh, then the *thud* of a body hitting the ground. The person who'd dumped it disappeared as Cadoc looked up. The ladder was pulled out of sight, and he heard a soft moan that made his stomach drop and his blood freeze.

The light of the single wall-fire flickered over the new prisoner. He was covered in blood and bruises, but that didn't hide the red hair, or the indicium that swirled up his arm and over the entire right half of his torso.

"Ancients, *no!*" Cadoc scrambled over as best as he could on all fours. He put his fingers to Rhys's neck, almost weeping in relief when he felt a strong, steady pulse. Beaten and barely conscious, his friend didn't give off the usual wash of power.

Rhys moaned and rolled onto his back, one neon-blue eye flickering open. "Cadoc?" Blood trickled from the corner of his mouth. Bruises covered one side of his face, and his right eye was swollen shut. He brought one hand up to his eye. He wore the same magic-blocking manacles as Cadoc, and they clinked softly as he moved.

Cadoc sat back hard. "I'm sorry. Rhys, I'm sorry. If I hadn't —" Cadoc put his hands over his face, too horrified by the memory of what he'd done in kissing Kai to finish the thought. "Where are the others? What happened?"

Rhys looked at his hands, then blinked blood out of his eye and looked at Cadoc. "How badly are you hurt?"

"I'm alive," Cadoc said bitterly. "And I seem to have my wits, if I ever did."

Rhys coughed. "Owain said...you told them where to find us."

Cadoc felt as if the world had dropped out from under him. "I didn't." At least, he thought he hadn't. He wasn't sure what he might have said while he was screaming. "I didn't," he repeated, less sure. He tugged at the shredded remains of his pants, tearing off strips and pressing the fabric into an oozing slash below Rhys's ribcage that was deeper than the others.

Rhys hissed in a breath. When he spoke, it was with diffi-culty. "Ashem wouldn't say... Where did...they catch you?"

Cadoc sat back and rubbed his face. "Twenty miles from the cave."

"That close?" Rhys coughed, and blood seeped from beneath the fabric Cadoc had pressed to the wound beneath his ribs.

"Hold on." Shaking, Cadoc tore another strip from his pants and pressed it to the injury, putting Rhys's hand on top. Once he was sure Rhys could hold it, Cadoc sat back and yanked on the chains around his hands. If he could get them off, he could cauterize the wound, stop the bleeding. But fine as they were, he couldn't break them. He swallowed against the tears of terror and frustration. "Fuck," he whispered. He took a breath, then another. The gravity of what had happened came crashing down.

Rhys, captured.

"How did it happen? Where are the others? What happened to Deryn?"

Rhys's face went even paler beneath the blood. Tears leaked from the corners of his eyes, and he shook his head once.

Cold crept up Cadoc's stomach, into his throat, choking him. "Where are they?"

"Dead." Rhys's voice held a flat finality that hit Cadoc like a blow. "Owain... He ripped her apart in front of me. There's no hope, *fy mrawd*." Rhys blinked and swallowed, tears still dripping down the side of his face. "It's over." Rhys took a ragged breath. "Twenty miles. Hard to believe if you'd made it twenty miles farther south, you'd have been home, and none of this would have happened."

Something about what Rhys had said seemed off, but Cadoc was too preoccupied with guilt and pain to care. If Deryn was dead and Rhys was here, it was over. The war was lost. The world was lost. And... "What about Kai?"

For the first time, Rhys sounded confused. "Kai?"

A rush of heat burst through the cold that had almost turned him to stone. "Kai," Cadoc repeated, his heart quickening. He spoke more deliberately. "What happened to Kai?"

There it was again, the split second of confusion, of hesitation. Then, with no trace of significant suffering, he said, "Dead, like the others."

Cadoc went still for a long moment. Something here was wrong.

If you'd made it twenty miles farther south...

He hadn't been flying south.

This was not Rhys.

Unable to hide his relief, Cadoc let out a rasping laugh. "You aren't Rhys. Rhys is safe. The others aren't dead. This is another illusion."

In a blink, his bloody, battered best friend disappeared, and Owain sat up where Rhys had been. He stood, an oddly approving look on his face. "You've lasted longer than I thought you would." Then he laughed. "It looks like you aren't as good at telling your kings apart as you thought you were."

Cadoc glared, flexing his fingers. The chains around them tightened. He met Owain's laugh with a mocking smile. "'Kings'? Rhys is the only king."

Owain's jaw tensed. "My mother was queen. The mantle was hers. It will be mine. My usurping cousin is no king."

A sudden chill bit deep into Cadoc's fingers. He bent them, but they were too stiff. Surprised, he looked down at them. They grew colder, and ice spread down his fingers and into his palms, blossoming into intense, burning pain. They grew colder still, and his skin took on frightening icy whiteness.

"It's been a thousand years, but I haven't forgotten what a pest you were. Always hauling around some noisemaker or another, blowing on it, plucking at it, disrupting the quiet." Owain knelt in front of him. "Wasn't your father a musician? Do you miss him less now?

"Put your hands on the ground."

The words held the weight of the mantle. Bile rose in Cadoc's throat. He couldn't speak. Couldn't fight it. The mantle had never been able to control a dragon's mind. However, it could control his body.

Like a puppet, Cadoc felt his arms jerk out and down. His palms pressed to the floor, fingers splayed numbly over the stone. Sweat beaded on his brow. The softest involuntary whimper escaped his throat. *At least Rhys is alive. They're all alive, and I'll keep them that way.*

Cadoc bit his tongue and forced himself to look up, away from his hands and into Owain's frosty, pale eyes. Owain stood and placed one booted foot over the fingers of Cadoc's right hand. "Where is Ashem hiding Rhys and Aderyn? You've already gotten us close. Kavar has returned from the pointless trip to Cadarnle Rhys commanded him to make—it's only a matter of time before he senses Ashem. Help me, Cadoc.

Twenty miles from where you were captured. Twenty miles in which direction? Help me, and I'll free you."

Tears burned behind his eyes, but Cadoc didn't speak.

Owain frowned. "You know, if I only freeze the bones, I think your fingers might even stay on your hand. Let's find out."

Owain brought his boot down hard, then lifted it and stomped again, grinding his heel into Cadoc's flesh. Hideous cracks and pops echoed in the small room. Cadoc's hand was numb, so he didn't scream. It was too horrible for screams, or tears, or knowing. When Owain finally stopped, Cadoc's hand was barely recognizable as hand. He couldn't wrap his brain around it. Couldn't comprehend it.

Music was lost to him forever.

"I'll give you another day to think. You've given us enough that we'll find him eventually. Make it easier on me, and you won't lose your other hand."

Owain left. Alone, Cadoc crawled on his knees and uncrushed hand to a corner and threw up bitter bile. Rhys, best friend and king, was safe. But even if Cadoc lived, he wouldn't be alive.

There was no life without music.

CHAPTER 32

JULI

Beep-beep. Beep-beep. Beep-beep.

Juli groaned. Dead tired, she tried to silence the hideously consistent alarm on her watch. Her arm wouldn't move. With another groan, she shoved at Kai's limp but warm weight until her friend sighed and rolled off. Juli shuddered at the sudden cold, then turned off her alarm and nudged Kai. "Get up."

Kai made a snuffling sound, but didn't move.

"Now! I thought you were worried about your cult following us." Juli crawled from the shelter of the rocks and shivered. The wind had picked up in the hour they'd slept, bringing in a sheet of clouds. It looked like it was going to snow.

Grumbling, Kai hauled herself out of the space in the stones and rubbed her eyes. Anticipating what Kai would ask, Juli fished around in her pack. She tossed Kai a strip of what she assumed was venison jerky.

Juli shivered as she thought about the caverns, the halls, the hoard. She wasn't stupid. Obviously there were things at play there. Things besides the cavern and its location that she couldn't explain. The white fires that didn't produce smoke or heat, the way the cavern was warm until you passed through a definite barrier onto the ledge, and a dozen other tiny things.

But Juli didn't want to know what those things were or what they meant. She just wanted to take Kai, get home, and get back to all the things she had planned. Medical school was well underway. Next, a doctorate in neurology, and then becoming the youngest expert in the world on the physiopathology of addiction. It was all on track. They just had to get back to humanity.

They didn't talk much as they stowed their blankets and took turns going behind the boulders to relieve themselves, then shouldered their packs and moved on. Not far from the boulders, they came to a narrow place where the river dove into a wide ravine, with the mountains rising like walls on either side. At the bottom, the river ran fast and deep. Before them, a narrow lip of stone hugged the canyon wall.

Kai indicated the ledge. "We'll have to walk along that and hope it doesn't end. Otherwise we'll have to turn back, or find some way to scale sheer rock walls to the top of these cliffs."

Juli wanted to protest, or at least to complain, but it was clear there was no other way. Though she leaned out as far as she dared, she could see no end to the narrow, twisting canyon. "What if the path disappears?"

Kai eyeballed the ledge. "If that happens, I may be able to get up the side. We've got rope. I can try to haul you up."

"I'm one and a half times your weight."

"With the right setup, I might still be able to do it."

"Hm." Juli glanced back the way they'd come, but unless they climbed out, there wasn't any other way to go. "Fine. We follow this ledge. But I don't like it."

Light snow started to fall as they edged along the rock shelf.

Well, Juli edged. Kai walked normally, strolling down the three-foot-wide ledge as if it were a sidewalk.

It made Juli's stomach turn. "Will you at least put your hand on the wall or something? I've already dealt with your death once this month."

Kai didn't turn, but she laughed and slowed her pace. "Better?"

Juli frowned. Only Kai could be kidnapped and come through it laughing.

An odd, heavy feeling washed over Juli, a kind of tension in the air, like a storm about to break. Juli looked up, but saw nothing.

In front of her, Kai swore softly.

"Keep moving," Juli said. "I want to get off this ledge. Those clouds are about to bury us in snow."

"It's not snow." Kai tipped her head back, gaze darting across the iron-gray sky. Suddenly, she looked at Juli, her eyes wide with alarm. "It's Rhys. We've got to run. If we can find an overhang or something he might fly over us."

"Fly over us? Have you lost your mind?" Had Kai heard a helicopter? And why should she fear Rhys specifically? He'd seemed to want to help her.

It was no use. Kai had already taken off. She glanced back. When she saw that Juli hadn't moved, Kai slowed. "Come on! We have to find somewhere to hide!"

Heart in her throat, Juli moved faster, hugging the canyon wall. Kai was looking back at her, but hadn't stopped walking forward. "Kai, watch where you're going!"

She didn't listen. "Hurry *up*!"

Time seemed to slow as Kai's heel caught on an uneven part of the stone. She stumbled. Her arms windmilled, reaching, grasping at the air. Before Juli could take a breath to scream, Kai fell.

With a splash, the dark water parted, then closed a mouth of white foam over her head.

She was gone.

"Kai!"

Wind tore through the canyon, and Juli's thrashing hair stung her face. She dropped her pack. A mountain climber Kai might be, but she was no swimmer. Juli, on the other hand, had been a certified lifeguard since she was fourteen. With ease born of long practice, she leaped from the ledge. Feet-first, knees slightly bent, arms crossed tightly over her chest, braced for the lung-spasming shock of cold.

She never hit the water. Something vast and black collided with her. It knocked the wind out of her as it caught her around the waist, wrapping her in what felt like thick, rough cables that caught on the fabric of her gloves.

Instead of falling, instead of saving Kai, she zoomed above the surface of the chill brown water. Then the river dropped away. Her abductor carried her higher, and the air pulsed rhythmically around her. Juli tried to scream, but fear tightened her throat and the scaly cables around her middle made it hard to breathe.

Far below in the river, a pale oval momentarily broke the dark surface. Juli found her voice. "Kai!"

Kai disappeared as the river slipped around a bend between the narrow canyon walls. The *thing* that held her had to climb, pulling her up close to it to avoid dashing her on the rocks. She couldn't see the water anymore. She screamed, desperate, reaching for the river. "Kai!"

Some huge, invisible disturbance shot beneath her. No more than a vast heat shimmer, it had a very real effect on the trees along the canyon's edge, cracking and bending them and sending sprays of pine needles and dust into the air. For an instant, the shimmer fell away, and Juli stared at a colossal impossibility with scales as crimson as blood. Then the red monster disappeared behind a ridge of rock, following Kai downstream.

Was that—no. The impossibility of the monster made Juli's vision go dark at the edges. Just then, the cables around her middle shifted. Juli looked down and realized they ended in claws.

Her world ground to a halt.

"I died," she whispered. "Clearly, I am dead." Her voice was breathy and high. "This is not what I imagined dying would be like."

The monster didn't respond. Higher they flew, upriver and around the mountain she and Kai had so carefully picked their way down last night, covering in seconds what had taken them hours.

They passed through another shimmer in the air, and the solid mountain gave way to an open archway bordered by a wide ledge. Juli, who felt like she was barely holding on to sanity, screamed as loud as she could when the beast passed her midflight from its back claws to its front.

Quiet, woman, a velvet voice growled in her head. A familiar voice. A voice used to giving commands. Though his flight was steady, Juli's world tilted.

The black monster flared his wings, and they alighted on the ledge outside the cave. Juli got a good look at her abductor for the first time.

He was a dragon, which, Juli thought, was somewhat rude. A sixty-foot spiked monstrosity with luminous golden eyes should not under any circumstances have the audacity to exist.

He set her down. In a weird, blinding flash of darkness, the monster disappeared. Ashem replaced it, anger snapping in his eyes... His golden eyes. Dizzy, Juli sat down hard.

275

"I'm dead," she said, dazed. "Despite being dead, I seem to be going into shock."

Ashem scowled, his expressive dark brows drawing together. "You aren't dead. You're too busy being a thorn in my side."

"I certainly *am* dead," Juli snapped. "Or else you drugged me. Yes, that's probably it. You gave me some kind of hallucinogen. You aren't a dragon, you're a helicopter. Where's Kai?"

She stood and looked out over the valley, panic rising. Kai's terrified face filled her mind, her misty green eyes wide with surprise and terror.

Ashem's gaze unfocused for a moment, and then he looked at Juli. His voice was tight. "She's still in the river. Rhys is trying to get her out. For your sake, your friend's, and the sake of all humankind, you had better pray he succeeds."

CHAPTER 33

RHYS

R hys ran alongside the canyon, his claws leaving deep gouges in the earth, his fear mounting with each second. Kai's face was a white oval against the dark water, and panic was clear in her choked-off screams. She swam for the side, but a rime of ice kept her from getting a grip on the wall. The current spun her, buffeting her against a rock.

"Rhys!" She coughed out water, reaching toward him. He must have dropped the veil in his panic. But if she could see him, it would give her hope. He wouldn't hide from her now. "Rhys, please!"

She went under. Terror dug icy fingers into Rhys's heart. *Kai!*

He tried to squeeze through the top of the canyon, but the opening was too narrow here, his wings too vast. Kai bobbed to the surface, but her movements were slow and uncoordinated. She reached for him again, coughing too hard to scream. Her head slammed against a rock, and Kai went under again.

She didn't resurface.

Rhys called the fire and changed in midair. The pain came

roaring back, and the wind whistled past human ears as he tumbled toward the black water, momentum carrying him forward.

He exploded through the freezing surface of the river, spinning and somersaulting. He smacked into rocks and debris, unable to tell which way was up or down. Fighting for control, he righted himself and broke the surface, gasping.

Rhys opened his mouth to call for Kai, but it filled with dirty water. He spluttered. It was all he could do to keep himself up and away from the walls as he fought the relentless current. He didn't see Kai, but he could feel her. She was close, and she was still alive.

Using his pain as a beacon, Rhys dove beneath the surface. Just as he was about to run out of air, his fingers brushed something soft and cold that sent an electric pulse through his body.

She was wearing some kind of huge coat and backpack that were waterlogged and dragging her down. He ripped it from her, then hauled her still, cold form against his chest and kicked until they broke the surface. She was unconscious, her face as white as the snow dissolving in the dark water around them, her lips purple. He held her against him with one arm, using the other to steer away from rocks and debris.

She was so cold. He'd been worried about her drowning; he hadn't realized she would go hypothermic in minutes. Humans were so damnably vulnerable. He couldn't warm her with magic while they were being battered by the river. There was too much of a risk that he'd lose concentration, pull too much power, hurt her. He couldn't transform for fear of dropping her or dashing them both against the sides of the narrow canyon, so he wrapped his arms around her and held on, doing what he could to keep them both afloat.

The river turned, its current too strong for him to fight. Rhys twisted, slamming his body against the oncoming rocks instead of hers. He gritted his teeth and grunted in pain, lying back to keep them both afloat.

"Hold on, Kai. We'll get out soon. We have to be close."

As if the universe heard, the ravine came to an end. The river spilled wide and shallow across a wintery meadow of yellow grass and leafless trees in a small valley between two shoulders of the mountain. Rhys's feet hit the rocky bottom and dragged for a minute before he managed to stand. He lifted Kai and limped to the bank, laying her on the snow-dusted earth. She rolled onto her side and vomited water.

He smoothed black hair away from her face. She was so pale and cold she might have been carved of marble, but the shock of skin-to-skin contact pulsed through his fingers.

Kai finished retching and rolled onto her back. She gasped and coughed, and her teeth chattered. She reached toward his face and ended up wrapping her fingers around his pendant. "Rhys. Hypo...hyp...river. Cold."

"I know."

"Donwannagoback."

"It's not safe out here. You have to get warm." The valley was as open as a bowl. One filling rapidly with snow. There was nowhere to build a fire, nowhere to lay her out of the elements or hide from enemies that might be scouting the area. He pulled her into his arms, where she shivered like a leaf in autumn wind. He opened his senses to her. Her temperature was still dropping, so cold that a blast of heat from him would shock her system and do serious damage.

Her eyelashes fluttered. "Juli...?"

"She's safe."

"Don' you tryda kiss me."

"I won't."

She took a shallow breath. "Pro...mise..."

"I swear." He would lose her if he didn't get her warm. Why were humans so fire-blasted frail?

He laid her down, not realizing until it was too late that she was still clinging to his pendant. The chain snapped, the rhombus with its citrine sun still wrapped in her hand. He tucked it into the pocket of Kai's hoodie; he'd get it later.

He jogged a few dozen feet away and transformed. As small as she'd felt in his arms, she looked even smaller now. The white halo of a heartsworn mate glowed diffusely around her, dimmer than it had been.

Stay with me, Kai. Stay awake.

"Tired..."

He gathered her up, holding her close to his belly as he could to offer some warmth, some protection from the freezing wind. He leaped into the sky, wings beating hard as he made steady, one-sided conversation. *Come on, George. Don't sleep. Not yet.*

Flight had never seemed so slow. He soared over the river, and the twinge in his shoulder turned into a scream as he pushed himself harder, forced his wings to move faster. He banked around the mountain, and the cave finally came into sight. He flared his wings, grasping the ledge with his back claws.

Inside, Juli crouched against one wall of the cavern, watching Rhys with terrified eyes as he hobbled inside, Kai clutched close. She made an odd, strangled noise, like she wanted to scream but wouldn't let herself.

Rhys settled Kai on the ground. He released the dragon body, sliding into human shape. When the fire of his transformation cleared, Juli was leaning over Kai. Like Kai, Juli wore an old coat and gloves, her body swathed from head to toe in layers. Cadoc must have shown Kai the hoard.

Cadoc.

Rhys swore. He had to take care of Kai first.

"She's unconscious and hypothermic." Juli's voice quavered, but managed to sound brisk. "She needs to get out of these clothes and get warm. I'll need—"

"No." Rhys scooped Kai from the ground, settling her against his chest. If someone tried to take Kai from him now, he would snap. "I'll need something warm, soup or a drink."

"Give her back!" Juli shouted, her eyes full of tears. "*I* will take care of her!"

With Kai in his arms, Rhys's pain had all but disappeared. Her head lolled against his shoulder. She was so, so cold. Cold, frail, and small. Where was her strength? Her energy? If she died because of him, because he had insisted on bringing her here, he would never forgive himself. Not that he'd have long for self-loathing if he lost her. "I can warm her up faster than you."

Juli grabbed him, teeth bared and eyes wild. "You can't have her!"

Urgency made his voice rough. *I do have her! She is mine!* But instead of shouting that at Juli, he said, "I won't hurt her."

"You aren't taking her out of my sight," Juli snapped. "You don't know what to do. She needs to shiver—"

"I *know*." Rhys shot a look at Ashem.

With a long-suffering sigh, Ashem approached Juli from behind. Carefully, as if she were a dangerous animal. A second later, she crumpled, and Ashem caught her, scowling down at her unconscious body still bundled in one of the enormous coats from the hoard.

"What do I do with her?" Ashem looked from Juli to Rhys as if he'd been handed a bomb.

"Take care of her." Rhys didn't have to look back to know Ashem was scowling. He carried Kai toward his room. He met the others in the hall.

"Kai!" Ffion pressed forward to look at her. "She's soaked. Is she all right?" She looked at Rhys. "Are you all right?"

He didn't stop. "Get something warm for her to drink."

Ffion ran off. Deryn followed him toward his room. "I'm glad you've both survived," she said, her voice deceptively mild.

Rhys shot her a look. Deryn would like Kai better for this escape attempt. "So am I." Rhys kicked open his door placed Kai on his bed, pausing briefly to conjure a large ball of flame and set it hovering a little above her. It gave off enough heat to help a little. "Owain has Cadoc."

Deryn gaped at him. "What?"

"Ask Ashem. He's known for days."

Deryn swore. "What are we going to do?"

"I'm going to go after him once Kai is warm again. You're going to stay here."

"Get fucked!" Deryn snapped. "I won't be left behind."

"We can't put both of us at risk." Kai's hoodie was unzipped, so Rhys slipped it off of her, then tore the sweater she wore underneath. When he got to the thin shirt that clung wetly to her skin, he paused. His hands hovered over the damp, sheer fabric. His throat went dry.

"Need help?" Deryn asked.

"No." Rhys tore the shirt away, revealing the smooth, pale curve of Kai's waist, the line of muscle up the center of her stomach, her ribcage, small breasts hidden beneath a wet white bra, the delicate lines of her collarbone and shoulders...

He had to step away, one hand tangling in his hair, breathing harsh.

Deryn pushed him aside. "Unless you've changed your mind about kissing her, let me finish this. If you want to be an effective little bed warmer, you might want to change out of those wet clothes. We'll talk about Cadoc later."

Rhys nodded dumbly, stripping and pulling on a dry set of

shorts. A moment later, Deryn stood, easily lifting Kai, who now wore only her bra and underwear. They were damp, but there wasn't anything to be done about that. Not unless he wanted to take them off.

He wanted to. But not like this.

"Hold her while I turn down the covers," Deryn said.

Rhys took Kai's limp body, feeling the pulse of energy as her icy cheek fell against his bare chest. Looking at her, his heart shifted, struck not by desperate, instinctive need, but conscious, voluntary wanting.

When Deryn finished, he placed Kai in the bed and stood, looking down at her.

"I think to warm her up, you have to get in too," Deryn said, her voice deceptively innocent.

Ffion came in holding a steaming mug. Rhys shot Deryn a withering look and took the mug, glancing inside. Tea. It looked too hot, but he wasn't sure what would burn a human throat.

"It should be fine." Ffion sat on his bed and pulled Kai into a sitting position. She shook Kai lightly. "Kai?"

Kai groaned.

Deryn crouched in front of Kai and snapped her fingers. "Oi! Wake up and drink this tea!"

Ffion shooed her away, took the mug from Rhys, and put it against Kai's mouth while he stood there, feeling like a useless idiot. Kai coughed, but after a minute, the tea was gone.

"That will do her some good." Ffion lowered Kai and cocked an eyebrow at Rhys. "Your turn."

Rhys forced his face to relax. He glanced at Deryn. "Convince Ashem that we need to go after Cadoc."

Deryn stopped smiling and nodded. Ffion followed her out, looking confused and uneasy.

Rhys eased himself down next to Kai and dragged the heavy blankets over both of them. He wrapped one arm around her waist and drew her close, fitting her freezing form against his body, trying to ignore the nerve-throbbing pulse. He pulled a thread of power from the inferno that lived inside him, pushing his body temperature up a few degrees. He would need to do the ritual again soon, but he had enough fire for this.

With a moan, Kai curled into him, pressing herself fully against him. She was like ice. Shivers racked her small frame.

With so much of her skin against his, the pain vanished. Rhys sucked in a breath, the sudden lack of agony a shock.

Was this all it took?

He lay there, feeling the lack of pain so acutely his eyes welled. He closed them, then opened them again, looking down at her.

"I almost lost you."

Eyes closed, breathing even, Kai didn't respond.

Rhys had never had the chance to study her face like this, uninterrupted, unobserved. His brows knit as he smoothed back strands of inky hair that clung to her cheek.

She was so beautiful. He hadn't thought so the night he met her, but that had changed even before he was heartsworn. Delicate features, big eyes, pointed chin, full lips. Sharp and soft at the same time.

In a moment of weakness, he pressed his lips to her mass of damp, dark hair. Doing so wouldn't endanger her—to complete the heartswearing, the kiss had to be on the mouth. He'd never known why, or why it was a kiss instead of something bigger, like sex, or something else entirely.

He tightened his arms, pulling her closer, reveling in the contact. Even the smell of the river couldn't cover her sweetly spicy scent. She was safe. She was here.

Instead of assuaging his need, allowing himself to kiss the crown of her head put a crack in his dam of control.

He kissed her hair again, then again. He pulled back, but it wasn't enough. His lips brushed the skin of her forehead and control skittered away.

"Stop," he commanded himself.

He couldn't.

He pressed his lips to her forehead again, then the bridge of her nose, then its tip.

"Stop."

He leaned his forehead against hers, a breath away from her lips, sweet and full. They were parted in sleep. The pain could end. He could have her. They would have such a long time together. If he did this, eventually, she might forgive him.

The memory of their conversation by the river lapped at his mind.

Don' you tryda kiss me.

I won't.

Pro...mise...

I swear.

Rhys pressed his forehead against hers. "You were so brave to leave. I'm sorry I couldn't give you a choice."

But damn everything, he wouldn't force her into a heartswearing while she was asleep.

With more will than it had ever taken to do anything, Rhys pulled back a few inches. He brushed his fingers along her cheek, then traced her palm, which was curled beneath her chin. He was surprised at the tough calluses on her fingertips and along the middle joints of her second and third fingers.

He turned her hand over, studying her scars, fighting feelings of tenderness. She'd wanted to escape him so badly, she'd risked death. To feel anything for someone so adamant about not being with him would be asking for pain.

Perhaps if he explained that he was king, she would heartswear to him without loving him. Or even liking him. Would it matter if she did it of her own free will?

Yes. He didn't want her pity or her sense of duty to humankind. He wanted her heart the way she was beginning to have his.

Weariness crashed down on him. The remnants of fear and days of sleep deprivation pulled him under, stronger than any river. Burying his face in her damp hair, he fought sleep. As soon as she was warm, he had to go after Cadoc. He had to go...

CHAPTER 34

ASHEM

Ashem scowled at Rhys's back. He would've shouted something, but they were both on edge about Cadoc, and Ashem didn't want to push him. It would be hard enough to keep him there when Kai was safely warm.

Ashem couldn't allow the fate of one soldier to compromise the safety of his king, even if that soldier was Cadoc.

Looking down, he sighed at the unconscious woman in his arms. Infernal Juliet King, a thorn in his side, though he'd known her less than a day. Kai was brave enough to escape, but this woman, she would have been the mastermind behind the common-sense preparations that kept them alive once they'd climbed away. Food and coats and whatever else they'd stolen from the hoard. Damn Cadoc, who must've shown it to Kai.

He placed her gently on the ground and allowed her to wake. A moment later, she sat up, her enormous coat puffed out around her, glaring daggers at him. "What did you do to me? Where's Kai?"

"I assume Rhys took her to his room."

Juli went white and shot to her feet. "Take me to her this instant!"

Ashem rubbed his temples. "If she is hypothermic, Rhys is the best person to care for her. He can do a damn sight more to warm her up than you."

Juliet whirled on him. "I don't know why you and your cult are so fixated on my friend, but you are going to let us go!"

Ashem barked a laugh. "No, I'm not. We're going to return to the plan. She can write letters for her family. You can deliver them. She stays, you go home."

Her lip curled. "No! I am not leaving her! Why did you kidnap her in the first place? Why are we in some kind of temple inside a mountain? And"—she strode forward and stabbed a finger into his chest—"what kind of hallucinogen did you slip me?"

"I assure you, you haven't been drugged. Though I would gladly sedate you."

She pressed her lips together. Any more and they would disappear altogether, and that would be a shame. "You'd love that, wouldn't you? To have a woman completely helpless and under your control."

Ashem pressed his knuckles to the bridge of his nose, willing his unruly mind to stay away from her lips and her perfect ass and her angry, beautiful eyes. "Ms. King, you *are* helpless and under my control."

Juli opened her mouth, closed it, and then opened it again.

"You do an excellent impression of a fish."

She made a noise somewhere between a sob and a frustrated shout, then whirled and ran toward the short hall that led to the kitchen. A few seconds later, a bowl shattered, the sound echoing through the cavern.

Ffion cocked an eyebrow at Ashem as she walked out of the kitchen with a mug of something steaming in her hands—the second one he'd seen her pass by with. That was good. It meant Kai drank the first.

Good luck, Commander, she thought, knowing him well enough after millennia to know he'd scan her mind to see what was going on with Rhys. *And by the way, Rhys may kill you for not telling us about Cadoc.*

It was necessary, he shot back at her. *Get Kai awake and her letters written. Sunder waiting for Evan and Morwenna. I want this one out of here before she breaks all our dishes.*

What about Cadoc?

Ashem's jaw clenched. He looked away and shook his head. Ffion bit her lip and hurried down the hall.

"Wʜᴀᴛ?" Juli whirled on Ashem as he entered the kitchen. Her dark eyes were red-rimmed and soft with tears. She threw down the overlarge gloves she'd worn and shrugged out of her massive coat.

He kept his voice dry to cover his discomfort and the pinch of guilt. Damn feeling guilt. He wasn't the one who ran away in the middle of the night. He wasn't the one who forced her to come looking for her friend, or who made Kai pick up a sword and attack Kavar instead of running away like she should have done all those days ago. "You're making noise."

"I am making *lunch!*" She slammed another bowl down on the counter with a bang. "You are going to bring Kai here *this instant* before your ginger henchman can do *anything* to her."

"It was your ill-conceived escape attempt that dumped her in a half-frozen river," Ashem snapped. "You are the one who can't be trusted to keep her safe."

All the blood drained from Juli's face. She strode forward

289

until they stood, toe-to-toe. Ashem inhaled. She smelled like chamomile and rage. "How *dare* you!"

She was perfection. He leaned down until their faces were so close, he could have tasted her. "You have no idea what I would dare, Juliet King."

Her hand flew back then rocketed toward his face. He caught her wrist, her palm centimeters from his cheek. He had a fraction of a second to notice the contrast. His large hand, her delicate one, his bronze skin, her fair.

The world contracted. His ears filled with rushing wind. Her wrist burned in his grip. Magic rose up like a tide, loosing the moorings of his soul. Power burned inside her, and he reached for it. Searching. Pressing. But it was as if an unscalable wall stood between them, and the darkness closed in.

If he didn't reach her, he would die.

Instinct rose, profound as hunger or thirst or the need to breathe, and Ashem knew.

He was heartsworn.

For a split second, he hesitated, teetering on the brink. He didn't know her. Didn't trust her. Already wanted her more than he could control.

He didn't care. He had a duty. He had to protect Rhys. Protect them all, and he couldn't do that if he was weak and in constant pain.

Ashem pressed Juliet King back against the counter, tipped her face up, and kissed her.

Her lips were soft as starlight. She lifted her hand like she'd try to hit him again, or drum her angry fist against his chest, but then she melted against him with a soft little moan of surrender that had him stiffening, sent his fingers delving into her hair, pulling her head back so she arched into him, and taking every bit of what she was giving. And Ancients, she was giving, but also demanding. She squirmed against him, and he grabbed her hips to hold her in place. Her hands came up to frame his face, pull him closer. She bit his bottom lip hard enough to make him growl, then sucked it into her mouth, claiming and soothing.

And then magic took them both.

Darkness swirled. Energy pounded, infusing him with strength. So much strength, all from her. The barrier between them cracked, opening, connecting. Magic poured into him. Their souls coiled together, fusing so profoundly it was as if they had never been two separate beings.

Ashem pulled back and stared into her face, astonished and lost. *Juliet?*

Ashem's kiss wasn't gentle. It was reckless, angry, edged with despair, and the most sensual thing she'd ever experienced. His huge, strong body pressed against hers, pinning her against the counter as his cock hardened against her stomach. His fingers twisted in her hair and pulled, and Juli gasped, riding the edge of pleasure and pain.

She wanted to squirm up onto the counter and feel that hard ridge in his pants against her center, right where she needed it. She would kick him back against the big, heavy kitchen table and climb on top of him and ride him until he broke or she did, or until they both saw stars.

He grabbed her hips to stop her from moving, so she grabbed his face, changed the angle of the kiss, and bit him hard. He growled, and she felt it in her core.

Screw Ashem and his golden eyes and constant commands. She'd kill him. She'd make him bleed. She'd have *all* of him.

Suddenly, a shockwave rolled over her. If Ashem hadn't already done it, she would have been thrown against the counter.

A veil over her mind was ripped away, revealing a frighteningly wide space. A creeping, tickling sensation inched from the back of her hand up to her shoulder. Power coiled through her muscles and blackness swam before her eyes, but she wasn't afraid. There was strength in the darkness, and power. A completeness that filled the deepest, loneliest parts of her soul.

Damn. She felt so satisfied, so serene.

Ashem straightened, breaking the kiss. His helpless expression rocked her to her core.

Juliet? The voice swirled through her mind, whispering her name like music on a desert breeze. She tried to mentally thrust it away. It wouldn't go. She put her hands against Ashem's chest and shoved him back instead. The darkness melted, and the kitchen seemed to coalesce around her. The comforting, alien presence remained.

She had to collect herself. Had to get back to that safe, angry place where no one could reach her. "What do you think you're doing?"

His rough hands fell from where they cupped her face. His eyes, so cool and collected a moment ago, were bewildered. He lifted his hand and touched his lip where she'd bitten him. His finger came away streaked with blood. He stared at it for a long time. "I'm...sorry. I have to be able to protect them."

Strange, crystal-clear scenes flicked through Juli's head in quick succession. A man who looked like Ashem but wasn't, smiling a horrible smile. A vast desert so dry it sucked the moisture from her mouth. Misty green mountains. Bowing to a red dragon. The sky. The sky, with black wings beating in the periphery of her vision.

"What did you *do*?" Juli spun away from him and cracked her elbow on the granite countertop. She gasped in pain. For some reason, he winced.

"I can explain." He said the words, but only seemed to be half listening, one hand to his head.

"Then explain," Juli demanded, rubbing her elbow. She would not think about kissing him again. About how he was still hard. About how all she wanted even now was to push him back onto the table and have her way with him.

He lifted his fathomless golden eyes to her face, blinked, and shook his head. A sharp twist of *want* lanced through her. Not lust, definitely not love. Craving.

When he spoke, his words echoed oddly, as if they were both in the air and in her head. He sounded surprised and confused. "We are heartsworn. It's...not at all what I expected."

Juli gaped at him. She opened her mouth, closed it, and then opened it again. *Heartsworn.* She'd never heard the word before, but somehow she knew what it meant. Mated. Bonded. Part of each other. She found her voice, but it shook. Her confidence had never failed her before, but now it cracked. "Is... Is this some kind of sick joke?"

No.

The completeness shifted inside her, all of the parts that weren't herself suddenly thrown into sharp relief. She could feel the places where it filled her up, made her *more.*

She leaned back against the counter. She should feel violated, but she could feel the way she had invaded him too. Her *self* had become suddenly, inextricably tangled with his, and he hadn't expected it. He had expected to retain control, but he was clinging to it by his fingernails.

She knew. Without having a clue how, she knew all of those things. "It's drugs. It has to be drugs. You...did something." She sidled away from him.

"Juliet..." He reached for her.

"Do *not* touch me." She held up a hand, stopping him. He

froze. He didn't want to frighten her. Something else she shouldn't know but did.

"It's the nature of the bond—" he started.

She cut him off with a vitriolic whisper. "I hate you."

He recoiled like her words were a spray of bullets that hit him square in the chest. Juli fled the kitchen, through the black cavern, not daring to stop until she'd thrown herself into Kai's room and bolted the door.

He didn't come after her, but she could still *feel* him, feel how irresistibly the thing between them pulled him to her. Pulled her to him. She was aware of him as he paced the kitchen, then the hall, then finally sat a little ways down from Kai's door, his back against the wall. She knew how lost he felt. Knew when he drew up his knees and dropped his head into his hands.

I'm sorry. I didn't know.

But Juli refused to believe. *It's all in my head. It's not real. It's not real.*

And if it was real, she would not forgive him. Ever.

CHAPTER 35

KAI

Consciousness lapped at Kai like waves. In: someone argued loudly with several other someones. Out: blessed blackness. In: the argument got louder. She heard Cadoc's name. Out: nothingness. In: something crashed. Fire roared.

Out.

In. Comfortable and deliciously warm, she burrowed deeper into the bed. Her hair was damp, but she couldn't remember why. At the moment, she didn't care.

"Mmm..." Clean, wild, and masculine with a hint of woodsmoke, the scent on the pillow made her curl her toes and sigh. In her mind, blue eyes flashed and lips turned up in a heart-stopping half smile.

Rhys. She was in a bed that smelled like Rhys.

She threw back the covers and tried to spring out of bed, but her feet got caught. Yelping, she hit the floor in a pile of pillows and blankets. Tangled in the sheet, she landed with her knees pressed to her nose.

"For the love of... Where are my pants?" She struggled

295

upright, digging her way out of the morass of blankets. She wore nothing but her underwear. "Where is my shirt?!"

"Here."

A soft mass of dark blue fabric flew at her from across the room. Without thinking, Kai caught it and held it up. It was a shirt. She shimmied into it—the hem hit her halfway down her thighs—before she dared look at the man who had tossed it to her.

Rhys watched her from across the room in a chair near the hearth, conspicuously shirtless. Gemstones were spread on a small table before him, along with the glass ball that allowed them to show records. The red scales of his indicium glinted in the light of a golden ball of fire that hung near his shoulder, which shed a brighter light on the stones and emphasized the sleek cut of the muscles on his chest and arms. His eyes clung to her, but for some reason, he looked utterly defeated.

She grabbed a blanket and yanked it up to her chest. "Rhys! Why the *hell* am I in your bed? And why didn't you just get me a shirt you weren't already wearing?"

"It's what I had." He rubbed his cheek, as if bringing his thoughts back from a distance. "As far as my bed, you don't remember?"

It was such a bad frat boy line Kai would have laughed if she hadn't felt sick. "If you roofied me, I will stab you."

Rhys's brow furrowed. "Roofied?"

"Drugged me and...and..."

His lip curled. "No."

Then she remembered the river. The darkness. The cold, cold nothingness. Warm, strong fingers that closed around hers and pulsed with life.

She sat down on the bed. "Holy shit. You jumped in the river."

He nodded, studying his hands.

Kai clutched the blankets harder. "You saved my life."

"I guess that makes us even, George." A ghost of a smile curved one corner of his mouth. "I couldn't just stand there." Then the smile disappeared. "Besides, if not for me, you wouldn't have been in the river in the first place."

She sighed, the fact that she was back here in the cave settling on her like a heavy weight—though not as heavy as she would have imagined.

Yesterday, she had thought she'd never see Rhys or the other dragons again. Only now did she realize how much she didn't want that. "Technically both of us made several choices that led us down the path from the moment we met to me ending up in the river. Regardless of how I got there, you risked your life getting me out. Thank you."

"Like I said, we're even." He stood, motioning to clothing hanging near the hearth. "Your jeans and hoodie are there. The shirts are ruined."

Kai reached for her clothes, but the rest of her memories returned in a sharp flash. "Juli! Where's—"

"Here. Safe. Angry. She wanted to be the one to care for you but I felt I might be better qualified to warm you up." He tipped his head at the ball of fire.

Relief washed over Kai and she pressed a hand to her chest. "Okay. You're sure she's okay?"

Rhys nodded.

"Okay. Good. Thank you for not leaving her out there." So much for their escape attempt. Again, Kai couldn't tell if she was angry or relieved. She felt like a cat. Let me out. No, let me back in. Just kidding, must escape!

Kai looked back at the rumpled bed, then down at her mostly unclothed body. It could be that when he said he was better qualified, he'd just warmed her up with his magic. But even though she had no conscious memory of his body against hers, of sleeping in his arms, it was almost like part of her could still feel his gorgeous, muscled, perfect body pressed against her.

"You warmed me up," she said.

"Yes."

"Without clothes."

"With some clothes," Rhys corrected, but his voice had gone rough.

"Did you kiss me?" Kai asked.

He sucked his bottom lip into his mouth, as if he had kissed her and could still taste her. Heat built in Kai's core, but Rhys shook his head. "No, I... If you were heartsworn, you'd know."

"Oh." Kai hesitated, then asked, "What would have happened to you if I had died?"

He crossed his arms and shrugged, a frown tugging down the corners of his mouth. "When one of a heartsworn pair dies, the effect on the survivor is... They recover, but it takes time. They're still heartsworn, though. They can't swear to anyone else."

Dread made a pit in Kai's stomach. She hadn't expected it to work that way. She'd been so sure that even if she lived to be an old woman, in time—not even that much time for a dragon—her death would set him free. "But—but we aren't heartsworn. Maybe you would've gone back to normal."

He shrugged again, face still troubled. "Perhaps."

Kai licked her lips. "Theoretically, if you knew my death *would* free you, would you have...?"

"I still would have gone in after you. Even if you refuse to choose me." Rhys's voice was soft. He didn't look at her. Instead, he tossed her the jeans and hoodie.

Kai swallowed, wishing he'd look at her. But no, actually, being pierced by those blue eyes would only make things worse.

Damn it. Now, on top of every other confusing thing she felt for him, he'd saved her life.

The clothes were still a little damp, like her hair, but she pulled them on anyway.

Someone knocked. "Rhys?"

It was Ashem, his voice tight.

"What is it?"

Slowly, Ashem entered. He looked troubled, but distant, his dark brows furrowed over eyes that didn't quite focus. "Juliet is asking for Kai."

Something about his tone made Kai's adrenaline kick into overdrive. "What did you do?"

He didn't answer.

"Ashem!" Rhys snapped.

He shook his head.

"Kai," Rhys said very quietly, "didn't you say you and Juli share blood?"

"Yeah, we're distant cousins. Why?"

Rhys stared at Ashem, and to Kai's shock, Ashem looked away. He looked ashamed.

"She's in Kai's room." Ashem's voice was pleading. "She won't come out."

"Why do you want her to come out?" Kai tried to stay calm, but she couldn't help the way her voice rose. "I thought you two hated each other."

"Well?" Rhys asked. There was no mercy in his tone.

"We... We are heartsworn."

"No!" Kai shouted. She strode toward Ashem, overwhelmed with helpless rage, thrusting a finger toward his chest. "No. *You* are heartsworn. Because I know even you are better than that, Ashem. I know you would not magically mate-bond my friend. My friend who doesn't even technically know dragons exist!"

Rhys's voice was flat. "He completed the bond. He always said he would."

Something happened to Kai then. The world went white, and the next thing she knew, someone was screaming and clawing and punching at Ashem so viciously the big man cowered away. It was only when Rhys pulled Kai off Ashem—*after* allowing her to pummel him for about twenty full seconds —that Kai realized the person screaming and clawing and punching was her. She shuddered, half choking on sobs.

When Rhys pulled her roughly against his chest, she let him, her tears smearing his skin as he held her close.

"Do it and be done." Rhys's voice rumbled against Kai's ear, mocking. His arms were around her so tight, as if he could protect her from this thing that had already been done, and not even to her. "You were wrong, Ashem."

"How did this happen?" Kai whispered against Rhys's chest. His skin was bare and soft over the steel of the muscle beneath. She could hear her own heartbeat and his, both pounding. "I thought heartswearing to a human was rare. How could you both heartswear to random girls you picked up in the woods?"

Rhys's fingers worked in small, comforting circles, massaging the tension between her shoulder blades. "Cousins. Predisposition runs in some human families."

Well. Shit.

For a long time, Ashem didn't speak. Finally, he said, "Juliet thinks she's hallucinating. She thinks I drugged her."

"I have to talk to her." Kai pushed gently away from Rhys, surprised at how reluctant she was to put distance between them.

When she broke contact, a muscle ticked in Rhys's jaw, but he nodded. "She needs you."

Ignoring the insistent instinct to linger, to go back and curl against Rhys's bare chest, Kai brushed past Ashem and into the hall, where she knocked on the door to her room. "Juli? It's me. Ashem isn't here."

For a full minute there was silence. Then the bold slid aside. Kai pushed open the door, entered, and turned to lock it behind her.

Juli was already climbing back into Kai's bed. Even from here, Kai could see her trembling. She'd always had a black-and-white view of what was and was not possible. Dragons would not fit into her world.

"I know he's not here." She scratched her left arm through her sleeve. "Or at least my brain is telling me I know he's not outside the door, because he's a little bit down the hall. But he did something to me. I can't trust my thoughts."

Kai padded to the bed and climbed in next to her best friend. "What happened?"

"I tried to slap him." Juli flopped back and put a pillow over her face, muffling her voice. "He caught my wrist. He must have slipped it to me then. Or else earlier. Maybe yesterday. Maybe it was slow-acting. Because today I swear..." Juli blinked, tears in the corners of her eyes.

Kai clicked a carabiner. Open, closed, open, closed. "You saw a dragon?"

Juli sat up, the pillow falling away. "Yes." She narrowed her eyes. "Have they been giving you the same stuff? Do you see dragons?"

Kai wanted to laugh or cry, she wasn't sure which. This reaction was so extremely Juli. Kai put a hand on Juli's cheek, forcing her friend to look at her. Focus on her. "Don't change, okay? Just don't ever change."

Juli frowned. "I won't." She shook her head. "Whatever drug he has, it's a strange one. I feel like he's in my head...and I'm in his."

"What do you mean?" Kai's stomach curdled. She remembered the violation of having Kavar in her mind. "Ugh. That's something he does. Juli, I'm so sorry. I'll tell him to stop."

Then her brain caught up with the last thing Juli had said. "Wait, you're in his mind, too? What do you mean?"

Juli blinked at her. "You want me to describe my hallucination to you?"

"Yeah. Sure. Hallucination." Kai shuddered. "God, why is he doing that? It must be awful."

"Awful?" Juli's nose scrunched. "He is insufferable, but it doesn't hurt, if that's what you mean. It feels...abnormally natural."

Juli looked close to breaking. In the silence that followed, Kai realized she knew it was no hallucination. She just couldn't deal with it any other way.

Juli took an unsteady breath. "It's like he's part of me. I can feel what he's feeling, catch glimpses of what he's seeing."

Kai felt sick. That didn't sound like what Kavar had done to her. Could it be that being inside each other's minds was part of heartswearing? None of them had told her that. They *knew* what Kavar had done to her.

They must have hidden it on purpose, because they knew it would only make her "no" that much more adamant.

Kai hugged herself and resisted the urge to run screaming into the tunnels beneath this place. "Juli... What if it's not a hallucination?"

"Of course it is," Juli snapped. Then she whispered, "It has to be. There are no such things as dragons. They are a cult, and I am drugged."

Kai sighed. She moved and sat at the very edge of the bed, waiting.

"Do you see dragons?" Juli's voice wavered on the edge of tears.

"Not at the moment."

Juli glared at her. "Seriously, Kai. I can't... Just tell me I've been drugged."

Kai smiled weakly at her friend. "I've been seeing dragons since a few hours after you went for help, and they didn't have a chance to slip me anything then."

"Well...shit."

Juli didn't curse much as a general rule. Hearing "shit" in her clipped, proper tones was so unexpected, Kai laughed. Juli looked at her, startled, then she started laughing too. They both laughed, hugging each other, until Kai's stomach ached. Despite the laughter, when it subsided, she knew the tears on both her cheeks and Juli's were not tears of mirth.

"My brain won't catch up with me," Juli said at last. She scratched her left arm hard. "I don't know what to do."

"Breathe for now. Is your arm all right?"

"It itches. I must be having some kind of reaction—"

Juli pulled back her sleeve, and they both gasped.

"What is that?" Juli demanded.

A pattern of spirals and whorls trailed up the back of Juli's hand, starting at her knuckles, climbing gracefully up her wrist and forearm. It was made of scales, like the dragons'. Unlike the dragons', these were translucent and colorless unless the light hit them at the right angle. Where it did, the pattern shone like an opalescent rainbow. It went higher than they could push her sleeve, so Juli pulled down the neck of her shirt. The scales coiled over her shoulder, trailing down a couple inches onto her chest and back before ending gracefully at the base of her neck.

It took Kai a long moment to find her voice. "You've got an indicium."

Juli touched the scales with one finger. She closed her eyes, released the neck of her shirt, and pulled down her sleeve, clutching the end tightly. "What is it?"

Kai clicked her carabiner. "The dragons have them. They're like scaly tattoos. I don't know if they do much."

They were silent for another moment. Kai was first to speak. "Juli... What's it like?"

"It itches."

Kai sighed. "No. Being heartsworn."

Juli closed her eyes. "It's like...addiction. I have an irresistible urge to be with him. It's not physical or emotional, just a *need*. Like he's a huge cup of coffee and I've gone a month without caffeine." She sat up abruptly. "This is asinine!"

Kai considered Juli's words. "Rhys is heartsworn to me."

Juli made a disgusted noise. "No wonder he wouldn't let me near you when he brought you in. If this is how he feels..." She trailed off. "Why aren't you with him? This feeling...it's uncomfortable."

Kai clicked her carabiner absently. "I'm not heartsworn to him. He hasn't kissed me."

Juli got up and paced. After three turns around the small room, she restlessly tidied the table near the hearth. When that was done, she came over to the bed and folded her arms. Kai sighed and rolled off. In less than a minute, the messy bed had been made, its covers impeccably straight, its pillows precisely arranged. Kai sat back down and Juli began to pace again.

"Would you like me to throw those papers off the table so you can rage-clean them again?"

Juli glared at her. "Don't be ridiculous."

"What's worse right now? The existence of dragons or the existence of Ashem?"

"Both. And the fact that it's you too." Juli's anger seemed to dissipate. She sighed and sank down on the bed next to Kai. She flopped back onto the pillows. "Dragons are incompatible with my five-year plan."

Kai smiled crookedly and smoothed her friend's hair.

"What a damn day. We rappelled down a cliff, hiked in the mountains, I almost died, and dragons want us as their mates."

"Obviously we have to run away again."

"Obviously," Kai echoed. But it felt less certain now. "What if you talked to him?"

"Don't be stupid."

"No, listen. There are three options." Kai ticked them off on her fingers. "A: We can sit here stewing for eternity. B: We can plan an escape from captors who can fly and have some supernatural way of tracking us, trek across a dangerous wilderness, and possibly die. Or C: We can stop fighting the unknown long enough to know it."

Of course, that meant she'd have to get to know the unknown too.

Juli put a pillow over her face again. "I don't want to talk to my hallucination."

Something in Kai cracked. Juli was heartsworn. It meant she didn't *have* to resist anymore. She could just give in to the whole idea. For reasons she didn't care to examine, it made Kai jealous. She pulled the pillow away from Juli's face. "Stop it. This is happening. It's real. Get over it."

Juli yanked the pillow back and leveled Kai with an icy glare. "Until yesterday, the universe had very clear rules. Now they're being broken left and right. Dragons. Magic. Mates. I need time to get my head around it all, and you are going to give it to me, just like I gave you time and space when you needed it."

Shame had heat rising in Kai's cheeks. "You're right. I'm sorry. But Jules, the world still has rules. We've just been playing with an incomplete set."

Juli nodded slowly. "I think I will talk to him. Tomorrow." With an air of determined denial, she turned over in the bed and immediately pretended to be asleep.

Kai watched her for a moment. She stuck her hands in her hoodie pockets, surprised when they brushed against something hard. She pulled it out. A gold pendant set with a single yellow citrine winked at her from her palm. It was Rhys's necklace. Its chain dangled, broken, from her hand. Kai frowned and stuck it in her pocket. She'd give it to him next time she saw him.

But Juli was right.

Tomorrow.

CHAPTER 36

RHYS

"You're wearing a hole in the floor," Ashem observed wryly from a chair by the hearth in Rhys's room.

Rhys turned away from Ashem and paced in the other direction.

"I did what I had to regarding Juliet *and* Cadoc. You know that."

"You should be crawling after her on your hands and knees begging for forgiveness, not in here justifying yourself to me. And we should be out there rescuing Cadoc!" Rhys rubbed his chest. The infernal burning would not stop. It wasn't anywhere near as bad as it had been this morning, but after having Kai in his bed and a few hours of near normalcy, it was maddening. "My heartswearing was going to cause enough problems, and now you, the head of intelligence, commander of the King's Vee, and a councilmember."

Ashem sighed. "I know."

Rhys's anger flared at Ashem's resignation, and so did the fire in the hearth behind him. "I don't know what you can do to atone for this, Ashem."

307

"Dragons aren't given a choice," Ashem barked.

"She is not a dragon!"

Ashem fell back into the chair, his hand over his face. "I will have thousands of years to make up for what I've done to her, and I will make that atonement to *her*. Not to you. We are still stuck in the wilderness. Owain is still out there. You are still only half sworn. Shout at me all you want when we're back at Eryri. Demote me. Exile me. But for now, I still have a duty to fulfill, and so do you."

"You cannot be serious. Right now? After what you just experienced, you're still telling me to heartswear to Kai?"

"You would be stronger."

Rhys didn't respond.

"You are being selfish, *Majesty*."

Rhys whirled on Ashem. "I'm giving her a choice, *Commander*, which is more than I can say for you."

Ashem closed his eyes briefly, but it was the only sign of shame he showed at the accusation. "Then we don't need Seren here to predict the future. Kai will choose to go back to her old life, unheartsworn. Then you die, either because Owain murders you or you can't stand the pain. Owain will gain full control of the mantle, and he will send us, *all* of us, out to commit genocide against the humans. Kai dies. Thousands will, hundreds of thousands, even, that first night. Now you're dead and she's dead. Humans retaliate and we're all dead. How *noble* of you, King Rhys ap Ayen ap Thân. How *selfless*." Ashem's voice dripped with contempt.

"My father died because he forced my mother into heartswearing. She left, and he was so weakened that his own nephew killed him." Heat built inside Rhys until his hands burst into flame. "I will not make that mistake."

Ashem shook his head. "Kai is not Mair."

Rhys shook his hands once, and the fire disappeared. He

barked a humorless laugh. "We both know the odds are that Owain is going to murder me, and given our current circumstances, it could be sooner rather than later. Better for me to suffer for a few days than to condemn her to a dragon-length life with a dead mate."

"Stop being melodramatic," Ashem snapped. "If you're dead, so am I. Then at least Kai and Juliet have each other."

A high, crystalline sound shivered into the air. Ashem drew his singstone out of his pocket and slid it over his ear. "Yes?"

His face changed as he listened, his grim expression falling away, turning into a smile. "They did? Excellent. Until then. Wind carry you well."

He pulled the singstone from his ear and grinned at Rhys. "That was Evan. They're with the Ironscales, and the winds are good. He believes they'll be here tomorrow."

His words struck Rhys in the gut like a hammer. *Tomorrow.*

Deryn would be safe. They could return to Eryri.

His time to convince Kai would be up.

Was he truly willing to die for this?

Yes. He would rather die than put another woman through what his mother had suffered.

Except Rhys's life wasn't his own. It had never been his own.

And Kai wasn't his only reason he needed more time. "Cadoc."

He was somewhere in these mountains, a captive of Owain.

Ashem's voice was rough. "Cadoc is lost."

Rage and denial flared in Rhys. "No! I will not leave him. Have the Ironscales take Deryn to Eryri if you want. You can all go. I'm staying here until I can free him or..." *Or can bring his body back.*

Ashem hissed through his teeth in frustration. "Today has

been long. Neither of us is in the right state of mind to discuss this right now."

"There will be no discussion."

"Will you put Kai in danger for him?"

Ashem's question caught Rhys off guard. "Kai doesn't need to be in danger."

"Oh, so you can suddenly fly as far from her as you like while you search for him? Were you going to teach her to ride dragon-back?" He scoffed. "Even full Wingless don't ride into battle. Or maybe you're going to allow Cadoc to wait for rescue until you can convince Kai to heartswear, and then go looking for him? That way you can fulfill your own prophecy of leaving her a widow within days of swearing to her."

Rhys felt like he was being strangled. Ashem was right. He wanted her to choose. He wanted to find his friend. If he was the soldier Kai thought he was, he could do those things.

But he wasn't a soldier. He was the fucking king. The only thing between the world and the destruction Owain would rain down upon it.

"Damn you, Ashem!" Rhys roared. "Get out!"

The commander rose, his face shadowed. "I am sorry, Rhys. You deserve a choice. She deserves a choice. But you know who you are, and her life is nothing to yours. You have one day."

Ashem left.

Rhys slumped in front of the fireplace and ran a hand through his hair. Perhaps he should have kissed Kai the first night. If he had, Cadoc wouldn't have.

And Kai. There was so little time, and he *hurt*. Would she hate him any less if he waited until tomorrow?

No. But she might hate him less if she knew that being with him would give that world she loved, that family she loved, their only chance to survive.

"Rhys."

310

Deryn stood at the door. From the look on her face, she'd been eavesdropping again.

She stepped into the room. Her long hair was pulled back tightly, emphasizing the sharp features of her face. "Ashem is right. Please don't put yourself through this any longer. It's stupid and useless, and Kai has a right to know the consequences of her choice. The true consequences."

Rhys shook his head.

Deryn's face turned to stone. "You ass. You're not protecting her. You're letting her condemn her entire race and ours without any clue she's doing it. I'm going to tell her. About the pain. About you being king. About the mantle. All of it."

"You might be right," he muttered. "But how can I tell her what's at stake without her feeling obligated? She'll resent me, Deryn. We'll end up just like our parents."

Deryn's face was cold. "She'll resent you either way. Or she won't. Tell her, Rhys, or I will."

Deryn strode from the room. Rhys stayed where he was, staring into the flames.

CHAPTER 37

KAI

The next morning, Kai watched as Juli went to go talk to Ashem with the air of a cat going to lay a trap for a dog. Kai waited for her to come back, then waited some more, reading the copy of *The Hobbit* she'd borrowed an eternity ago. After two hours, she'd had enough of waiting. She needed to talk to Ffion.

Kai rolled off the bed and opened the door to head into the hall. To her surprise, she met Deryn, who had her fist raised as if she was about to knock. When she saw Kai, she stepped back. She folded her arms, hands gripping her elbows so hard the knuckles were white. Her lips were also white, pressed into a tight, thin line.

"Is something wrong?" Kai glanced up and down the hall, hoping to see someone else. No such luck.

"Did he talk to you?"

Kai frowned. "He who?"

"You have to stop what you're doing to Rhys."

Kai's brow furrowed. "I don't know what you're talking about."

Deryn shoved her against the wall, and Kai yelped, more in shock than pain. She squirmed, but Deryn had pinned her in place. "Your little midnight run nearly killed him! How do you not realize that? He could've been captured going after you! Cadoc *was* captured. Did you know that? Owain has him. That's why he hasn't returned. He might be dead!" She let go.

Kai staggered. Her stomach became a lead weight. "Owain has Cadoc?"

Deryn shoved Kai again, but this time Kai was ready for it and didn't hit the wall. "When Cadoc flew off, Owain caught him." Her voice broke. "He's dead, Kai. And if he isn't dead, he probably wishes he was."

Kai gaped at Deryn, her mouth working soundlessly. She couldn't breathe. "What—what are we going to do?"

Deryn's breath caught, and she blinked rapidly. "Nothing. We're doing nothing. There aren't enough of us. Ashem can't put Rhys or me at risk."

Kai felt like she was falling. "You or Rhys? Why?"

Deryn laughed humorlessly, dashing tears from her eyes. "You are dense, aren't you? First of all, Rhys is in no condition to fight. Every second the heartswearing is incomplete, he's in agony. Real, physical pain. How have you not noticed?"

Kai swallowed hard. The knowledge that she *had* been lying to herself was difficult to process. "How could I know? No one told me!" Her thoughts jumbled. Cadoc, dead. Rhys, in agony. "So Ashem can't go after Cadoc because Rhys can't fight?"

Deryn laughed derisively. "Ashem can't go after Cadoc because Rhys is the *king*, and he cannot be risked to save a simple soldier."

The world reeled. She might have known Rhys was in pain on some deep level, but she hadn't known this. "Rhys is *what?*"

"*Y Ddraig Goch.* The Red Dragon. The King of Dragons.

The person who *should* have the power to completely control every dragon on earth." Deryn clenched her hands into fists and snarled, like she wanted to shake Kai but was resisting. "When Owain killed our father, the mantle ripped somehow. Each of them only has half. If Rhys dies, his part of the mantle —we assume—goes to me. I am the next closest blood heir. If Owain kills both of us, he gets the whole thing."

"But Cadoc...?"

"If we try to save Cadoc with Rhys half sworn like this, unable to fight, barely able to fly, he *will* die."

Kai's mind reeled. *Rhys is king. Save Cadoc. Rhys is king.* "What if I kiss Rhys and we're heartsworn? That would make him stronger, wouldn't it? Could you go after Cadoc then?"

Deryn seemed to deflate. Without anger, she was close to tears. "The Ironscale Vee will be here tomorrow, and Ashem said we'll see what we can do for him then. But if you think Cadoc's capture is the most important thing I've just told you, you're stupider than I thought. Rhys is the *king*, Kai."

Kai's mind flashed back to a conversation she'd had with Rhys days ago. *It's broken right now. Weak because it's torn between them. One king wants to maintain the status quo with dragons hidden from humans. The other wants to force dragons to commit human genocide.*

"Rhys is the good king," Kai said, wonder flooding her.

Deryn swiped at her watery eyes. "Yes. And Rhys won't be able to do anything without you. There's nothing either of you can do about it, so please just kiss him so he doesn't hurt anymore."

Kai opened her mouth, then closed it. Rhys was king. If she heartswore to Rhys, that would make her...

Kai blanched. "I—I didn't ask for this."

Deryn shot her a contemptuous, teary look. "And Rhys did? People don't ask for natural disasters or accidents or war, but

315

they happen. Things *happen*. Deal with it. Because if you can't, you're taking everyone down with you. I thought you should know."

Without another word, Deryn strode away down the hall. Kai watched her go, unable to move. Unable to think.

The sound of pounding feet echoed down the hall. Kai braced herself for Deryn's return.

"Kai!" Juli appeared. To Kai's surprise, Ashem trailed reluctantly after her, his hands in his pockets. "You will not believe what these idiots are hiding from you!"

Kai rubbed her face. "Try me." She tried to keep her voice light, but it came out sarcastic.

Juli turned suddenly to face Ashem, who hadn't spoken. "You shut up! He's an idiot. You both are."

Ashem grimaced, and Juli turned back. "Kai, he's their king. Rhys. The one who's heartsworn to you."

Kai barked a laugh. "Yeah, so I heard." She shifted her gaze to Ashem, and her voice went hard. "And I heard about Cadoc. Deryn told me."

Juli snorted at Ashem. "Clearly, Deryn is more intelligent than you."

"Then you know why I haven't gone after him." Ashem's face was a neutral mask, but to Kai's surprise, Juli's face softened. Then she seemed to realize what was happening, and her brows drew together again. "Stop that," she barked at Ashem. "I will not feel sorry for you."

"Feel what you want, Juliet King."

"Why do you use my entire name every time?" Juli snapped.

"Let me think." Kai twisted her finger through her carabiner tight, then tighter, until the metal bit into her flesh and it felt like her bones might break. Cadoc, she couldn't help. But Rhys could. If she saved Rhys, he could save everyone else.

All it would cost was her freedom. All it would cost was her life.

Juli tugged Kai's hands away from her carabiners and held them, eyes full of compassion. She pulled Kai into a tight embrace. "What are you going to do?"

Kai hugged her back, squeezing tight. Throw up. Jump into a wormhole that would erase her existence so Cadoc would be okay. Go home and hide under the covers. Tears burned the backs of her eyes, and she had to let Juli go before she lost it entirely. Kai's stomach dropped at the thought of home. Her family. Human genocide.

Rhys had wanted to give her a choice, but to believe she had one was a lie. If he'd told her everything, everyone could've avoided so much suffering.

Well, everyone except her.

She didn't want a man who was with her because of mating magic; she wanted a man who loved her.

What if she fell for Rhys and he never fell back?

Kai swallowed. On the grand scale of things, her and Rhys's love, or lack of it, didn't matter. "I'm going to go talk to him."

"Rhys?"

Kai was in luck. He was alone. He'd cleared a wide space on the top tier of the amphitheater where the hoard was kept, next to a rack of weapons. He stood facing away from her, shirtless. The bandages were gone. Daggers hung from both his white-knuckled fists. The muscles of his back heaved with every breath, and his skin glistened with sweat. He'd been pushing himself.

He bowed his head as she approached. Kai curled her fingers, her nails digging into her palms. Deryn's revelation beat against her skull. She wished she knew Rhys better. That he didn't frighten her sometimes. That she could trust him to be a friend, an ally, like he had been when Ashem confessed to bonding Juli last night. That she had some idea how her life might go.

She wished she could trust him enough to tell him how utterly unsuited she was to be queen.

She wished he knew her well enough to know he could have trusted her.

Finally, he turned to face her, looking confused at her presence. "Kai?"

His voice slid across her name like silk. The single syllable wrapped itself around so many meanings: a greeting, a *what are you doing here*, and beneath that, soul-deep yearning.

God, what a privilege it was to be woman who heard her name spoken like that.

"I spoke to Deryn. By which I mean she shouted all your secrets at me," Kai said.

He crossed the room before the daggers could clatter to the floor, eyes blazing. His fingers wrapped around her upper arms like gentle bands of steel, the skin of his palms a hair below painfully hot. His scent washed over her, wild and masculine with a hint of smoke. It rocketed along her nerves and made her want to bite her lip and breathe deep.

His gaze skimmed her, and his strong fingers feathered down her arms. "Did she hurt you?"

"No!" The memory of Rhys almost killing Cadoc made her say it louder than she meant to. Her face must have shown her fear, because the light in his eyes died. He closed them and turned away, running a hand through his hair before smoothing it again.

He was leaving. This wasn't how it was supposed to go.

"Rhys." Kai stopped him with a touch on his arm, and he froze. "You're in pain. You didn't tell me."

"I didn't want pity to be a factor in your choice."

"I don't really have a choice, though, do I?"

He was silent. Kai spoke again. "Me being in the room helps, doesn't it? And being close...touching?"

He gave a single, tight nod.

She licked her lips. "You should have told me who you are."

"What would I have said?"

Kai threw her hands into the air. "'Hey, Kai, I'm the only thing that stands between genocide and the human race' would have been nice."

He turned to face her, his brows arched in surprise. "You believe Deryn? Maybe she's lying. Trying to make you feel guilty so you'll swear to me."

Without breaking his gaze, she pressed her palm to his chest then pulled it away. Rhys gasped and then half succeeded at stifling a groan. The sound and the look on his face had her swallowing a sound of her own, her breath coming short.

"She's not lying," Kai whispered.

A muscle in his jaw jumped. As if he couldn't help himself, Rhys captured Kai's hand and pressed her palm flat against his heart again. His skin was heated, smooth, perfect. His smoky scent was everywhere. Awareness burned through Kai's body, warmth pooling low in her belly. He leaned into her touch, and she had to tilt her head back to keep eye contact. His face hovered over hers, eyes darkening. "All the more reason for her to tell you a tall tale about me being some last hope."

Kai tilted her chin up and splayed her fingers over his chest, like doing so would allow her to feel more of him. Take more of him in. Her voice was barely a breath. "So tell me it's not true."

His mouth curled in a derisive smile. "I have more reason to lie than she does."

"Then tell me it's not true," Kai bit out, harsher.

His smile faded. As if it took everything out of him, he said, "I can't."

I closed her eyes and let the truth of it wash over her. His heart was steady under her palm. He didn't let her go. Finally, she opened her eyes again. "I know about Cadoc too. That he's —" Her voice shook. "It's my fault. I'm sorry."

He stiffened at the sound of Cadoc's name, but then shook his head. "It's all of our faults."

Kai rubbed at the wetness that threatened to spill from her eyes with her free hand. "Why did you keep so much from me?"

"I wanted..." His jaw worked. "I wanted you to choose without anything forcing your hand."

Kai let out a frustrated breath. "Not very practical of you, Your Majesty."

Rhys sighed. "I've seen too many relationships based on obligation turn to poison, and that poison turn to intrigue that led to death."

Kai considered this. "Stuck between a rock and a hard place, then."

"Yes. But it would be a lie to say I didn't also want to be chosen for myself."

"You planned on heartswearing to a dragon. They would've known who you are and what it all means. And they wouldn't have been able to say no."

"But you aren't a dragon."

Kai tried not to wince, but the words stung, even if they were simply the truth. "Yes. I'm keenly aware of that." She paused, then said, "If I heartswear to you, can you go after Cadoc?"

"You would heartswear to me to save him?"

"Of course."

He flinched, then released her hand and stepped back. "But not when I needed you."

Even though he was less than two feet away, the gulf between them felt endless. "You aren't being held captive. You don't need to be saved."

He let out a hollow laugh. "Don't I?"

He turned and walked to the wall, then stopped and glanced around, like he didn't know what to do with himself but couldn't stand to look at her anymore. After a moment, he started to fiddle with the weapons on a rack. He was obviously planning to ignore her until she walked away.

Kai wanted to walk away. This conversation was awkward and terrible, and she'd never wanted to escape someone so badly in her entire life. But that wouldn't solve anything.

"Rhys!" He still didn't turn.

Kai marched over and inserted herself between him and the wall.

Mistake. She knew it as soon as he looked down, his surprised, electric gaze locking first on her eyes, then her lips. "What are you doing?"

"We aren't done talking."

"Fine." He lifted his hands and pressed his palms to the wall on either side of her, fencing her in. The scant inches of air between their bodies grew so hot Kai expected it to spark and steam. Her breath caught. Desire flared in her core. This close, he took up the world. He dipped his head close to hers and enunciated every letter when he said, "Speak."

Words fled as desire flooded her body, her mind, sharpened by the barest razor's edge of fear. "That kiss—" Her gaze fell to his lips. "—didn't mean anything. I never felt anything for Cadoc but friendship. I was afraid, and I did something terrible so that I could feel in control."

His voice was low and rough. "I don't blame you for wanting him. Cadoc is easy to talk to."

"Wanting Cadoc?" Kai flashed back to the feeling of Rhys's arms around her on the ledge. To waking up in his arms, soaked and shivering and safe from the river. To the first time he'd called her George.

"Rhys." Even now, Kai was battling the urge to arch her back, expose her neck, grab his hand and put it on her body the way he'd held her hand against his own heart moments ago. God, she wanted his hands on her. Could almost feel how good it would be. "Cadoc is gorgeous, funny, and kind, but he's never stopped my breath by saying my name."

He exhaled sharply, his head bowing like she'd just set a heavy weight on his shoulders. It brought his mouth even closer. So damn close.

"Rhys..." There was no other choice. "Kiss me."

His eyes widened and his head jerked back. "What?"

She licked her lips, telling herself she was ready and this was right. "Kiss me. I'll heartswear to you." She couldn't catch her breath. "As long as it's what you want, too."

He laughed, a sound so unexpected Kai jumped. "What I want?" He raised a hand to her face and traced the rough pad of his thumb along her cheek, his touch crackling along her every nerve. His eyes went hazy, and he brought his other hand to the back of her neck, sliding his fingers through her hair to cradle her head. "I want you like breath, Kai. Like sun. Like wind under my wings." He ran his thumb across her bottom lip. "I. Want."

He leaned down. Kai tried to be ready. She'd thought she was ready. But her body tensed. Panic blossomed. Tied to Rhys, who was still a stranger. Thrust into being queen of a people at war. Her breath came fast and shallow. She raised had a hand on his chest, and flexed her fingers, willing herself not to push him away.

Rhys froze, his mouth hovering an inch over hers. Their eyes locked, and she felt seared by the blue flames his.

Then he stepped back and turned his face away, refusing to meet her gaze. He closed his eyes and cursed beneath his breath.

Kai sagged. She felt like a balloon someone had blown up and then released, all the air going out of her at once. "What's wrong?"

A muscle in his jaw jumped, and she traced the movement down the taut lines of his neck to his chest and the rigid line of his shoulders. "You're still frightened half out of your mind. I want. You don't."

She pushed away from the wall. Her head spun with being so near him. Her body screamed that it was well past time to kiss him. Hell, it was past time for her to climb him like a tree and get out all of those dirty raccoon dumpster thoughts. "Rhys, this is inevitable. We might as well get it over with."

He pulled a long silver spear off the wall, hefting it. Kai waited.

Rhys tossed her the spear. Without thinking, she caught it. It was surprisingly light. Kai looked at him questioningly.

He took a staff from the rack of weapons. "We have tonight and tomorrow. Stay with me. We can get to know each other as well as we're able."

Kai didn't know what to say, and was uncertain if prolonging the inevitable was wise, or if it would make much of a difference in the end. But then again, maybe it would, and the fact that he was concerned enough to handle her fear with so much care made her heart twist. "I don't know how to use this."

"I'll teach you. You have so much pent up energy, George. I can feel it in you. Let's take the edge off and see where we are."

"What about heartswearing?"

Finally, he looked at her. She wasn't sure what to make of the expression on his face. Sadness, wariness, hope. "I want to make this as easy for you—for both of us—as possible. Maybe when the time comes, we'll both be less afraid. But for now? Let's get too tired to think."

Kai hesitated, then nodded, giving the spear an experimental twirl. A headache had started at her temples, pounding like distant drums. Cadoc was dead or being tortured. In the next twenty-four hours, she'd kiss Rhys and lose her old life forever.

"Not thinking for a while sounds good to me."

CHAPTER 38

RHYS

R hys taught Kai the first form of the spear, knowing how
short their time was. She memorized the dance-like
moves after two demonstrations, but they spent a couple of
hours practicing. He tried to keep his eyes on her hands and
feet, but, Stars, it was both pleasure and torture to watch the
way she moved, the way her long shirt clung to the curve of her
waist and hips and breasts.

Kai was unafraid to sweat. Graceful and agile, she could be
more than a passable fighter; she could be a warrior.

Not that it mattered. Wingless didn't fight.

She slammed the butt of the spear against the ground in the
final stance, breathing hard, and grinned at him. Perspiration
plastered inky wisps of hair to her forehead. Her cheeks were
rosy with exertion, her eyes bright beneath their fringe of black
lashes. She was so beautiful, so proud of herself, Rhys couldn't
help grinning back.

Kai relaxed and leaned the spear against the wall. "Can we
get some water?"

He nodded, absently tapping fingers against his chest. It

didn't hurt, exactly. Forms required hands-on teaching: adjusting her arm here, repositioning her foot there. His hands on her waist, her body cradled against him, her dark head level with the top of his chest.

"Let's go up."

Kai kept pace at his side. Despite how long they'd been working, she bounced like she had endless energy. "What's next? Another workout?"

The temptation to take her hand, or rest his on the small of her back, was so strong. He wanted a reason to touch her. She obviously liked physical activity, and there were so many ways to make her sweat. Ways to take the edge off. So many things they could do that didn't involve kissing her on the mouth.

They walked to the black cavern. The sky, visible through the archway, was dark and dusted with stars. No one else was around—Rhys assumed they'd all gone to bed. They went into the kitchen. Rhys got water and handed the full cup to Kai. Their fingers brushed, and a wave of heat coursed through him.

They took chairs across the table from each other, drinking in silence. After a minute, Kai set her empty cup on the table. A second later, she picked it up and rolled it between her palms. She was never still.

"I know all I've done since I arrived is ask questions. But I think, given the circumstances, there are a few more things I need to know." She studied the squatty brown cup like it was the most interesting thing she'd ever seen.

He examined the bottom of his own empty cup and rolled his shoulder. The scarred skin pulled, but the pain was gone. Aside from the burning in his chest, he was healed. "More?"

She seemed hesitant. "More about the war. About Owain. About you. All the things I didn't realize I needed to know before."

Rhys set down his cup, relief clashing with unease. It could only be a good sign that Kai wanted to hear the details, but it wasn't a story he enjoyed telling.

Her cheeks pinked. "Do you want me to sit next to you?"

Rhys tried not to groan in relief. "Yes."

She stood and moved around the table, settling in a chair next to him and dragging it as close as she could. They watched each other awkwardly for a moment. The space between their bodies seemed to shriek and pulse.

Kai gave him an uncertain smile. "Begin at the beginning, I guess. How did the war start?"

Rhys took a breath, settling back. "The story is a long one."

"In that case..." Kai leaned back and moved as if she'd put her feet in his lap. But she hesitated. "I still have my boots on. Is that okay?"

He swallowed. "You could take them off."

"We were just sweating."

Rhys pulled her booted feet into his lap and gingerly laid his hands along her calves, muscular and strong. "I don't care."

With Kai so near, the pain in his chest had gone to nearly nothing. Rhys cleared his throat and began the tale.

"More than a thousand years ago, my aunt, Rigani, was queen. She was quite a bit older than my father. I don't remember very much about her, except that she always used to give me sweets." He half smiled.

Kai smiled with him. "I assumed your father was king."

"He was, later." Rhys traced his fingers over her calves, trailing them up her boots, wishing he could touch her skin, reveling in the fact that even without being able to, she shivered at his touch. "But first, my aunt was queen. She had only one child, my cousin Owain. He's always been obsessed with magic, especially the artifacts the Ancients left behind."

"The ones who built this place," Kai said. "The ones Ashem is always cussing by."

327

Rhys chuckled. "Yes. Ancient dragons. True dragons, who didn't have the power to become human. But that's its own story. You wanted to know about the war."

Kai nodded.

Rhys continued. "Owain used to be a fire Draig, like Cadoc and me. Like my father. In his search to rediscover the powerful magic the Ancients used, Owain murdered a handful of dragons for their blood and scales. But the magic backfired. His powers inverted. Instead of creating heat, he could only take it away."

He looked up. Kai was silent, her eyes fixed on his face.

Rhys ran his hands over her calves again and continued, "Rigani was horrified when she heard what Owain had done. There have been so few dragons for so long that murder, especially in pursuit of power, is unforgivable. Without telling Owain, Rigani gathered our greatest mages and transferred the inheritance of the mantle from Owain to my father, her brother Ayen. In doing so, my father should have received the mantle upon my aunt's death.

"It didn't go as planned, though no one knew it until later. Like the artifacts, the mantle is magic of the Ancients. We're a fading race, and the secrets our people held during our peak are lost to time. According to my father, Queen Rigani meant to tell Owain that she'd transferred the inheritance of the mantle. But she never had the chance."

"Why? What happened?" Kai's expression was rapt. She was always so curious. So full of questions, and she listened so carefully to the answers. Rhys decided then that he loved telling her stories, even stories as tragic as this.

"She died."

Her eyes widened. "How?"

Rhys faltered. "Slaughtered by humans for sport. It happened, back when they knew of us."

328

Kai pulled her legs out of his lap and leaned forward, taking his hand, she opened her mouth to speak but paused as the electricity of the contact rolled through them both. When it passed, she said, "I'm sorry."

He shrugged with more nonchalance than he felt. "Dragons have killed greater numbers of humans for less purpose. Dragon–human history isn't peaceful."

"Oh." Kai's troubled expression deepened.

Rhys siphoned off the smallest bit of power inside him, spinning it into a ball of fire no larger than a robin's egg. He rolled it across his free palm and back again; his other hand was fully occupied with holding Kai's. "It's been better in the past millennium. Since dragons have been warring amongst ourselves, we've left humans alone. You've left us alone in turn. So much alone, in fact, that your people decided we never existed."

Kai pressed her lips together at that but didn't speak, watching the fire in his hand.

Rhys levitated the fire above his palm and called four more tiny flames into existence, pulling a few drops from the well of power he'd refilled that morning, setting them to orbit each other. "Owain accused my father of setting Rigani up—of bespelling her, killing her, and framing humans so that Ayen could take her power. Owain refused to believe that his own mother had disinherited him, no matter what he'd done.

"Owain left Eryri—the original Eryri, in the place you now know as Wales—and many dragons followed. They believed, as Owain did, that my father had stolen Owain's birthright and murdered Rigani. Another group broke off, declaring that they would follow neither. Today, they call themselves free dragons. My people—the people of Eryri—call them rogues. They scattered across the globe, some living in groups, most living in isolated families in the wilderness, or hiding among humans.

"And so, as I told you a few days ago, a third of the dragons stayed with my father, a third went with Owain, and another third swore they would follow no king and take no part in war.

"Owain stayed in exile for a few hundred years. We didn't hear much about him, except that as he grew older, his followers grew in number. Mostly from among the rogues, but some of my father's people defected as well. Still, Father didn't worry. Not the way he should have."

Kai squeezed his fingers, leaning in. It felt so natural, so *right*.

The fires over his other hand zoomed faster and faster, until they seemed to stretch and become lines of light. "Father seemed to forget about Owain. He had his own problems, the foremost of which was my mother, a Wingless woman named Mair. A woman he'd heartsworn against her will. She was unhappy, and he didn't treat her well. One day, my mother went missing. That night..."

Rhys's fingers curled into a fist, suffocating the fragile flames. "My father woke up in agony. Pain that makes even this pain look like nothing." Rhys traced fingers over his heart, lost in the past. "As the story goes, my mother hated my father so much that she went to Owain with a plan to kill him. Owain used his piece of the mantle—a piece that had gone to him despite his mother's intentions—to sunder my parents."

"Sunder? Another curse. But I don't know what that one means."

Rhys flipped their hands so his was on top and traced his fingers over the delicate skin of her wrist. "It means he broke their heartswearing."

Kai's eyes fluttered half closed as he continued to slowly stroke her wrist. "Ffion said there was a way."

"It can only be done by someone who holds the mantle. I

don't know how, but I think Owain needed something of them both to do it. A strand of hair, maybe. Or blood. Or tears.

"Before my father could recover fully, Owain attacked. My father was the only one who could fight Owain without being killed outright, because both controlled a part of the mantle. My father, his power being so much greater, should have beaten Owain easily. But he was too weak from the sundering, and Owain slaughtered him."

Rhys swallowed. The memories were still so vivid—the heavy air of the summer night, the roaring, the sounds of death, and then power unlike anything he'd ever imagined. "The instant my father died, I knew. In killing him, Owain gained a full half of the power of the mantle. I inherited the other half. We're perfectly matched."

Kai's eyes were still partially closed. She'd leaned in so close, if he dipped his head...

A few more hours. I can wait a few hours. He stared hard at the woodgrain of the table. It was far less tempting than her mouth.

"What happened to your mother? Did she die when your father died? Because she was Wingless?" she asked.

Rhys jerked one shoulder in a dismissive shrug. "I don't know. The Council claims she died, but everything was chaos. I don't know who killed her or what happened to her body. In all honesty, she was never much of a mother to me. Though I know Deryn misses her. I don't think Wingless die just because their mates do. As far as I know, even sundered, the Wingless retain their powers." He paused. "It changes you, Kai. Once you're Wingless, you're no longer human. You're a dragon with no dragon form."

"If—When I become Wingless, will the mantle have power over me?"

She sounded frightened of the idea. Rhys didn't blame her.

"No. Wingless are still not subject to the mantle's powers."

"So you're at war with Owain. He killed your father. Do you hate him?"

Rhys leaned back, surprised at the question. It took him a moment to find words. "No. I don't hate him. I don't even want to kill Owain. He's family. When I was a boy, he was like an older brother to me."

"He sounds sort of enthusiastic about killing you."

"Owain has always been very good about pursuing his goals," Rhys said drily.

"But he can't use his part of the mantle on you, can he? He can't just command you to walk into the ocean or something. And he has no power over someone you've already commanded not to listen to his orders."

"Correct."

"So what's the point of the mantle at all?"

Rhys laughed without mirth. "As of now, I try not to use it unless absolutely necessary. Ultimate power has never sat well with me. Some think I'm a weak king. But my father used it too freely. When all these things happened, dragons who might have supported him went rogue or followed Owain, who promised to control them less."

"You're a weak king for not using it, but people followed Owain because he promised to not use it?"

Rhys shrugged. "Politics. And really, those are two different groups of people."

Kai rolled her eyes. "That would drive me insane. I'd be tempted to use it just to get people to shut up."

"That is the greatest temptation, certainly. But that much power is heady. Seductive. It's better to let it lie unless you absolutely cannot." He didn't tell Kai that he didn't use the mantle because he was afraid. Afraid of becoming his father, who had been obsessed with control. Or Owain, obsessed with using the mantle for vengeance.

Rhys shook his head to clear his thoughts and went back to the story.

"Ashem got us out: my vee, Deryn and I. Deryn didn't have a vee yet, she was too young. So she came with us. Ashem, though he wasn't much older than us, kept us alive and helped me make alliances. The Mo'o of the South Pacific took us in, and we moved Eryri to an archipelago in the middle of the ocean—as far from Owain's stronghold in the north as we could get."

Kai was stroking his wrist now too. It felt good, as if energy and comfort flowed from her skin into his. She was intoxicating. Even just her hands—the silky, scarred skin on the back, the rough calluses on her palm, won in battle after battle against gravity and stone, the delicate but strong tendons in her wrists. He could spend hours learning those hands. Centuries learning the rest of her.

Silence settled between them, and Rhys broke it before it could become awkward. "So that's why there's war."

Kai was frowning, distractedly running her fingers over his palm now. It sent electricity and heat all the way through him. He should ask her to stop, but he wouldn't be able to bear it if she did.

"I know I asked, but that's—I mean, Rhys, it's a lot. War and death and revenge. It's for stories. Heroes. It's not something for people like me. I'm just...normal. I shouldn't be trusted with world-breaking decisions."

Rhys squeezed her hand. "It's normal people—people who want nothing but peace, family, and happiness—who die because some idiot wanted some grand thing." Rhys thought of his people, who would pay the price for Owain if Rhys failed.

"It's normal people who fight the fiercest, having those things to defend."

She drew a troubled breath and let it out slowly. "And you can't stop, can you? Because Owain... He's after a grand thing. The elimination of humans. The only thing stopping him is that you hold half the mantle. And he doesn't dare start a war with the humans without every single dragon he can get, but they won't all fight for him unless he can force them to."

Rhys nodded. "Though if I die, my half of the mantle passes to Deryn. He'd have to kill both of us to get all of it."

Kai frowned. "What about your other sister? The one who can see the future?"

"No. Being the Seeress prevents Seren from holding the mantle."

Kai laid her head on his shoulder. "What I said is still true, though. You and Deryn are the only things stopping Owain from killing everyone. What you're fighting for is the normal thing. Peace. Family. Happiness."

"Yes. Which is why when I fight Owain, he won't win." Rhys cupped Kai's cheek and used a thumb to hook a strand of black hair behind her ear. "It's why I think he wouldn't stand a chance against either of us."

Kai's cheeks flushed. She took a breath, as if to speak, but feet scuffed on the stone floor. Rhys looked up to see Ffion, who winked at him before taking a bowl of leftover dinner from the shelves that kept them magically cool, then ducked out of the kitchen and disappeared into the darkness.

Rhys sighed and dropped his hand. "It's late, Kai. You should sleep."

Kai smiled. "*We* should sleep. You're looking kind of sickly."

"I am not sickly."

Kai snorted. "Okay. You're strong and impressive." She yawned.

Reluctantly, Rhys stood and pulled her to her feet. He didn't want to let go of her hand, nor did he look forward to another night of pain and sleeplessness—he couldn't bring himself to take Ashem's drug again, no matter how much his eyes felt like sand.

She tugged his hand. "Come on."

He followed her into the cavern, where he saw not one figure, but two. Griffith and Ffion together on watch. Griffith sat in the center of the archway, just inside. Ffion leaned against him, munching on the food she'd retrieved. When she noticed them, Griffith turned as well.

If they noticed Rhys and Kai's linked hands, neither of them commented. Out loud, anyway.

"Griff," Rhys whispered.

"Mm?" Griffith rumbled.

"Go to bed. You and Ffion."

"We have to keep watch," Ffion whispered back.

"Let Ashem do it. He's probably just sitting in the hall pining after Juli anyway. The two of you deserve a night together."

Ffion smirked.

Griffith's smile was white in the dark, but his words, as always, were quiet. "If you're sure?"

"I am."

Griffith took Ffion's hand, and they stole away together into the hall. A few seconds later, a grumpy-looking Ashem appeared, glared at Rhys, then stood outside on the ledge.

They walked to the hall outside Kai's room. She lingered, as if she didn't want this—their conversation, their time together—to end. "I suppose we should say goodnight."

"I suppose we should," he echoed.

He didn't want it to end. He didn't want to be apart from her, even if it only meant she was down the hall.

Kai hesitated, then said, "Unless we just...don't."

Rhys froze. The moment balanced on a razor's edge. He didn't want to say the wrong thing. Didn't want to do anything that might make her change her mind, that might scare her away. Finally, he managed, "What should we do instead?"

Kai's cheeks turned a deep rose pink, but she lifted her chin. "We can go to your room."

"My room?"

She nodded. "Yeah. And...sleep."

"Sleep?"

The pink deepened. "I'm laboring under the assumption that unless we're ready to heartswear, that's all we can do."

Rhys's blood heated, and his voice came out a rough whisper. "The only thing that will complete the heartswearing is a kiss on the mouth."

Kai frowned. "That's strange. It seems like it should have to do with the exchange of bodily fluids."

"It's magic. Symbolism, not science."

"Hm."

"About the...sleeping."

"You think it's a bad idea?"

Rhys searched her face, searching for any sign that he should say yes. Any hesitation or look of fear on her part. He saw none. "I want you in my bed, Kai. I don't want to be apart from you."

Kai released a slow, unsteady breath. "Is it only because of being heartsworn?"

"No." Rhys reached out and tucked a stray strand of black hair behind her ear, savoring the softness of her skin. "I wanted you before. Since the first day here."

"Oh." The word was a soft exhale. Kai looked down at

herself. "I smell. I am going to shower. I'll meet you in your room in twenty minutes. Don't fall asleep."

Rhys only smelled what he ever did from her, sweetness and warm spice, but if she was cleaning up, it would give him time to do so, as well. "I won't."

Kai grinned and slipped into her room. Rhys washed in the small bathroom at the far end of the hall, the time passing torturously as he imagined Kai in her own shower, water sluicing over her skin, dripping over her breasts, sliding between her legs.

"Fuck," he muttered, wiping water from his eyes.

Were they just going to sleep?

Rhys returned to his room. Time stretched, and he was sure she'd changed her mind.

Then there was a soft knock on his door.

CHAPTER 39
KAI

Kai spent her shower debating what to do, weighing it all, trying to consider everything about her situation from every angle. What was smart? What was best? What was the most responsible?

"Fuck it," she growled, and turned off the water. "Fuck it all."

The reality was, they liked each other. They wanted each other. He was a goddamned dragon. A goddamned *king*. And he seemed like a good man. There were worse fates.

She was going to his bed.

When she knocked, Rhys opened the door wearing nothing but a pair of gray sweatpants riding low on the deep V of his hips. The usual white fires that lit the room were out. In their place, he'd lit a small fire in the fireplace.

The warm light played lovingly across the sculpted lines of his muscles, glimmering gold in the crimson swirls of the indicium that disappeared tantalizingly beneath his waistband. He smiled, huge and genuine, and it stole the thoughts from Kai's head, the breath from her lungs.

Wordlessly, he reached out. She put her hand in his. He pulled her inside and led her to his huge, luxurious bed.

He helped her in, then climbed in after her. Kai slid between the dark silk sheets, Rhys's wild, increasingly familiar smell closing around her.

Technically, they'd done this before, when he warmed her up after she fell in the river.

So many things had changed in so little time.

Kai thought the moment would be awkward, but Rhys settled on his back and lifted his arm, and it was the most natural thing in the world to slip into the offered space, cuddle against his side and tangle her legs with his.

As soon as she touched him, it was like Rhys's entire body unwound, relaxed, and melted into the bed. "Kai. You feel so good."

His voice was fervent, almost desperate. Heat rolled through Kai's body. "I haven't done anything."

"You don't have to," he murmured. He turned toward her, cradling her against him, slipping a knee between her thighs, and brushing his knuckles from her neck up to her cheek. "Just touching you is paradise."

"So now we...sleep?" Kai grinned and lifted her nose to nuzzle hot, sensitive skin just below the corner of his jaw and was rewarded with a groan from Rhys that rumbled through his chest.

Rhys captured her hand in his and pulled it to his lips, placing a biting, open mouthed kiss below her thumb that had Kai gasping at the heat and wetness and sharp edge of almost-pain.

He exhaled, warm breath unsteady against her palm. "If you want to sleep, I'll hold you, and be still, and treasure every blessed second until dawn. If you want me to touch you in a way that is purely comfort, I'll rub your back or play with your hair or stroke the perfect skin of your face, your hands, your arms until you tell me to stop. If you want pleasure... I swear, Kai, I'll make you feel so unspeakably good, and hold you while you come apart in my arms, and then if you let me, I'll do it again."

Kai's lips parted, her breath coming fast and shallow. "Shouldn't we both feel good?"

He closed his eyes and kissed her palm again. This time, it was feather-light, right in the center. "If you put your hands on me, I don't know if I could stop myself from claiming you. I want the moment it happens to be your choice. But if you let me bring you pleasure, I promise to take mine in my own way."

She turned the hand he was kissing so that her fingers interlaced with his, and pulled his hand to her chest, the heel of his palm pressed to her racing heart, his callused fingertips brushing her collarbone and the base of her neck. Immediately, he curled, then extended them again, stroking her skin.

Even just that small contact was so good, it sent sparks all through her body. Her breasts ached. Need flared and grew insistent between her legs.

"Make me feel good, Rhys. Touch me."

The fire was low enough now to leave them in near-darkness, and his eyes, never leaving hers, luminesced starfire blue.

Rhys's hands went to her waist, and the next thing Kai knew, he'd flipped them so he was beneath her and she straddled his hips. He was hard, and his erection pressed against her right where she wanted it. She moaned and couldn't help moving against him.

Rhys shifted, lifting his hips into her, and let out a satisfied sound. Kai was wearing a loose-cropped shirt and pajama shorts borrowed from Ffion. The shirt left a strip of her belly exposed, and the way Rhys had positioned her rucked the shorts all the way up her thighs.

"If we do this, I am in control. I won't kiss you. I won't take off any of my clothes. We won't go further than touching. If you tell me to stop, I'll stop. That's the word you use, Kai. 'Stop.' Otherwise, I'm going to touch you, explore you, make you whimper and moan and cry out my name at my leisure. That's what's going to make me feel good. Do you understand?"

Breathless, Kai nodded.

"Say it."

"Yes. I understand."

"Good." He ran his hands along the exposed skin on the outside of her thighs, palms flat and fingers splayed as if he wanted every iota of contact he could get. He continued up over the shorts to her bare waist and under the hem of her shirt, until he held her just below her breasts, his thumbs stroking back and forth over her ribs. "Take this off."

In her days here, Kai hadn't heard Rhys issue many commands. Compared to Ashem, he was laid back. A man who brought people into his way of thinking instead of forcing them there.

But holy shit, when he wanted to take control, he took it.

Tentatively, Kai reached for the hem of her shirt, then pulled it up and over her head. She wasn't wearing a bra, so the move exposed her small breasts.

Rhys swore in a language she didn't understand. The blue of his eyes was a thin ring around the blackness of pupils blown wide with desire, his gaze fixed on her pebbled, pale pink nipples.

"You are perfect," he breathed.

Heat rose in Kai's cheeks. She wasn't exactly shy, but the intensity of his stare made her self-conscious. "Perfect is pushing it. There's not much going on there."

His eyes broke from her chest just long enough to meet hers. "Perfect," he growled. Achingly slowly, he shifted his hands upward so his thumbs brushed the curve of the under-side of her breasts.

Kai forgot to be nervous. Her eyes drifted closed and her head lolled back as he touched her again, higher, until he grazed the hard peaks.

Pleasure jolted through Kai like lightning, and she cried out, jerking her hips forward. With her sex pressed against his, the motion set off another burst of pleasure in her body.

"Rhys," she gasped, bracing her hands on the hard ridges of his abdomen.

If anything, he seemed more captivated by her pleasure. Slowly, deliberately, he ran his thumbs over her nipples again. Already, that spot between her legs felt twisted almost painfully tight. It had been so long since she'd been touched this way, and she wanted him so much, it would take ridiculously little for him to send her careening over the edge and flying into ecstasy.

As if he could sense it, he slid his hands down her back and grabbed her waist again, this time flipping them so that she was on her back and he was braced over her. "Not yet."

Kai slid her hands up his chest and cupped his face. He was so unbelievably beautiful. "It's not my fault you're so good at this."

He gave her that wicked half-smile, then dipped his mouth to place a line of biting kisses down her neck, then between her breasts. Kai shifted, searching for contact where she needed it.

Rhys kissed lower, until he was at her belly button, then the waistband of her shorts before he moved back upward. When he got to her chest this time, he captured one of her nipples in his mouth.

Kai cried out and arched at the sudden, sharp pleasure that zinged straight from her nipple to her core. Rhys settled his body between her parted legs, cupping her other breast, squeezing it, toying with the sensitive peak as he sucked and licked the other, then pulled back just far enough to blow cold air over it.

"Rhys!" His name tore from her mouth, a plea. But he was merciless. When she tried to squirm, he pinned her hips in place with his free hand and went right back to torturing her with his mouth, switching from one breast to the other and back again.

Rhythmic whimpers escaped her. Kai might not be a virgin, but she wasn't *that* experienced. She'd never felt anything like this. The need for friction between her legs was a looming wall that threatened to crush her.

Rhys shifted so that he was on top of her. His weight pinned her to the bed. His mouth went to the place her shoulder met her neck, spreading more kisses over her heated skin. Kai cried out as the ridge of his cock pressed into her sex again, sending building little waves rolling through her as she arched up and he finally let her grind against him.

"Rhys, please. Please!"

"Almost," he murmured against her ear, gently taking her earlobe in his teeth. "You're doing so good, Kai. You can take more."

Half out of her mind with pleasure already, Kai wasn't sure she could.

Rhys's arm went around her waist, and he shifted their positions again. This time, he was mostly beneath her, and she lay on her back, sprawled on top of him.

Kai whimpered at the loss of friction again as Rhys cupped her breasts in both hands and worked them until Kai was thrusting her hips uselessly into the air.

Then finally, blessedly, one hand slipped down over her abdomen, teased her waistband, and then his big, capable hand was in her shorts.

He cupped her sex, then delved one finger into her folds.

Kai cried out as he found her clit and stroked it once, then twice, then started making tiny circles. Her legs fell open, and she pressed back against his bare chest.

"Does that feel good?"

"Yes," she whispered. "But I need..."

Kai wasn't sure how to tell him what she wanted. She wanted to feel full. Penetrated. Claimed.

Like he could read her mind, Rhys's fingers slipped downward and circled her entrance. Then he slid his middle finger inside.

Kai gasped and arched so hard her back lifted from his chest.

Rhys bent his head and lightly bit her shoulder, his other hand rolling her nipple between his fingers as he slowly drew his finger out of her body and then pushed it back in again.

Her eyes were open, but she felt like she couldn't see the room anymore. Couldn't hear anything but the rush of her own blood and Rhys's harsh breathing. She lost the capacity to do anything but feel all of the ways he touched her, pleased her.

He added a second finger, and the added fullness brought her so close to the edge Kai almost cried. "Please, Rhys. Please."

"Come for me," he growled in her ear.

At the same time, he rolled her nipple, thrust his fingers into her, and pressed down on Kai's clit with his thumb.

She exploded. She'd never had an orgasm like this before. Not in her limited experience with other partners, nor her much more extensive experience with herself and various toys. It gripped her by the throat and rode her in wave after wave of mind-melting ecstasy. She screamed Rhys's name, moaned it, whimpered it.

Finally, the pleasure ebbed. Kai collapsed back onto Rhys,

boneless. He rested his palm over her breast. He stopped circling her clit, but kept his fingers inside her.

Kai didn't care. With him touching her like this, she felt possessed by him. Claimed in a way no one else had ever claimed her. She wasn't in a hurry to let that feeling go.

At length, Rhys finally slipped his fingers from her body. Instead of wiping them off, he put them in his mouth and sucked every drop of her off of them.

"Good?" he asked.

"Good."

She snuggled closer, and he held her. She reveled in the feeling of her body, wrung out and boneless. She also reveled in the feeling of his, so hard and strong and wrapped around her.

Kai closed her eyes, and for the first time since discovering dragons, she drifted off easily, unafraid, wondering if this might work.

Tomorrow, she was going to kiss him. She'd do it now if she wasn't so damn tired.

She was no longer afraid.

CHAPTER 40

CADOC

C adoc wished for death, but it didn't come. He gritted his teeth against a moan as feeling returned to his shattered right hand. Even after days of torture, he'd felt nothing like it. The *wrongness* of bones splintered into flesh, healing where they shouldn't. His fingers and the top half of his palm were a swollen, twisted mass, though his thumb was still intact. Where skin was visible through the dried blood, it was purple and black. In some places, bones were visible. He pressed his face into the dusty stone floor and screamed.

He could hear movement and voices above, but no one came for him. Finally, the agony from his hand, the torture, and days without food or sleep got the better of him. He blacked out.

He flickered in and out of consciousness, awakening once to realize that the normal scuff and rumble that signified the occupation of the cave above had stopped. It was silent for a long time, then the voices were back. The horrible, cold *slap* of the ladder hitting the stone floor of his prison jerked him awake. His tongue was parched and swollen, his vision blurred.

"Just kill me," he rasped, more a plea than a command. Unbidden, tears leaked from his eyes. *I won't tell. I won't tell. I won't tell.* He'd chanted the words so often in the past days they'd almost become meaningless.

"Cadoc?"

A feminine voice, but soft, nothing like Izel's sultry growl. It plucked at the back of his brain. He opened his eyes. A ball of golden fire hovered at her shoulder, throwing her features into shadow. Cadoc turned away from the bright light.

"*Bachgen gwael,*" she murmured, placing a cool, dry hand on his forehead. *Poor boy.* "What have they done to you?"

Cadoc shuddered at the kind touch, blinking until the shadows on her face formed themselves into features.

"Deryn?" Ancients, please, no more illusions.

Her hand froze. He coughed, and she smoothed back his hair. "No, not Aderyn."

"Aderyn...?" The coughing stopped, and he blinked away the tears. She was older than Deryn, more dignified. Her features were soft instead of sharp, and her long auburn hair was streaked with gray. The clothes she wore—a simple belted tunic and high boots—were of expensive fabric, but cut in a way humans hadn't worn for over a thousand years. Besides, Deryn couldn't make fire. Not like—

He jerked away from her, horrified. "Mair!" But it couldn't be. She was dead. It was nothing but an illusion. He croaked a laugh.

She withdrew a little, her eyes full of pain. "Why do you laugh?"

"Once, shame on you. Twice, shame on me. Thrice, I'm an idiot. I'm an idiot anyway, but I'm not falling for this again. I don't understand the choice of illusion. Lady Warbringer—"

She bared her teeth and hissed, "Don't you *dare* speak that name in my hearing, Cadoc ap Brychan. Not when I'm here to set you free."

Cadoc laughed again. He felt dangerously close to insane.

"Enough!"

The tone was so familiar, Cadoc's mouth snapped shut automatically.

She flipped long hair behind one shoulder and gave him a stern glare. "Do you remember the last time I saw you?"

"I remember the last time I saw Mair."

"Don't be impertinent. The last time I saw you, I smacked you good with a wooden spoon for eating all my blueberries."

Cadoc blinked. "I... You were going to bake a tart." And no one else had known. He and Rhys had snuck into the kitchen while the others were all out training.

She nodded. "And my *son* was supposed to be your lookout, was he not? It seems he takes no better care of you now than he did when you were younger."

It was why they'd never told anyone. Rhys had been ashamed that he'd left Cadoc behind to take the punishment alone, and Cadoc hadn't been particularly keen on everyone knowing he'd been walloped by his best friend's mother.

All humor left him. If this really was Mair, there was nothing funny about it. "Owain makes war and hunts your children because of you, and you don't even have the decency to be dead like the Council said. Fuck me. First Uwan, now this. Maybe I'm the one who's dead."

Mair's face tightened. "The Council lies. *They* banished me when Ayen died. *They* wouldn't let me come home. They sent assassins to kill me, so I hid. I've been hiding. Watching. Waiting." For a moment, her face paled. "The night the heartswearing broke, I was in so much pain I hardly knew what was happening. I couldn't help Ayen when Owain attacked." Her gaze went distant.

Cadoc had hardly known what was happening either. Ashem had burst into their room, overturning Griffith's bed when he didn't get up fast enough. They'd been youths, but Cadoc had killed for the first time that night. Later he'd held Rhys back with bloody hands as Ayen's dying scream pierced their brains. He'd still been holding Rhys as the power of the mantle washed over him and his friend went from boy to king.

"Cadoc?"

His head gave a hard throb, and he took an unsteady breath. A strange, dizzy coldness had washed over him at the thought of Rhys, and he couldn't seem to shake it.

"Cadoc? *Bach?* How badly are you hurt?"

When he didn't answer, Mair, if it really was her, reached into her pocket and pulled out a water bottle. Light from the fire glittered off the translucent scales that spiraled over the back of her left hand. They shone iridescent in the dim light, at once all colors and none.

She took a small vial from a different pocket and dumped it in the water bottle. "Drink. It will take away your pain for an hour or so. You'll need to be able to fly."

Cadoc didn't resist when she lifted his head and put the bottle to his lips. He didn't care if what she'd put in it was poison. Glorious, cool wetness hit his tongue, and he drank, relishing the feeling of the water as it slid down his throat.

It wasn't poisoned, however, which surprised him, considering his luck. Whatever painkiller Mair had put in, its effect was instantaneous, like fire in his veins. He drank the bottle dry, then rose unsteadily. She hadn't noticed his hand, and he cradled it against his body to hide it from her.

"Put these on. Your clothes are rags." She handed him a bundle of clothes, then went to the ladder and looked up, speaking to whoever was above.

He hesitated. It could still be Owain, still be a trick.

But it could also be his only chance.

Using his good hand, Cadoc eased the shirt over his head, grateful for the painkiller as some of his deeper cuts broke open and bled. He got his torn, bloodied pants off all right, but it took some work to get the new ones on one-handed. Finally, he managed. "I'm ready." He wondered if his voice would ever sound normal again.

Mair nodded her approval. "Let's go." She indicated the rope ladder. Cadoc limped over. He put his good hand on the rung level with his face, then stood there, numb.

"Go on," Mair urged.

Cadoc let go of the ladder and turned to her, revealing his right hand. Mair glanced down and gasped. "Oh, *bach*."

"Do you have a way to take off these sundering chains?" Cadoc asked through gritted teeth. They'd embedded in the skin in places.

Wide eyes never leaving his mangled hand, she nodded. "We got a key off one of the guards."

Shaking, she reached over his maimed fingers and pressed an intricately carved piece of quartz into an indentation in the cuff. It clicked open. With a sickened look on her face, Mair reached down into her boot and pulled out a small knife.

Cadoc's stomach turned at the sight of the knife. "How did you find me? How did you even know to look?"

"Let's just say I have a friend you might not expect. Tell me, do you have any magic?" Mair held out the blade.

"Scraps." Cadoc took it. He hesitated, licked his lips, then sliced the skin that had healed over the fine chains and peeled them out, grateful for the numbing effects of the painkiller. He held up his left hand, and Mair unlocked that cuff. The chains slid off easily. She secreted both binders into a pocket.

"You go first," she said. "I'll hold the ladder steady. It will be easier that way."

Cadoc nodded, realizing it would be this way from now on. He'd lost a hand. He wasn't a warrior; he definitely wasn't a bard. He was a liability and a burden.

It took him long minutes and a hard struggle to make his way up the unsteady ladder. Mair's weight on the bottom helped, but he was seven inches taller and a few dozen pounds heavier than her. He panicked for a moment when, at the top of the ladder, three pairs of hands reached down to haul him out.

"Relax," Mair said, climbing up in less than a quarter of the time it had taken Cadoc. "They're with me." She took something from a stocky, bowlegged Quetzal woman whose nose had been broken at least twice. "Penelope, was there trouble?"

Another woman, a tall, beautiful Derkin with olive skin and soft eyes, answered, "No. Everything went as planned."

The last woman, a mousy, nondescript Draig with a silver indicium, nodded.

Penelope grinned and swept her gaze down Cadoc's body. "I bet you're pretty when you haven't been beaten to a pulp."

He smiled, his dry bottom lip cracking. "Pretty as a song."

"Cadoc, Tlalli is a healer," Mair indicated the Quetzal woman with the broken nose. "We need to get you somewhere safe so she can inspect your wounds.

But he was already backing away. "No. I'm grateful to you for coming to my rescue. But I'm afraid I've got to fly. Owain... He knows where the cave is, or close enough. I've got to get to them before he does."

Mair, who had been inspecting the object the Quetzal handed her, slipped it into her pocket. "He does? Then yes, it's urgent you get back to Rhys. I would come with you, but my hold on power is tenuous, for now. But when I heard Owain had you, I couldn't let this chance pass."

That strange coldness flooded him at the mention of Rhys's name again. "I..."

Mair put a hand on his arm and glanced at the others. "Wait here. I'd like to talk to him alone."

They nodded, and Mair led Cadoc through a tunnel to the outside. He put a hand over his eyes, blinking in the bright light, still reeling in disbelief. Daylight. He was free. Mair was alive. It had to be a dream, an illusion. But when his eyes focused, he saw the bodies of two dead guards on either side of the cave.

"What happened to them?" Cadoc asked.

Mair smiled. "We did. Izel escaped, but we cut two from Owain's number."

Nausea roiled through his stomach at the thought of his torturer still alive. "I don't have time to talk. I have to get to them."

She grabbed his arm. "*Bach—*"

Cadoc shrugged her off. "Don't call me that. I'm not a child."

She shook her head, tendrils of auburn falling into her face. Age had made her no less beautiful. "I'm sorry, it's how I still see you in my mind. All of you. But I wanted to ask about Aderyn."

"What about her?"

Mair frowned. "Is she all right? Has she grown tall? A mother shouldn't be away from her daughter so long."

"You have two daughters, Queen Dowager."

She sighed. "Seren was never truly mine. The Council took her from me the day she was born, flame the lot of them. I suspect you know her better than I ever did."

Cadoc's thoughts drifted to Seren. Impatient, he pulled them away. "Aderyn is well. She's sarcastic and makes Rhys do all the cooking. You'd be proud." The foggy cold washed over him again, and he shook his head to clear it.

Mair smiled. "I am proud. I have a message I need you to

carry. Tell my children I'm alive. Tell them I can help. I won't see Owain take the throne and the mantle from my flesh and blood."

Cadoc nodded, his injured hand once again held close to his body. "I will. And I have to go. Rhys isn't..." Dizziness. "They'll need me."

"Wait! He isn't what? Is he injured?"

Cadoc shook his head. "When I left he was... There was a girl..." Why was he telling her this? He shouldn't be talking.

Mair grabbed Cadoc's arm again, her voice sharp. "He's heartsworn?"

Cadoc couldn't stop himself from answering. "He is, but she's not. At least, she wasn't. I have to go."

Ancients, he was tired.

"She's human?" Mair's voice was flat. "He'll force her. He's just like his father."

Cadoc frowned. "Neither of them have a choice. If he dies or goes mad, we're all at Owain's mercy."

She snorted. "What's the girl's name?"

Cadoc closed his eyes for a moment, his thoughts blurring. "Kai."

"Kai." Mair smiled. "Heartsworn to a human girl. Like father, like son." She laughed a little, deep in her throat. "The Council will be thrilled. Now, go to him. Perhaps you'll be in time to stop a tragedy."

Cadoc nodded. "Thank you."

"Wind carry you well." She put a hand on his shoulder, then walked back into the cave.

Cadoc called his fire. For a moment, nothing happened. Icy terror trickled down his spine. He inhaled, fighting for calm, and tried again.

Fire flared around him, and this time, he became the dragon. Holding his shattered right foreclaw off the ground, he opened his wings and threw himself into the air. He was exhausted enough to lie down and never move again, but rest would have to wait. He had to warn Rhys.

Ignoring another flash of numbing cold through his mind, Cadoc glanced back.

He was alone.

CHAPTER 41

KAI

K ai crouched near the bed, considering the best way to wake Juli without getting pummeled. Juli gave a particularly loud snore. Kai sighed and wondered how late she'd been up speaking with Ashem. Since yesterday, when Juli had gone to see him, there had been a definite shift in their chemistry.

Kai flipped the covers off her friend and leaped backward.

Slap! The sound of a hand against the mattress where Kai's head had been only seconds before.

"Ouch!"

Kai sniggered. Juli opened one eye and kicked at her. Kai smacked her leg, then Juli grabbed her and dragged her onto the mattress. The wrestling match devolved into a slap fight, and for the second time in days, Kai ended up on the floor in a swamp of bedding. Except this time Juli's bony elbow was poking her in the thigh.

"Stoppit!" Juli groaned, then face-planted into the pile of blankets. "It's too early."

Kai poked Juli in the side. "You're supposed to be annoyingly chipper in the a.m. Late night?"

357

Juli sat up. Her short blonde hair stood out at crazy angles, at odds with the prim eyebrow she arched at Kai. "Not as late as you, seeing as you never came back. Are you heartsworn?"

Heat rose in Kai's cheeks at the memory of Rhys. His hands on her body, the way he took control. She cleared her throat. "No. Being partially heartsworn causes him pain unless I'm close to him. He can't sleep. I thought it would be nice for him to get a full night's rest, so I stayed with him."

"In his bed?"

"Yes."

Juli took in Kai's blush and scoffed. "Right. I'm sure the two of you did *so* much sleeping."

"We did enough."

Juli scoffed again.

"How much not-sleeping did *you* do?" Kai retorted.

Juli made a noise of disgust. "I am not going to dignify that with an answer. He did inform me yesterday that the other dragons are supposed to arrive by tonight, which means he's busy. Thank goodness. It's keeping him out of my head at the moment."

Kai had been feeling good, if nervous, about what she needed to do today. At the mention of Ashem being in Juli's head, the one fear she hadn't been able to put to rest returned. "That's good, right?"

Juli nodded, but she seemed distracted. "Kai... I know you're going to heartswear to Rhys today. I want to tell you not to do it. I want to tell you to run. But, assuming all of this isn't a drug-induced delusion, I've seen Ashem's memories. Dragons live so long, most of them remember a time when they were the dominant species on the planet. Many of them want that back. With Rhys out of the way, Owain would be a step closer." She hesitated, then added delicately, "Though, if you can't bear to do this, just remember, there's still his sister. If Rhys dies, his half of the mantle goes to Deryn."

Kai, who was in the process of disentangling herself from the sheets one limb at a time, stopped and stared at Juli. "Wow. That's cold, Jules."

Juli looked away and shrugged one shoulder. "You're my friend. He's not."

Finally free of the blankets, Kai straightened. "I'm doing this. I just want to talk to Ffion. I'll be back in a little while." She just had a few final questions about heartswearing.

Juli rose. "I'm coming with you. I wouldn't mind learning more about this heartswearing nonsense. Just let me get dressed."

Kai frowned. Had she told Juli why she wanted to talk to Ffion? She must have.

Once Juli was ready, Kai led the way to the room Ffion shared with Griffith. Ffion greeted them at the door and let them in, saying Griffith was sparring with Rhys and Ashem.

This room had been carved with rivers and waterfalls and water creatures. Ffion showed Juli and Kai to two things that were not chairs in front of the fireplace, then settled onto a third. It was like a short couch that swooped up on one side.

"Are these Roman reclining couches?" Kai asked.

Ffion nodded. "I've always preferred them. Old habits. Don't believe what human historians say about them just being for the men."

Juli lay gracefully on hers, propping herself up on one arm as if ancient Roman furniture was part of her daily life. Kai just sat on hers.

"So... I know we haven't talked much in the past few days," Kai began.

Ffion gave an elegant one-shouldered shrug. "It's understandable."

"Right. Anyway, I know about Rhys. There are things you tried to tell me that night about heartswearing. I'm sorry I didn't listen. I was hoping you would tell me now. What do I need to know?"

Ffion sat up a little. "Of course." She tapped her lips with her fingers. "Well, first, there's the magic. Juli, perhaps you've noticed?"

Juli kept her mouth shut and her expression neutral.

"What magic?" Kai turned to Juli.

Ffion sat up farther, her voice taking on a lecturing tone. "When a human becomes heartsworn to a dragon, they're changed. They aren't truly human anymore, but a dragon without a dragon body. Therefore, Wingless. As Wingless, you have the same magic as your mate. So, Juli, you're probably able to hear the thoughts of those around you. Kai, if or when you heartswear to Rhys, you will be able to manipulate heat and fire."

Kai opened her mouth. Closed it. Turned, blinking, to Juli. "Have you been reading my mind?"

Juli shrugged. "It isn't very strong. Impressions. A gut feeling about what's on someone's mind. Nothing I'd call mind reading."

"It will be weak at first, but you have the same raw potential as Ashem, if not his precision. Your power should develop fully in anything from a few days to a few months, but it will take time and training to learn to use it." Ffion tilted her head. "Though I've read somewhere that Azhdahā female magic works slightly differently than the males'. More subtle when it comes to reading minds. More like wind through the cracks instead of a hammer against a wall."

"Great," Kai said. "That's just what I need. Juli reading me even better than she does now."

Juli shot Kai a narrow-eyed look. "It's not my fault you think every thought you have with your face."

"Will we have to do the rituals you all do in the mornings?" Kai asked, ignoring her friend. She'd only really seen Rhys's once, but she'd passed by Ffion's open door once and seen her standing in the middle of a swirling gust of air, face tilted upward, some kind of gnarled staff gripped before her in both hands.

"Ashem showed me something last night," Juli said. "We cast down a handful of black sand and inscribed runes into it. Then we meditated, sort of. It made me feel...more."

Kai looked at Juli with wide eyes, but Ffion didn't seem surprised.

"It's good that Ashem made your first ritual a priority. Yes, to realize your full potential, you'll have to do the rituals. You'll only have the barest hint of power without them—not enough to do anything but make your own fingertips warm, Kai. The two of you will also get magic unique to the Wingless. You'll be able to provide a power boost to yourself or to a dragon. That magic does not require a ritual."

Kai sat back in her cushion, recalling how Cadoc wove fire through his fingers. She rubbed her thumb against her fingertips. When she heartswore to Rhys, she would be able to do magic too. She grinned.

Abruptly, Juli craned her neck, trying to see down the passage. "Idiot man. He's hovering."

Kai turned, but she didn't see anyone.

Ffion gave a quiet laugh, and Juli glared at her. "Don't worry, the need to be together all the time eases up after a few days. When Griffith and I swore, it was like being followed everywhere by the world's most colossal puppy."

Juli sat up straighter. "So this obsessive *wanting* will stop?"

Ffion shook her head. "It's always there, but it goes down to manageable levels. In any case, magic and...attraction aren't the only changes. I'm sure you've noticed Juli's indicium."

Kai and Juli nodded. Juli ran her fingers over her left arm.

"Wingless indicium are, as you can see, translucent and iridescent. All of them are like that, no matter who you're sworn to. And I told you already, Kai, that you'll have the lifespan of a dragon."

Juli went pale. "What do you mean, 'lifespan of a dragon'?"

Ffion's smile faded. "Ashem didn't..." She trailed off as footsteps echoed through the short passage.

Juli looked thunderous. "Go away, you bat-winged cretin!"

Ashem's deep voice came through the door. "If you want me to leave, petal, you're going to have to come out here and make me."

"Petal?" Juli half shrieked the word.

Despite everything, Kai grinned. "What a perfect couple."

Juli stood, outrage in every line of her body. "Fine, you titanic iguana. You want to talk again? Let's talk." She stalked to the door, giving Kai a not-so-gentle whack on the back of the head as she passed. "And you watch it, Monahan, or I'll tell your ginger lover you wet the bed until you were seven."

"I was five! It was anxiety!"

Juli raised an eyebrow, then yanked the door open and marched into the hall. Kai caught the surprising white flash of Ashem's smile before the door closed. Juli started shouting, but the sound faded as they walked away.

Ffion lay down on her side on the couch again, her head resting on her fist. "She's good for him. What other questions do you have?"

Kai reached for her carabiner, then stuffed her hands between her knees instead. "The lifespan. If I heartswear to Rhys, I'll save my family and the people I love, but I'll lose them anyway, won't I? Cadoc said he was over two thousand years old."

Ffion's expression turned sad. "I'm afraid so."

Kai felt the blood drain from her face. That kind of time was unimaginable. She opened her mouth to speak, and then closed it again.

Thousands of years.

She'd had her problems with her family, but... They'd all die, and she'd barely age a year. Their children would die, and she'd still be the same. By the time her body was thirty, she'd have lost track of her brothers' descendants altogether. "How do you do it? How do you live so long without going insane?"

Ffion tilted her head and focused her eyes somewhere in the distance. "Time is relative. When things are good, it flows like a fast river. At times like this, when we're at war, it seems to stretch and warp. Every day feels like a year might have felt before. I imagine it's how you experience time on a regular basis."

"That's...interesting."

"Relationships help. Friends, the family you'll gain from being with Rhys. Someday you could have children too, if you want them. I've been told time with young children both flies and drags. I wonder how that will feel." Ffion toyed with the hem of her shirt, her voice almost dreamy.

Kai refused to think about children. She had enough on her plate just dealing with Rhys. "Another question, given how fast this all happened—Rhys has never given me any reason to believe he's anything but single, but I just want to be sure. He doesn't have someone waiting for him at home, does he?" Her stomach knotted.

"No. Not that I know of."

Ffion's answer was a little too quick. Kai waited for more,

but the dragon woman's face remained serene. "Any other questions?"

"Just one," Kai inhaled, then let it out slowly. "I wanted to talk to you about what it's like to have someone in your head all the time." She wasn't sure why, but it felt like she was asking Ffion something supremely intimate. "I mean, obviously Ashem is in Juli's head. She doesn't like it, but she's not reacting the way I did when Kavar..."

Ffion's eyes lit like a light bulb had gone on in her brain. "Oh, Kai, is that what you've been thinking? What Juli is experiencing with Ashem as his heartsworn is not the same as what Azhdahā can do with their magic. Heartswearing is nothing like what Kavar did to you. First of all, Rhys is not Kavar. Second, you'll be bonded. As much a part of him as he is of you."

Kai frowned. Could it really be that different? A person's mind was their mind, how many different ways could there be to experience someone else getting inside it? "Do I want to be in someone else's head?"

"You don't have to be all the time."

"Do you keep Griffith out?"

Ffion smiled. "Not usually."

"Oh." Kai rubbed her temples and barked a short laugh. "You know, I just realized Juli is the dragon version of married. But also not, because it's not like it was her choice. This is a mess, Ffion."

Ffion blinked at her, the air of concern deepening slightly. "If you're just now realizing that, perhaps I should point something out."

"What?"

Ffion cleared her throat. "If you heartswear to Rhys, you'll be queen, which I'm sure you've realized. But after what happened with Mair and Ayen, the fact that you're human is going to cause problems."

Kai thought back to Rhys story, and a new fear churned in her stomach. Queen. Ruling. She'd dropped out of law school to avoid being in the position to ruin lives, and now she was faced with this. It was so much responsibility. "I imagine it will. Will Rhys be able to deal with it?"

Ffion's mouth flattened into a line. "I'd like to see anyone give him trouble while I am at his side."

"You, all of you, are good friends." Kai sighed. There were no more questions. She had no reason to delay. She stood. "I'm going to go find him."

Ffion smiled encouragingly. "They're finished sparring. I believe—if Griffith is correct—you'll find Rhys out on the ledge."

Kai nodded numbly, then rose and went where Ffion had instructed.

Rhys was, indeed, out on the ledge, his gaze lost somewhere beyond the mountainous horizon. She could tell he'd been working out because his hair was damp at the temples. As she watched, he pulled up the hem of the black t-shirt he wore to blot his forehead, revealing the glorious expanse of his abs and back, which gleamed with a fine sheen of sweat.

Standing there, surveying the mountains, powerful body relaxed, Rhys looked exactly like the king he claimed to be.

He tilted his head and turned, as if he'd sensed her. His mouth curved into that heart-stopping half smile. The thunderstorm feeling rolled over her as she stepped out of the cave to join him in the bracingly frigid, clear air. "How's it going?"

The smile grew a little. "All right."

"I talked to Ffion."

He watched her.

"She said that Wingless have magic."

Rhys nodded, his smile still in place. Kai found herself mesmerized by the curve of his lips. "Wielding fire magic sounds intimidating. Maybe not as intimidating as mind invading magic, but—"

Rhys folded his arms across his chest. "You think Ashem's magic is better than mine?"

Kai grinned and bit her lip, enjoying her body's reaction to the annoyed rumble of his voice. She shrugged, just to goad him and hear it again. "I mean, *reading minds*..."

"Follow me." He strode past her into the cavern.

Intrigued, Kai stepped inside. The black cavern was empty. The others were probably getting ready to move.

Kai hesitated just inside the cave mouth as Rhys walked to the middle of the cavern, then turned to face her. He stood, as it always seemed in this room, in a sea of stars. She opened her mouth, but he held up a hand.

The tiny fires that illuminated the area died, swallowing Rhys in darkness. He held his hands in front of him, palms toward each other. The air between them rippled as his eyes began to glow. A spark of light appeared between his hands, swirling lazily. It grew into a single tongue of flame that danced, flickering from blue to yellow to red and back again.

He dropped his hands. The flame became a softball-sized ball of fire. Other fireballs winked to life, surrounding him. They moved, weaving in and out of each other with such quick complexity they became streaks of light, searing an intricate afterimage into her vision.

The pattern surrounded Rhys, forming a golden cage, never still, a whirling, changing pattern with him at its heart. The cage collapsed, forming a pool of fire at his feet. It stretched outward, mini-geysers of flame shooting into the air. Flowers bloomed, vines put out leaves and curled back upon themselves, spiraling outward. They grew, covering the cavern walls, then the ceiling, until the entirety of the cavern was laced with flame in beautiful, dizzying designs.

A pathway opened, parting the garden of flame. Rhys stood at the other end, perfectly still, body tense. He held out his hand.

Kai swallowed and stepped onto the path. Suddenly nervous, she looked back. The fire wasn't closing in as she'd thought it would; he left a way for her to escape.

Confident now, she moved toward him, mesmerized by those starfire eyes. He seemed just as enthralled by her.

She wasn't sure who moved first, but their fingers intertwined. A shockwave pulsed through her body. She moved forward, or he pulled her, or both, but suddenly she was in his arms, crushed to his hard body with desperate intensity.

She closed her eyes and laid her head on his chest, and he buried his face in her hair. He was shaking; his heart pounded beneath her ear. The fire coalesced around them, a column of rushing flame that reached from ceiling to floor. But he'd left the way out. A gap in the flame to her right, a space just large enough for her to escape if she wanted.

She didn't. Maybe it was the time they'd spent together last night, or seeing Juli interact with Ashem, or talking to Ffion, but Kai was no longer afraid.

To hell with freedom. Give me fire.

She was aware of every perfect inch of him, aware that he smelled like wind and smoke and the scent that was specifically *Rhys* and made her nerves zing.

She tilted her chin up just a fraction, her nose brushing his jaw. He lowered his eyes, his head angling down a fraction. If she moved, if she lifted her mouth another centimeter, they would kiss.

She traced her fingers along the flame-like indicium that

covered the right side of his chest, down his ribcage to his stomach. His breathing became unsteady. She grinned.

His fingers feathered down the back of her neck, down her spine to the hem of her shirt. They found a stripe of skin and slipped, warm and rough, under the fabric. He caressed her back, then skimmed the curve of her waist from her hips to her ribcage, his thumbs making small circles on her stomach.

Her eyes drifted closed. All she wanted was to feel his hands on her again. To hear the way his voice dropped and turned into a possessive growl while he pleasured her. "Rhys…"

He kissed the side of her neck, and she buried her fingers in his hair. His teeth nipped her skin and she gasped. He kissed her neck again, then tucked her head beneath his chin, holding her for another minute, his hands against her skin.

She pulled away just enough.

It was time.

Suddenly, Rhys froze, his eyes on the sky beyond the cave mouth. The garden of fire collapsed.

"Cadoc," he whispered. He released Kai. She saw pain flicker across his face, but he didn't take her in his arms again.

"Cadoc?" Her voice sounded oddly flat. Dizzy, she couldn't process what had happened. Why hadn't they kissed?

Rhys spun to look at Kai. "Move to the side. I need some space to transform. He'll be injured. I want to make sure he can find us."

Kai craned her neck, but couldn't see any dragons in the sky. She gave Rhys the space he needed. Fire blazed up around him, and he was the dragon. He gave her a lingering look with his starfire eyes.

Stay inside. The wind from the downbeats will knock you off the ledge.

And then Rhys was gone.

CHAPTER 42
CADOC

adoc's wings faltered, and he dropped several dozen feet before catching himself. His right foreclaw was curled tight to his body, as twisted and mangled as it had been as a human hand. He needed to sleep so badly that keeping his eyes open was a torture nearly as wrenching as anything Izel had done.

The ground sped away beneath him. He forced his weary head up to look at the horizon and blinked bleary eyes. The mountains in front of him unwillingly coalesced, forming a shockingly familiar pattern. He was nearly to the cave. A few hundred yards, only. Close enough to call out. *Ashem! Anyone!*

Ashem answered immediately—he was the only one who could respond in human form, after all. *Cadoc! You escaped! How?* The Azhdahā's mental touch skimmed over him, then he swore softly. *Land somewhere and wait. Don't come here. Something is wrong.*

Cadoc groaned. If he landed, he wouldn't take off again. *I'm almost there.*

Power washed over him and a flash of crimson caught the

corner of his eye. Rhys had come up beneath him. Cadoc hadn't even seen him approach.

Cadoc! Rhys flew closer and did a roll around Cadoc, looking him over. *Blood of the Ancients, your hand. Get inside. Go see Ashem.*

The contradictory orders from commander and king made Cadoc laugh, an out-of-control giggle. He was so tired.

Rhys. A chill creeped over Cadoc's mind, and conscious thought slowed to an icy crawl. He tried to shake the cold, but it wouldn't go. It had to be the exhaustion, the stress. *I'm...sorry. I came to...warn... Owain and Kavar are close. I did it. I...*

The cold grew more intense, sliding through his veins until his entire body was numb. He faltered again as a red haze rose up to blanket his mind. A voice seemed to echo through his brain, murmuring and hissing: *Rhys ap Ayen must die. Kill the dragon king. Lladd y brenin ddraig.*

Cadoc watched in horror from some distant, shrouded place as he dove for Rhys's back, drawing in a breath, igniting fire deep in his belly to incinerate the delicate membrane where it stretched between the bones of Rhys's wings.

In his mind, Ashem shouted a warning to Rhys.

As undeniable as blood, the voice whispered, *Kill the dragon king.*

CHAPTER 43

JULI

J uli sat in the library, glaring at Ashem over the top of the book she wasn't even pretending to read since their last "conversation" had again devolved into him being an ass. Ashem ignored her, manipulating some kind of holograph that floated above a glass sphere.

Ashem! Anyone!

Juli jumped at the sound of the stranger's voice. She'd been practicing eavesdropping on Ashem without him knowing, like he did to her. Now his hand hovered in midair, the holograph forgotten. She "watched" him respond, then give the stranger, apparently the Cadoc person Kai had told her about, a mental once-over.

Something was very, very wrong with his mind.

Juli knew it was bad when Ashem swore only once, his voice soft. That single, murmured curse held more vehemence than any of his normal strings of obscenities. *Land somewhere and wait. Don't come here. Something is wrong.*

Cadoc didn't stop. Ashem rose. So did Juli. Whatever was wrong with Cadoc's mind, it put Ashem on edge.

Then they heard Rhys mind-speak. Ashem swore again, strode toward door, and then paused and fixed his golden gaze on Juli. "Stay here."

Juli snorted and rose to follow. "No."

Ashem glared, sent out a mental call to Ffion, Griffith, and Deryn, then put his hands on her shoulders and spun her around. "Go back to your book. Or your room. Just. Stay. Here!"

She smacked his fingers. When that didn't work, she twisted her head and tried to bite him. Only half listening to the conversation between Rhys and Cadoc, she froze at Cadoc's next exhausted words.

I'm...sorry. I came to...warn... Owain and Kavar are close. I did it. I...

Ashem released her and sprinted out of the library. Juli followed, running through the long halls and into the black cavern. She caught a glimpse of Kai out on the ledge, holding her ever-present sea-green hoodie tight around her. Beyond her, two red dragons flew. One had scales the red-orange of flame, and his wingbeats were slow and unsteady. The other, crimson as blood, flew smoothly below him and to one side. Juli's breath caught and she came to an abrupt halt.

Dragons. She hadn't seen one since Ashem had brought her back to the cave after the ill-fated escape attempt. There they were, as plain as day. Freaking. Dragons.

Juli sensed, as Ashem did, the moment Cadoc lost control. She watched the red-orange dragon pull his head up and back, fire and blood hot in his brain.

Rhys! Dodge left! Ashem's mental voice boomed. Rhys twisted away an instant before Cadoc's flames seared the air. *Something's wrong with Cadoc! Can you bring him down with the mantle?*

Rhys cursed. *I've been too weak for the ritual. I could perform it now, maybe, if I had time.*

Ashem made an audible sound very much like a growl. Mentally, he said, *There is no time.*

Obviously! Rhys snapped. *We'll have to bring him in.*

Get away. I'll knock him out, and we can figure out what's wrong with him when we get to Eryri.

Ashem turned to Juli. "Get Kai and get out of this place, *jāné del-am.* Have one of the others take you down to the valley floor and hide." *If Kavar finds out about you...* He pulled the shutters over his mind too fast for her to hear the end of the sentence, but not before she sensed his fear.

"Wait!" It shocked them both when Juli rose on her toes and pressed a kiss to his mouth. She didn't know why she did it. Nor did she expect the roiling wave of emotion that crashed over her, but Ashem's lips were warm and softer than they had any right to be.

He wrapped his arms around her waist and pulled her against the hard lines of his body, lifted her so their faces were level, and claimed her in a searing clash of lips, tongues, and teeth that somehow both lingered and moved too fast. His mind was heavy with so many things: guilt, fear, sorrow. Too soon, they tore away from each other. Ashem let her slide down his body, gave her one confused, almost vulnerable look, then turned and ran.

"Kai, move!" Juli shouted.

Darkness gathered around Ashem, coalescing and growing until the man disappeared. Juli blinked, and the blackness became an ebony dragon. Kai dove out of the way as he reached the edge and plunged over, his vast wings like a patch of night that had somehow survived the sunlight.

You really are a dragon, Juli sent.

Ashem didn't reply.

Next to her, Kai was pale and shaken. "Cadoc is alive! What's going on? Did Rhys lose control again? Is this still because of that stupid kiss?"

Before Juli could answer, footsteps pounded across the cavern. Ffion, Griffith, and Deryn.

"What's happening? Where did Ashem go?" Ffion asked, breathless.

"Something is wrong with Cadoc." Juli snatched her fingers away from her lips, which felt oversensitive and swollen. Breathing was hard, and her body ached with wanting. "Cadoc isn't in control of himself. He's trying to kill Rhys."

Jāné del-am, Ashem had called her. She'd seized the meaning from his mind as he'd closed down on her. *Jāné del-am.* Life of my heart.

Sure. The life of his heart, whom he'd known for days.

What was time, she supposed, when you lived partway inside the other person's head? When she knew just from the little time they'd spent together who he was inside and out? An angry, hard man. A man who wrung every drop of effort and perfection from the people under his command.

A man who would die for the people he loved. Who demanded more from himself than he did anyone else.

A man who had very much in common with her.

If Kai's life was on the line, if Juli's future dangled on the thread of a returned kiss, she would have taken it from Ashem, too.

Juli snapped back to the present. The dragons were gaping at her. "Why are you standing there? Go help them!"

The cavern filled with the sound of wind, wave, and shifting earth. Where there had been three humans, now three dragons stood: silver, blue, and green. Now the vast cavern seemed very small. Juli's mouth dropped open in an O of amazement at the sheer size of them.

She closed it. "Ffion!"

The smallest of the dragons turned her finely sculpted head in Juli's direction. Her wings were translucent silver, and her scales glittered like thousands of mirrors. Juli found herself confronted by soft gray eyes the size of dinner plates.

Yes?

Juli took a step back. Ffion was perturbing enough as a tiny woman. Now she was at least forty feet long. Juli tilted her chin up the smallest bit. "Ashem wants Kai and me out of here. We could rappel down, but it would be faster if someone carried us. Can you do it?"

Ffion gave her a look Juli supposed was the dragon equivalent of an arched eyebrow. *I believe I'm capable.*

Juli repressed the instinctive fear of prey looking up at a predator and nodded, keeping her face perfectly calm. Oddly, the spike of fear made her want to reach out to Ashem. She'd a thousand times rather ride down on his broad, black-scaled back than this fine-spun creature of Saran wrap and silver glitter.

You're broadcasting. Ffion's mental voice was dry. *I can hear you.*

"Well, pardon me for being uncertain," Juli snapped.

It was odd, hearing the dragon in her head. It wasn't like the little mind reading she'd managed since heartswearing to Ashem. Neither was it like speaking to Ashem in her own mind. Of the three, the dragon speech was the most like talking. Very much on the surface, without any to hint at what the speaker was thinking beyond tone or intensity.

Reading minds, she was able to pick up a bit more of the thoughts behind the speech. With Ashem, she got everything.

Intention, tone, words, images, emotion, and sometimes hints of memories—flashes of sight, sound, or smell.

A quarter mile away, Rhys, Ashem, and Cadoc had turned into a writhing ball of black and red, Cadoc fighting like a rabid animal.

Kai had gone out to the ledge. Juli tugged her inside. "Come on."

Griffith and Deryn took off while Ffion waited.

"But why is this happening?" Kai asked, resisting.

Kai and her endless questions. Juli touched Ashem's mind enough to observe his surface thoughts. "Ashem thinks Cadoc is under a curse, which sounds insane. They're trying to subdue him, not hurt him. Cadoc says Owain and Kavar are coming. We have to leave. Hold on."

Leaving Kai looking dumbfounded, Juli sprinted to their room, grabbed the coat she'd worn when they tried to escape, then snatched the thick comforter from Kai's bed. If things went wrong, she didn't know if they'd make it back up here. It was better to prepare.

By the time Juli got back to the cavern, Ffion was bent low to the ground and Kai was scrambling up her back, seating herself between the ridges at the base of Ffion's neck.

Juli tossed the blanket to Kai and put the coat on. With one last, steadying breath, she clambered up Ffion's silver side.

Here we go. Ffion lifted her wings and stepped off the ledge. Air whistled past Juli's ears. Kai's hair came loose from its messy bun, filling Juli's mouth when she took a breath to scream. She coughed instead, spitting and shaking her head.

"This would be the best moment of my life under different circumstances," Kai shouted, whooping with involuntary laughter.

"Clearly, you are insane!" Juli still had her eyes tightly closed.

I think I can manage not to drop you, Ffion snipped.

Juli opened her mouth to make a sharp retort, but Kai gasped. "Oh, Cadoc."

Juli looked. Cadoc was surrounded by the others now. He fought, but his body had been driven beyond exhaustion. The others rebuffed his every attempt to break their circle, holding him in one tight place in the sky.

Tentatively, Juli reached for Ashem again. Through him, she heard the dragons shouting to each other and at Cadoc, trying to communicate with him. Only Ashem remained grimly silent. He knew talking was no use. He was focusing his power, trying to knock Cadoc unconscious.

Juli started in surprise when Ffion hit the ground with a soft *thud.* Kai slid from the silver dragon's neck, feet crunching into a thin crust of snow.

Juli followed, stumbling. Still absorbed in the aerial battle, she felt Ashem gain some headway. Juli observed, fascinated, as he shut down Cadoc's conscious mind bit by bit. She gave Cadoc a tentative mental touch. When nothing alarming happened, she began to mimic Ashem like a small child clumsily imitating a parent. Still, it seemed to be effective. Either that or Ashem was suddenly working faster. Another minute and Cadoc's attacks slowed. His wings faltered. He beat them once, twice, then his mind went dark.

Cadoc plummeted from the sky. Kai shouted, but Griffith slid beneath Cadoc and Rhys held him from above. Even so, the mountain shook when they hit the ground.

Juli and Kai ran down the slope into the sparse copse of aspen and pine where the dragons landed. Ffion bounded ahead, her wings carrying her there in a few great leaps.

They'd all become human. Cadoc lay prone at the center of the circle, still unconscious. Juli could feel Ashem fighting against the weird magic that pushed, even now, to bring Cadoc's body back online.

"You can't be here when he wakes up." Ashem stood in front of Rhys, blocking him from reaching Cadoc. "His mind isn't right. It feels like Quetzal blood magic."

"That isn't the only thing wrong with him." Ffion's birdlike voice was filled with distress. "Look at him."

"Look at his hand," Rhys demanded. "Ashem, let me be and look at it!"

"I'll look at it when you move away," Ashem growled.

Juli watched. The air between king and commander sparked with angry energy. Deryn put a hand on Rhys's arm, murmuring softly. Finally, Rhys nodded. He turned and marched back uphill, casting one final, worried glance at the unconscious newcomer.

Deryn couldn't take her eyes from Cadoc. "We're going to keep watch. Hurry, Ashem." Rhys and Deryn transformed and took flight.

Kai tried to get closer, but Juli held her back. "You can't help him, Kai."

Ashem crouched next to Cadoc. He didn't say anything out loud, but in his mind he swore softly for the second time that day. Juli slipped between the others and knelt next to Ashem. She had a strong stomach, but at the sight of Cadoc's twisted, mangled hand, bile rose in her throat. The bones had been well and truly shattered, then healed horribly. Slivers were even visible through some parts of his purpled, blood-crusted skin.

Can dragons fix that? Juli asked into Ashem's mind.

He looked at her, his eyes bleak. *No. Even the Quetzals, gifted as they are, haven't come so far as to be able to completely reform a limb. The gold dragon, perhaps...but Cadoc isn't heartsworn.*

In Ashem's memory, Juli saw a woman in a golden gown

and golden veil, saw her lay her hands on someone's head, saw them stand from a stretcher and walk. That woman, she somehow knew, was not allowed to touch the unheartsworn.

Next, Juli heard a strain of music and laugher. Apparently Cadoc had been a musician. He wouldn't be playing instruments anymore.

The sound of ripping fabric split the air, and her attention jerked back into the real world. Kai had given Griffith the comforter, and the huge, dark man was shredding it into strips. Wordlessly, Ashem took the first few and bound Cadoc's injured hand to his chest. Just as silent, Juli examined the blood crusted on his forearms, which surrounded countless long, thin scars. It looked like someone had used a very sharp knife to turn his skin into ribbons.

Deryn's panicked thought cut through all of their minds. *Kavar is coming! The Talon is here!*

Juli felt Ashem's heartbeat pick up. Kavar would have to be some distance away for Ashem not to have sensed him first. There was still hope. *Head for the apartment in Seattle. We'll catch up.*

We can't. Rhys spoke this time, voice tense. *We're surrounded. They're closing in.*

Fear filled Ashem's mind, and Juli's own heart began to pound. He looked at her. "Stay here. Keep Kai and Cadoc calm." He used the strip of fabric in his hands to blindfold Cadoc. "Don't let him take this off, don't talk about Rhys where he can hear, don't let him go anywhere. Do your best. If he transforms, run."

Juli nodded, not wanting Ashem to leave. *What happens to me if you die?*

Ashem shook his head. "Griffith, take Cadoc there." He indicated a denser patch of dusty green pines that would hide them. "Ffion, let's go."

He spared a brief glance for Juli before he turned to run uphill. *For both our sakes, Juliet, pray you don't have to find out.*

Shivering, Juli followed Kai and Griffith deeper into the trees. Griffith laid Cadoc down gently, nodded to Juli and Kai, and walked out. The earth shook with his transformation. Overhead, flames split the sky. The battle had begun.

CHAPTER 44

KAI

K ai crouched on a bed of dry, brown needles, the scent of pine all around her. For a second, there was no sound but the harsh in and out of Juli's breath. Then a dragon roared, a sound like thunder. Kai jumped.

Juli didn't. Her tennis shoes made a soft swishing sound as she paced back and forth through the pine needles, her head tilted to the sky, her gaze far off, as if she saw things Kai couldn't. Things Ashem was seeing as well.

Kai held Cadoc's unbroken left hand. His right was a distorted lump beneath the strips of fabric Ashem wrapped over it, but she'd seen. Guilt curled her insides. Whoever hurt Cadoc had taken his assortment of bracelets, armbands, and necklaces. He looked oddly plain without them.

Something in Cadoc's breathing changed. Juli paused. "He's waking up."

Kai glanced at her. "Is he going to be himself?"

Juli shrugged, her attention still clearly on Ashem.

Cadoc groaned. His injured hand twitched beneath the

bandage, and the groan turned into a gasp. He shot into a sitting position and clawed at the blindfold.

Kai touched his shoulder. "Cadoc?"

He jerked away. After a few deep breaths, he spoke. "Kai? They... They don't know about you, do they? You can't be an illusion."

His smooth, melted-chocolate voice had gone rough. Kai fought the burn of tears. "I don't think so. It's hard to tell what's real, the past couple of weeks. Leave it," she said as he reached for the blindfold. "Ashem wants you to leave it on for now."

Cadoc released the fabric and reached out, searching. His fingers found her cheek, her hair. She pulled him into a gentle hug. Beneath the smell of sweat and blood lingered the scent of cedar wood and lemon oil.

Cadoc's hand fisted in the back of her shirt, and he pulled her tight to him, shaking hard enough to break. "Real. Blood of the Ancients, you're real. I'm free."

Kai stopped fighting the tears, and they spilled down her cheeks as she clung to him, rubbing a hand along his back. She buried her face in his shoulder. "I'm sorry. I'm so sorry."

A gust of wind rattled the trees, a glimpse of azure flashing by as they swayed. Another roar, louder and closer, and then a noise like a thousand voices screaming. Cadoc released her, reaching for the blindfold again.

"Leave that on," Juli snapped. She'd wandered to the edge of the thicket, still craning her neck to look at the sky. Her face was white. She turned frightened eyes on Kai. "It's not going well."

"Who's that?" Cadoc asked.

"My friend Juli. She's heartsworn to Ashem. Long story."

Lightning cracked, a deafening peal of thunder sounding in the same instant. Kai wondered if it had come from Ffion or some other silver dragon.

"Ashem is sworn?" Cadoc shifted.

Kai put a restraining hand on his shoulder. "You have to stay here."

He reached for the blindfold again and shoved it onto his forehead. His amethyst eyes blinked, flicked over the thicket, and then met Kai's. "Ah, *brânwen*. It *is* you."

More thunder. He tried to stand, but Kai held him still. "You can't go out there."

"But what's happening? Where's..." He shivered.

Fear tingled at the back of Kai's neck. "You don't remember?"

Cadoc shook his head. "I remember calling out to Ashem... and..." His body went tense. "Rhys."

Juli was suddenly on his other side. "Don't think about him," she commanded. "Don't talk about him. Don't say his name. Ashem says you're under some kind of spell. Blood magic. You attacked him."

Cadoc's breathing had gone ragged. "I attacked Rhys? But — Stars, I...feel cold."

"Don't think about him," Juli said, her voice firm. "You're stronger than us. You have to stay in control."

Cadoc didn't seem to hear her. "I remember... *Lladd y brenin ddraig...*" His eyes unfocused, amethyst irises flat and cold as glass.

"No!" Kai took Cadoc's rigid fingers in her own. She had to distract him. "Hey, do you remember that night I came up on the ledge? You were on watch? It was, what, my first or second night?"

Cadoc blinked, his eyes still glassy. Slowly, he nodded.

"You sang to me."

He nodded again. The movement looked easier this time.

"Sing to me now?"

His right arm tensed, pressing his injured hand into his chest. "I can't."

Kai hated herself. Nothing like prodding an open wound to get a man's attention. "You can. Please."

Another roar. Cadoc tensed, his muscles like steel beneath her hand. His voice shook. "They're my family."

Kai squeezed his fingers. "I know."

Juli stood from where she'd crouched on his other side, her voice uncharacteristically soft. "If you go up there, you'll lose control and attack again. Your mind is still...wrong. Fogged."

"Ashem's heartsworn." Cadoc gave Juli a ghost of his old grin. "He didn't do too badly."

Juli arched an eyebrow, and he laughed softly.

Wind whipped over them again, bringing a sudden, searing heat that made it hard to breathe. Cadoc closed his eyes, inhaling, and the heat disappeared as if he'd sucked it from the air the way he'd pulled fire from Rhys's hands. His voice was unsteady. "Rhys is using magic." He opened his eyes. They'd gone glassy.

Kai put her hands on either side of his face. "Sing to me."

He took a deep breath, then another. "*Brânwen—*"

"Sing, Cadoc!"

Soft and hesitant, he began.

"Fel 'roeddwn i ryw fore hawddgar,
Yng nghwr y coed ac wrth fy mhlesar,
Ar frig y pren mi glywn ryw glomen,
Yn cwyno'n glaf— 'Ow, beth a wnaf, am f'anwyl gymar?'"

The tune was heartbreaking. His voice gained strength as he went. Tension drained from his face, and his shoulders relaxed.

384

"'Rhyw g'ledi mawr sydd yn fy mynwes,
Wrth gofio'r cur a'r poen a gefes;
Wrth gofio'r mab a'r geiraiu mwynion,
I'm calon rhoes drwm glefyd loes—Fe dyr fy nghalon.'"

When the song ended, he shook his head, wincing at the sound of a dragon's scream.

"I can't stay."

Even rough, his voice was magic. Kai was still partially under its spell. "What?"

"I can't stay. I know he's here. I recognize his roar, I feel his power. I've got to leave before I lose control again."

Kai's brow furrowed. Rhys. Was he all right? Were they winning?

She wrenched her mind from thoughts of Rhys. She had to talk Cadoc out of being stupid. "What about your hand?"

He wouldn't meet her gaze. "It's too late for my hand. Tell them... Tell him Mair is alive. She's been hiding among the rogues. She wants to help."

"Mair? Isn't that his mother?" Kai looked to Juli for help. If anyone could browbeat a dragon into obeying orders, she could. But Juli had wandered to the edge of the trees again, attention completely captured by the battle. "I don't even... Cadoc, you're hurt. We're in the middle of a battle."

Cadoc pushed himself up on shaky legs. Kai had forgotten how tall he was. He smiled at her.

"Don't worry about me, love. Nothing in the wilderness is as frightening as a dragon."

Juli eyed Cadoc warily. "Do not leave these trees without putting that blindfold on."

"Don't leave the trees at all!" Kai protested, standing as well.

Cadoc's face was so innocent it looked positively wicked. "I will be Orpheus leading Eurydice from the underworld."

Juli narrowed her eyes. "Orpheus looked back."

Suddenly her face went pale.

Kai stepped toward her. "Juli?"

"Ashem," Juli whispered. She took off, sprinting uphill, dodging between trees.

"Juli!" Kai swore. She turned to Cadoc, torn. "Stay here. Please. We'll win. I know we will. And then we'll take you to Eryri, and they can fix your hand and your mind, and everything will be okay."

Cadoc smiled sadly at her again. "I hope you fall in love with him, *brânwen*. You both deserve to be happy."

"Just stay," Kai pleaded.

"I can't. But I will see you again."

He cupped her cheek in his hand. "Even in the days I've been gone, you've changed. Grown. You'll do wonderfully. Just wait and see."

"Cadoc..."

There was a scream. Cadoc winced. "Go, Kai. She needs you, and so will he."

Kai hesitated for a moment, trying to memorize the sight of him, then took off after Juli.

The sky was filled with streaks of color on vast wings half obscured by branching blue-gray pines and the last of autumn's leaves. They wheeled and dove through clouds, spitting poison and flame.

Afraid to call out, Kai searched through the spindly white trunks of aspen trees for Juli. It suddenly hit her how cold it was, and she hugged herself, shivering. The trees on her left seemed thinner, so she veered that way. The aspens ended, and a cliff loomed above her, towering a hundred feet over her head.

"Juli!" she called, her voice hardly more than a whisper. "Where are you?"

No answer. No sound. Not even small animals or birds in the trees. Then a dragon roared.

She turned her face to the sky, but couldn't see. Before her, the cliff was weathered and cracked and perfect.

She climbed, wedging quickly numbing fingers and toes into the fissures and crannies that offered themselves up beneath her hands and feet. She passed the point where the fall would leave her broken on the leaf-littered floor of the aspen grove, then twice that distance.

The wind picked up the higher she went, snatching at hair and clothes with cold, greedy fingers. Once, her foot slipped. She spent a mind-thrashing second dangling by her hands before her feet found holds again. Now above the golden canopy, she clung to the rock, pressing herself to the cliff's frigid face every time a roar or thunder vibrated through her. She didn't think about Rhys, didn't think about Juli, didn't think about the dragons who clashed behind her. There would be time for all of them when she made it to the top. She had to be able to *see*.

She pulled herself onto level ground, scooting on her belly until she was far enough from the edge to stand. Her legs shook like jackhammers, and her arms were getting weak. Above the cliff, the slope was wide and gentle except for an upthrusting of rock about a dozen feet away. The wind smelled of ozone and smoke. With shaking breath that misted in front of her, she counted her dragons.

"One, two." Ffion and Griffith fought together maybe a third of a mile directly in front of her. Ffion's mirror-scaled body glittered as she flitted this way and that, seeming to surround two of the enemy dragons on her own as she drove them toward Griffith. He raked three-foot-long claws down the belly of a bronze dragon. It screamed, a horrible sound that made Kai clap her hands over her ears. Ffion opened her mouth, and lightning crackled along the hide of the bronze dragon's companion, who jerked and twitched as thunder rolled over the valley.

Kai turned west. "Three." Deryn led two more dragons on a zigzagging chase. As Kai watched, she flared her wings. One of her pursuers twisted in the air to avoid collision. As it passed, Deryn opened her mouth. From this distance, Kai couldn't see anything, but she did hear the enemy dragon scream.

"Where are you, Rhys?" Kai muttered. "And where's Ashem?"

As if in answer, the air *whooshed* as an ebony dragon soared over her head from behind. Great red gashes in his belly rained fat drops of blood as he passed, spattering in the dust not ten feet from where Kai stood. *Whoosh, whoosh, whoosh.* Three more dragons appeared, giving chase. Ashem skimmed low across the aspens. They bent and swayed from the wind of his passage, and golden leaves swirled in his wake like fistfuls of coins flung at the sky.

He spiraled upward. When they'd fallen behind several body lengths, he let himself fall back to the earth, head down, jaws open. A cloud of yellow vapor blew from his mouth directly into the face of his closest pursuer. The dragon faltered, beat its wings weakly for a moment, then plummeted. The ground shook when it hit, and tree trunks shrieked as they splintered under its weight.

The other two dragons banked away from Ashem and his deadly mist. The path of one brought it close to the mountain, and a blood-red dragon launched itself from a rocky crevasse, breathing a white wall of flame that made the enemy dragon's pale blue hide crack and blacken like an overcooked hot dog.

"Rhys!"

He and Ashem flew toward the center of the valley to rejoin Ffion, Griffith, and Deryn. The enemy dragons were regrouping as well. Kai counted. Eight enemies left, and no black dragon among them. Hope bubbled up within her. Maybe Kavar was dead.

Behind her, stone ground against stone.

Pressure filled Kai's skull. Nausea soured her stomach. Knowing what she would see, she turned. Kavar crouched on the outcropping above her, a mass of huddled darkness.

Hello again, baby ape. His baleful silver eyes roved over her. He flexed his right foreclaw, the one she'd stabbed.

"Get out of my head!" Kai pressed her hands her ears as the pressure grew. She fought the urge to throw up. His presence was thick and oily and *wrong*.

But I owe you pain. With a flick like the careless swatting of a fly, Kavar's mind smashed into hers.

Kai staggered and cried out through numb lips. She fell to all fours, gagging.

Disgusting. Kavar smashed down harder. The pain was so intense, Kai thought her brain would liquefy. She wanted to die.

He leaped from the top of the rocks, landing in front of her with an earth-shaking *thud.*

Kai! Another voice in her mind, a voice that felt like shelter. She pushed toward it, but she couldn't reach, couldn't connect. Out of the corner of her eye, she caught the flash of sunlight on crimson scales, too far away to matter.

She gave Kavar a mental shove. The pressure relented a little. She tried again, pushing outward hard. With a curl of his lip, Kavar lashed her with his horned tail.

Kai dodged, bringing her arms over her face. A horrible, burning pain tore down her arm. Her roll brought her within a foot of the edge of the cliff, one heel hanging over nothing. Hot blood gushed from the slash he'd opened in the underside of her right arm, soaking her torn sleeve and dripping to the ground.

Rhys spoke into her mind, low and urgent. *Jump, Kai!*

Memory flashed. Her own voice. *What would you do if I jumped off this cliff?* Rhys's response, utterly confident. *I would catch you.*

Kai rose, turned, and jumped. The wind whistled past, and the golden crowns of the aspen trees rushed to greet her. For one eternal moment, Kai knew she was going to die.

Red-scaled claws closed over her shoulders, gentle and unbreakable. Rhys swung her up, away from the cliff, pulling them into the sky.

Kavar roared. As Rhys looped around the mountain and over the peak, the black dragon sprang into the air and hurtled after them.

Rhys skimmed across the slope, dangerously close boulders and dry, windswept grass. He caught his wingtip on a spur of stone and his flight went erratic. He dropped so low, Kai had to run her feet along a grassy strip of mountainside.

Kavar gained.

Rhys thrust down with his wings, heaving them back into the air. But their speed was gone. Kavar was on them. The Azhdahā reached forward with scythe-like claws and raked Rhys's back leg. Rhys roared and twisted, shooting white fire. The black dragon flared his wings, pulling back.

Below them, a ravine opened. Rhys flipped sideways and arrowed through the opening to the narrow canyon with Kai pressed against his warm, scaled belly.

Behind them, there came a crunch of stone and a roar of anger and pain. Kavar had tried to pull the same maneuver as

Rhys and crashed into the wall. Apparently dazed, Kavar clung to the cliffside like an enormous, disoriented bat.

Rhys angled them around a sharp bend, and Kavar disappeared from view. He released Kai—who fell ten feet to the ground, rolling as she hit—and landed. *Run for that cave.*

Kai staggered, dizzy from the flight and loss of blood, then got her feet under her and sprinted toward a small opening at the base of the canyon wall. She dove inside. Fire flickered on the canyon walls, and Rhys ran flat-out toward her, human, sliding into the tiny cave like a baseball player stealing home.

As Rhys hunkered down next to Kai, Kavar flew around the sharp curve in the canyon. The black dragon didn't even pause, but flew on.

Chest heaving as he panted, Rhys turned to her. "Are you all right?"

Dizzy, Kai looked down at her arm. Blood still sheeted from the long slice. She felt very, very cold. She staggered, then sat down hard on the ground. Her vision blurred. Her breath came fast and shallow.

Rhys knelt and took her injured forearm in strong, warm hands, and pulled back the bloody fabric. "*Uffern dân.* I'll kill Kavar, I swear it."

"Not if I kill him first." Kai's voice was oddly breathy. She noticed a damp red stain spreading across the calf of his pant leg. "You're bleeding too."

"I'll be fine. *Mae'n ddrwg, cariad.*" Rhys's voice shook, but his hands were steady as he smoothed back her tangled hair. His fingertips brushed her skin and she felt the shockwave of his touch as if from a distance. Suddenly, his hands froze. He took in a sharp breath.

"What...?"

His fire-blue eyes stood out in sharp contrast to his pale, strained face. "It's Ashem. Griffith is wounded."

Kai didn't want him to go. "They need you."

Fists clenched, Rhys looked toward the cave entrance, then at Kai. "You first. I depleted myself with that damn fire garden, but I have enough for this."

He moved behind her and pulled her down so her back was cradled against his chest. With his left hand, he grasped her bleeding wrist. Kai almost passed out at the sight of the gaping, sliced skin. Her entire forearm was soaking red and still dripping.

With a loud tear, he ripped away the sleeve and tossed it aside. The first finger of his right hand hovered over the top of the ragged cut. "If you need to scream, scream into me. This is going to burn."

He touched her. Searing pain rocketed through Kai's body, and the sick, sizzling smell of burning flesh wafted through the air. She turned, pressed her face into his broad chest, and screamed.

He ran his finger steadily along the length of the cut, cauterizing her flesh, breathing hard. He leaned his cheek against the top of her head, murmuring words she didn't understand. *"Mae'n ddrwg gen i, mae'n ddrwg gen i. Bydd yn drosodd yn fuan."*

After some indeterminable amount of time, he released her arm. She turned it toward her and bit her tongue to keep from throwing up at the sight of the shining, angry red line of blood-stained skin that ran from wrist to elbow.

Rhys shifted as if to stand.

Kai tensed. "What are you doing?"

He wouldn't meet her gaze. "If I don't come back, wait a day, then keep going through this canyon. When you get to the other end, head southeast. There's a town. It might take you a day or two to get there, but you can."

She was half turned toward him now. He raised a tentative hand to her face, running one finger along her lips. It felt like goodbye.

Kai wasn't ready for goodbye. She slid her own hand up to press his to her cheek, ignoring the screaming pain in her arm. The heat and rushing flame of the fire garden he'd made only an hour ago seemed to surround them, invisible, the air sparking in the scant inches between their bodies. One of his arms came around her waist.

His clean, wild scent surrounded her, his warm breath brushed her skin. "I wish we could have known each other better." His gaze went to her lips for a long moment, then he released her and leaned back.

He was leaving, and if she didn't do something, he wouldn't come back.

"No." She grabbed a fistful of his shirt and tugged him toward her. He didn't budge. With a soft growl of frustration, Kai changed directions. She pushed him backward, overbalancing him and landing on his chest, straddling his hips.

"Kai..." His hands went to her hips and he held her to him. His voice was half question, half desperate plea. "Please..."

Their lips collided, soft and hot. His fingers dug into her hips, and Kai relished the bruising edge of pain as he pulled her hard against him and arched into her at the same time.

Rhys took control, fisting a hand in Kai's hair and angling her head so he could delve into her mouth with his tongue, taste her, devour her. Kai melted into him and made a sound between a gasp and a moan.

The cave disappeared, and they fell into darkness and silence, a place where no one and nothing existed except for them. Then came the sound of rushing wind. Her arm itched, but she hardly noticed. Her mind opened, and something new flooded in. It felt *right*, as if she'd been waiting her entire life to become more than she could ever be alone.

Fire scorched her veins, searing away pain, searing away cold. Like smoke, their souls flowed together, twining and merging until there was no distance, no difference. The world burned, and they were flame.

CHAPTER 45
RHYS

Y^{es.}
   No.

Ancients...

A torrent of energy cascaded over them, washing away the ache in his chest as if it had never been. Rhys was no longer only himself; he was more. Better. Complete. He was *aware* of her, the way her heart pounded, the way her arm throbbed, the way her body ignited where it pressed against his. Fire licked through his veins, leaving power in its wake.

He could burn the world.

With her weight on top of him, he forgot everything but the soul-deep need to come closer, destroy every barrier. *Knowing* she wanted him as much as he wanted her was going to drive him mad.

Griffith! No! Ashem's anguished mental shout pierced Rhys's mind like a shard of ice.

Kai pushed away. "What?"

Ashem's voice was like a river of cold. *Rhys, Griffith... He's dead.*

395

The world narrowed into one fine point of light. No sound but harsh breath. Rhys sat up, his insides constricting. "No."

Kai put a hand to her head and slid from his lap.

Ashem spoke again. *That bastard Demba killed him.* He paused. *They're distracted. Take Kai and run.*

The part of Rhys's mind not wrapped up in Griffith's death was aware that Kai was registering the changes in her body. The new strength. The sudden dampening of the pain in her arm. The magic that burned through her, allowing her to sense and manipulate heat.

Grief made it hard to speak. He tried to shove it back. Later, he would have time to mourn. He could still save the others. "I've got to go."

Kai blinked at him. "Did I just hear Ashem saying Griffith...?"

Jaw set, Rhys nodded, fighting down another wave of choking emotion. "I need you to stay here."

Kai stood straight, clutching her injured arm. "He can't be dead. I just saw him! He carried Cadoc into those trees."

Rhys could feel her numbness, her confusion. She'd never lost a friend to quick, violent death. And Ffion...

"He's gone, Kai." Rhys's eyes burned, and he dug his nails into his palm. Later. Feelings were for later. "Ffion won't be able to fight. She'll be in too much pain. I have to get to her, or we'll lose her too."

She was blocking his way out of the cave, her expression half fear, half wonder. "You think you're going to die. I can sense it."

Rhys pushed her gently aside. It wasn't as easy as it had been a few minutes ago. She was Wingless now. Stronger. Faster. Even so, Wingless didn't stand a chance against dragons. It was why they didn't fight. "As long as Deryn survives, there's hope."

Kai folded her arms over her chest. "I'm coming with you." Behind the words, he heard the thoughts. *Don't leave me alone here. Please, don't go without me.*

"Sunder me," Rhys muttered, then clenched his jaw as the full meaning of the words hit him. Kai was a virtual stranger, and yet, if they were sundered, if anything happened to her... He pressed his knuckles into his eyes. "I'll take you close enough that you can see what's happening, but that's all. I can't —I *can't* put you in danger."

"Fine."

"Fine." He turned and strode into the canyon, and its tall walls cast the wide bottom in uneven shadow. His leg hurt where Kavar had raked it, but it was healing.

He felt Kai follow him, physically aware of her location, her health, her body...

She gasped, and he spun. But she was only examining her uninjured left arm. A pattern of fine, translucent scales swirled up the back of her hand and wrist, shimmering with rainbow iridescence in the sunlight. She pulled up her sleeve, turning her arm this way and that, tracing her fingers along the intricate whorls and loops. She pulled her shirt up, revealing a taut stomach and narrow waist.

Rhys studied the pattern that covered the entire left half of her body, as his covered the entire right half of his. He bit back a groan. The instincts of just being heartsworn screamed at him. There could not be a worse time to be distracted by all of the things he wanted to do to her. *Needed* to do. "The takeoff will be rough. Are you sure you can hold on?"

She nodded, dropping her shirt and hooking a fall of thick black hair behind one ear. "Yes."

He moved into the center of the ravine and opened his mind. It was harder than usual. He'd gone from dragon to man and back again more than he could ever remember doing in one day. Thoughts of Griffith and his new sense of Kai kept intruding.

Finally, Rhys wrenched the fire over himself through sheer strength—a strength he hadn't had ten minutes ago. The world shrank. Rhys looked down at Kai, who was surrounded by the white halo that marked her as his heartsworn. Energy crackled through his bones and fire sang in his blood. Time seemed to have slowed just slightly, or else he had sped.

No wonder the Council preferred their soldiers to be heartsworn.

Kai scrambled deftly up his shoulder and settled in the hollow above his wing joints, far enough away that she wouldn't interfere with flight. It felt good to have her there, a small weight that balanced instead of hindered. Small comfort, but comfort nonetheless.

"I'm ready," she called.

Hold on. He leaped, sweeping his wings down. Their tips brushed either side of the small canyon's walls as he labored into the sky. Above the cliffs, he caught a thermal and soared. The mountains unfolded beneath them in waves of pine and aspen, and the sun flashed off a blue lake snugged among the trees.

He flew up the mountain, back toward the battle, and they burst over the peak. On a clear, gentle slope about halfway down the other side, Deryn flew in low, tight circles around Ffion, who was crouched over Griffith's unmoving body. She lifted her head and gave a wailing keen.

Five of Kavar's vee orbited them like buzzards. Across the valley, too far to tell which was which, Kavar and Ashem clashed like warring patches of night.

They were closer to Deryn and Ffion now, and Rhys could see that Griffith had become human, as dragons did when they died. He lay on his back, his neck twisted at a nauseating angle.

Rage exploded. Rhys had believed Ashem, but seeing Griffith drove out all coherent thought. Griff, the kindest, most patient man Rhys had ever known, was dead.

He couldn't lose Deryn and Ffion too.

There was no time to let Kai down, but he didn't sense any fear in her. Like him, she was angry. Ready, even eager, to fight.

He dove.

One of the five dragons darted in, only to be driven off by a screeching, deranged Deryn. As he approached, he could see blood running red from slashes in her azure hide and smeared around her mouth.

A faint tingle brushed the back of Rhys's mind. Fire magic. Rhys swore. *Stop, Kai. You're too new to the magic. If you draw too much, you'll injure yourself.*

She shouted something, but the wind of their flight snatched it away.

Speak with your mind.

When she did, it wasn't like the mind-speech of dragons, but a language deeper than words that went straight to his heart, where he could feel her desperation. *I want to help!*

As one, the attacking dragons broke off, wheeled around Ffion and Deryn, and dove for them. One for Ffion, three for Deryn.

Fear clamped cold teeth into Rhys's chest. One of Deryn's attackers was Demba, the huge, sleekly muscled Bida. Even from this distance, Rhys could see blood spattered over his scales.

Griffith's blood.

Fire filled Rhys's chest, surging up his throat. Too far. *Too far.* He pushed himself harder, seconds dragging between heartbeats.

I would love your help, Kai, but you haven't done a fire-

calling ritual. Without it, you won't have anything but a whisper of power.

Kai felt indignant. *Ffion said Wingless can give power boosts. That we don't need a ritual for that, like you don't need a ritual to transform.*

Demba opened his jaws. A silent ripple of air emanated outward, nearly invisible from this distance. It slammed into Deryn, and she was knocked wings over tail. She hadn't been flying high, and she crashed hard into the ground and skidded downslope, leaving a furrow of overturned earth in her wake.

No! Rhys came within range of the nearest dragon, a male air Draig about twice Ffion's size, and blasted him with flame. The silver dragon screamed. Rhys didn't stop, but careened into him, ripping and tearing, barely conscious of the other dragon's claws and teeth as they slashed through his own scaled skin. Carried by forward momentum, he wrenched the silver dragon sideways as they crashed.

Kai went flying. She hit the ground and rolled. Horror froze Rhys, but he could still sense her. The fall had knocked her unconscious, but she was alive.

A rock shifted behind him. Rhys brought his tail around, scoring a long line of red down the mirrorlike hide of the silver dragon, placing himself between it and Kai.

The silver recoiled. Rhys darted forward and bit at the dragon's neck. It reared onto hind legs, and Rhys surged forward, knocking the silver onto his back. Rhys's claws sank deep into the other dragon's belly and he dragged them through soft flesh.

The silver tried to take an awkward, running leap into the air. Rhys opened his mouth and bathed his opponent in flame. The silver dragon's dying screams echoed through the valley, became human, then cut off. Nothing was left of the enemy but a pile of ash and charred bone.

Regret clouded the edges of Rhys's mind. The world held one less dragon.

His eyes found Ffion, still in her dragon body and hunkered over Griffith's human one. One of her attackers lay on the ground a short distance away. She favored one side, swaying dizzily and making pitiful keening noises.

Likely thinking her weak, one of Deryn's attackers peeled off and headed for Ffion. Rhys vaulted toward her—when Iain had died, Morwenna had been barely conscious for days—but with a crazed roar, Ffion met the enemy in a flash of silver wings and lightning. She fought like a rabid beast, protecting Griffith's body.

Something whistled past Rhys's ear. Deryn's attackers had noticed him. One, a large male Quetzal, raised its foreclaw and shot two poisoned spurs at him, one right after the other. An hour ago, they would have hit him. But Rhys was heartsworn now; his body reacted faster.

He dodged, then lunged at the Quetzal as Deryn led Demba, her last pursuer, in a spiraling chase. Rhys let the full weight of his body slam into the Quetzal and snapped his jaws, closing them on the Quetzal's wings. His mouth and eyes filled with rainbow-colored feathers.

The Quetzal buried long teeth in Rhys's right shoulder, the same shoulder Kavar had torn to shreds. Rhys roared and grabbed the Quetzal by the feathered frill that ran down the back of his neck. He wrenched the other dragon's teeth from his shoulder, losing chunks of flesh. The Quetzal hissed and sunk his claws into Rhys instead, gouging them deep into his neck and chest.

Rhys swung around, ramming his enemy's head into the nearest boulder over and over again. The Quetzal's body went limp, claws releasing. Light glittered off him as if shining through a million prisms, and the Quetzal shrank into a man, blood pumping from a hideous wound in his head. The gush slowed to a trickle. The sight made Rhys sick. So few dragons. So much death.

There you are, cousin.

Rhys's heart turned to lead. Something huge and white slammed into his injured shoulder, sending him sprawling.

Owain. The Quetzal had been nothing but a distraction.

Like a lion on a gazelle, Owain smashed Rhys across the face with one huge foreclaw and lunged, clamping his jaws around Rhys's throat. Owain bit down, cutting off Rhys's air. Rhys opened his mouth, gasping, but air didn't come. He tried to breathe fire, but it pooled in his throat. Owain started to twist, straining the muscles of Rhys neck too far.

The movement exposed the scales underneath Owain's chin. Rhys slashed, drawing blood. Owain's grip didn't loosen, but he stopped twisting and hunkered down. *Stop fighting, Rhys. Our people need a strong king, and I need the entire mantle to be strong. This is the only way.*

Rhys thrashed, his lungs screaming. *Our people need to survive. You'll pile human and dragon bodies so high, neither race will be able to see the sun.*

Owain flicked his wings. *I am the savior of dragonkind.*

Rhys writhed, instinct taking over. He needed *air*. But his movements only drove Owain's teeth deeper into his flesh. Memories danced before Rhys's eyes. Early memories. Owain flying with him. Owain teaching him the first form of the spear.

Owain sending assassins after him the night Ayen died.

Black spots appeared in Rhys's vision. *You can't win against the humans. All of us will die!*

Owain's voice held sorrow. *I would rather kill every last dragon with my own teeth than see our people diminish and disappear, hiding in holes in the ground.*

Thirty yards away, the ground boomed with the impact of

another body. Ashem had fallen from the sky. Dozens of slashes covered his belly, and his entire body glistened darkly with blood. *Hold on...* He dragged himself toward Rhys, but Kavar slammed down on top of him. Ashem roared, claws and teeth flashing. Fighting. Dying.

Rhys... Ashem's mental voice was little more than a whisper. *Hold on, they're almost—Juliet, no!* Juli had appeared from a thicket of trees, running for Ashem.

Rhys? Kai's horror flowed over him as she regained consciousness and realized what was going on. She sat up.

Kai. Her presence brought comfort and grief. His consciousness flickered. *Run.*

She was running. He felt her legs pumping, her body flushed with adrenaline, her lungs sucking in the oxygen that his were denied. But she wasn't running away; she was running toward him, fumbling with magic she had no idea how to use, magic hardly there at all.

But she was Wingless.

His dimming brain registered her power. Not the fire just sparking inside her; the innate reservoir of Wingless magic that could fan that spark into an inferno. She could save them, but she had no idea.

She would hate him, but Rhys was out of options.

With a mental lunge, he shoved into her mind and grasped the brand-new core of heat at her center, pulling it toward him, feeding it her Wingless magic, drawing it out through channels that weren't readied by the ritual that would have allowed her to call on her own fire.

She stumbled and cried out, falling to her knees in front of Owain.

Rhys thrust an image into her mind. With a sharp cry of pain but no hesitation, she raised her hands and pointed her palms toward Owain. Rhys *yanked* with every ounce of strength he had left. Jets of flame shot from Kai's fingers straight toward Owain's face.

Flesh popped and hissed. Owain released Rhys's throat and roared in agony. Rhys gulped enormous breaths of sweet, cold air one after another.

Fire still flew from Kai's hands. She was screaming. It was too much, too soon. No ritual. She was burning.

Horrified, Rhys shoved his way into her mind once again. *I'm sorry, Kai. I'm sorry. I'm sorry!*

Absolute, mindless panic. She fought, pushing him back, but he had to stop her before she killed herself. He pushed deeper, finally shutting off the flow of power. Kai collapsed.

Owain was roaring, swiping his claws back and forth in blind agony. There was a bloody, melted mass where his right eye used to be. He lunged at Kai, who scrambled out of the way.

A red mist rising before his eyes, Rhys caught Owain's back foot and hauled the white dragon away from Kai. Bone crunched between his jaws. Scales sheared from flesh. Blood ran over his tongue, and Rhys reveled in it. Vengeance. Justice. Hurt the one who hurt those you love.

Rhys released Owain's back leg just as a midnight-blue body slammed into the white dragon, knocking him away. Owain shoved the blue dragon off and pulled himself up, favoring his back left leg and slashing at the newcomer.

The red mist cleared, and recognition snapped Rhys back to the present. *Evan?*

Sorry, boyo! We came as fast as we could!

Rhys was still taking great, heaving breaths, terrified of the pleasure he'd taken in hurting Owain. Above, a dozen new dragons joined the fight.

Evan, Morwenna, and the Ironscale Vee had arrived.

Owain backed away from Rhys and Evan, hissing a cloud of ice. Evan stopped.

A shadow passed overhead, and red-black Morwenna landed between Rhys and Owain as well. *We outnumber you, Firelost,* she hissed.

Owain exhaled more of his icy mist. Evan drew back. Touching it would have the same effect as plunging into liquid nitrogen.

Owain's white lips drew back over whiter teeth in an expression that was part grin, part snarl. He leaped into the air. *Withdraw! Kavar, leave him!*

Around them, Owain's dragons rose into the air. Kavar went last. As he took off, a bleeding Ashem collapsed to the ground.

We need to leave too. Evan blinked coal-gray eyes at Rhys. *He may have reinforcements in the area. He could come back.*

Rhys needed to be human, to go to Kai, touch her, make sure she was all right. He needed to hold her before the grief he'd held off during the battle crashed down and crushed him.

Griffith is dead, he said, unable to contain the words.

Evan went still. Morwenna let out a keening cry. *Who killed him? I'll blast them to char and eat their bloody heart!*

There was no time. He leaned in to the weight of duty, using it to prop himself up. *Vengeance will keep. Get Griffith's body. Protect Ffion. Evan is right. We need to gather what we can and leave. Now that Owain knows where we are, it will never be safe here again.*

Still keening, Morwenna lifted off. Evan followed, and Rhys could finally turn to face Kai. At some point, she'd taken shelter behind a cluster of small boulders.

She sat up, hugging herself. Tears streaked her face. Like swinging an ax, she slammed a mental shield over her mind.

Rhys staggered.

"Don't you *ever* force your way into my head again!" Tears threatened to strangle her voice as she pulled herself to her feet. "My mind belongs to *me*. I will not be violated by dragons anymore. Stay out, or I swear I will find a way to end this."

Rhys felt as if the ground dropped out from under him. *Kai* — A void gaped where her mind had been, an emptiness populated by nothing but a cold, howling wind.

"No! Ffion said it wouldn't be like Kavar." She hugged herself, her face gray, like she might be sick. "It was worse. Oh God, it hurt so much. *Stay out.*"

He started to change so he could look her in the eyes, make her see reason, when a shrill voice rent the air.

"Rhys!" Juli ran toward him, her eyes wide. "He's losing too much blood. He's dying. Help me save him!"

Beyond Juli, Ashem was on the ground, human. Blood pooled around him.

Griffith dead. Cadoc cursed. Ashem dying.

Rhys gathered himself. There was nothing else he could do.

Later, there would be time for grief. There would be time to beg for Kai's forgiveness. Now, tired to his soul, he called the change, diminishing into his human body. He'd failed Griffith and Cadoc. At least he could help Ashem.

CHAPTER 46

KAI

Wind whistled in Kai's ears from her place on Commander Tane's back, but it didn't cool the scorched feeling that had settled deep into her bones. Nor did it help the throbbing headache, or the burning pain in her forearm, though that was mostly gone now.

Dragons flew in a V formation around them, making it obvious where they had gotten the name for their military units. Tane was on the inside, protected by the others because he carried Kai on his back. Now that she was heartsworn, Kai could see through the veils the dragons pulled over themselves. There was still a shimmer in the air around them, but it no longer hid what was inside.

Tane's skin wasn't like the others', she observed numbly. It was smooth instead of scaled, more like an amphibian than a reptile. He was Mo'o—a dragon from the South Pacific—and the commander of the reinforcements who had saved them.

She glanced toward Rhys, who flew next to a sleek red female. If Kai was right, that dragon would be Morwenna, the haughty-looking woman from that first night. There was something possessive about the way she flew so close to Rhys. Something intimate. Their movements didn't have the strange synchrony that Ffion and Griffith's had had, but they definitely knew each other well.

Rhys turned her way, and Kai was assaulted by the memory of him forcing himself deep into her mind. Accessing power she, herself, hadn't even had time to feel. For a minute, she thought she might throw up all over Tane's dappled skin. She hadn't thought a mental invasion could get worse than what Kavar had done.

Wrong.

She checked the shield over her mind, trying to ignore the feeling of being alone in pitch darkness on the edge of a cliff. It had only been hours since she'd heartsworn. This feeling would go away. It had to go away. Because there was no way in hell she was letting Rhys back in.

They flew over pine-covered mountains and snowy wilderness, tense and on edge. Ashem and Juli rode on Evan's back. Ashem's wounds had been crudely bandaged, and he leaned, half-unconscious, on Juli. To Kai's surprise, her friend clung to him. For someone who'd only known him a few days, she was utterly undone by his injuries.

Heartswearing was sick that way, Kai decided, shooting another glance at Rhys. He stared straight ahead, sometimes turning toward Morwenna, as if they were talking. Her heart wrenched, fear battling with idiot longing. Things had been going well, but he had hurt her. In hurting her, he had kept himself alive. She wanted him to be alive. Did that make what he had done less awful?

She couldn't decide.

She lay against Tane's neck, trying not to think of Rhys, watching the Mo'o's wings. They reminded her of lionfish fins, frills streaming in the wind of his flight.

A town passed beneath them, breaking the monotony of forested mountains. Eventually, the mountains sank into dry, brown, eastern Washington with its scattered towns and farms. A couple hours later, the land rose once again into forested hills. They landed, according to Tane, about an hour outside of Seattle. Tane set down in a stretch of mountainous forest between two towns like gentle rain. Several cars were parked in a lonely garage painted the same grays and greens as the trees around them.

"What is this place?" Kai looked at Tane, who had become a large Polynesian man with tattoos on his cheeks and a short, gray-streaked black ponytail.

"We can't just go flying into the city." Tane smiled at her, though it looked small on his broad, brown face, like he was more used to laughter and giant grins. It didn't even crinkle his tattoos. "We keep cars here, become human and drive into town. Less mass hysteria."

Kai wished she could return the smile. She wished she could feel anything at all. But if she let the tsunami of her suppressed emotions crash down on her, she would drown.

The dragons drove four dark SUVs out of the garage and onto the narrow gravel road that led away into the forest. Kai followed Deryn and Evan to the closest one. In a rare display of dragon strength, they yanked out the middle seats. Someone produced blankets from the garage, and they laid them on the floor of the SUV before they put Griffith's wrapped body inside.

Ffion had spent the trip unconscious, her tiny human body cradled in the claws of a dragon who looked like it had escaped an ancient Chinese painting. Awake now, she crawled in with Griffith. Weeping and clutching her stomach, she curled up and put her head on Griffith's chest.

Ashem limped over, his face drawn, and pulled a vial from

his pocket. When Ffion saw it, she nodded. He unstoppered the top and dripped a single drop onto her tongue.

"Sleep," Ashem said. "We'll get you both home. There will be time to mourn."

Ffion's tear-filled eyes drifted closed.

Grief clawed at Kai, rending her heart. It wasn't fair. Though Griffith had been the largest of the dragons, he'd been the least frightening. He'd been kind, and smiling, and so obviously in love with Ffion.

Hot tears dripped down Kai's face, and she covered it with her hands, remembering what Rhys had said that night he'd first held her hand. *It's normal people—people who want nothing but peace, family, and happiness—who die because some idiot wanted some grand thing.*

No one had deserved peace and happiness more than Griffith and Ffion.

"Kai?" Evan was watching her from the driver's side of another SUV.

Kai wiped her eyes. "Yeah?"

"Ashem wants you to ride with me and Deryn."

Kai nodded. She looked around for Juli, wanting to make sure her friend would know where she'd gone.

Juli was hovering behind Ashem, watching him with worried eyes. Ashem had one arm clamped over his quickly-bound abdomen and was pulling himself into another car, pain written on his face. Juli met Kai's gaze and nodded, as if Kai's concerns had been spoken aloud and Juli had heard them.

Maybe she had.

Kai climbed into the back of the SUV Evan indicated, then leaned against the seat. Deryn climbed into the passenger seat and slammed her door. As soon as it was closed, her silent tears became audible weeping. Evan reached over and wrapped her in a hug, kissing her hair. They held each other, and Kai wiped at her own face, leaving trails of salt across her lips.

Griffith. Gone. Just gone. As sudden and shocking as the snap of a rubber band, leaving Ffion alone. Kai covered her face with her hands, crying as quietly as she could so she didn't intrude on the others' grief.

The SUV rocked and the side door slammed shut. The seat dipped beside her. Surprised, Kai took her hands from her eyes and jerked back. "Rhys." She'd thought she'd seen him get into a car with Morwenna.

His scent washed over her, at once strange and familiar. Evan put the SUV in gear, and they followed the vehicle that held Ffion and Griffith down the bumpy road.

Rhys didn't look at her. Bruises ringed his neck, black and purple already fading to yellow. His eyes were red, though his face held no evidence of tears, only tight control.

"I'm sorry," he murmured. His voice was barely audible above the rumble of the SUV's engine.

Kai didn't respond, torn between the repulsing fear of being invaded and the deep, unrelenting *need* to be close to him. Closeness won. Tentatively, she reached out and touched his cheek. As if the touch broke some invisible spell, Rhys crumpled. He wrapped his arms around her waist and buried his face in her stomach, shoulders heaving. A man who had lost one of his best friends since childhood. A brother.

Kai stroked his hair. It hurt so much, wanting to comfort and be comforted, but being so angry, so afraid of letting him in. Still, with him close, something desperate inside her eased. When he would have moved, she held on to him, and he laid his head in her lap. They stayed like that for an hour or more, until his bruises faded into nothing and skyscrapers peeked over the omnipresent trees. Then the city was all around them, the buildings so tall Kai had to lean her head against her window and crane her neck, and still she couldn't see their tops. Rhys didn't move until Evan pulled up behind a pair of ritzy-looking towers and Evan parked the SUV.

Rhys sat up, but his hand lingered on hers. "I'm sorry," he whispered again before letting her go. Then, "Kai... Don't say anything about our heartswearing. Not yet."

Before she could ask why, he climbed out and went to help the others. Tane, Evan, and a tall East Asian man carried Griffith's body into the building. Rhys scooped Ffion into his arms and followed them.

The sight broke her heart. Still, Kai couldn't bring herself to let him into her mind.

CHAPTER 47

JULI

Blood clouded the water. Juli dipped the rag again and wrung it out, watching the pink liquid stream back into the bowl. *Plink, plink.* The water rippled again when her tears hit the surface. Tightening her jaw, she turned back to Ashem, who was seated on a plush gray chair draped with towels.

The apartment was luxurious, all white walls and dark hardwood floors and decidedly boring after days in a dragon's lair. Though she'd been in the ancient complex mere days, Juli felt a sharp ache for the beauty of the ancient underground palace. After retrieving what they could, they'd destroyed the entrance rather than leave anything behind for Owain. A place hundreds of thousands of years old, if Ashem's memories were to be believed, just gone.

Like Griffith.

Juli thought she might drown in the guilt, and it wasn't even hers.

Light from the gas fireplace flickered across Ashem's bronze skin, highlighting the elegant lines of his face, the heavy muscles of his shoulders, chest, and stomach. The firelight also warmed the cool white and gray of the room and turned the remaining blood on Ashem's torso to ugly black streaks and splotches.

She'd sponged off the worst of the mess, but it still covered at least half of his claw-marked body. They'd had to use some kind of discreet dragon back entrance to get him, Ffion, and Griffith's body into the building without causing a scene. Angry red welts and lines of dark sutures ran parallel over the ridges of his chest down to his lower abdomen, already almost healed. The sutures weren't her finest work, but she'd get better if she had to.

At least Ashem would survive.

He reached for her. *Thanks to you*, aziz-am.

Shush. Juli turned from him and dunked the cloth in the water again.

During the battle, she'd darted from tree to tree, staying as close to Ashem as possible without being seen, trying to slip into the mind of whichever dragon he fought. Making them slow, distracting them. And Kavar... Juli flung the rag back into the bowl, and blood-tinged water slopped over the edge onto the mahogany table.

"We survived." Ashem's velvet voice startled her out of her thoughts. She caught a flash of devastating grief. *Most of us*.

"You were lucky," Juli snapped. "He would've killed you, you idiot! I don't care if he's your brother, you can't—" She took a shallow breath.

She'd been inside Ashem's head during the fight. He could have killed Kavar so many times, but he hadn't. Instead, Kavar had nearly killed him.

"You can't—" Another shallow breath, then another, faster and faster until the room spun and tilted.

Ashem's mind surrounded her at the same time his arms came around her from behind. He steadied her, body and soul, and it made no sense, but being cradled against his chest with him all around her felt more like coming home than anything ever had.

There was no way she could leave him now.

Another surge of guilt from Ashem. "You would have made an excellent doctor."

Juli snorted, but calmed, timing her breathing to the measured beat of his heart. "I still will. You won't stop me."

"I won't. I will help you." His fingers traced down her back, sending prickles of heat and desire racing down her spine. His spoken voice was light, but his mental voice was pure anguish. I failed them.

"I did a horrible job with the stitches. You'll be covered in scars." She twined her arms around his neck and stroked the soft hair at his nape. It's not your fault.

He didn't respond to her thought, only veiled his more in shadow. "I can make a salve. You won't notice the scars in a week."

Juli snorted. "Scars are the least of our worries. Kai might want some salve, though. The one on her arm will be bad." She pushed him away. "You're getting blood all over me."

"You were covered in it already."

Juli drew away from him, from his safety and tempting heat, and looked down. This morning her shirt had been cream and sky blue. Now it was mostly splotches of brown and bright red, as were her arms. Even her hair had sticky spots in it. Perhaps the fallen weren't the only reason they'd had to sneak in the back.

"I'll clean up when I'm done with you." She wet a new rag and wrung it out. It was stained red already.

She threw her hands up in frustration. "This water is disgusting." Of all the ridiculous things, tears burned behind her eyes. Why on earth should she cry? She hadn't been hurt. They had lost Griffith, but it wasn't like Juli had known him well. Kai would live. Juli would live. Ashem...

She moved to pick up the bowl, but he wrapped his hand around her wrist. She glared over her shoulder.

He scowled. "You need rest."

"Sit down."

Ashem sat, but didn't release her wrist. He wrestled the bowl from her hand and yanked her onto his lap, letting out a muffled grunt of pain.

"I beg your pardon! I hope that hurt!" She struggled into a sitting position, and it served him right if she elbowed him somewhere tender. Served him right for being so stupid and getting so very close to dying days after heartswearing to her without even giving them a chance to have time with each other—

"Damn it, woman! Don't blame me. I still have to do my job. I didn't expect—"

Juli struggled again, but his muscled arms were bands of iron cinched around her waist. She beat her fists against his bare chest, though that was like iron, too. "Let me go! I don't even care! Go ahead, go fight battles and die! I've been alone. I'm strong enough to keep going on alone!"

But the image of Ffion curled next to Griffith's body flashed through Juli's mind. She pressed her hand against her mouth and stifled a sob.

He gripped the back of her neck with one big, warm hand. It felt so good. It was such a relief to have him there, alive. She stilled, and he leaned his forehead against hers.

His mind opened. Anger. Guilt. Relief. Desire. Fear. The fear was the strongest, swirling over everything else. A knee-knocking kind of fear Juli had only felt once, after some drunken idiot drove her off the road and she wrapped her car around a tree. It was seeing death and surviving.

Ashem hadn't feared his own death. He had been afraid for her.

You are strong enough to go on alone, jāné del-am. *Not me.*

Juli grasped his shoulders, holding on, using the strength coiled in his body to steady herself. His forehead still rested on hers, downcast eyes hidden by thick, dark lashes. But she felt what he was feeling. Embarrassed by his emotions, afraid of rejection...and damn it, it felt good to hold her, to feel that she was safe. Her skin was like sun-warmed silk. He wanted...

Juli's cheeks grew warm. "Stop. This...what we're feeling, it's the magic, or whatever silly thing you want to call it. It's not real."

"What is real?" He lifted golden eyes to her face, and she felt trapped in the molten heat of them. "I would have chosen you."

Juli swallowed. "You don't even—"

He kissed her.

She hadn't seen it coming, this soft, dark kiss. She melted into it, allowing the scant mental barriers she'd built to slip. She let him experience what she'd felt that hellish hour he'd been in the sky. The desperation and terror, the need for him to survive. His grip on her tightened, and the kiss intensified, becoming tongues and teeth, wandering hands and soft moans. They broke apart, and each took a shuddering breath.

"You should go in the bathroom and clean up the rest of the way," Juli said, staving off a wave of emotion so tender it made her ache. "You're covered in blood."

He raised his eyebrows. "As we've established, so are you."

She had an involuntary longing for a hot shower. A long, thorough, steaming shower...

The gold in Ashem's eyes deepened. When he spoke, his voice was gruff. "Go. You'll feel better."

Maybe it wasn't the right time for this. People were dead. Grief weighed down the very air in this place. But Juli was alive, and so was Ashem. Still, somewhere deep inside her remained cold with the fear of losing him, like death had touched her and left an icy mark.

Juli didn't want to be cold. She wanted heat. She wanted to feel like they were both alive.

She touched his cheek. "I don't want to go alone."

Ashem made a strangled sound, then scooped her up so that he was cupping her bottom. She made a startled sound, wrapping her arms around his neck and her legs around his waist. She opened her mouth to complain about him ripping out his stitches, but he silenced her with a kiss.

Fuck my stitches. Let me show you how alive we are.

He kicked the bathroom door open so hard it banged off the wall. Inside, the bathroom was all cool stone tiling and potted plants on the floor and in hanging arrangements on the wall, meant to give the impression of a forest grotto. A deep, wide tub was sunk into the floor, and one open corner held a square rainfall showerhead above a drain.

Ashem headed for the shower, and she broke from his mouth with a gasp. "Your stitches. You can't get them wet for forty-eight hours."

A growled rumbled low in his throat. "Quiet, woman." He lifted her for another kiss, and she turned her head.

"Don't be an idiot. The risk of infection—"

There is no risk. I'm not a human man.

"I've noticed," she muttered. Well, if he wasn't worried, she wouldn't be, either. Ashem pressed her against the tiled wall just below the waterfall showerhead. She arched in his arms, pressing her center to his hardening length, reveling in the way it felt to be pinned between his body and the cold tile. Heat like a stirring fire rose in her core, and she arched again. He was so hard already. *Your anatomy seems similar enough, if a bit larger.*

He groaned, his breathing unsteady. "You are a curse."

She bit his bottom lip. "Poor man. How you suffer."

Ashem reached down, and Juli gasped as cold water sluiced over them, soaking her filthy clothes, dampening their hair, and beading on Ashem's skin.

He slid his thumb along her jaw and lifted her chin. "Let me suffer at your hands for the rest of eternity."

He dipped his head, leaving a trail of desperate, hungry kisses down the sensitive skin of her neck, sucking and biting in a way that would absolutely leave a mark. The pain added a glorious dark edge to the gathering pleasure between her thighs. Between his heat and the water's coolness, it was almost more than she could take already. Her nipples pebbled, and her breasts felt heavy and aching.

Ashem lifted his head, leaving her neck cold. She sensed his intention to tell her that he would be gentle.

She buried her hands in his wet, dark, beautiful hair and pulled his mouth back to her neck before he could even speak. "No. Mark me. Touch me. When it's my turn, I won't be gentle with you."

He moaned a curse, his lips hot against her neck, this time moving up to the corner of her jaw, then nipping at her ear. Juli whimpered and moved against him, searching for friction, but he had her pressed against the wall too tightly to move. His hand slid down and cupped her breast through the fabric of her shirt, his thumb grazing her peaked nipple.

"Yes!" she hissed. "More. Now!"

Pinning her in place with his hips, Ashem slid his fingers just beneath the collar of her ruined shirt. The muscles of his

419

forearms flexed, veins moving beneath his skin, and the fabric tore down the center like wet tissue, revealing the pale skin of her chest and stomach, and what had been a sensible white bra. Now, however, it was just as grimy with blood and dirt as her shirt.

Slowly, reverently, he slid the torn shirt from her body, memorizing every inch of skin as it was revealed.

Ashem growled with pleasure. There was no other way to describe the noise that rumbled from his chest as he drank her in with his eyes, traced her lightly with his hands. She leaned forward, and with a flick of his fingers, the ratty bra came free and joined her shirt on the ground.

There was something voyeuristic about being inside his mind when he looked at her like this. Knowing exactly which parts of her made his dick strain harder against the front of his pants—the dip of her waist, the curve of her generous breasts, the perfect circle of a small mole on the skin just below the right side of her collarbone.

As their minds intertwined, the flaws she saw when she looked in the mirror faded, until she was only what Ashem saw. Still herself, but more. A creature altogether more ethereal, more perfect, more beautiful.

My goddess. My curse. Mine, forever mine.

He released her just enough that she could slide down the wall and his body, and land on the ground with unsteady feet. He planted fevered kisses in a line down her sternum, between her breasts, until he was on his knees pressing his lips against the soft, chilled skin of her stomach.

"Ashem!"

With a deft movement, he flicked open the button on her jeans and dragged down the zipper. Then his fingers were in the waistband, and he was working the fabric of her jeans and underwear down over her hips and thighs, until she could kick them off, leaving her exposed to him.

"Beautiful," he whispered. "Mine."

He rose, running his hands up her naked, wet body, cupping her breasts and circling his thumbs over her nipples. Blinding pleasure shot directly to her core.

"Blood of the fucking Ancients." Ashem stripped off his own wet pants, and then he was naked before her as well. Glorious and broad, the heavy muscles of his chest giving way to the flat plane of his abdomen and the vee of his hips, where he stood erect and every inch the size she imagined he'd be. Dark hair scattered his chest and started in a faint line beneath his naval, thickening the farther down it went.

"Beautiful," she whispered. "Mine."

Ashem reached for the bar of soap, and they took their time washing each other, exploring each other's bodies until Juli was sure she was about to melt. When they were clean enough, she reached for him, but Ashem interlaced their fingers and pinned her hands to the wall behind her, then sank to his knees again.

"I'm going to taste you, Juliet. And then I am going to have you."

Steadying her with one hand, he used the other to hook one of her knees over his broad shoulder. Juli gasped at the sensation of being so open to him. She might have felt self-conscious about the way he was seeing everything, but his satisfaction with her body and need for her drove all thought from her mind.

Ashem slipped a finger into her folds and cursed again. "You're already so wet."

Juli could only moan and press her hips toward him. Nothing had ever felt as good as this man's hands on her pussy.

That was, until he opened her and pressed his mouth to her clit.

Juli bucked as pleasure jolted through her, a cry torn from her throat. Ashem closed his lips around her and sucked, his tongue swirling against the sensitive bud. Juli buried her hands in his hair and did everything she could to not go completely boneless and slide to the floor.

He released her clit just to slide his tongue down the length of her, then swirl it around the edges of her opening before plunging it inside.

Juli bucked and cried out again as he replaced his tongue with one finger, then two. He thrust them in and out of her, gently at first, then harder, curving them to stroke just the right spot. He closed his lips over her clit again and sucked hard, and she felt herself get close, the tension in her body ratcheted so high she felt like she was going to break.

Ashem fisted a hand around his cock and stroked once, reveling in the pleasure it sent through them both.

Julie's entire body arched off the wall and she screamed as the orgasm broke over her in wave after rolling wave. Ashem didn't stop, didn't let up until he'd wrung everything from her. Until her body slumped, and he had to stand and take her in his arms to keep her from sinking to the tile floor.

"That was the most exquisite thing I have ever seen," Ashem breathed.

Juli couldn't speak, so she took his face in her hands and guided his mouth to hers.

Unlike their other kisses, this one was gentle. She tasted herself on his lips, and she could feel in their bond how he relished it.

Ashem wrapped her in his arms and ran his hand down her back, cupping her bottom to press her against him. His body was as tight as a wound spring with how much he still wanted, still craved her.

That need fed her own, and even though she'd just come

harder than she ever had in her life, she moved against him, restless and wanting.

"I want the rest of you," she demanded. "Now."

Ashem lifted her, once again pinning her to the wall, and held her there. Juli lifted and parted her thighs and Ashem dipped one hand down to stroke her still-sensitive clit.

"Ah!" Suddenly, all she could feel was how empty she was. How much she ached. How much she needed to be filled.

Ashem leaned forward, sliding his cock against her most sensitive place and then down into her wetness. She moaned and rocked against him, sensation exploding across their bonded minds. "Now!"

"Demanding thing." Ashem tangled a hand in her hair and tilted her head so that he could devour her mouth. "I've waited thousands of years for this. I am going to savor it."

He dipped his head to kiss her again, sliding the wide head of his cock in just an inch before pulling out again. Julie made a noise like a frustrated cat, clawing his back and opening her mouth, drawing his tongue deep, her teeth clashing against his. She arched and whimpered and demanded, and every time he gave her just a little more before withdrawing. The pleasure rose in her again, twisting tighter, until Juli felt like she was going to shatter from the tension of it.

"Ashem," she gasped, half in rapture, half in rage, "I thought you were going to fuck me."

With a smug chuckle that turned into a gasp, he thrust all the way inside.

Julie arched, near-mad at the perfection of the fullness, the completion, the way he held her so bruisingly tight, as if she were the only thing keeping him in the world.

All barriers gone, all space eliminated, they began to move. Slow at first, a sweet, deep rhythm. Then they quickened, their bodies slipped and slid, the water sensitizing their skin, every sensation was exquisite. It went on until pleasure neared the point of pain. Until the universe shattered, and he cried her name into her mind, and she gasped his into the steaming air.

They stayed braced against the wall for a long time, holding tight, breathing and hearts slowing, mutually loathing the idea of separation.

Finally, he pushed from the wall and carried her back into their room, to their bed.

"The sheets will get wet!"

He dumped her into them even as she protested, then climbed in after her. "They'll dry."

He braced himself on one arm for a long moment, lying on his side and looking at her, until finally, he spoke.

"Ancients," his voice was a low echo of one of the first things he'd said just after they'd become heartsworn. "I didn't know it would be like this."

Neither had she. Of course, she hadn't known to expect anything. A week ago, all she'd wanted was to find Kai, and now here she was, stuck with a dragon for the rest of a long, long life.

"I am a practical woman." Julie knew she sounded desperate, but she was so utterly out of her depth, and the man who had thrown her into this bottomless ocean was the only lifeline she could see. "And all of this is so impractical. I shouldn't feel this way about you."

The emotion thrumming between them shifted. Ashem wrapped an arm around her, pulling her close. "Heartswearing is not a kind thing. I'm sorry."

Juli knew she would have done the same, she knew she didn't want to be without him, but she hadn't quite sorted all of her emotions yet. "It isn't."

Ashem traced her cheek, moving damp hair off her face. His golden gaze moved across her features like he was memorizing her face. Like he would never be able to get enough of simply looking at her. Juli had never felt so safe. So known. So treasured.

"Even so, perhaps we can learn to live with each other, Juliet King."

She buried her face against his shoulder and breathed him in. "Perhaps we can."

CHAPTER 48

KAI

K ai balled her fists on her knees, staring at her upturned forearms. A long, angry scar puckered the skin of her right. Her sleeve hid the opalescent scales that swirled over the left.

I'll never be able to wear short sleeves again.

She tensed and relaxed her fists, trying not to squirm on the plush, white couch. After a week amid the ornate majesty of the underground palace, the elegant, minimalist lines of the furniture and fixtures in the penthouse apartment were disorienting. Luxurious as it was, it felt mundane.

She glanced up at the remaining members of the vee gathered in the kitchen. Rhys sat on a stool at the bar, hunched over with his head in his hands. Morwenna stood behind him, rubbing his back. Heat flooded Kai's cheeks as she watched them. Rhys hadn't even tried to talk to her since they'd gotten out of the elevator an hour ago.

Renewed sobbing drew Kai's gaze across the room to where Evan leaned against the counter, red-eyed, his arms around Deryn, whose shoulders shook with the force of her cries.

427

Though there were more people here than Kai had seen since being kidnapped, they were diminished. Ashem was keeping Ffion sedated. Griffith was dead. Cadoc, once again, had gone. Some of the Ironscale Vee had searched for him while Rhys, Kai, and a few others retrieved things from the cave, but Cadoc was nowhere to be found.

Kai looked back at her arms, fighting off the burn of tears. She turned her hands palm-down, grasped her knees, and studied the subtle way light played off the newly acquired scales that peeked from below her sleeve. She ran her fingers along the swirling, sheer rainbow that reminded her simultaneously of flowers and flame until her fingers hit the bottom of her sleeve. She pushed it up a few inches.

A chair scraped, and Kai looked up. Rhys was coming toward her, his brows furrowed. Kai tensed, torn between craving and a tiny, tingling edge of fear.

Morwenna moved to follow him, Rhys waved her away. The couch sank as Rhys sat next to Kai. He lifted a hand, hesitated, then tugged down her left sleeve, his fingers lingering on her wrist. He touched Kai's other arm, turning it over to examine the scar, sliding a finger along the raised red skin. Kai flinched and pulled away. It hadn't hurt, but unlike her indicium, the scar felt ugly and wrong.

"You're healing," he said, too low for anyone in the kitchen to hear.

"Looks like it." Kai wiggled her fingers, pulling the scarred skin, and sighed. She wanted to lean against him, but something in the way he kept shooting glances back at the kitchen—at Morwenna—stopped her.

Rhys reached out with a finger and brushed the callus on her thumb. "Thank you."

Kai shivered at the softness. "For what?"

He raised his gaze to meet hers. "For saving my life. Again."

Kai opened her mouth to respond, but a muted thumping heralded Ashem's descent down the stairs, followed by Juli. They looked almost...normal. As if they'd found something in each other that took the edge off the sadness that sliced everyone else to bloody pieces.

"*Gwaladr.*" Ashem jerked his head toward the kitchen. Rhys stood and followed, and Juli settled into his spot. She gave Kai a tight smile. "How are you?"

Kai watched Rhys go. Beyond him, Morwenna arched one eyebrow and smirked at her. Kai gave Morwenna an icy stare, then grabbed the remote and turned on the TV, mindlessly flipping through muted channels. "I'm fine."

Juli snorted. "Clearly—" She clamped a hand on Kai's arm. "Go back!"

Sighing, Kai did as she was told.

"Stop!"

Kai's mouth fell open and she stumbled forward. "Mom?"

The quiet talk in the kitchen ceased. Leila Monahan's face took up most of the large screen. Her green eyes, so like Kai's, were red and puffy. She dabbed them with a wadded tissue, dark with tears and streaks of mascara. Words scrolled across the bottom of the screen.

—MISSING OVER TWO WEEKS. JULIET KING, MEDICAL STUDENT, MISSING DAYS LATER IN SAME LOCATION. AUTHORITIES SUSPECT DISAPPEARANCES ARE LINKED. KIDNAPPING—

"The volume! Where's the volume?" Juli shouted.

Kai tapped the button on the remote, turning it up. Suddenly, her mother's voice filled the room. Kai's gaze snapped from the words to her mother's face.

"—just want to thank everyone for coming out. If they

could see...how many people..." She broke off, then looked directly into the camera. "Kai, baby, if you're watching this, we love you. You and Juli come home if you can." Fresh tears welled in her eyes. "If you have my daughter, please let her go. Let both my girls come home."

"Mom." Tears burned Kai's eyes, spilling hot and wet onto her cheeks. She touched the screen, standing on tiptoes to trail her fingers along what parts of her mother's image she could reach. "Mom, I'm—" A sob caught in Kai's throat. Reality came crashing back in a wave. Dragons, war, tragedy—all that belonged to someone else's life, not hers. "I'm okay. I promise I'm okay."

A reporter came on the screen, looking somber. "If you'd like to help search for the missing women, please contact..."

Juli walked over and put her arms around Kai. Blinded by tears, Kai collapsed into her, weeping. Suddenly, more than anything in the world, she needed to see her family. Juli smoothed Kai's hair and made soothing sounds. Her breath hitched a few times, but she held together. Juli always held together.

Kai took a breath, then another, borrowing strength from Juli's steadiness. On the television, the news had moved on to coverage of the previous night's football game. Her mother was gone.

Kai straightened and wiped her eyes. Beyond Juli, Rhys stared at her as if he'd been sucker punched in the gut. They held each other's gaze for a long moment, then he turned and murmured to Deryn.

Someone knocked on the door, an intricate rhythm of raps and rests Kai couldn't follow. Ashem peered through the peephole and unlocked the door.

Tane and half a dozen unfamiliar people filed in. "The sky is secure. Owain's people didn't follow."

Ashem nodded and looked to Rhys.

"Let's meet in the dining room. It has the largest table." Rhys gestured toward the open space with a huge table in the center, a massive wooden slab that would seat at least a dozen people. The dragons wandered over and took seats, the newcomers standing so that members of Rhys's vee could sit. Juli squeezed Kai's hand and went to take a seat by Ashem.

When Kai moved to follow, Rhys stopped her, looking troubled. "You should rest. There are bedrooms upstairs."

Kai looked beyond him to the others. "Why?"

He shook his head. "If I had time, I'd explain."

In a blink, Kai's grief turned to rage. She remembered what he'd said about the dragon Council, about people being angry he'd sworn to a human. "You can't just shove me in corners when I'm inconvenient, Rhys."

His brows drew together. "I'm doing what's best. For you. For me. For everyone. Trust me. You should sleep while you can. You'll be traveling sooner than you think."

The thought of going anywhere made Kai so tired she could melt. She closed her eyes, and visions of the past few hours flashed through her brain. Her mother's stricken face. Griffith's body loaded into the SUV. Cadoc's mangled hand. What Rhys had done.

Kai rubbed her temples, willing away the headache that had plagued her since he jumped into her brain and used her nascent power. "Fine. Just... Fine." She turned her back on the meeting and walked up the stairs. A few hours of oblivion sounded like heaven anyway.

CHAPTER 49
RHYS

"Why does she do this?" Rhys rubbed his fingers over the barely-healed skin of his neck, frowning at Evan over the polished reddish wood of the table. The blond man had a finger pressed to his ear, listening to someone—probably Harrow—on the other end of the quartz and silver singstone. The Council had just sent word. Seren, Lady Seeress, had run away from Eryri.

Again.

They sat in the dining room. Four of the chairs were filled with the remaining, functional members of the King's Vee—Rhys's vee. Five if he counted Juli, which he did. The other four chairs and two people standing represented half of the Ironscales. The other half was outside, guarding the building.

Rhys suppressed a growl. "I was only gone three weeks. It didn't take the Council long to lose her."

Evan shoved wheat-colored hair out of gray eyes, his glance flicking to Deryn, as it did every sixty seconds or so. "I think it was...a particularly difficult vision. We wouldn't have gotten here on time if Seren hadn't sent the Ironscale Vee out to meet us. She left shortly after sending them out. Protector Iolani thinks she's somewhere in North America this time."

Rhys shook his head. He was fairly certain that Protector Iolani, who was charged with the care and keeping of the Seeress, *let* her run away more often than not. "Citlali?"

The pretty, bronze-skinned Quetzal woman seated next to Deryn blinked innocent black eyes and twirled the beads threaded into her dark hair. "Yes?" On the other side of her, Feng Sung-ki, her heartsworn, gave her a sideways glance.

Rhys raised his eyebrows. "Half the time she goes missing you're with her, *and* you sit on the Council. Do you know where she is?"

She shook her head, smiling ruefully. "Not this time."

Rhys sighed and glanced at Ashem, who seemed weirdly content. "Have you found Cadoc?"

"He's keeping his distance, but I've sensed him a few times. He thought we'd come here, so he's hiding in the mountains outside the city."

Rhys nodded, feeling the smallest trickle of relief. "How is he?"

"Alive." Ashem pressed his lips into a thin line. "For now, he won't be rejoining us. He'd attack you again." He nodded to Citlali. "The councilwoman is going to advise me on blood magic. We'll decide what to do about Cadoc from there."

Rhys nodded, remembering Cadoc's hand and knowing what it meant. Without his music, "alive" was a relative term. "Next time he checks in, send him after Seren. If he can't come home, he'll need something to occupy his mind."

"That's not a good idea." Morwenna curled in her chair like a cat. She'd taken the one exactly opposite Rhys, so he couldn't escape looking at her. "What if the curse he's under activates on contact with any member of the royal family?"

Citlali snorted loudly. "It won't."

Rhys ran a hand through his hair. The Quetzal were few in number to begin with. Most of them were free dragons. Citlali's knowledge was rare among Rhys's people. At the moment, she was the only person he'd trust to help them understand the finer points of Quetzal blood magic. "Will you explain?"

She pushed a beaded strand of black hair behind her ear, then tapped the edges of her hands on the table. "Owain isn't an idiot." Her hands rose in the air, indicating an imaginary crowd. "If he killed the Seeress, rebellion. Ninety percent of his supporters *poof* in an instant." She snapped her fingers. "The gold dragon is sacred. The curse won't touch her."

Evan shifted. "Unfortunately, Seren might be the least of your worries. There are other whispers. There's a leader among the rogues who... Rhys, she's claiming to be your mother."

Rhys stared. Deryn stood so abruptly that her chair fell backward. "Mother? Alive?"

Evan shook his head. "I haven't seen her myself, *annwyl*, but there are enough rumors—"

"Where?" Deryn leaned forward, both hands on the table.

"Somewhere in the north, in Canada or Alaska," Evan said, his face troubled.

"Where did you hear this?" Rhys's voice was as sharp as Deryn's.

Evan looked to Tane.

The big Mo'o shrugged. "From the Council. Maybe that male Wingless who was taking reports in Ashem's absence. What's his name? Harrow."

Rhys's brain seemed to have stopped. His mother. Queen dowager. Warbringer. Alive.

He looked down the table to Deryn, who still stood, eyes blank, face pale. It had been a thousand years, but if Rhys knew Mair, her reemergence now would hardly be a coincidence. She had something planned.

He pushed back his chair, and they all stood. "My mother, alive or not, is a concern for when we've returned to Eryri."

"But—" Deryn began.

Rhys cut her off with a sharp shake of his head.

"Four more vees are waiting to escort you, *mo'i*," Tane said. "They're in the Cascades. Owain won't engage a force of that size. There would be too many casualties."

Rhys nodded. "Good. If there's nothing else—"

Juli cleared her throat, and the dragons all turned to her with expectant eyes. "Kai needs to go home." She met Tane's eyes. Evan's. Morwenna's. "She isn't heartsworn. She has no reason to stay."

"Of course." Though Rhys had been the one to tell her to say it, his pulse jumped. He saw Kai in his mind, straining to touch her mother's image with gentle fingers, both of their faces stricken and tearstained. Griffith had been right that night on the ledge. Kai needed time, and so did he. The news of Mair only made the situation more urgent. If Warbringer was alive and making trouble, dragons would be even less likely to accept another Wingless queen.

"I'll take her." Ashem's voice was only slightly less flat than the table. He didn't approve of the plan, cobbled together as it had been in the last few seconds before the meeting. "My heartsworn has some business to finish at home before she can join us. I'll stay with her, and we can take Kai back with us."

Also as planned, Deryn spoke. "We can hardly afford to lose you for that long, Ashem." Her voice was even flatter than his. In her words, Rhys was "being a relentless idiot."

"It shouldn't be a problem, if the Ironscale Vee will come back with us." Rhys glanced around, and the others nodded. "Good. Ashem will go with his heartsworn and take Kai home."

This was why he hadn't wanted her at the meeting. Kai had to remain a secret. She would be safer, and he wouldn't lose followers. Only Owain had seen her, and the others had shown up so quickly after, Rhys hoped his cousin would think she'd been with one of them. Though there wasn't really a good explanation for a Wingless on the battlefield, ever.

He ignored a sharp feeling of loss. Surely, she could only be happy to go home. "If that's all?"

The others nodded and dispersed. Ashem approached as they left. "I need to talk to you about Ffion."

Rhys bowed his head. "I should have been there."

Ashem looked away, his jaw clenching briefly. "She's pregnant."

"She's...what? Shit." Cold fear knotted his stomach. The trauma of Griffith's death would put Ffion in serious danger of losing the baby. A baby who would grow up fatherless. He felt a sudden, fierce determination. "We can't let her lose the child, Ashem. She's been talking about babies for a century. It's all"— his voice broke—"all of Griff she'll have."

"Yes. And we can't keep her sedated. Not with the draught I have—long-term use is too dangerous. We need to get her back to Eryri."

Rhys nodded, realization dawning. "That's what they were arguing about. She didn't want to go back to Eryri, where it was safe for her. Because of me."

Ashem looked at the floor. "Rhys, we're sworn to protect you. Ffion hasn't told me any of this. I took it from her mind. She didn't realize she was expecting until after we'd left Eryri. Griffith wanted to go back, but she didn't. She's going to blame herself, though it was too late for them to leave anyway, with Owain flying around like a sundering murderous seagull." He shook his head. "But if I'm to go to Colorado with Kai, you'll need to get Ffion back to Eryri as quickly as possible."

"I will." Rhys had hoped he'd have more time with Kai to

explain. To apologize. Ffion's need, however, was more pressing. "Tell everyone to prepare to leave. I have to speak to Kai."

Ashem ducked his head and was gone.

Rhys gripped the back of his chair hard enough that his knuckles went white and the wood groaned beneath his hand. Cadoc, gone. Griffith, dead. Ffion in danger of dying or losing her child or both. Even Ashem would be gone. His vee—his family—was falling apart, no matter how tightly he tried to hold it together.

There was a splintering sound, and he looked down. The back of the chair had cracked beneath his hands.

CHAPTER 50

KAI

S eattle really was as rainy as everyone said, though Kai thought it felt more cozy than dreary as she leaned on the railing. Across Lake Washington, the nebulous lights of the city proper glowed yellow against a navy sky. She knew she should be cold, but didn't seem to feel it anymore. Without cold, wetness wasn't much of a bother.

"Are you all right?"

Kai spun. A tall, beautiful East Asian woman in red and black stood next to her. Her sleek hair was pulled back in an elaborate twist held with a pair of enameled combs and dripping with charms. "Who are you?"

The woman smiled. "Jiang." She tilted her head. "Who are you?"

Kai looked out over the city, her mouth twisting. "No one. Just a human who happened to be in the wrong place at the wrong time."

Silence fell over them. After a moment, the woman spoke again. "I'm a member of the Lung Clan. We're empaths."

Kai pressed her lips together, trying to bring her brain into the present. "You can sense emotions?"

Jiang nodded.

Kai laughed without humor. "And mine are violent enough to bother you?"

Jiang shook her head. "No, but, feeling the way you do, I didn't want you to be alone."

Kai opened her mouth to ask Jiang to leave, but she suddenly felt lighter. Warmer. She would be going home soon, after all. She should be happy about that. Instead, she said, "Thanks."

Another silence fell. Minutes passed. Kai blinked tears and droplets of misting rain from her eyes and pulled up her dripping hood. "What are you doing out here?"

Jiang looked out over the city. "Guarding the roof. I'm part of the Ironscale Vee, but still in a trial period."

Kai got the distinct impression Jiang wanted her to ask about the "trial period," but the sound of the door sliding open distracted her.

The outer walls of the penthouse were glass, the panes held up by thin, stylish columns of white. Rhys stood in front of the rain-beaded windows and closed the door behind him, his storm-heavy presence adding pressure to the air.

"Majesty." Jiang bowed, pressing the first two fingers of her right hand to her forehead.

"Lung Jiang." Rhys dipped his head. "I didn't expect to see you. I thought you were at Cadarnle."

"Not for the next few months. In fact, I have a proposal for you, Majesty. If Commander Ashem Azhdahā and Commander Tane Mo'o approve. It involves Kavar."

Curiosity crossed Rhys's face. "Speak to them now."

Jiang bowed again and went inside.

Rhys came and stood next to Kai, then leaned over the railing. He was so close she swore she could feel the heat of him. She waited for him to get closer. He didn't.

To distract herself, Kai looked down forty stories to the street below. The cars looked like beetles with headlamps, and the rain and height dampened the noise of traffic. "How was your nonhuman meeting?" she asked. "Oh, except it wasn't nonhuman, because Juli was there."

Rhys straightened and tapped the railing with his fingers. Twitchy again. So much energy coursing through that big, capable body. "It was fine."

"Right."

Silence.

"Did you come out here to talk?" Kai asked after a long moment.

"Yes. I came to tell you again how sorry I am. I was out of options. I didn't know what else to do."

Kai internalized his words, his bleak tone. He'd used her to save himself today. But Rhys wasn't just "himself." He was the bulwark shielding the human world from Owain. And he had saved her countless times. In the first battle, in the river, today. He'd done his best to protect her from the heartswearing, once he was able. The one night they had managed to be together, he'd brought her so much pleasure.

But then he'd *hurt* her. So much.

Kai shoved the entire mess to the back of her mind. "I was surprised we didn't lose more people."

He still wasn't coming any closer. Did she want him to? The heartsworn part of her absolutely did. Her entire body thrummed with the certainty that there could be no safer place than wrapped in Rhys's arms.

Her mind heartily disagreed.

"Owain wants as many dragons alive as possible when he

takes the mantle," Rhys said. "The more he has, the more humans he can kill."

Ah, Rhys. Never one to mince words.

Kai glanced at him out of the side of her eye. "I've never heard of a war where the point was to *not* kill the other side."

"We're a careful, long-lived people. In a thousand years, we've only lost perhaps a hundred dragons to this war. We've only had a true battle once. Ten years ago, when Iain died. It's still too many."

"You definitely don't do war like humans."

"The results are close enough." His expression was distant, and despite her feelings, seeing that distance made Kai's chest ache. "And I was arrogant enough to think the stalemate might last forever. That's why I thought it was safe for Deryn and me to leave Eryri at the same time."

They fell into silence again. After a minute, Rhys said, "I thought you might want to know that Ashem has been in contact with Cadoc. He's fine. He's close, actually."

Rhys glanced to the southeast, where the Cascades and Mount Rainier would be visible in daylight. "My sister, Seren, has run away again. I'm putting Cadoc in charge of the search for her."

"How generous of you." Kai's voice was dry.

He gripped the railing. "He's cursed, Kai. He can't come home."

Kai threw her hands in the air. "Then maybe you should have him try to free himself. Maybe you should help him. He's been tortured. He needs rest."

"Citlali will look into breaking the curse. I'm trying to keep him too busy to wallow."

"Oh." A memory tugged at the back of her brain. "He wanted me to tell you...your mother is alive. She wants to help."

Kai expected some kind of reaction from Rhys. His parents

played such a huge role in the way he saw the world. But Rhys just looked over the city and nodded. "Evan said something similar. I didn't entirely believe it, but maybe I should have."

Kai blinked, confused at his lack of reaction. "I thought your parents were dead."

"So did I."

"What are you going to do?"

He shook his head. "I won't truly believe it's her until I see her myself."

Kai wiped rain from her face, frowning, her own mother's agonized plea flashing through her mind. "Cadoc seemed sure."

Abruptly Rhys said, "I'm sending you home, Kai. Go back to your life for as long as you can. It's...better that way, for both of us. Safer."

Kai stared at him. She couldn't have heard right. "Go home?"

Rhys ran his hand through his hair, shaking water from it. He looked like a king again, so stern and yet so beautiful with rain gathering on his lashes, on his cheeks. "If I take you to Eryri, Owain will find out about you in days. You'll be a target. If he hurts you, he hurts me. This way he won't know you exist. Not even Evan and Morwenna know. That's why I kept you from the meeting. Being heartsworn to a human could cost me soldiers and support on the Council. If I lose too many people, Owain will win."

"But...I don't understand. Don't they already know that we're heartsworn?" She gestured at her left arm. "Didn't they see?"

Rhys shook his head. "No, and I don't think Owain knows either. At least, not that you're heartsworn to me."

This is what I wanted, she reminded herself harshly. She had to see her family again, to reassure her parents and brothers that she was alive. But even though she was angry with him, she also wasn't ready to leave Rhys. The thought of not seeing him hurt her heart. "When?"

Rhys looked toward the city. He was dripping, his hair almost black from the rain. "Now. It will be safer if you fly at night, and I have to get Ffion back to Eryri."

"Now?"

"Yes. Now." The word was final.

"Does Juli know?"

Rhys nodded. "She and Ashem are going with you."

The iridescent scales of her indicium blurred beneath droplets of rain. Somehow, in just over a week, dragons had become reality and her family a dream. Then she'd seen her mother on the news, and everything snapped back into place. "How long will I stay at home?"

"Until it's safe."

"But you're going back to the islands in the Pacific."

"I'm the king."

Kai squeezed the slippery railing beneath her hands. *Without you, who will teach me to control the fire? Who will walk me through the ritual to call it?* She stopped short of asking. Rhys wasn't being cold, exactly, but he was so matter-of-fact. Kai didn't want him to be matter-of-fact. She wanted the Rhys who'd held her last night. Who made gardens of fire. Who'd kissed her in that cave.

Maybe she didn't need the help of this new, cold Rhys. She'd seen him with his golden bowl and knife. She might be able to figure it out. And if she couldn't, Ashem probably knew.

"Before you go..." He hesitated, his gaze far away. "Would you take down your shields?"

Kai grasped one of her carabiners. Open, closed, open, closed. "So you can be in my head?" Nausea pooled in her belly, remembering how he'd shoved her aside, so much stronger than her. She could never be his equal. She might as well be his pet. Swallowing the bitterness, she shook her head.

His voice was low. "Kai, please. I... Then we could at least talk."

Her patience snapped. "I don't think you understand. I'm glad you did what you did. I'm so happy you're alive. I just... *can't*. I'm tired, Rhys. All this shit is happening and you're jerking me back and forth like your personal emotion yo-yo. You want me, then you want me to leave. You need me, but I'll make you lose the war." She hadn't meant to say the rest, but it burst from her in a flood. "You terrify me. You made me a puppet in my own body. Even Kavar couldn't do that." She dashed tears from her eyes. "You hurt me. My head *still* hurts."

He flinched like she'd struck him, then reached for her, his hands wrapping around her wrists, tugging her toward him. "I'm sorry."

She closed her eyes at the anguish in his voice. "I know you didn't mean to, but I need time. If I'm leaving, I'd better go." She turned toward the door but couldn't bring herself to let him go. Reluctant, even now, to part from him.

Fuck heartswearing.

"Wait." He tightened his fingers on hers and pulled her against him.

Then Rhys was kissing her, hard and desperate, like he was trying to brand her lips, to sear himself into her memory so that no other kiss, no other man, would ever be enough.

She kissed him back, opening for him. He moaned and slipped a hand into her hair, taking control of the angle and pace. His hand slid up to her neck, his thumb gently brushing over the hollow of her throat before moving down to her breast.

Heat built in her center, and she moaned into his mouth. Her hand went to the front of his pants, and she felt how much he wanted her, just from this. How much he needed her.

Her resolve wavered, threatening to crack.

Then again, if he needed her, if he cared, they'd be working this out. Instead, he was sending her away.

She broke off the kiss, feeling empty even though she was still in his arms. Rhys stared at her, starfire eyes ablaze, chest rising and falling as he gulped in air.

"It's... It's not forever," he breathed. "I just have to figure things out."

Kai licked her lips, tasting salt. "It's never going to be perfect, if that's what you're waiting for, Rhys. None of it will ever be perfect."

She had never done anything in her life so hard as stepping away from him. Feeling their bodies break contact. Knowing she wouldn't touch or be touched by him again for some indefinite, yawning amount of time. That *something*, that potential brightness between them, put on hold until who knew when.

He lifted his hand as if to touch her again, then let it fall. "I want this to work, Kai. I want to be happy." He hesitated. "I want us to be happy."

Suddenly overwhelmed, Kai turned and stumbled into the apartment, leaving a trail of rainwater and tears along the hardwood floor from the sliding glass door to the bathroom. She closed the door, hugging herself. She only needed a minute, just a few seconds to breathe before Juli saw her and started asking questions.

I want us to be happy. But there were too many emotions crowding her mind to think of something as simple as happiness.

When she pulled her hands from where she'd been clutching her hoodie, two black scorch marks remained. She stripped it off with a frustrated noise and threw it into the corner. It was shredded and covered in blood and dirt anyway.

Something clicked against the tile. Kai bent and picked up

Rhys's sun pendant, which dangled from a broken chain. She piled it in her palm, watching light catch in the yellow stone, the fine gold links glinting at her.

She let her imagination run wild for a moment. Imagining, as she had a hundred times, that she and Rhys had met under different circumstances, that he was normal, just a guy at the climbing gym. A guy she could flirt with and fall for. A guy she could get a burger with, go on hikes with, and bring home to her parents. She suppressed a small, bitter laugh at the idea of Rhys sitting in the living room, talking to her father, who would periodically push up his small, gold-rimmed glasses as he polished his shotgun.

Did she want to be happy with Rhys?

Yes. The thought was surprising, desperate, and terrifying.

A knock sounded, and the image shattered. "Kai?" Juli's voice was muffled by the door. "Did he talk to you?"

Kai stuffed Rhys's pendant and chain in the pocket of her jeans. "Yeah." No matter what happened, there was no question that she'd have to go to Eryri, to be with Rhys, someday.

"We're ready to go. I have a poncho for you." A pause. "It's a long flight, but we'll be with your family in time for your mom to make pancakes and bacon." Kai opened the door, and Juli gave her a crooked, sympathetic smile. "They're going to be so incredibly happy to see you."

Kai returned the smile. "And you."

Home. Her family. Her life. Her house. Her bed. A shower. Her smile grew into a grin as she walked past Juli. "Come on. Let's not keep your giant black iguana waiting."

Kai didn't see Rhys as they climbed back onto the roof. Ashem was ready for them, a harness around his neck and back. Juli grumbled, but Kai climbed up with ease. Following Ashem's directions, they strapped themselves in.

Ashem took off, swooping from the side of the building and

banking around. Rhys stood in one of the windows, a palm pressed to the glass, starfire eyes ablaze. Kai gripped the harness until it dug into her hands and her knuckles turned white. No matter how angry or afraid she was, she'd count every second until she saw him again.

The city below fell away, and Rhys disappeared from sight. One-one-thousand. Two-one-thousand. Three...

AUTHOR'S NOTE FOR THE FIRST EDITION

When I started this story, it only had the Elemental (European) dragons. It was the first book I'd ever tried to write, and it wasn't until a few drafts in that I realized how silly that was. Dragon mythology comes from all over the world; obviously, so should dragons. In expanding the dragons' world, however, I created a problem for myself. I haven't had much opportunity to experience other cultures firsthand. I did my best, but I'm sure that I've glossed over, missed out on or misinterpreted elements of each of my dragons' originating cultures. For this, I apologize in advance.

Some of you may also have noticed that my dragons, ancient as they are, speak quite modern languages. Unfortunately, this came down to resources. I would have loved to include dragons speaking proto-Celtic or Old Persian, but I had a hard enough time finding people to check the languages still in use today. Let's just say dragons keep up with language as it evolves.

ACKNOWLEDGMENTS

At the time of this publication, this story has been over a decade in the making. First written in 2011, first published in 2015, and now given a second life in 2023. Because of that, there are a lot of people to thank.

I always mention my brother Jordan first when I talk about this book. The only reason I ever finished a novel in the first place is because he harassed me into writing on a daily basis. Thanks, dummy.

The second person I want to thank is my husband, Will, who believes in me so profoundly I tear up when I think about it. Thanks, love. You are the only reason I've held on to sanity as long as I have.

The third person—who is actually the most important in regards to this book and, honestly, the fact that I'm still writing at all—is my BFF, critique partner, podcasting buddy, personal cheerleader, and now publisher Charlie N. Holmberg. I might not be writing today if it wasn't for Charlie, and you definitely wouldn't be reading this book. Though I met her after the original draft of *Soul of Smoke* was finished, she was vital in helping me brainstorm the rest of the trilogy and generally keeping my dreams alive. Also, she sends me cookies when I'm stressed. Charlie, you are an incredible person, a generous friend, and a gifted writer. There aren't adequate words for the gratitude I feel for everything you've done for me. Thank you so, so much.

Thank you to my mom, my sisters Kristin and Lindsay, and my friend Ashlyn for reading the project in its early stages and letting me talk at them for countless hours while brainstorming. Thanks to my dad, for always telling me I was smart enough to do anything I wanted. Thank you to my friend Diane for making me stick with it (and inspiring many of the Juli-est parts of Juli). And of course to my amazing mother-in-law, who watched my three daughters (who were very young and chaotic at the time) for entire weekends so I could go to writing conferences. Thank you to those same children, who are older now, for being supportive of me pursuing my dreams and for growing into generally awesome, smart, funny, kind, compassionate people. Love you guys.

Thank you to Mikki and Tricia. You guys are my lifeline, amazing critique partners, and the best of friends. One of my biggest and only regrets about leaving Utah is that I can't hop in the car, drive ten minutes, and hang out with you.

Thank you to my Dungeons & Dragons group, who have also been key in helping me stay sane over the last few years: Mikki (again), Cole, Nathan, Raylene, Joon, and Will (also again).

Thank you to my writer friends. To my first critique group: Deb, Julie, Leah, Alison, Erin J., Sabrina, and Christina. Thank you to my later critique partners Jenny, Kim, Rae, Laura, and Erin S., and to the amazing writers in the Utah writing community who taught me and befriended me.

Thank you so much to my former agent, Marlene Stringer, for believing in this story so much you pulled it out of a slush pile. I appreciate everything you've done for me.

Thank you to everyone who helped me with research, especially Professor Taylor for correcting my Welsh. Any mistakes in the Welsh in this story are my fault, not his.

Thank you to every author whose books I've devoured over

the course of my life and especially to Gail Carson Levine, Brandon Sanderson, and the countless other selfless writers who share their knowledge of craft online for free. Without you I never would have known how to begin.

Most of all: thank you, thank you, thank you to anyone who reads this book. Whether you liked it or not, I'm so grateful you gave me a chance.

ALSO BY CAITLYN MCFARLAND

Dragonsworn Trilogy

Soul of Smoke

Shadow of Flame

Truth of Embers

Daughters of the Shattered Moon

Echoes of Night

ABOUT THE AUTHOR

After spending most of her adult life in UT, Caitlyn McFarland has returned to the Midwest and currently lives by a lake in Missouri with her husband and three daughters. She has a Bachelor's degree in linguistics from Brigham Young University. When she's not writing romantic fantasy, Caitlyn can be found wandering the woods, crafting, or playing TTRPGs.

www.ingramcontent.com/pod-product-compliance
Lightning Source LLC
Chambersburg PA
CBHW020518110726
47899CB00004B/1150